The Shipyard Girls on the Home Front

Nancy Revell is the *Sunday Times* bestselling author of the Shipyard Girls series, which is set in the north-east of England during World War Two.

She is a former journalist who worked for all the national newspapers, providing them with hard-hitting news stories and in-depth features. Nancy also wrote amazing and inspirational true life stories for just about every woman's magazine in the country.

When she first started writing the Shipyard Girls series, Nancy relocated back to her hometown of Sunderland, Tyne and Wear, along with her husband, Paul, and their English bull mastiff, Rosie. They now live just a short walk away from the beautiful award-winning beaches of Roker and Seaburn, within a mile of where the books are set.

The subject is particularly close to Nancy's heart as she comes from a long line of shipbuilders, who were well known in the area.

Why YOU love Nancy Revell

'I read it in one day and couldn't put it down. I'm only sorry I've got to wait until February for the next book in the series to be released'

'I absolutely love these books and as *A Christmas Wish for the Shipyard Girls* is the ninth in the series I feel like all the wonderful characters are like family'

'Once again an astounding follow-on book in the Shipyard Girls series'

'Nancy Revell brings the characters to life and you get totally engrossed in their lives and hope things turn out well for them. Have read all of the books now and can't wait for the next one. Please keep them coming'

'The Shipyard Girls is one of my favourite series of all time'

'How wonderful to read about everyday women, young, middle-aged, married or single, all coming to work in a man's world. The pride and courage they all showed in taking over from the men who had gone to war – a debt of gratitude is very much owed'

'I love these books and am always eagerly awaiting the publication of the next one in the series. As a Sunderland lass myself who knows the area where the stories are set, I can appreciate that these books are very well researched. Keep up the good work, Nancy'

'It's a gripping, heart-breaking and poignant storyline. I couldn't put it down and yet didn't want it to end'

'I felt I was there in those streets I know so well. This series of books just gets better and better; a fantastic group of girls who could be any one of us if we were alive in the war. Could only give 5 STARS but worth many more'

'What a brilliant read – the story is so good it keeps you wanting more . . . I fell in love with the girls; their stories, laughter, tears and so much more'

'I thoroughly enjoyed *A Christmas Wish for the Shipyard Girls*'

'I absolutely love these books . . . Nancy Revell manages to pull you in from the first page and you can't wait to finish each book but at the same time don't want it to end. I am delighted there is going to be a book ten and can't wait to see what all these lovely people are up to next'

What the reviewers are saying ...

'Well-drawn, believable characters combined with a storyline to keep you turning the page'
Woman

'The author is one to watch'
Sun

'Our favourite author, Nancy Revell . . . Heart-warming, emotional and gripping as ever'
Take A Break

'A riveting read in more ways than one. Nancy Revell knows how to stir the passions and soothe the heart!'
Northern Echo

'The usual warmth from Revell, featuring lovable characters and heart-warming storylines'
MyWeekly

'Researched within an inch of its life; the novel is enjoyably entertaining. A perfect way to spend hours, wrapped up in the characters' lives'
Frost

'Nancy Revell has created a fantastic saga that could literally have fallen from the TV. As a reader you feel like you are right there watching all the action take place'
Chellsandbooks

'Nancy Revell gives the usual warm fuzzy feeling of having caught up with my old, familiar friends'
Clyde's Corner

'This series goes from strength to strength, and each new book in the series surpasses the previous book'
Gingerbookgeek

'Another superb read from Nancy Revell. Full of all the hope, humour and heart that have become her hallmarks'
Bookish Jottings

'You can always rely on Nancy Revell to offer up a story that is full of hopes, struggles and valuable friendships'
A Novel Thought

'This series keeps getting better and better. Nancy Revell always manages to make the drama new and fresh'
Over The Rainbow Book Blog

Also available by Nancy Revell

The Shipyard Girls
Shipyard Girls at War
Secrets of the Shipyard Girls
Shipyard Girls in Love
Victory for the Shipyard Girls
Courage of the Shipyard Girls
Christmas with the Shipyard Girls
Triumph of the Shipyard Girls
A Christmas Wish for the Shipyard Girls

The
Shipyard Girls
on the Home Front

Nancy Revell

arrow books

1 3 5 7 9 10 8 6 4 2

Arrow Books
20 Vauxhall Bridge Road
London SW1V 2SA

Arrow Books is part of the Penguin Random House group
of companies whose addresses can be found at
global.penguinrandomhouse.com.

Penguin
Random House
UK

First published in Great Britain by Arrow Books in 2021

www.penguin.co.uk

A CIP catalogue record for this book is available from
the British Library.

ISBN 9781787464285

Typeset in 10.75/13.5 pt Palatino
by Integra Software Services Pvt. Ltd, Pondicherry

Printed and bound in Great Britain by Clays Ltd, Elcograf S.p.A.

The authorised representative in the EEA is Penguin Random House
Ireland, Morrison Chambers, 32 Nassau Street, Dublin D02 YH68.

MIX
Paper from
responsible sources
FSC   FSC® C018179
www.fsc.org

Penguin Random House is committed to a
sustainable future for our business, our readers
and our planet. This book is made from Forest
Stewardship Council® certified paper.

To Gina Wilson, poet, novelist, psychotherapist,
and a very special person.

Thank you x

Acknowledgements

Thank you to all those who have taken the time to tell me about or write to me about their wartime experiences, or about their female relations who worked in the Sunderland shipyards during the Second World War. In particular: Iris Lindsay and her daughter Ann Robinson; Angela Stevenson, whose grandmother Catherine Jameson worked as a comptometer operator at Thompson's; Marie Dale for her wonderful anecdotes about her mother Margaret Graham, who worked as a crane driver at Bartram's and went on to nurse injured soldiers at the Ryhope Emergency Hospital; Ann Moss, whose mam, Doris Wilkinson (née Hope), worked as a lathe operator at Greenwell's; and Marilyn Campbell whose mother, Joan Tate, worked as a French polisher at Austin & Pickersgill's.

Thank you also to all the lovely staff at Fulwell Post Office: postmaster John Wilson, Liz Skelton, Richard Jewitt and Olivia Blyth, who have supported the Shipyard Girls from the off. Thank you to the wonderful booksellers at Waterstones Sunderland, the Sunderland Antiquarian Society – especially Linda King, Norm Kirtlan and Philip Curtis – researcher Meg Hartford, Jackie Caffrey of 'Nostalgic Memories of Sunderland in Writing', Beverley Ann Hopper, of The Book Lovers, journalist Katy Wheeler at the *Sunderland Echo*, Simon Grundy at Sun FM, and Lisa Shaw and her fantastic producer Jane Downs at BBC Newcastle.

To artist Rosanne Robertson, Soroptimist International of Sunderland, and Sunderland City Council for their continuing work to make the commemoration to the real shipyard women a reality. To Ian Mole for bringing the series to life with his *Shipyard Girls Walking Tour*.

To my former editor Cassandra Di Bello, now publisher at Simon & Schuster Australia, for planting the seed of one of the major romantic story lines in this book.

To my present editor and publishing director Emily Griffin and the whole of 'Team Nancy' at Arrow who have worked so hard to make the Shipyard Girls series a *Sunday Times* bestseller, and to my wonderful copy editor, Caroline Johnson.

Special thanks, as always to Diana Beaumont, of Marjacq Scripts, for being a such a fabulous agent.

And, of course, to my mum Audrey Walton (née Revell), and my husband, Paul Simmonds, for listening to me, encouraging me and for the love they give.

Thank you, all.

'As we give, we find that sacrifice brings forth the blessings of heaven. And in the end, we learn that it was no sacrifice at all.'

Spencer W. Kimball (1895–1985)

Chapter One

The Tatham Arms, Tatham Street, Sunderland, County Durham

Christmas Day 1943

'I reckon this little girl's ready for her bed,' Helen said, nodding at Hope.

The two-and-a-half-year-old was her half-sister, not that Helen saw the gorgeous, dark-haired girl curled up on her lap as a 'half' sibling – it didn't matter to Helen one iota that they had different mothers.

'Yes, yer right,' Gloria agreed reluctantly, leaning across and pushing her daughter's fringe away from her eyes, causing her to stir. 'I've been putting it off.'

'Because you're having to go back to a cold, empty flat? On Christmas night?' Helen ribbed as she hoisted Hope onto her hip; her little sister immediately clamped her hands around her neck and wrapped her legs around her waist.

'Don't rub it in,' Gloria said, standing up and putting on her coat. She sighed. 'I don't know – I must be getting soft in my old age.' She picked up her boxed-up gas mask and her handbag, swinging them over her shoulder.

'Come on then, sleepyhead.' Helen kissed Hope on the cheek.

Gloria followed Helen through the throng of Christmas revellers, her daughter's cherubic face watching her, chin resting on her big sister's shoulder as she desperately tried to keep her eyes open.

When they reached the hallway, Helen handed Hope over.

'You don't fancy coming back for a while?' Gloria asked. She really did *not* want to go back to a cold, empty flat. The cold she could tolerate, but not the emptiness. Or rather, the absence of the one person she wanted to be there more than anyone in the world: Jack Crawford. Hope's father. The man she had loved for as long as she could remember. The man she'd been forced to live apart from these past two years.

'Yer could have a hot chocolate 'n tell me what *really* happened today? Yer won't have to worry about anyone eavesdropping,' Gloria said. It had been obvious something had happened when Helen had turned up earlier with Pearl Hardwick and her daughter Bel Elliot.

'I think I'll stay here for a bit longer,' Helen said, tipping her head towards the lounge door of the pub, where there was life and laughter and plenty of festive cheer. 'I'll come around tomorrow and tell you everything, OK?'

Gloria forced a smile. 'I look forward to it.'

Pulling open the front door, Gloria stepped out into Tatham Street. It was quiet, and the virgin snow meant there was no need for her little electric torch. As she started the short walk back to her flat, it felt as though her mood was getting heavier with each step.

Yer should be happy, she berated herself. It had been a lovely Christmas, spent with those she was close to – and with a slap-up dinner at Vera's, in spite of rationing. Then they had all walked to the Tatham Arms and continued the festive celebrations, stepping out and listening to the carol singers when the Salvation Army band had turned up. She'd even had the bonus of getting a Christmas card from her boys, Bobby and Gordon, both serving in the Royal Navy.

Gloria thought of Rosie with her husband behind enemy lines, Hannah, a Jewish refugee from Prague with parents in a German concentration camp, and Polly, who'd just had a baby with a man who was spending the war yanking limpet mines off the hulls of Allied ships.

If they could all keep their spirits up and a smile on their faces, then so could she.

Gloria looked down at Hope. At least Jack was just over the border and safe – or as safe as could be these days, working in an industry that was one of Herr Hitler's prime targets.

But, Gloria thought as she trudged towards the end of Tatham Street, it didn't matter how much she argued with herself, she still couldn't stop feeling totally despondent about ever seeing her lover again, never mind Hope ever having a father in her life.

Reaching the T-junction at the top of the street, Gloria turned left into Borough Road. Crossing over, she kept her eyes on the ground, not wanting to slip and fall with Hope in her arms. The snow on this stretch of road leading into town had been churned up by traffic, making it a mix of slush and ice.

Reaching the pavement on the other side, which, thanks to the lack of footfall, was still carpeted in a thick white layer of snow and unspoilt, Gloria's attention was caught by the outline of a figure standing outside the entrance to her flat. A dark, man's figure. He had his back to her. A duffel bag was slung over his shoulder.

Gloria slowed her pace.

As though sensing her approach, the man turned round, causing Gloria to stop dead in her tracks.

It couldn't be? Could it?

3

Was her mind playing tricks on her? Did she want this so much her mind had fabricated it?

'Gloria!' Jack's voice sounded out loud and clear as he dumped his bag in the snow and strode towards her. *'Hope!'* The joy in his voice was undisguised.

Gloria stood immobile, unable to speak as the man she loved reached them and wrapped his arms around them.

'Jack! Oh, Jack!' Gloria's voice was muffled. She could feel her heart thumping against her chest. 'I can't believe it!' She looked up, needing to see him, to be reassured that this was not a dream.

She watched as Jack stepped back and took Hope, kissing her on the head and lifting her high in the air.

'My beautiful little girl!' He smiled up at his daughter and spun her round.

It was only when Gloria heard Hope's tired but excited little voice cry out 'Daddy!' that she knew this was for real.

Only then did the tears start tumbling down her face.

The initial rush of euphoria Gloria felt was quickly pushed aside by fear and panic. She blinked to clear her vision, which had become blurred by the sudden onset of tears at seeing Jack and watching him with his daughter. Hope's shrieks of joy and excitement were filling the air, breaking the silence of this unforgettable Christmas night.

'What yer doing here, Jack?' Gloria asked, furtively looking up and down the street. The rapture in her face was gone, anxiety now at the fore. 'Yer shouldn't be here. What if someone sees you? What if Miriam finds out?' Jack's wife had blackmailed them after finding out about their affair, threatening to expose some of the women welders' secrets should Jack ever return to his hometown.

'Don't worry,' Jack was quick to reassure her as he lowered a giggling Hope back down, 'it's all right. Everything's been sorted.'

Gloria pushed her curly brown hair away from her face and looked around, still terrified that someone might come out and clock them. Clock Jack. With Hope in his arms. Outside her flat. Then shoot across to the other side of the Wear and sell them out to Miriam.

'Let's get inside!' She hurried to the top of the steps to her flat, quickly scanning the street before clomping down to her front door. Jamming the key into the lock and pushing open the door, she flicked on the light and ushered Jack inside. He ducked slightly, at the same time kissing the top of his daughter's head. As soon as they were over the threshold, Gloria closed the door and dropped the latch. Only then did she allow herself a sigh of relief. They were safe. Away from prying eyes.

'What on earth possessed yer to come back?' Gloria said, taking off her coat and automatically going over to the electric gas fire and switching it on. She turned to see Jack gently putting Hope down; he was smiling as he ruffled her mop of raven hair.

Gloria walked towards the man she still couldn't quite believe was here as he put his hand out and pulled her close, kissing her gently at first and then with more passion.

'It's safe,' he said. 'I wouldn't have taken the risk otherwise. Trust me.' He cupped her face in his hands and kissed her again, savouring the feel of her lips on his. Her mouth tasted of sweet berries. Port. Her favourite tipple.

Gloria gave up trying to question him, believing him, knowing he would never put others in danger to satiate his own selfish needs. She kissed him back. The feel of his lips reassuring her that this was real. That he really was here.

'*Daddy!*'

5

They both looked down to see Hope staring up at them, her hand grasping Jack's trouser leg as she started to tug it.

'Come here, my gorgeous little girl.' Jack let go of Gloria and reached down. 'My, my, someone's grown up since I saw them last.' He picked Hope up again and kissed her little button nose, causing her to scrunch up her eyes and giggle. 'Two years. Two whole years.'

Gloria heard sadness and a shred of bitterness. Hope had just been six months old when he had last seen her.

'*Daddy*,' Hope said again, as though practising a new word. A word she had only ever spoken into the receiver of a black Bakelite phone.

'Aye ... *Daddy* ...' Jack suddenly felt his throat constrict with emotion.

Hope's face creased into a smile and she touched his face with one hand.

Gloria felt the tears welling up.

'I'll tell yer what – ' Jack looked at Gloria and then back at his daughter ' – why don't I read yer a bedtime story, eh?'

Gloria looked at Hope and pulled a happy face, mouthing the word 'story'.

'*Story!*' Hope clapped her hands together.

A wide smile spread across Jack's face and he took a step towards Gloria and kissed her again. Nothing, he vowed silently, would ever part them again. Nothing.

'I don't think I've ever felt this happy in my entire life,' he said, his eyes glistening with the sting of tears.

'Nor me,' Gloria said, as she kissed him back.

Gloria watched as Jack read Hope her favourite bedtime story, Beatrix Potter's *The Tale of Two Bad Mice*. It had become her favourite after they'd been forced to spend the last air raid with a rather frantic mouse that had been scurrying around in Mr Brown's Anderson shelter.

Looking at Jack, Gloria saw the physical changes the past two years had brought: his hair was more grey than black and his face looked tired and weather-beaten, but physically he seemed strong, certainly more muscular than when she had seen him last on that awful day when they'd been forced to say a rushed farewell in the porch of St Peter's Church.

Gloria looked at Hope. Her dark lashes were lowering as she tried desperately to stay awake. Jack's voice was soft as he relayed the mice's tale of mischief in the doll's house, knowing that the lilting rhythm of the words would soon send his daughter into a deep slumber.

Sensing her eyes on him, Jack glanced back at Gloria and winked before turning another page of the hardback book. Gloria noticed how full of life he seemed.

At the familiar sound of her daughter's gentle snoring, Gloria stood up, careful not to make any noise. Jack followed, putting the storybook down on the stool by Hope's cot and tiptoeing out of the room.

As soon as they were in the hallway, Jack pulled her close and they kissed. This time for longer. And without interruption.

'God, I've missed you,' Jack murmured.

'Please – tell me yer here to stay? For good?' she asked, her voice barely a whisper.

'I'm here to stay,' Jack reassured. 'For good.'

Gloria kissed him again, curious to know more, but not wanting to talk. They had spoken on the phone so much since Jack's exile, she suddenly felt tired of words. She only wanted the feel of his mouth on hers and his body pressed against her own.

Sensing her passion, Jack looked at Gloria. 'I've waited two years for this moment,' he said, his breathing becoming heavy. 'I don't want to wait another minute.'

'Me neither,' Gloria said.

And with that she took his hand and led him into the bedroom.

After making love, Gloria and Jack lay in each other's arms, simply holding one another, enjoying the feel of each other's bare skin and the warmth of their bodies.

'So …' Gloria said, kissing Jack's bare shoulder '… tell me, tell me everything. How come I've got yer back? I'm guessing it's got something to do with Helen?'

'Aye,' Jack said. 'She rang me from the old man's house and told me I could come back home.'

Gloria knew that Helen and Miriam had gone to Mr Havelock's for Christmas dinner.

'Thank God I offered to work Christmas Day – she'd have had a job getting hold of me otherwise.' He looked at Gloria. 'She told me that Bel 'n Pearl had turned up out of the blue. All she said was that I had to trust her – that she'd tell me everything later, but that I could come back.'

'It must have been something big for Miriam to allow yer to return,' Gloria said.

Jack blew out air.

'*Allow.*' He repeated the word with undisguised resentment. 'That woman has been ruling our lives for too long.' Gloria knew Jack wasn't just thinking about his banishment to the Clyde, but about the fact that Miriam had lied and manipulated him into marrying her all those years ago, pretending she was pregnant to get him down the aisle and then telling him she'd had a miscarriage, by which time it was too late – he had a ring on his finger and an invisible shackle around his ankle.

'Well,' Gloria said, snuggling up to him, 'all should be revealed tomorrow when Helen comes round.'

Gloria smiled as Jack switched off the light and pulled her close. *No wonder Helen hadn't wanted to come back to the flat*. She'd known Jack would be waiting for her. She had done well to hide her excitement. It had been Helen's mission for a long time to get Jack back – to put right the wrong she felt partly responsible for – so that Hope could finally have her daddy home where he belonged.

Her final thought as sleep came was that Helen too would now have her father back in her life – something, Gloria knew, that would mean the absolute world to her.

Chapter Two

Boxing Day

As Helen drove across the Wearmouth Bridge, she automatically looked to her left, her eyes scanning the river, crammed as always with an eclectic mix of boats and barges, cobles and colliers, the odd schooner and, of course, ships – those in the making, as well as those docked for repair. She caught a glimpse of the J.L. Thompson & Sons shipyard on North Sands through an archway of overhanging cranes, before forcing her attention back to the road. Whenever she saw her place of work, she never failed to feel a swell of pride.

Driving down Bridge Street and turning left into High Street West, she spotted a couple of billeted Admiralty leaving the Grand Hotel and her mind swung to her mother. She had heard her return late last night, stumbling up the stairs to her bedroom, having undoubtedly drunk the bar dry with her friend and fellow lush, Amelia.

Helen indicated and turned right down Norfolk Street.

Parking at the bottom of the street, she climbed out of her beloved green sports car, admiring it for a moment. Even though she had bought it several months ago, the novelty of owning such a swanky motor, and driving it rather than being chauffeured, had not worn off.

Looking at her watch, Helen saw it had just gone half ten. Enough time for Gloria and her father to have had a lie-in and enjoyed their first breakfast together with Hope as a family, but not so late that they might have ventured out – something she knew they'd be loath to do until they'd been told exactly what had happened yesterday.

Walking through the melting snow towards the end of the road, Helen turned right into Borough Road. As she approached the steps that led down to Gloria's flat, she imagined how wonderful it must have been for her father to finally be reunited with Gloria and Hope. Her heart warmed at the thought of it.

Knocking on the front door, Helen called out, 'Only me!'

Seconds later, the door opened. Jack stood with Hope in his arms.

'Dad!' Helen held her arms out wide and hugged them both.

'*Daddy!*' Hope shouted out, copying her big sister.

'Yes,' Helen said, cupping Hope's heart-shaped face. 'Daddy's back!'

Looking over her father's shoulder, Helen saw Gloria coming out of the kitchenette. She didn't think she had ever seen her look so happy.

Having fussed over Hope playing with her toys on the clippy mat by the coffee table, Helen sat down in the armchair next to her and watched as her father settled with Gloria on the sofa opposite.

'So, come on, don't keep us in suspense any longer,' Jack said.

'Well,' Helen took a quick sip of her tea, 'it's a long story, which I will try and keep as short and succinct as possible.'

She kept her word, briefly telling her father about Bel's true paternity, how she had initially suspected that she might be a Havelock after seeing Bel and Miriam at Polly and Tommy's wedding last Christmas. The similarities between the two had hit her like a slap on the face: the same corn-blonde hair, the same button nose, the same lips and the same blue eyes. Both pretty and petite. She relayed how she had ended up employing a young female private eye, whom she had nicknamed Miss Marple, to find out the truth. Armed with the information she'd been given, Helen had decided she would only know for sure if she confronted Pearl and Bel; something she had done last May in the Tatham Arms.

'So, you've known all this time?' Jack asked, surprised that Helen hadn't told him.

'I have,' Helen said.

'And I have as well,' Gloria said, looking at Jack. 'But Bel said she wanted as few people to know as possible. She said it was all right for Helen to tell me as she knew how close we are.'

'So,' Jack said in disbelief, 'the old man is Bel Elliot's real father?'

Helen and Gloria looked at him and nodded.

'Pearl used to work as a scullery maid way back when—' Helen stopped short.

'And he got her in the family way?' Jack said.

'More like *raped* her,' Helen said.

Jack looked to Gloria for affirmation. She nodded, her face grim. He felt a shiver go down his back. Charles Havelock had been his father-in-law for over twenty-five years. This was shocking.

'And I learnt yesterday that Pearl wasn't the only one,' Helen continued. 'One poor girl called Grace never got over what had been done to her. Her mother came home one day to find her daughter hanging from the bannisters.'

Gloria's hand went to her mouth. 'Oh, that's terrible.'

Jack stood up and paced across the living room. His face was red and his jaw clenched.

12

'So,' Gloria said, 'I'm guessing when you 'n yer mam were at yer granddad's for yer Christmas dinner, Pearl 'n Bel turned up – and Bel told Mr Havelock that she was his daughter?'

'Yes,' Helen said.

'And *I'm* guessing,' Jack said, his face still flushed with anger, 'that Bel said she'd tell everyone about what he'd done to her mam – 'n that she was the result – if I wasn't allowed to come back.'

'More or less,' Helen said.

'And what about Miriam?' Gloria asked. 'I can't imagine she took all of this lying down.'

'No, she didn't.' Helen sighed. 'She accused Bel and Pearl of being liars, at which point Bel showed them the private eye's report, which detailed all the evidence that pointed to Grandfather being Bel's father.'

'What? You gave Bel the report?' Gloria didn't try to hide her surprise.

Helen nodded.

'Bel said she'd make it plain that Pearl was in no way a willing participant in her conception and that she would tell the judge and jury and anyone else who would listen to her that Grandfather was a rapist. A "sick and perverted old man". And that Pearl had only been fifteen years old at the time, which, she pointed out, was below the age of consent.'

'Blimey,' Gloria said, beckoning Jack to come and sit down.

'And very clever,' Helen said. 'She had Grandfather in a corner. Even if it couldn't be proved he'd raped her, it would still be an offence because of Pearl's age.'

Helen watched as her father sat back down next to Gloria.

'Bel said that in exchange for her silence, she wanted Dad to be able to return home to be with the woman he loves, but more than anything so that he could be a father to Hope. She did what she did for this little girl here,' Helen said, looking at Hope playing intently with her dollies. 'So Hope could have a father in her life.

'But,' Helen went on, raising her eyebrows, 'that wasn't the only shocker to come out of yesterday's very eventful Christmas dinner.'

'There's more?' Gloria said.

'There is indeed.' Helen looked from her father to Gloria. 'Grandfather said that he'd also been doing his research and knew Bel had a half-sister called Maisie who had been adopted as a baby.'

'Which everyone knows already,' Jack said.

'They do,' Helen said, 'but not many know that she is also a *call girl* – and that she works in an upmarket bordello which is run by Rosie's friend Lily.'

Helen looked at her father and Gloria. Neither looked at all shocked.

'Did you know that already?' she asked accusingly.

'We did,' said Gloria. 'But it wasn't our secret to tell.'

Gloria and Jack waited for Helen to ask more about Lily, the eccentric woman with the orange hair and fake French accent, and her connection with Helen's head welder, Rosie Miller, but she didn't. Much to their relief.

'So after Grandfather showed his trump card,' Helen continued, 'he told Bel that if she said anything to any-one about him being her father, then he would inform the authorities about the bordello, and also make sure all the women welders' secrets would be bandied about town.' Helen sighed. 'And, of course, that he would take great pleasure in finding ways of ruining not only Bel's life, but the lives of all those she holds dear.'

Jack shook his head in disbelief.

'So, how come he agreed to allow Jack back?' Gloria asked.

Helen arched an eyebrow. 'Pearl. Unbelievably, it was Pearl who saved the day.'

'How come?' Jack asked.

Helen watched as Hope got up, squeezed her way past her mammy and started climbing on to her daddy's knee.

'Well, Pearl said that if he did grass them all up, Lily's little black book would undoubtedly find its way into the hands of the police. And that every one of those businessmen, judges, lawyers and those high-up in the police would know it was Grandfather's fault that they were being pulled in for solicitation.'

'She had him by the short and curlies then,' Jack said.

'She did, but Pearl had one more card to play to totally secure the deal,' Helen said.

'And what was that?' Gloria asked.

'Grandmother,' Helen said simply.

'What do you mean?' Jack asked.

'Well,' said Helen, sucking in air, 'it would seem that my dear grandmama is not in fact dead, but is very much alive and living – or should I say incarcerated – up at the asylum under an assumed name: *Miss* Henrietta *Girling*.'

'What? At Ryhope?' Jack was incredulous.

'Yes,' said Helen.

Jack had met Henrietta a few times in the early days of his marriage to Miriam. He'd never forgotten her look. She was eccentric, certainly, but not mad.

'Why's she at the asylum?' Jack asked.

'That's the pertinent question,' Helen said. 'Grandmama Henrietta has been locked away in the local mental hospital because of Grandfather.'

There was silence as Jack and Gloria digested what they'd been told.

'So, he got her sectioned?' Jack asked.

15

'He did. Greased the necessary palms. And she's been there ever since,' Helen said.

'Are you sure about this?' Gloria asked.

'I've seen her with my own eyes.' Helen looked at their shocked faces. 'I drove there last night and Genevieve the old receptionist took me to see her.'

Gloria and Jack looked at Helen and then at Hope, whose attention was now also focused on her big sister.

'And she's *lovely*,' Helen said. 'Really lovely. Obviously, she comes across as a bit doolally, but who wouldn't if you'd been shut away in the local loony bin for the past two decades.'

Jack and Gloria were speechless.

'And you'll never guess who her doctor is.' Helen was looking at Gloria.

'Not Dr Eris?'

'The one and only,' Helen said, wide-eyed.

Jack looked puzzled. 'Who's Dr Eris?'

Helen stood up and sighed. 'A story for another day.' She looked at her watch. 'Gosh, look at the time. I've got to get back to the yard.' She got up and looked at her father, Hope on his lap and Gloria sitting next to him. She smiled. 'I'll come and see you all later.'

As she left, she turned. 'And Dad … it's great to have you back.'

'I'll second that,' Gloria beamed.

As she closed the door, Helen heard Hope's squeals of delight. They weren't the only ones to be over the moon to have Jack back.

As Helen walked to the car, she thought of Dr Parker. He was never far from her thoughts, especially when she was excited or upset or she had some news to tell – and boy did she have some exciting, as well as pretty scandalous, news to impart. She wished she could go and see him now, just drive over to the Ryhope and have a good catch-up over a pot of tea and an iced bun. John's favourite. But she had to get back to work; although, even if she didn't, it was likely that John would be busy in the operating theatre, doing his rounds or on call. And if he wasn't, there was an equally good chance he'd be with that awful woman – Claire Eris. *Dr* Claire Eris. Helen didn't like her one bit. And not just because she'd got her claws into the man Helen wanted for herself – the man she was in love with.

The moment she had first met Claire that day in the canteen on a visit to see John, her hackles had risen. There was something about Claire that she didn't like. It was hard to pinpoint exactly what. Outwardly, Claire was a lovely, intelligent, attractive doctor – a psychotherapist, no less – doing a wonderful job of helping others, of *mending minds*, as she put it. But Helen suspected that inwardly all was not so perfectly lily-white – that Claire had a mean, conniving streak in her, and could be ruthless when she wanted something.

Still, those were thoughts she'd have to keep to herself. She was going to have to learn to deal with Claire, as there was a good chance that she'd bump into her when visiting her grandmother at the asylum. Claire was Henrietta's doctor, after all. Typical – out of all the doctors working in the asylum, Claire was her grandmother's shrink. But at least Helen's visits to Ryhope would give her the opportunity to see John.

As she got back in her car, Helen's mind wandered back to two days ago, to Christmas Eve, when they had been squashed up in the Tatham after the christening. John had seemed genuinely sad that they hadn't seen much of each other lately. He'd been in a reflective mood and had talked about how close they had become over the years, which was true, and how they had been there for each other, which wasn't entirely true. He had been there for her – throughout her four-month pregnancy, her miscarriage, the sickening revelations about her grandfather – but she honestly didn't think that she had really been there for him, other than as a companion.

Starting up the engine, Helen indicated and pulled out, turning left into Borough Road. She just wished she had realised she was in love with him sooner. But at the beginning she had been too wrapped up in her girlish crush on Tommy; then she'd become involved with Theo – lying, cheating, married Theo – who had used her like a rag, tossed her aside and returned to his pregnant wife and two children. John had helped her pick up the pieces, and as time had gone on she had realised, too late, that she was in love with him. Although even if she had realised sooner, it would still have been hopeless. John would not want her as a wife. As her mother had repeatedly told her, she was 'sullied', after all.

As she drove through the town centre and then across the Wearmouth Bridge, Helen recalled John saying how much he valued their friendship. '*I think we've got something special,*' he'd said. And she'd told him that she agreed. That she was glad she wasn't losing him, despite his relationship with Dr Eris. And she had meant it.

She couldn't imagine a life without John in it, even if it was just as a friend.

Chapter Three

New Year's Day 1944

'Happy New Year!'

Rosie, Polly, Gloria, Martha and Hannah looked up to see Dorothy and Angie, arm in arm, walking across the yard towards them.

'Health, wealth and happiness!' they declared, their voices loud enough to cause most of the other overall-clad workers in the vicinity to glance up. Seeing that it was the two gobby welders from Rosie's squad, they turned back to their own conversations.

'Happy New Year!' the women chorused back in unison. They had been bracing themselves for the arrival of the squad's 'terrible two'. The pair were pretty much inseparable. They worked together and lived together in a little flat in the centre of town, yet they were like chalk and cheese. Dorothy was tall and dark-haired and came from a relatively well-off background. Angie just nudged five foot and had strawberry-blonde hair and came from a mining family in the Barbary Coast, known as one of the poorest areas of the town.

'They don't look too worse for wear.' Gloria spoke out of the corner of her mouth to the group's gentle giant, Martha. They were both holding their hands up against the warmth of the five-gallon brazier they had managed to get going as soon as they'd arrived at their workplace, a stone's throw away from the quayside. The fire was now flickering and spitting, providing them with some much-needed heat to combat the bitter cold and biting winds slicing across the yard from the North Sea.

'*Yeah!*' Dorothy let go of Angie and marched over to Polly. 'She's back!' She threw her arms around her work-mate and squeezed her. 'We've missed you! Didn't we?' She looked at Rosie, Gloria, Hannah and Martha. They all nodded, smiled and muttered their agreement.

Polly had been forced to give up her job when she had nearly miscarried in the third month of her pregnancy. After having a cervical stitch put in, she had kept on working in the yard in more sedentary positions, first as timekeeper and then as a clerical worker in the admin department. She'd worked right up to giving birth to Artie, who had come almost two weeks earlier than expected and had been born amidst great drama on the sorting table in the middle of the main office. That had happened four months ago and today was her first day back with the women welders.

'Eee, yer knar, Pol, I can honestly say it's not been the same without yer,' Angie said, her face serious.

'Ah, thanks,' said Polly, pushing a strand of her thick chestnut-coloured hair back into her headscarf. She'd almost forgotten what a battle it was to keep her hair away from her face. Thompson's was located on the bend of the River Wear, making it perfectly positioned to take the full force of the north-east's unrelenting weather.

'I have to agree,' Rosie said. 'It's going to be good to have you back – and not just because I won't have to find a replacement.'

Polly looked at Rosie and then at the rest of her friends.

'It feels good to be back,' she said, a wide smile appearing on her face. 'Even if the weather's awful.' She looked up at the dark morning sky, which was only just starting to lighten with the break of day.

'You don't think you'll miss Artie too much?' Hannah, the group's 'little bird', asked. She was still considered one of the squad, even though she had left welding when Rosie got her an apprenticeship in the drawing office, where she had excelled; pen and paper suited her much more than a rod and metal plates. Hannah's question about baby Artie had been one that had gone through all their minds on seeing Polly back in her overalls this morning.

'I hope not,' Polly said, looking at Hannah, who had on double layers of everything. A muffler as well as a scarf. A hat as well as her hood pulled up. You could only just see her face peeking out and the blunted fringe of her bobbed black hair.

'I'm only going to be working normal hours, no overtime,' Polly explained to all the women. 'So I'll be with Artie from the minute I get back from work until the minute I leave. And all weekend.'

'But today's Saturday?' Martha asked, genuinely puzzled.

'That's just to get me back into the swing of things,' Polly said. 'You know, with it being a short shift.' In reality, Polly had been chomping at the bit to get back and had argued the case with her mam, Agnes Elliot, to start today rather than Monday.

'I suppose it's the start of the New Year. A clean sheet and all that,' Gloria said.

'A clean sheet. Exactly,' Polly agreed. 'And I really don't think Artie will miss me at all.'

'That's a bit harsh,' Rosie said.

'Yeah,' Dorothy agreed. 'I'm sure that won't be the case. Little Artie adores you.'

Polly let out a splutter of genuine laughter. 'Honestly, since the twins arrived in his life, he's only had eyes for his two younger cousins.'

There was a collective 'ahh' at the mention of Gabrielle and Stephen, the newborn babies Bel and Joe had adopted on Boxing Day. The women had gone to meet the two new additions to the Elliot household earlier on in the week and had all been instantly smitten.

'Well, I for one,' Dorothy said, 'have a good feeling about this year.'

'Why's that?' Martha asked, giving the fire a poke with a pair of metal tongs.

'Yeah,' Angie chipped in, 'yer been looking into that crystal ball of yers?'

'The stars are aligned,' Dorothy explained. 'Gloria's got Jack back.' She looked at Gloria and smiled. 'And Rosie's heard from Peter.' They had all been there when Dorothy's beau, Toby, had told Rosie on Christmas Day that her husband, Peter Miller, an undercover operative in France, was alive and well. 'And Angie has *finally* – ' Dorothy's eyes went to the heavens ' – got it together with Quentin.' Thanks to a little meddling from Dorothy and their neighbour, Mrs Kwiatkowski, Angie and Quentin had become girlfriend and boyfriend after he had surprised her on Christmas Eve, having got leave from his job with the War Office and travelled back to his hometown to tell the woman he had been in love with for over a year how he felt.

'And,' Dorothy said, pausing for dramatic effect, 'I'm pretty sure that I might well be wearing something shiny and diamond like on my left hand before the year is out.'

'Really?' Hannah asked. She and Olly had been courting for over a year and neither of them had even thought about getting engaged. Or at least *she* had never thought about it.

'Why are yer so sure?' Gloria asked.

'I'm *so sure*,' Dorothy said, 'because Toby kept going on about meeting my parents when he was here at Christmas. And we all know what that means.'

22

'It means he wants to meet yer mam 'n stepdad,' Angie said, rolling her eyes.

Dorothy ignored her.

'He clearly wants to ask their permission for my hand in marriage,' Dorothy explained. 'Like a proper gentleman – not that I want to jinx it.'

'Haven't you just jinxed it by saying it out loud?' Martha asked. She had nearly been jumped on when she'd started to say that they'd not had an air raid since the end of May last year.

'Blimey, there's nowt like being sure of yerself, is there?' Angie gawped at her friend.

All the women laughed loudly, although none of them thought that it was so improbable. They had seen Toby and Dorothy together on Christmas Day when he had turned up at Vera's café looking very dashing in his army uniform. There was no doubt they were well suited – both were from educated, middle-class families – and it was as clear as day that Toby was well and truly taken with his sweetheart.

'*Love!*' Dorothy put both hands on her chest. 'There is to be a lot of love this year! I can feel it in my bones.'

As soon as the midday klaxon sounded out, the women downed tools and hurried across the yard towards the sanctuary of the canteen.

'I've just got to pop up to see Helen,' Rosie said. 'I want to catch her before she heads over to Doxford's for the launch of *Arabistan*.'

'More like heading off for a schmooze with the scrumptious Matthew Royce,' Dorothy declared.

Matthew Royce Jnr was the new manager at Doxford's, who had made no secret of his amorous feelings for Helen.

'I don't think Helen sees him that way,' Gloria said.

'Is the woman totally blind?' Dorothy gasped.

'Who's blind?' Angie sidled up next to her best mate.

'Helen,' Dorothy explained. 'Glor reckons she doesn't fancy the irresistible Matthew Royce.'

'Never!' Angie sounded equally amazed.

Rosie and Gloria exchanged exasperated looks.

'Tell her Happy New Year from us,' Dorothy said. 'And to have a *luverlee* time with lover-boy Matthew this afternoon.'

Dorothy and Angie hooted with laughter and ran to catch up with Martha and Polly, who had just been joined by Hannah and Olly hurrying over from the drawing office.

Gloria followed them, thinking that Helen *was* blind when it came to Matthew. But she knew that was because she only had eyes for one person – Dr Parker.

'Get a move on, Glor!' Dorothy shouted over; she was holding open the canteen door.

Gloria quickened her pace. Everything seemed to happen so much faster these days. You had to walk quicker, work quicker – get married quicker. Gloria sighed as she reached the entrance to the canteen and Dorothy made a show of bowing and waving her through the entrance with a flourish. The girl was as nutty as a fruitcake, and such an attention-seeker, but she had a heart of gold.

'I feel for Toby,' Gloria ribbed Dorothy as she walked into the warmth of the cafeteria.

'Why's that?' Dorothy let the door swing shut.

'Because if he does propose,' Gloria said, 'he's gonna have his hands full, that's for sure.'

'What? Little ol' me? A handful?' Dorothy's words were followed by a robust cackle.

As they dumped their flasks and luncheon boxes on the table they had commandeered as their own after first starting at the yard, Muriel waved at them from behind the counter.

'Good to see yer back, Polly!' she shouted over. 'Bet yer wish yer were up in the office today, though? Brass monkeys out there.'

Polly laughed. As did the rest of the women. They knew it didn't matter how bad the weather was, Polly would always choose welding over office work.

Taking a bite of her sandwich, Dorothy pulled out a copy of the *Sunderland Echo* from her haversack. 'Time for our lessons in current affairs.' She looked across at Polly, whose idea it had been initially, although Dorothy had taken on the mantle of head teacher.

Polly nodded and pulled out her copy of the *Daily Mirror*, which she always bought because it reminded her of Tommy's granddad, Arthur; it had been the only national newspaper he would read. Arthur had died a year ago, but she still felt his presence – still wanted to feel his presence. Looking around the table, Polly saw that she and Dorothy were the only two who had remembered to bring a paper to work with them.

'You go first, Pol,' Dorothy said magnanimously, 'seeing as today is your first day back with the troops.'

'Consider yerself honoured,' Gloria japed.

Polly spread out the paper on the table and scanned the headlines. 'Looks like the Chinese are having some success against the Japanese in Burma,' she said, her eyes scanning further down the page.

'That's good,' Martha said, taking a big bite of her corned beef and potato sandwich.

Everyone mumbled their agreement.

'And there's more on General Eisenhower and him being officially named head of the expected invasion of Europe,' Polly continued.

'I thought it was France they were gonna invade?' Angie asked, her eyes glued to Martha's sandwich. She was always in awe of the packed lunches Mrs Perkins managed to put together for her daughter.

'France *is* Europe – well, a part of Europe,' Dorothy said, rolling her eyes.

'I think the plan is to start with France and then push through to the rest of Europe,' Olly informed them.

'Would I be right in saying that this means Peter will be a part of it all?' Hannah asked quietly, checking over her shoulder that Rosie was nowhere in sight.

'Well, now that you mention it,' Polly said, 'I would guess there's a good chance he will be.'

They were all quiet for a moment. Peter's work was very hush-hush, and although no one knew for certain what he was doing over the Channel, it didn't take a genius to guess he'd be helping the Resistance prepare for the anticipated invasion.

'I think we should keep any chatter about what's going to happen in France down to a minimum when Rosie's about,' Gloria suggested.

Everyone agreed that ignorance was bliss in this case.

'You heard anything from your boys yet?' Hannah asked.

They all knew that Gloria's sons, Bobby and Gordon, were able seamen on the destroyer HMS *Opportune*, and that it had been part of the Battle of the North Cape, which was being hailed as a significant victory for the Allies. It hadn't been without casualties, though. A battleship, a destroyer and a cruiser had been damaged and twenty-one men had been reported dead, with more injured.

'She got a telegram from them the other day,' Dorothy answered for Gloria.

Gloria sighed. 'I am capable of speaking for myself, Dor.' She looked at Hannah. 'Thanks for asking. They said they were all right, which was a huge relief.'

'They sound nice boys,' Hannah said. 'Knowing how anxious you'd be and putting your mind at rest.'

Gloria nodded. It was true she'd been worried sick the moment she'd seen the headlines. The telegram had lifted a massive weight off her shoulders, but, like just about every other mother with sons at war, she wouldn't be happy until they were back home.

'So, what about news here? What's in the *Echo*?' Hannah said, looking across at Dorothy, who did not need further encouragement to take her turn in the relaying of the day's news bulletin.

'Well, I have to say the editorial seems as sure of victory as I am about Toby's proposal.'

There was the expected rumble of groans around the table. They all knew this was all they were going to hear from now on. They could only hope that Toby dropped down on one knee post-haste to save them all months of earache.

'It reads …' she declared, taking a quick sup of tea '… "This is the year of Victory".'

'Who says that?' Martha asked.

'The editor of our local newspaper,' Dorothy said, again rolling her eyes. 'That's why it's called an "editorial".' She took a deep breath and continued. '"This is the year, the year of Victory, the end of the European war."' She paused. 'Notice how he said *European* war – not the war *worldwide*.'

Angie emitted a loud sigh. 'Gerra a move on, Dor, we've not got all day. Yer might like the sound of yer own voice, but that's not to say the rest of us dee.'

Everyone chuckled. Angie was doing a valiant job of keeping up the banter with her best mate, but her words lacked any kind of sting. It was obvious to them all that she was too much in love for there to be any kind of genuine sharpness or edge to her words.

Dorothy rustled the paper and continued to read. '"The year in which we believe all our troubles, real or imaginary, will come to an end."' She looked up to see Hannah listening attentively. Poor Hannah. Her worries were most definitely not imaginary.

'Well, let's hope so,' Polly said.

They all hoped so. Gloria for the sake of her two boys, Rosie for Peter's sake, Polly for Tommy's, and Hannah for the safety of her parents, imprisoned in the notorious Auschwitz concentration camp in Poland.

The women – like countless others across the length and breadth of the country – prayed with all their hearts that the words penned by the editor of the local paper in a town on the north-east coast of England would come true.

As Rosie made her way over to admin, she felt happy. She hadn't read the *Sunderland Echo*'s editorial, but she too had felt a sense of hope ever since Toby had told her that Peter was alive. She'd wanted to beg him to tell her more when he'd turned up at Vera's café, where they had all been having their Christmas dinner en masse, but she knew it wasn't fair and that it didn't matter if she pleaded, Toby would not have been able to give her any more information, for he was part of 'Churchill's secret army' – formally known as the Special Operations Executive.

It was Toby who had recruited Peter for the SOE's French division while Peter had been working as a detective sergeant. Since Rosie had said her goodbyes to Peter in Guildford, where he'd gone for his training two years ago, she had only seen him the once, when he had turned up for an overnight stay in the summer of 1942. Since then she'd only had a short but very beautifully worded message from him, transcribed by a wireless operator. Since then, not a whisper. An entire year had gone by, during which time she had become increasingly worried and convinced that no news was not actually good news at all, so on Christmas Day when Toby had told her that Peter was alive and well, the relief had been overwhelming. She had failed to keep her emotions in check, which was unusual for her, and she had wept openly in front of everyone.

In the days that followed she'd decided that she would continue to revel in the good news for as long as possible – before the worry set back in. She'd even allowed herself to imagine what life might be like if – no, *when* – Peter came back from the war. For the first time in a long while she began to believe that dreams really could come true – it didn't just happen in the Hollywood films which Dorothy dragged them all to see. The dream of having a family could become reality – not a family in the traditional sense, of course, that would never happen, but a happy-ever-after with her husband and sister living in the house in Brookside Gardens, with Peter back working for the Borough Police and Charlotte continuing her education. She might even be able to convince Lily to go legit. Rosie laughed at herself as she pulled open the main doors of the offices. *As if that would ever happen.* Lily and legit just didn't go together.

Taking the stairs two at a time, she reached the door to the open-plan office and yanked it open. A dozen faces looked up momentarily to see who it was before their attention returned to their typewriters or comptometers. There was a skeleton staff as it was Saturday and New Year's Day at that.

'Happy New Year!' Marie-Anne called out as soon as she saw Rosie. She got up from her desk and hurried over.

'Happy New Year to you too,' Rosie smiled.

'Thanks,' Marie-Anne said, her face suddenly becoming sombre, 'but I have to admit, I'm going to miss Bel terribly … I'm already missing her and it's barely been a week.'

Rosie smiled again. She knew Marie-Anne had loved having Bel as her second in command. The two had got on well.

'And she's going to be hard to replace – that's *if* I get a replacement.' Marie-Anne pushed back a stray curl of her unruly ginger hair and looked over to the manager's officer. 'Are you here to see Miss Crawford?'

Rosie nodded and Marie-Anne walked her over to the small office, knocked and opened the door.

'Mrs Miller to see you, Miss Crawford,' Marie-Anne said in her best King's English, just a hint of an Irish accent sneaking through.

'Ah, Rosie.' Helen waved her in. 'Perfectly timed. Marie-Anne has just made a pot of tea.'

'Ask if you need anything else,' Marie-Anne said as she made to leave, jumping as Winston, the office tomcat, shot past her.

'I will,' Helen said, reaching down to stroke the cat, now rubbing up against her legs and purring loudly. 'And Marie-Anne – I just wanted to say thank you for all your hard work. I do appreciate it, you know.'

Marie-Anne's pale, freckled face lit up; she was beaming as she shut the door.

Rosie gave Helen a sceptical look. 'I take it you're not replacing Bel, then?'

Helen shook her head. 'Am I that readable?'

Rosie didn't say anything but just smiled. She had known Helen from first starting at the yard. They'd both risen through the ranks in their areas of expertise. Rosie through skill and hard work, Helen also through hard work and long hours, but helped along by a good dollop of nepotism and a nature that could be both wily and a little ruthless.

'I'll make it up to her,' Helen defended herself. 'A promotion, title and a small pay rise.'

Rosie sat down in the chair in front of Helen's desk.

'You got everyone to work through their lunch break?' Rosie asked, surprised.

'No, no, I'm not that much of a slave-driver, although I'm sure Marie-Anne would argue the case. I'm letting everyone go at one o'clock. It *is* New Year's Day, after all.' Helen fished around for her packet of Pall Malls. 'So, tell me, how's things?'

'All good, thanks,' Rosie said. 'My squad told me to wish you a Happy New Year.'

'That's nice,' Helen said, lighting up a cigarette. 'I think I've finally been forgiven for all my past misdemeanours, of which there are many.'

Rosie laughed, thinking of the old Helen, the one who had tried unsuccessfully to split up Polly and Tommy, and failing, had then tried to split up Rosie's squad of women welders. There had been a lot of water under the bridge since then and Helen had more than proved her worth by saving Gloria from her violent ex-husband, Vinnie, after he'd attacked her in the yard, and later when she and Martha had pulled Gloria and Hope from a collapsing building during the Tatham Street bombing.

A little frostiness had returned to the women's relationship with Helen when they had found out she had been the one to tell Miriam about Gloria's affair with Jack and about Hope, but that had completely thawed after recent events. Any resentments towards Helen that the women might have still been hanging on to had been well and truly severed after hearing how Helen had helped Bel by giving her the private eye's report on her grandfather.

Helen and the women welders were now firmly bonded. They all now knew the truth about Bel's true paternity and the real reason Charles Havelock's wife was in the asylum. Just as they all knew that the truth must never get

31

out. Henrietta was the axe over Mr Havelock's head, but it would only remain there for as long as Henrietta was a closely guarded secret. The women were well aware of the importance of keeping shtum, even Dorothy.

'So,' Rosie chose her words carefully, 'is everything all right at your end? No repercussions from your grandfather – or your mother?'

'Not yet,' Helen said, taking a deep drag. 'Mother's done a bunk and gone to stay with my aunty Margaret and uncle Angus up in Scotland. I've not spoken to Grandfather since, but I know there will be repercussions of some sort. Perhaps not immediately, but sometime in the future.' She blew out a long stream of smoke, thinking of her grandfather and his obsession with winning at all costs. 'But when that time comes, I'll deal with it.'

'And Jack?' Rosie asked. 'Gloria said he's got back his old job at Crown's.'

'Yes, he has.' Helen's face brightened, as it always did nowadays when her father was mentioned. 'He went straight round there on Boxing Day and saw the MD, who couldn't get him started quick enough by all accounts.'

'That's brilliant,' Rosie said. She'd always had a soft spot for Jack since he'd stuck his neck out for her and given her a job after her parents had died.

'And the twins are settling in?' Helen asked, making a mental note to ask Dr Billingham to pop round and give them a once-over. Dr Billingham was the obstetrician who had helped Polly when she had nearly lost her baby.

Rosie laughed. 'According to Gloria after she dropped Hope off this morning, there's absolutely nothing whatsoever wrong with their lungs.'

Helen chuckled. She had popped in to see Gabrielle and Stephen at the Elliots' a couple of days after Bel and Joe had brought them back from the orphanage on Boxing Day. She had become close to Bel since she'd learnt the truth about her grandfather; it was a closeness that they were both keen on maintaining. On top of which, they were family: Bel was her aunty, which made the twins her cousins.

'I've a sneaking suspicion that much as Polly loves her new little niece and nephew, they have also contributed to her urgent need to get back to work.' Rosie chuckled.

'And Pearl? Has she set a date?' Helen asked. They had all been a little taken aback to learn that Bill Lawson, landlord of the Tatham Arms, had proposed to Pearl on Christmas Day – and that Bel's errant ma had said yes.

Rosie shook her head. 'Apparently she won't get married in the winter. It being her least favourite time of year.'

'I think we'd all agree with that,' Helen said, looking out at the dark afternoon skies threatening rain.

They were quiet for a moment. Helen would have loved to have taken the opportunity to bring Lily into the conversation – to ask Rosie about her connection to the woman Helen now knew to be a madam. But despite the urge, it just didn't feel appropriate.

'So,' Helen said instead, 'let me fill you in with the latest wish list from the Ministry of War Transport.'

Rosie felt herself relax. She had wondered if Helen would ask her about Lily's; she must be curious about her connection to the bordello. She'd prepared an explanation – a lie – but didn't want to use it unless forced to.

'Why does the sound of a wish list make me nervous?' Rosie said.

Helen let out light laughter. 'Because you know as well as I do that it means hard graft, lots of overtime and nigh-on impossible deadlines.

'Go on,' Rosie said, 'tell me the worst.'

'Well,' Helen said, opening up a green hardback ledger lying on her desktop, 'we've got to get *Empire Pitt* down the ways as fast as humanly possible.'

Rosie groaned. The cargo ship had a way to go before she was ready for launch.

'I'm going to get everyone working on her,' Helen said, looking up at Rosie. 'So, can you spread the word that overtime is expected?'

'For those who can,' Rosie added, thinking of Polly.

'Of course,' Helen countered.

'Is there a particular reason the Ministry of War Transport want her ready so quickly?' Rosie asked, sensing there was more to this than the usual need to increase Britain's shipping capacity in order to offset those lost to German U-boats.

'There is,' Helen said, stubbing out her cigarette. 'It looks like we're going to be concentrating on producing LCTs for the next five to six months.'

Rosie looked surprised. LCTs – Royal Navy landing craft tanks – were not usually vessels they were asked to build.

Helen caught her look.

'For the anticipated invasion of France,' she said simply. 'They need as many as they can get their hands on. All the yards here are being asked to knock them out. The Yanks are mass-producing them as well.

'Ahh,' Rosie said. She had read about what the papers were calling the planned assault on Fortress Europe. 'Of course, it makes sense. They need to get troops and tanks onto the beaches.'

Helen looked at her watch. 'But we can chat about it in more detail later. I just wanted to give you a heads-up.'

'Of course,' Rosie said. She felt momentarily disorientated. Any mention of France always knocked her for six.

Helen picked up her handbag. 'I'll follow you out. My presence is needed at Doxford's.'

Rosie snapped herself back into the here and now and turned to leave.

'Say hello to Matthew from all of us,' she said as they walked out of the office.

'I will,' Helen sighed.

Chapter Four

Tuesday 4 January

'At ease,' Toby said, looking at the roomful of men and women whose eyes were all trained on him. He strode to the brand-new blackboard at the front of the ops room. As he did so he was aware of some of the younger women watching him with particular interest. He knew he cut a fine figure in his army uniform and his rank always gave him an extra edge with the opposite sex. Reaching the blackboard, he picked up a stick of chalk. There were certainly some lookers in the room. There was a time when he would have earmarked at least one of them for a date, but not now that he had Dorothy. The moment he had first clapped eyes on her at Lily's, he'd fallen for her. Well and truly.

'We are here today,' Toby said, his voice commanding and serious, 'to be a part of one of the most important special operations of this war.' Toby knew how to inspire those under his command so that they gave it their all, making them feel that what they were doing was just as important as being out in the field. 'The purpose of the work you will begin today, and will most likely continue to do over the next six months or more, is to enable the successful delivery of military supplies, and the parachuting of weapons and equipment to resistance groups in enemy-occupied

36

countries. Namely, France, Denmark, Norway, Belgium and Holland.' He paused. 'There will also be times when personnel – specialised agents conversant in transmissions, demolition or armaments – will be dropped into the field and occasions when they will be brought back.'

Toby looked at the military personnel and civilian workers standing, listening intently to every word he spoke. He smiled. 'You can all sit down.'

He waited until chairs had been scraped back and the room was once again quiet.

'This operation that you are now all a part of is called ...' he turned and started scrawling on the blackboard before facing his audience again and pointing at what he had just written '... Operation Carpetbagger.'

He waited a beat before continuing. 'It will be written about in years to come. It *will* be a success. And it will be a success because of people like you, working day in, day out, often throughout the night. Everyone in this room will be an important cog in the wheel that takes us to victory.'

You could hear a pin drop – the swell of patriotism was all-pervading.

Half an hour later the room was abuzz with activity. There was a huge pinboard detailing the various categories of supplies, which ranged from sewing kits and bikes to grenades and guns, and where exactly they were to be dropped. Looking down at his watch, Toby left his sergeant, who had been transferred down south with him, in charge. He spoke with a broad Scottish accent and was a natural-born leader.

Walking out of the ops room, Toby headed along the corridor and into the deputy group commander's room. As soon as he walked through the door, he was greeted by a lower-ranking officer who quickly introduced himself as

Officer Kayle and took him over to a huge operational map covering the back wall of the office.

'One inch equates to ten miles,' he explained. 'As you can see, topographical features such as elevations, rivers and forests are clearly marked out.' He tapped the map with a long wooden ruler. 'Any areas where Special Operations flights are prohibited are clearly indicated.' Another tap.

'Anything from London?' Toby asked. He'd been informed on arrival that the base was to expect communications via a scrambler phone direct from Air Operations headquarters in the Office of Strategic Services (OSS), an American intelligence agency based in London.

'Yes, sir.' Officer Kayle stood up straight. 'S2 has just been given a list of approved targets.' Toby knew S2 to mean the intelligence officer based on-site.

'Good stuff,' Toby said as Officer Kayle took him over to a nearby desk and showed him the list of target drops, which were designated by names and numbers – everything was coded: 'Joes' were agents and 'nickels' referred to bundles of propaganda leaflets.

Toby saw that there were a series of planned drops over Caen, in northern France. It was where Peter's unit of men were presently positioned. *Talk about being in the middle of a nest of vipers.* Toby often wished he could have been an undercover operative like Peter, but his French, although good, was not good enough. Looking at what was planned over the next few months, and the danger that men like Peter, working alongside the Resistance, would undoubtedly encounter, he had to admit that he was glad to be on this side of the water.

Chapter Five

'Jack! It's grand to see yer!' Agnes ushered him into the house, nearly tripping over the two dogs, Tramp and Pup, who were trying to beat her to greet the visitor.

'Yer look well, very well,' she said. 'No Gloria and Hope?'

'They won't be long,' Jack said, patting the two small dogs. 'They just had to run a few chores first.' He shook off his coat.

'Here, give it to me,' Agnes said, not giving Jack any option. 'I'll stick it by the range, see if we can't get it dry.'

Jack smiled. It had been two years since he had seen Agnes. Her Irish brogue seemed more pronounced and her hair greyer, like his own, but other than that she hadn't changed a bit.

'We can't say enough how wonderful it is to have yer back,' Agnes said, pushing him down the hallway. The dogs scampered ahead excitedly. 'And Gloria – well, I've never seen her so happy in all the time I've known her.' They both walked into the kitchen.

'Oh, Jack!' Bel's face broke into a wide smile. 'How lovely to see you!'

'And you too,' Jack said, looking at the two small babies nestled in Bel's arms. 'Glor told us about the bairns.' He leant forward to get a good look at their scrunched-up faces. 'Bonny, eh?'

Bel laughed. 'I think so, but of course, I'm prejudiced.' She got up and put the twins in their Moses basket by the side of the range, praying they didn't wake up.

'Come here ...' She reached up and gave Jack a hug. 'Your return has made so many people happy.'

'Made possible because of you – and Pearl,' Jack said, hugging her back.

Agnes had shaken Jack's coat out and was now stretching it across an old, rather rickety wooden clothes horse. She looked down at the two dogs, adopted a stern expression and pointed to their bed next to the range. Jack smiled as Tramp and Pup complied.

'I've been wanting to come 'n see yer since I got back,' Jack said to Bel, 'but when Glor told me about yer new arrivals 'n that it had been quite chaotic here, well, I thought I'd let things settle first.'

Agnes let out a hoot of laugher as she went into the scullery. 'Yer can say that again.'

Bel chuckled. 'You couldn't have timed it better. I think this is the quietest it's been.'

'Joe not about?' Jack asked.

'He's out with the Major – apparently there's some kind of meeting to discuss "the future of the Home Guard".'

Jack nodded. He knew Joe spent every spare minute with his unit and Major Black, who had also become a good friend of the family. He was also aware that as the country was no longer under any real threat of invasion, questions were beginning to be asked about the real need for an armed citizen militia.

'And Polly's just taken little Artie to the park in the pram,' Bel said, as the sound of light footsteps could be heard hurrying down the stairs. 'Leaving just me, Agnes and – ' Lucille burst into the kitchen ' – cheeky chops here.'

40

'My, my!' Jack said. 'Someone's shot up.' He was genuinely surprised to see how grown up Lucille was. 'The last time I saw this little lassie, she was only so high.' Jack put his hand out level with Lucille's waist. 'How old are you now?'

'Five and a half,' Lucille said, leaning against her mammy, her big blue eyes looking up at the strange man in their kitchen. Her vision fell to the parcel under Jack's arm.

'Ah, a bit of fish from the docks.' He took the filleted pollock that had been wrapped up in greaseproof paper and handed it to Agnes.

'That's very kind, but unnecessary, Jack. Yer don't have to come bearing gifts. It's just nice to see yer.' A flash of sadness suddenly crossed Agnes's face. 'Yer just reminded me of Arthur there. Always bringing me a bit of fish or a few crabs.'

'That sounds like the old man,' Jack said.

Agnes touched Jack's arm. 'I'm sorry yer never got to say a proper goodbye.' Miriam had refused to allow him back to attend the funeral of the man who had been a father figure to him when Jack was young, and a trusted friend as he had got older. 'I know how close yer both were.'

'We were,' Jack said solemnly, 'but I know he'll be happy now he's back with his Flo. I don't think there was a day went by that he didn't miss her.'

Agnes nodded, thinking of how she had found Arthur in his bed the morning after he'd seen his grandson married. He had looked so peaceful and had been holding a picture of Flo to his chest.

'*Hello!*'

Everyone turned on hearing Gloria's voice. Seconds later, she appeared in the kitchen with Hope by her side.

'Gloria, lovely to see you,' Bel said. The two women embraced. 'Come in, take your coat off and sit down.'

41

Gloria unbuttoned her coat and pulled out a gift that she had been keeping dry.

'This is just a very small thank-you present,' she said, looking at Jack. 'From us both.' She handed the present over. 'Helen helped me choose it. We went to Risdon's.' Bel widened her eyes. Risdon's was the town's top baby store. 'She says to tell yer that she'll probably pop in 'n see yer later.'

Bel opened the present and pulled out two beautiful romper suits – one pink and one blue. 'Oh, they're adorable,' she gushed, putting them both to her face and feeling the softness of the fabric. 'But you shouldn't have.' She gave Gloria a hug. 'Thank you. That's incredibly kind.'

Lucille, who was still standing by her side, quietly observing the grown-ups, pulled on her sleeve.

'Mammy, can I show Hope my new bedroom?'

Bel looked down at her daughter. 'Yes, but make sure she's careful going up the stairs. Keep hold of her hand.'

Bel looked at Gloria as Lucille took Hope's little hand and left the room. 'We've let her have Pearl's old room, next to Agnes's.'

'Pearl's moved out?' Gloria was surprised.

'She moved in with Bill today,' Agnes said, coming back into the kitchen and putting a pot of tea on the table. She waved at everyone to sit down.

'Oh,' Gloria said, surprised. 'I didn't think she'd move in until after the wedding.'

Bel chuckled. 'You know my ma, never one to conform to society's conventions.'

Jack and Gloria looked at each other as they sat down. They too were living in sin.

'Ma said it was a good idea as it would give Bill a chance to back out before it was too late,' Bel said, deadpan.

Everyone laughed. It sounded exactly like the kind of comment Pearl would make.

'Bill, of course, was over the moon.'

'We're going to pop 'n see her after we've been here,' Gloria said.

'Any reason?' Bel asked, looking over at Gabrielle and Stephen, who, thankfully, were still sleeping soundly.

Jack laughed.

'For the same reason I'm here today – to tell her how indebted I am to her. To say thank you for what she did.' Jack shook his head. 'Thank you just doesn't seem enough.' He paused. 'I don't think you have any idea how much what you and yer ma did has changed our lives ... How happy you've both made us. Me, Gloria and Hope.'

'And Helen,' Gloria added.

Bel looked at Jack and Gloria. 'I'm just so glad the idea came to me.'

'As are we,' Jack said. 'I want yer to know we'll never forget what yer did for as long as we live, will we, Glor?'

Gloria nodded. She forced herself to swallow back tears. She still felt overwhelmed by what Bel and Pearl had done.

Bel smiled, feeling her own eyes become hazy with the onset of tears. She wanted to tell them that she, too, had much to be grateful for. She had also thanked her ma, as well as her sister, Maisie, and her 'niece', Helen – they had all provided her with the ammunition she needed for her battle with Charles Havelock. A battle she was certain would have ended in defeat had she fought it on her own.

'I'm just so glad it all worked out in the end,' Bel said, not trusting herself to say more. She looked across at the twins, who were just starting to wake up, their little clenched hands reaching out for their mammy. She had been rewarded tenfold.

*

'Ah, the wanderer returns,' Pearl said on seeing Gloria and Jack walk into the pub. She made it sound as though Jack was a travelling troubadour who had finally decided to come back home.

'Hello, Pearl.' Jack strode over to the bar and put out his hand.

Pearl dried her hands on a tea towel and shook it. After everything that had gone on, she felt as though she knew him, even though in the past they had barely exchanged more than a few words.

'All right there, Jack ... Gloria.' Bill walked from the far end of the bar and stuck out his hand. 'Good to see you both. What yer having?' he asked.

'A port and lemon 'n a pint of Vaux – and whatever you two are having,' Jack said, putting his hand in his pocket.

'No,' Bill said, 'this is on the house.'

'No, it's not,' Jack countered. 'This is the least I can do.' He looked at Pearl. 'For everything yer've done.'

Jack and Gloria knew that Pearl had visited Henrietta regularly at the asylum, her instincts telling her that Henrietta was sitting on a pile of dynamite. And my goodness, had she been proved right.

'We both wanted to thank you – properly,' Jack said.

Pearl sparked up a fag and blew smoke into the air.

'No offence, Jack,' she said, looking about to make sure none of the regulars propping up the bar could hear, 'but I did what I did for my Isabelle.' She laughed, then coughed. 'I won't say no to a Scotch, though.'

Jack chuckled and Bill shook his head in despair.

'And congratulations on getting engaged,' Gloria said as Bill placed their drinks on the bar.

'Thanks,' said Bill, pouring himself a pint. 'I've just got to get my future wife here to set a date so I can get us booked in with the registrar.' He winked at Pearl as she helped herself to a shot of single malt from the optics.

'Patience is a virtue,' Pearl said, raising her glass.

'I don't know about that,' said Bill, 'but "Cheers" anyway.'

Everyone clinked glasses.

'And wishing yer lots of happiness in yer home,' Jack said before taking a sip from his pint.

Bill and Pearl gave each other the briefest of looks.

'Eee, I dinnit knar, news travels fast round these parts,' Pearl said. 'Had to get out of there, it's like a nursery now, what with the twins, baby Artie and LuLu. It's the only reason I said yes to this heffalump.' She threw Bill a playful look.

Just then a crowd of shipyard workers came bustling into the bar, full of laughter and cigarette smoke. Gloria and Jack made their excuses and headed over to a quiet corner of the pub.

'She's a tough nut, isn't she?' Jack said as they sat down.

'She is, but I think Bill's softening her up.'

Jack laughed. 'Brave man. It must be love.'

As they both took sips of their drinks, they looked about, sitting quietly for a moment, enjoying the novelty of being out together as a couple. Bel had kindly offered to look after Hope, chuckling when they'd said they wanted to thank Pearl for her part in bringing Jack back. She'd predicted her ma would be having none of it.

For a while Gloria and Jack chatted about Crown's and Jack's new job, or rather the return to his old job, and Gloria filled him in with the latest from Thompson's, the women welders and how Dorothy was already planning her wedding to Toby.

'Poor bloke hasn't even had a chance to ask her yet,' Gloria said. 'Sounds like he's been moved to some base down south.'

45

'Where's that?' Jack asked.

'He can't tell her, but he's promised to try and get up to see her in the next few weeks. Even if it's just a fleeting visit.'

Jack knew Gloria was the mother hen of the women welders and ended up being a stand-in mum, in particular to Dorothy, whose own mam didn't seem to have the time of day for her, and, of course, Helen, Miriam not possessing a single maternal bone in her body.

'It's a shame *Helen* can't find herself a nice bloke to start a family with,' Jack said.

'I know,' Gloria agreed. 'I really had high hopes that Dr Parker might be the one, but that just seems destined never to happen.'

'I remember he seemed like a decent lad. Very caring manner. Didn't have that attitude some doctors have, yer know what I mean?' Jack had got to know Dr Parker a little during his convalescence after coming round from his coma.

'I know exactly what you mean. And he's been a good friend to Helen while you've been gone,' Gloria said, thinking of how Dr Parker had saved Helen when she'd nearly haemorrhaged to death miscarrying. Not that she could tell Jack. Helen had sworn her to secrecy about the whole Theo debacle.

'So, what happened? I can't imagine him not liking Helen.' He laughed. 'Mind you, I might be a bit biased – she is my daughter, and as such can do no wrong.'

'I think it's complicated,' she said.

Seeing two sailors come into the pub, Jack knew this was the perfect chance to broach the subject of Gloria's sons – Bobby and Gordon. He took a sip of his bitter and decided to just come straight out with it.

'When yer gonna tell yer boys about us?' Jack asked, his eyes on Gloria. She had also noticed the two sailors, who looked to be in their early twenties, around the same age as her sons.

Gloria sighed heavily. 'Yer must have read my mind.'

Jack smiled and reached over to squeeze her hand. The past few weeks had been filled with such joy and happiness. *Finally*, he was with the woman he loved. *At last* he could be a father to his little girl, and, of course, to his eldest daughter – not that Helen needed him. She'd grown up a lot since he'd been banished to Scotland. But now that he was back, it was time to confront certain concerns – one of which was Gloria's boys and the fact they had no idea their mam had divorced their dad and was now living with another man – a married man – with whom she'd had a baby.

'Do yer think yer should write to them?' Jack suggested. He knew Bobby and Gordon were presently stationed on HMS *Opportune* somewhere in the Atlantic Ocean. 'It's going to be an awful lot for them to take on board when they *do* come back.'

Gloria let out another heavy sigh and took a sip of her port. 'I know it is. I wish I'd at least told them about the divorce.'

'And there's no way *he* would have written and told them?' Jack couldn't bring himself to say Vinnie's name. Just the thought of him made his jaw clench with anger. How he wished he had been able to give Vinnie a taste of his own medicine to make up for just a modicum of what he had forced Gloria to endure over the years.

'No, they'd have told me if he had,' Gloria said. 'Vinnie's not exactly one for writing, and I certainly don't think they would have written to him. Why would they? They both hate the man, even if he is their father.'

Jack knew that Bobby and Gordon had left home as soon as they could. They'd both done a couple of years as apprentice riveters at Bartram's before joining the navy as soon as they were old enough. From what Gloria had said, it hadn't been a calling, more a case of them wanting to escape the atmosphere at home, which had become increasingly charged and violent as they had grown into young men.

'I just don't think it's a good idea to tell them everything in a letter,' Gloria said. This had always been a slightly touchy subject between her and Jack. It had cropped up before in conversation, but had never been properly discussed – it had been hard chatting to Jack over the phone at work; there were always people coming and going, or he had to dash off when he was needed in the yard. Lately she'd had Hope with her, which had made it even more difficult.

'I mean,' Gloria said, rotating her glass of port on the wooden table, 'how are they going to feel hearing that not only have I divorced their father, which is pretty shocking in itself, but I'm now living in sin with a married man … and we've had a child together.'

Jack took a mouthful of bitter but didn't say anything.

'And it won't take them long to work out that I was having an affair with you while I was still with Vinnie – and that I'd already had Hope before I'd even started divorce proceedings.'

Jack exhaled. 'Put like that, it does not sound good.'

Gloria looked forlorn. 'I want to be there to answer their questions. To explain. I'm worried about how they'll react if I tell them in a letter … If they get upset or angry … I wouldn't want anything to take their minds off what they're doing and for something to happen to them as a result.' Gloria looked at Jack, desperate for him to understand.

'I think yer might be being a bit overprotective there, Glor.' He paused, knowing that Gloria would not appreciate

48

what he really thought, but unable to hold back. 'They are both grown lads now. How old are they again? Twenty-two? Twenty-three?'

'Bobby's twenty-three. Gordon's about to have his twenty-second birthday.' Both her sons' birthdays were somehow even more ingrained than usual in Gloria's memory these days. Her boys were the only two good things that had come out of her unhappy and abusive marriage.

Jack was quiet. He and Gloria saw eye to eye about almost everything, but she did have a tendency to hold back information for fear of causing upset. She'd not told him she had been pregnant with Hope before he left for America, worried about how it would affect him. And she hadn't told him about Vinnie's violence when he was recovering from amnesia; something that had ended up having dangerous repercussions for herself.

Holding back from telling her boys about divorcing their father made it so much harder now to tell them that she had met someone else – never mind that she'd had another child. Gloria, he realised, had boxed herself into a corner. There was not going to be any easy way out.

'At the moment I just want them to get back. Safe and sound,' Gloria said eventually.

They were both quiet; they had just heard that *Empire Houseman*, a cargo vessel Doxford's had built, had been hit by two torpedoes. Two lads from the town who were on board had been lucky to survive. One of their crew hadn't been so fortunate.

'I don't know what I'd do if they didn't get through this war,' Gloria said. 'I can deal with anything – anything at all – except that.'

Jack knew it was true – in the light of what could happen, worries about what her boys might think of her changed domestic situation seemed insignificant. He still thought, though, that she should write and tell them.

'Come on, let's go and fetch Hope,' he said, getting up. He helped Gloria on with her coat.

'Anyway,' he added, trying to lighten the mood, 'there's one thing you don't have to worry about with yer two lads ...'

'And what's that?' Gloria asked.

'The pair of them won't be able to help falling in love with their little sister.'

Gloria smiled.

'That's true,' she said. 'They're both suckers for a pretty face.'

Chapter Six

Saturday 15 January

'*John!*'

Helen called out and waved over the sea of heads in the canteen.

As soon as Dr Parker spotted Helen, he stood up. He watched as she manoeuvred her way around half a dozen tables to reach him. Her stunning looks and hourglass figure drew admiring glances from the men she passed, and envious once-overs from the women. When she reached him, he put his arms out and gave her a kiss on the cheek.

'I know it's a bit late, but Happy New Year,' he said.

'Only two weeks late,' Helen laughed, enjoying the feel of his body close to hers, fleeting though it might be. 'And Happy New Year to you too.'

Dr Parker pulled out her chair.

'Forever the gentleman,' she said, smiling up at him as she sat down.

If only he hadn't always been a such a gentleman.

Helen had thought about this a lot lately and was sure that John had desired her but had been too principled to make a move on her, knowing he would never want them to be serious. As her dear mama had reminded her many times this past year, she was 'soiled goods'. Men like John

– a surgeon no less – did not want second-hand goods. Not as a wife, anyway. And now John was with Dr Eris – had been courting her for more than eight months – he would never stray. John was not the kind to play away from home. And besides, Claire was a very attractive woman. Bel had commented that she reminded her of Katharine Hepburn, and Helen had been forced to agree.

Dr Parker poured the tea and looked at Helen; her emerald eyes never failed to mesmerise him. 'Why do I sense you have lots to tell me?' he asked.

Helen smiled and took her tea. 'Is it that obvious?'

Dr Parker laughed. 'It's good to see you happy.' He wondered whether Helen's sparkle was down to Matthew Royce. The pair had been pictured in the *Sunderland Echo* again, at a charity do at the museum, looking, as always, like some Hollywood couple. He'd tried not to dislike the bloke. But it was hard. He was a typical lady's man.

Helen took a sip of her tea and quickly looked around the cafeteria, making sure there was no one she recognised – or, rather, that Dr Eris wasn't anywhere in the vicinity. She hoped John hadn't mentioned they were meeting up; if he had, she'd bet her boots she'd turn up to check up on them.

'It's Father,' she said, leaning in so that those on the table next to her couldn't hear. *'He's back!'*

'What? Back from the Clyde?'

Helen nodded and took a sip of tea.

'Well, that *is* news,' he said, a perplexed look on his face. 'How's he managed that? I thought your mother had him over a barrel?' John knew all about the secrets of the women welders, and how Miriam had been using those secrets to keep Jack in exile. John looked into Helen's twinkling eyes. 'Or should I say, how did *you* manage that? I'm guessing it was you who orchestrated his return.' John knew that ever since Helen's father had been banished over the border, she had been plotting and planning to try and get him home again.

Helen put her cup back on the saucer. 'Actually, it wasn't me. Although I like to think I did help a little. But no, all the credit really has to go to Bel – and Pearl.'

'*Pearl?*' John did not attempt to hold back his incredulity.

Helen chuckled. 'Yes, *Pearl.*'

And with that she proceeded to regale John with the compelling events of Christmas Day and how the drama played out in her grandfather's dining room had led to Jack's return – as well as to the discovery that not only was her grandmother alive, but she was just down the road in the asylum.

'She's here – in Ryhope – in the asylum?' John was gobsmacked.

'She is indeed,' Helen said, enjoying telling a story that for once had a happy ending.

'But I would have thought I'd have known – would have heard her name mentioned. Henrietta Havelock is not a name you'd forget.'

'That's because she's been living under an assumed name for over two decades …'

Helen paused. 'My dear grandmama is now known as Miss Henrietta Girling.'

'Miss Girling?' John repeated.

Helen nodded.

'But that's one of Claire's patients.'

'I know,' Helen said, eyes wide. 'Talk about coincidence.'

She watched as John combed his mop of sandy-coloured hair back with his fingers.

'Does Claire know? I'm sure she would have said something if she did.' He paused. 'Or perhaps not. Patient confidentiality and all that.'

53

'She doesn't know,' Helen said. 'No one knows. No one *can* know. As far as Claire's aware, Grandmother is some mad spinster who's been here for as long as anyone can remember. Part of the furniture. I think the technical word for it is "institutionalised". Claire thinks Mother is some distant great-aunty.'

'What? Miriam visits her here?'

Helen nodded. 'Only occasionally, although she won't be about for a while as she's scarpered off to Scotland to my aunty Margaret's.'

John sat back and blew out air. 'Dear me. This really is shocking.'

'Henrietta's actually why I'm here today,' Helen said, lowering her voice conspiratorially. 'Apart from to see you, of course.'

John let out a bark of laughter. 'And there was me thinking you'd made the trip all the way over here just to see me.'

Helen gave John a look he couldn't read. 'Actually,' she said, 'I thought this would be a great way for us to bob in with each other, stay friends, like you said after Artie's christening. Whenever I'm here visiting Grandmama, I can grab you for a quick cuppa. That's if you're free, of course.'

John smiled. 'I think that's a great idea. And if you ring beforehand, I can make sure I *am* free.' He paused. 'I meant what I said. About our friendship. About us having something special.' As he took in her beautiful face and bewitching eyes, framed by loose curls of glossy black hair, he wondered if she'd known how he'd felt. How in love he had been with her.

If she had, she'd never let on.

'I have to ask you, though,' Helen said, her face becoming sombre, 'if you can keep everything I've told you – in particular about Henrietta – from Claire. It's not that I don't trust her,' she lied, 'it's just that if it gets out, Grandfather

54

has made it perfectly clear that he will run amok. He will make sure all the women's secrets are trumpeted from the treetops – he'll destroy Bel and Pearl and anyone they're close to.'

Dr Parker nodded. Of that, he had no doubt. He knew Charles Havelock.

Helen looked up at the clock. She had another half-hour until visiting time over at the asylum.

'Have you got time for another cuppa?' she asked.

Dr Parker smiled. He'd made sure he wasn't to be disturbed unless it was an emergency. 'I certainly have.' He narrowed his eyes at Helen. 'Why do I think that you haven't told me everything?'

Helen poured them each another cup from the pot and added milk.

'You know me so well,' she said, with a mischievous smile. She took a sip of her tea.

'*Well*,' she said, 'you know Bel's sister, Maisie?'

'Yes,' said Dr Parker. He had met Maisie several times at various functions Helen had taken him to in the past.

'Well,' Helen leant forward, her teacup cradled in her hands, 'you wouldn't guess in a million years what she does for a living …' She paused. 'And who her boss is …'

Rosie had just about caught up with the bookkeeping and was now in desperate need of a nice cup of tea. She got up from her desk in the bordello's front reception room, which had been converted into an office, and stretched her arms high. They felt stiff from the overhead welds she had been doing all day. Her whole body felt physically shattered, and now, after hours of doing the books, she felt mentally exhausted as well. She wasn't sure which was worse.

Since the start of the New Year, work at Thompson's had been full on. Then again, when wasn't it. But at least they were on schedule for launching *Empire Pitt* at the end of the month. As it was Saturday, she and her squad had just worked a half shift, although it had been an unrelenting and hard half shift – was, in reality, a three-quarter shift, as they'd worked through till half-past one and had only had a short lunch break. After Dorothy, Angie, Martha and Gloria had left, and she'd had a chat with Jimmy, the head riveter, about preparing to start work on the first of the commissioned LCTs, she'd nipped up to have a word with Helen, but she had left on time for a change, leaving Marie-Anne to finish up for the day. Rosie had stuck her head round the main door to see Helen's personal assistant commandeering the room, telling all the clerical staff to make sure their work areas were spotless and they had everything prepared and ready to go for Monday morning, when they would all be in at nine o'clock sharp. Not for the first time, Rosie had thought Marie-Anne would have fared well in the ATS.

Hurrying home, Rosie had bathed and changed into her favourite cream-coloured slacks and cashmere V-neck, before making her way up the long, steep stretch of Tunstall Vale to West Lawn, where she had done a solid few hours on the accounts.

She had to admit, it felt good to be able to come to the bordello without having to worry about Charlotte. Much as she loved her younger sister, Rosie was glad she was away for the day, visiting her friend Marjorie. The two had been best buddies when they were at boarding school in Harrogate and had remained close after leaving.

Charlotte had been very clingy since she'd found out the truth, but like Lily had said, she seemed happy and was doing really well at school – all good signs. And thankfully, the revelation that Lily was in fact a madam and her home a bordello had not seemed to perturb

Charlotte at all. Her sister had made it clear she loved its splendour, and even more, the people in it. Lily, George, Maisie, Vivian and Kate had become Charlotte's family – a dysfunctional and very peculiar family, but a happy one all the same.

Walking out into the hallway, Rosie heard Maisie and Vivian chattering away upstairs as they got ready for the evening. Hearing Maisie's soft southern accent and Vivian's faux-American one always made her smile. Kate, she knew, would be at the Maison Nouvelle, her boutique-cum-seamstress-shop in the town centre, until well after six. Lily and George would be either out shopping, upstairs or in the scullery. They tended to go into the back parlour only when the bordello was open for business and there were clients to entertain.

Pushing open the heavy oak door to the kitchen, Rosie saw that Lily and George were at the large wooden table in deep discussion. George, a veteran of the First War with an array of medals to prove it, was sitting, back straight, looking dapper as always in a dark blue suit, his hand placed on top of his ivory-handled walking stick. Lily had a heavily jewelled hand round a large brandy glass and was tapping ash from her Gauloise into a rather ugly red, white and blue ashtray that Charlotte had made in her pottery class, and which Lily viewed as a work of art.

'You two seem serious,' Rosie said.

Her sudden appearance startled them both.

'*Ma chère!*' said Lily. 'Come in. Wonderful to see you've lifted your head out of those wretched books.'

'You'd soon be complaining if I didn't do them,' Rosie said, going over to put the kettle on. 'So, come on, what are you two plotting and planning?'

'We're talking about the future,' Lily said.

'Really?' Rosie was genuinely surprised. 'That's unusual. I thought you were all for living in the moment. *In these uncertain times.*' She looked at George.

'New Year always gets one thinking,' George said, looking at Lily.

'As well as that horrible, horrible man ...' Lily added, reaching for her fan, which she always kept close to hand.

'You mean Charles Havelock?' Rosie asked.

George nodded and got out a cigar from his jacket pocket.

'That explains the sombre faces. Go on,' Rosie said. She was leaning against the Aga, waiting for the kettle to boil.

'We were just discussing what would happen if he did report us to the authorities,' Lily said, taking a deep drag on her cigarette and fanning herself.

It had been Maisie's refusal to grant Mr Havelock membership of the Gentlemen's Club that had led to him finding out about the bordello and threatening to report them if Bel were to expose him. Lily and Maisie might well have coached Pearl on what to say when she went head to head with Charles Havelock – that they'd get off lightly with a mere slap on the wrists – but Lily knew that was the best-case scenario. If they got a particularly puritanical judge, they could all be looking at spending time behind bars.

Hearing the kettle start to whistle, Rosie took it off the heat and poured steaming hot water into the teapot. 'So, what were you thinking?' she asked.

'Just ideas at the moment,' George said. 'You know, ways of pushing any spare cash into bona fide businesses. Perhaps expand the Gentlemen's Club.'

'As well as expand La Lumière Bleue,' Lily chipped in. Lily's London bordello was in the heart of Soho. 'That place is as safe as houses – half the top brass at the Met go there.'

'And,' George continued, 'I've always got half an eye out on any properties in which it might be worth investing.'

Rosie took the teapot and placed it on the table.

'More so at the moment,' he added. 'This war won't last for ever. Thank goodness. It might even be over by the end of the year ...'

Lily rolled her eyes. 'Enough war talk! I feel like I'm drowning in it.'

Rosie poured herself a cup of tea. She was actually over the moon to hear Lily was thinking of going legit; it was something she had never thought she would even consider.

'We'll work something out,' George said. 'Just need to get the old brain percolating a few possibilities.' He tapped the side of his head to make his point.

'Well, keep me in the loop, won't you?' Rosie said. 'You know me, I'm all for being "bona fide". And if I can do anything, you must say.'

'Of course we will,' Lily said, stubbing out her cigarette.

'And talking about make everything legal – have you two finally decided when you are going to tie the knot?' Rosie arched an eyebrow.

'Not yet, *ma chère*,' Lily said, glancing at George. 'But don't worry, you'll be the first to know. Now, tell us about our favourite girl. How's she doing?'

Rosie smiled. Lily adored Charlotte. As much as Charlotte adored Lily.

'Charlotte is presently whooping it up with Marjorie in Newcastle,' Rosie said.

Lily laughed. 'Oh, *ma chère*, much as I think Marjorie is a lovely girl, I can't see her being one for *whooping* it up. At least you know Charlotte will be keeping on the straight and narrow when she's with her friend from the Tyne.'

Rosie took a sip of tea and smiled.

'It's a shame Charlotte can't come here after school,' Lily said tentatively. An agreement had been made that Charlotte could come and have breakfast with Lily before she went to school, but other than that the house was out of bounds. 'It would make life easier for you, so long as she stayed in the kitchen or in your office, of course.'

Rosie sighed. 'Don't you start. Charlie's already giving me enough earache about coming here as it is.'

Rosie wondered, though, if perhaps the reason Lily was nudging towards legitimacy, something she had always railed against, was Charlotte. This wasn't the first time the bordello had been threatened with exposure, but it *was* the first time since Charlotte's return. Was Lily fearful of the effect it would have on her new charge if the bordello and those in it were ever exposed? Did Lily really want this wonderful house to be a proper home that Charlotte could consider her own and where she could come and go as she pleased?

Chapter Seven

A freezing fog had enveloped the shipyard, but it had lifted as the day had worn on. It's absence, however, seemed to make the bitterly cold air even more biting. Rosie looked up at *Empire Pitt*, waiting to be sent down the ways. The launch couldn't come quickly enough for her. She was itching to get started on the LCTs they had been commissioned to build.

Normally, work enabled her to switch off from her worries about Peter as there was always so much to do. Compartmentalising her life was one of her survival techniques. She had done it when she had first started working at Lily's – keeping the work she did at the bordello separate in her mind from her work at Thompson's. It was now a well-honed skill, which had helped her get through life. But since hearing about the planned invasion of France and being told by Helen earlier on in the month that they would be building the actual vessels that would take troops and tanks across the Channel, her work and her worries about Peter had merged. How could she push thoughts of him away when she was helping to build the ships that would help liberate France? And why would she want to? Work might no longer afford her a way of switching off from her anxieties about the man she loved, but it gave her an enormous sense of purpose – even more than she'd already had. It made her feel closer to Peter; they were in this together, fighting shoulder to shoulder – metaphorically speaking, anyway.

She had sensed George and Lily's reticence in speaking about the war, or rather, about anything to do with France, since they'd seen her outpouring of relief and tears when Toby had told her Peter was alive. She'd guessed they were trying to spare her more heartache, but she had sat them down yesterday and told them that she was done with running away from her fears. It was no longer possible. And in some ways, it was liberating. There was to be no more compartmentalising. 'This is my way of helping Peter,' she had told them both. For the first time in ages, she'd told them, she felt hopeful. 'If France is liberated, that means Peter's work will be done and he can come home.'

And just this lunchtime, when they'd been going over the latest news stories and Dorothy had read out an article on the Allied troops' ongoing assault on Anzio in Italy, which, if successful, would lead to the eventual capture of Rome, and about the Red Army reclaiming Leningrad, she'd felt it was further evidence that they were pushing towards victory.

Rosie looked at her squad shuffling about in the cold, waiting for the launch to get going. They'd worked hard to get *Empire Pitt* ready. She just hoped they hadn't burned themselves out. She needed them to be strong and give everything they had these next few months. No one knew for definite when the invasion would happen, but it was looking likely to be sometime in the late spring, early summer.

Rosie looked at Gloria, who was pulling on her gloves and stamping her feet on the ground. They'd all been talking about her dilemma as to whether or not she should write to Bobby and Gordon to tell them about Jack and Hope. There was a general consensus that she *should* tell them; Dorothy had even offered to help her write the letter.

Observing the rest of her squad, Rosie could tell that they were tired, their pale faces still visible through the black smears of soot and dirt.

'I'm freezing,' Dorothy moaned, wrapping her winter coat around herself tightly as the rest of the women welders shuffled about, trying to keep warm by the side of the slipway. 'We should have stayed in the canteen for longer.'

'If we had, we wouldn't have got prime position for the launch.' Angie argued the point a little half-heartedly; she was also chilled to the bone.

'I thought you wanted to support Marie-Anne,' Gloria said, tightening her headscarf, which was fluttering about in the wind.

'We do.' Dorothy and Angie spoke in unison as they linked arms.

'I still can't believe Marie-Anne is launching a ship,' Martha said, looking up at the towering bow of the cargo vessel. She was standing behind the women, so as not to block their view and to provide a buffer against any pushing and shoving from the throng of shipyard workers gathering behind them.

'It's something new they've started to do,' Dorothy informed them. 'A typist launched a collier at Austin's on Tuesday.'

Hannah and Olly arrived, squeezing their way through and catching the tail end of the conversation.

'We heard they did a ballot and she got to smash the bottle,' said Hannah.

'Is that what happened with Marie-Anne?' Martha looked at Rosie, who was standing to the side of the women. 'Did she win the ballot?'

'I believe she did,' Rosie said, flicking a look across to Gloria. They had both agreed it seemed a coincidence that Marie-Anne had 'won' the ballot around the same time

Helen had broken the news to her that she would not be replacing Bel.

'Where's Polly?' Gloria asked. 'I thought she left the canteen with us.'

'She nipped to see Marie-Anne. Bel asked her to say that she was sorry she couldn't come, but to wish her luck.'

'Here she is,' Martha said, looking over her shoulder and seeing her workmate weaving her way through the sea of flat caps.

'Made it!' Polly said breathlessly, taking her spot beside Rosie.

'Is Marie-Anne all right?' Dorothy asked.

Polly chuckled. 'She seemed a bit jittery.'

'Who wouldn't be?' Angie gasped. 'Standin' in front of this lot, swinging a bottle of champagne. I'd be terrified it didn't smash.'

'That seemed to be her main concern too,' Polly said. 'She's been told to really give it a good whack.'

Everyone knew that if the bottle didn't smash, it was a bad omen and the ship would be cursed. It was a suspicion dating back to when ships were made of wood and sail.

Now more than ever these ships made of steel needed every bit of luck they could get.

'You nervous?' Helen asked Marie-Anne as they left the warmth of the offices and walked across the yard towards the little platform that had been erected at the top of the slipway.

'A little,' Marie-Anne admitted.

'Enjoy it – and feel proud,' Helen said. 'You're a working-class girl done good. You deserve the honour as much as anyone.'

Marie-Anne was taken aback. She knew Helen was being extra nice to her because she wasn't getting another clerical assistant to replace Bel, but it didn't matter, she'd take any compliments she could get.

'Is that my favourite granddaughter?'

Helen could feel herself stiffen, and it wasn't the cold weather.

'Grandfather!' She stopped in her tracks and turned around, forcing a smile on her face as she greeted the man she despised. She was irked to see him in such rude health. He looked positively dapper. Underneath his grey woollen winter coat, he had on his best navy blue Savile Row suit with matching tie, a starched white handkerchief poking out of his top pocket. The ornate walking stick he was swinging forward and stabbing into the ground as he walked towards her proved to Helen that it was not really needed and that his moans and groans about his physical health were overblown. He did not look nearly eighty years of age. He was opening his arms to embrace his granddaughter when Helen spotted Matthew running across the yard to catch them up.

'Ah, Matthew,' she turned, rebuffing her grandfather's embrace and raising her hand to wave. 'Glad you made it.'

Mr Havelock hid his ire at having been stonewalled by his granddaughter.

'Apologies for my tardiness,' Matthew said, breathlessly. He smiled at Helen, Mr Havelock and a nervous-looking Marie-Anne.

'Ah, Royce Junior!' Mr Havelock put his hand out to Matthew. 'Good to see you. How's your father?'

The two men shook hands.

'He's well. Taking it easy these days.' Matthew's father had suffered a stroke and had handed the reins over to his son. 'Miriam not here today?' he asked. It seemed unusual to see Mr Havelock without Helen's mother by his side.

'Not today, old boy. She's having a break up north. Gone to stay with her sister Margaret and that son-in-law of mine on their country estate near Loch Lomond.'

'Ah.' Matthew nodded, although he couldn't think why anyone would want to have a break in the wilds of Scotland in January. Strange that Helen hadn't mentioned it. Not that she was particularly forthcoming about her family life.

'Come on, let's get this done before everyone freezes to death,' said Helen.

Mr Havelock stuck close to his granddaughter's side, forcing Matthew and Marie-Anne to walk behind.

'I didn't expect you to be here,' Helen said, glancing at her grandfather. 'I heard you were at the launch of HMS *Nunnery Castle* at Pickersgill's on Wednesday.'

Helen had not seen her grandfather since Christmas Day, but she kept her ear to the ground and knew exactly what he was up to. He'd been keeping a low profile. Until now.

'Nothing escapes your notice,' said Mr Havelock.

'Not like you to attend the launch of a lowly merchant cargo vessel?' Helen probed.

'Every ship counts,' he said, waving at Harold, the shipyard's manager, who was waiting with Basil, the head draughtsman, on the makeshift platform. 'Merchant Navy or Royal Navy – they're all in it together. All equally important.'

Helen looked at her grandfather. *Why was he really here?* She didn't trust him one bit.

'Couldn't agree more, Mr Havelock,' Matthew said, having manoeuvred himself so that he was back at Helen's side. 'Especially after hearing about SS *Fort Buckingham*.' The merchant vessel had been torpedoed and had sunk in the Indian Ocean a few miles off the Maldives. Thirty-eight of the crew had perished, including a twenty-one-year-old gunner from the Southwick area of town.

They walked in silence for a moment.

As they neared the small gaggle of bigwigs by the ship's bow, Helen turned to her grandfather.

'There'll be no celebrations afterwards,' she lied. She had just sent one of the office juniors out to fetch cakes from the local bakery up the road in Monkwearmouth. This was the first time a ship had been christened by a female worker from the yard. They would mark the occasion.

'Don't worry, my dear,' Mr Havelock said. 'I know there's *work to do – a war to be won* and all that. I'll be on my way as soon as the old gal's gone down the ways.' He looked at Matthew. 'I might even pop in and see Royce senior, if you think he's up to it?'

'Of course,' Matthew said, full of enthusiasm. 'He'll be over the moon. He misses the cut and thrust of work – and the company – not that he would admit it.'

'Splendid,' Mr Havelock said, slapping Matthew on the back. 'Splendid.'

Helen looked at her grandfather. He'd never had a good word to say about Matthew's father in the past. Why did she feel that he was ingratiating himself with Mr Royce senior because she was chummy with Matthew? Was he trying to wheedle his way into her life? Was it a subtle way of saying he could spill the beans on Helen's tawdry past to any potential beau – or potential beau's family? Her grandfather knew all about Theodore, her pregnancy and ensuing miscarriage – enough to make most suitors run a mile. Well, he was barking up the wrong tree if he thought she was interested in Matthew. The man she really loved already knew all about her past.

*

'Oh. My. God,' said Dorothy, trying to keep her voice low but not so low that her workmates couldn't hear. 'Look who's with Helen and Marie-Anne.'

The women all looked to see a smartly dressed Charles Havelock swinging his walking stick with gusto as he crossed the yard with Helen by his side. Behind them was Matthew Royce, looking as dashing as always, and an apprehensive Marie-Anne.

'What's he doing here?' asked Gloria. Helen would have mentioned it to her if she'd known he was showing his face today. She had been anxious about seeing her grandfather; unlike Bel, she couldn't simply cut him out of her life and ignore him. People would talk. It would draw attention to the family. Helen had wondered if the best course of action would be to treat him as though nothing had happened, which by the looks of it, she was having to do now, whether she wanted to or not. Her decision had been made for her.

'Has the man no shame?' Hannah said quietly, but not so quietly that they could not hear. It disturbed her greatly that his wife was imprisoned in the Ryhope mental hospital.

'Men like that don't feel shame,' Rosie said. When Bel had told them how Mr Havelock had raped her ma and that she had been the result, Rosie had been catapulted back to her own past; to her own rape at the hands of her uncle Raymond. Seeing Mr Havelock for the first time since she'd learnt what a monster he was, she felt the anger swell up inside her. His presence at the launch had somehow defiled the occasion.

'I didn't think he and Helen got on now ...' Martha hesitated '... since Christmas Day.' She too had been shocked by what she'd learnt. It had frustrated her that yet again the truth about her birth mother being a child killer was being used as a chip to stop the truth from coming out. It had been bad enough when Miriam had used it to send Jack to the Clyde, but for it to be used now to enable one of the town's VIPs to get away with rape *and* imprisoning his wife, that angered her – a lot.

'They don't,' Gloria said. 'I think this is his way of saying to us all that he might have been knocked down, but not out.'

'There's nothing he can do, though, is there?' Angie asked. Just looking at the old man made her skin crawl. She hated that her mam having a bit on the side had given him power. Even more power than he already had.

'Bastard,' Dorothy mumbled under her breath so that only Angie could hear. She still wasn't sure what would happen if the law found out her mother had committed bigamy.

Polly didn't say anything, simply observed as Mr Havelock chatted and smiled and shook hands. Thank goodness Bel had decided not to come to the launch. She hadn't said as much, but Polly knew it was unlikely her sister-in-law would ever go to another again; certainly not if there was the remotest chance that Mr Havelock or Miriam would be there. She had told Polly that from this point forward she would not let any of their toxicity near her or her family – her new, extended family.

Looking at Helen as she walked onto the platform and was greeted by Harold, Polly thought she would bet her boots that Helen would have loved to do the same – simply erase her grandfather from her life. But today had proved that was simply not a possibility. That man would be a bane in her life – in *all* their lives – for as long as he lived.

Still, she reassured herself, Bel and Pearl had won the day. They'd got Jack back, and providing Henrietta's secret was never revealed, the women's secrets would also remain intact.

The women watched as Marie-Anne put on a long protective glove that looked rather like the ones they used for welding, only cleaner. She then smiled nervously as Harold passed her the bottle of champagne, which was dangling from a rope and had been covered in a loose netting so as to prevent any broken glass from going flying. Taking a deep breath, she pulled her arm right back, as though she were about to throw a javelin, and with all her strength hurled the bottle at the bow.

It smashed instantly, covering Marie-Anne and Harold, who was the nearest to her, with a spray of champagne.

There was a huge cheer and Marie-Anne looked over to the women welders and beamed from ear to ear – a smile of unadulterated relief.

They all shouted out 'Hurrah!' and waved back to Marie-Anne as the *Empire Pitt* slid majestically down the ways, huge chains unravelling behind her until she hit the water, at which point the chains became taut to prevent her from hitting the docks on the south side. Flat caps were thrown in the air, and the yard was filled with the sounds of cheers, whistles and the blowing of horns. Another ship had been born on the Wear.

Chapter Eight

One week later

Friday 4 February

Rosie, Dorothy, Angie and Martha were standing around their five-gallon barrel fire.

Rosie looked around the yard at the various squads of platers, riveters, caulkers and general labourers, then up at the yard clock, just about visible through the dirt and grime. It was only a few minutes to go until the klaxon sounded out the start of the morning shift.

'It's not like Gloria and Polly to be late.' Martha said what Rosie was thinking.

'They might have got held up with Hope – or baby Artie,' said Angie.

'Or the twins,' Dorothy said. 'They've probably spent too much time fussing over them and made themselves late. They're so gorgeous, you can't help it.'

'That's if they're not screaming their lungs off,' Angie said. The twins could be the most perfect babies one minute, all sweetness and light, smiles and gurgles, the next minute the worst, screeching and shrieking with all their might.

'Yeah,' Martha chuckled, showing her gapped front teeth, 'they're worse than any air raid siren, that's for sure.'

'Is that why yer never give them a cuddle?' Angie asked.

'I'm always frightened I'll hold them the wrong way and hurt them,' Martha confessed.

'I think babies are pretty robust,' Rosie reassured her, thinking that Martha herself was a prime example, her birth mother having tried to poison her.

'Yeah, providing you don't drop them on their head,' said Angie.

'Like your mam did with you,' quipped Dorothy.

Angie was just about to bat back a reply when Gloria and Polly came hurrying through the main gates, quickly grabbing their clocking-on cards from Davey, the young timekeeper, and breaking into a jog to make it over to their workplace by the quayside.

'Glor doesn't look too happy,' said Dorothy.

'She doesn't, does she,' Angie agreed.

'I hope nothing's wrong,' Martha worried.

'Everything all right?' asked Rosie as soon as they were within earshot.

Polly's face looked grim.

'Yes 'n no,' Gloria said, puffing as she reached them and dropping her haversack on the ground. 'It's my Bobby. He's been injured.'

'Oh my God!' Dorothy said, going over to her friend.

Even though none of the women had ever met Gloria's sons, they all felt as though they knew them, especially as Gloria often brought their letters and postcards to work and read them out. The loud blare of the yard's horn suddenly sounded out, making any more talk impossible as the noise of the shipyard instantly started up.

'You all right to work?' Rosie shouted into Gloria's ear as a nearby worker turned on his pneumatic drill.

Gloria nodded.

'Bobby'll be fine,' she shouted back, more to convince herself than anyone else.

*

At half-past ten Rosie made the sign of a T and they all downed tools. Seeing her grab her haversack, they all did the same, following her across the main deck of the ship they'd been welding, to the tip of the bow. It was far enough away from the other workers, most of whom had also stopped for a break, to allow a modicum of conversation.

'So, what's happened?' Rosie said as they all sat down with their backs to the railings.

Thankfully, the wind had dropped and the temperature had risen to just about bearable.

'He's suffered some kind of head injury,' Gloria said, her face full of concern.

Dorothy made a gasping sound and was instantly glowered at by the rest of the women.

'But he's not too bad from what I can tell.' Gloria forced a smile and looked at Dorothy. 'He's not been made a vegetable or anything. He managed to write to me, which says a lot.' Gloria fished around in her bag and pulled out his letter.

'His writing looks a bit ropy,' Dorothy said, looking over her shoulder.

'That's because he's out at sea,' Martha said.

'Yeah,' Angie laughed out loud, 'yer writing would be *ropy* if yer were having to write while yer ship was gannin up and down like a bleedin' seesaw.'

Polly looked at Rosie and rolled her eyes.

'So, what exactly does he say?' Polly asked as Rosie handed Gloria a cup of tea from her flask.

'Thanks,' Gloria said, taking a sip.

'Give her one of yer mam's flapjacks,' Angie commanded Martha. 'She needs sugar. She's had a shock.'

Martha did as she was told, offering them around, as Angie had hoped.

'So, come on, what does it say?' Dorothy said impatiently, her eyes darting down to the page. Bobby's writing was small and spidery, making it impossible for Dorothy to read from where she was sitting.

'He says,' Gloria straightened out the letter, 'that he and Gordon didn't want to worry me, but during the "tussle they had with Jerry a few weeks back—"'

'Does he mean the Battle of the North Cape?' Dorothy interrupted.

'I guess so,' Gloria said.

'Why doesn't he just say the Battle of the North Cape?' Dorothy said. 'I mean, it's not as if it's a secret. All the papers were full of it.'

'Bobby's like that,' Gloria said. 'He can be a bit vague sometimes.'

'Or it's his head injury,' Dorothy suggested.

'Or he's not wanted to worry his mother,' Rosie said, giving Dorothy the daggers.

''Cos a tussle makes it seem like it was nowt,' Angie said. 'A few fisticuffs 'n then they were on their way.'

'Go on,' Dorothy nudged Gloria. 'What else does he say?'

'He says, "the ship got hit, but not badly," and at the same time he got hit on the head, "but not badly".'

'But *badly* enough for him to tell you.' Dorothy said what the rest of the women were thinking.

'He says,' Gloria read from the letter, 'that they've got him "sat twiddling my thumbs" until they give him the green light to get back to "thrashing Jerry's backside".'

'Well, I think they've done a good job of that already,' Rosie said. The sinking of *Scharnhorst* meant that for the first time in the war the Allies were free from the threat of German battleships raiding their convoys in both the Arctic and the Atlantic.

'But there must be something wrong for whoever's his boss' – Dorothy was unsure of the naval pecking order – 'to have him sat *twiddling his thumbs*?'

Gloria looked up. 'He just says that he's got a bit of an ear infection, and it's taking time to clear up.'

Dorothy breathed a huge sigh of relief. She put her arm around her friend. 'Eee, thank goodness it's nothing serious, eh?'

Gloria smiled.

'Exactly,' she said, finally taking a bite of her flapjack.

As they all trudged across the yard at the end of the shift, too tired to rush to beat the crush at the timekeeper's cabin like some of the young apprentices, Dorothy tapped Gloria on the shoulder.

'You still all right with me and Ange coming round tonight before we go to the Ritz?'

'Yeah, we understand if you want to just be on yer tod,' Angie said.

'Because of Bobby's letter?' Gloria smiled. She'd had the day to mull over her son's letter and felt reassured that he really was fine. That there was nothing serious to worry about.

'Aye,' Angie said, wrapping a scarf Quentin had given her around her neck. It was soft wool and smelled of him.

'We'd all love to see you,' Gloria said. 'Especially Hope.'

'Great, we'll bring her favourite sweeties,' Dorothy said.

Gloria smiled. Her daughter was a lucky girl. She'd got her daddy back, a godmother who sacrificed her sweet ration for her, the best big sister anyone could want in Helen, and a bunch of unofficial aunties in the women welders. And one day soon – when this war was over – she'd also have two lovable big brothers who would totally adore her. Once they got over the shock, of course. Which they would. Hearing that Bobby had been injured had momentarily blindsided her, but it had also made her realise that she needed to tell them about her situation, about her divorce from Vinnie, and the fact that they now had a little sister. It wasn't fair to keep them in the dark any longer. Like Jack said, they were grown men – brave men – they could deal with what she had to tell them.

Chapter Nine

Monday 14 February

Helen looked at the beautiful red roses that Marie-Anne had carefully arranged and put in a vase for her. They had arrived this morning with a note saying *From your not-so-secret Admirer*, followed by a solitary kiss. She didn't have to be a super-sleuth to work out they were from Matthew; he might as well have just signed his name. But that was Matthew for you – not exactly subtle, certainly not when it came to how he felt about her. Helen wondered where on earth he'd managed to get roses during these times. There were barely any florists in the town still trading. Losing herself in her thoughts for a moment, her mind wandered to John. How she wished the flowers had been from him – that *he* was her secret admirer.

Those musings were followed by less palatable ones. *Had he bought Claire flowers? Had he arranged to take her out on a romantic date?* Helen pushed back the green-eyed monster. Would it be easier to accept John's relationship with another woman if she liked Dr Eris? Helen laughed to herself. *Who was she kidding? Of course it wouldn't.*

Picking up the vase of roses, she moved them from her desk to the top of the filing cabinet. Hearing a quick rap on the frosted glass of her office door, she looked up to see Marie-Anne standing in the doorway. Helen no longer bothered to shut her door as lately there seemed to be a constant stream of people in and out: constant queries from the yard manager, as well as just about every head of department.

'They really *are* lovely,' Marie-Anne said, her eyes fixed on the roses. She had just been gossiping with Dahlia, Matthew's Swedish secretary, about them on the phone and the fact that Dahlia had been asked to make a reservation for two at the Grand on behalf of her boss. Marie-Anne thought he was pushing his luck. Matthew might have most women swooning at his feet, but her boss was not one of them.

Helen looked at Marie-Anne, and thought she seemed a little flushed.

'Please don't tell me there's someone *else* wanting to see me,' Helen said wearily. This morning she'd already had Jimmy the head riveter in, followed by Billy the platers' foreman, then Rosie. The two LCTs being built in the dry docks were of a far simpler design and much easier to produce than your average cargo vessel, but for some reason there seemed to be a litany of queries and concerns, the latest being whether the length of the hull would put too much stress on the suspension system. She'd wanted to scream at them that it wasn't their job to question the design, just to get the ships down the ways in time. All the same, she respected their knowledge and expertise and had promised to talk to Basil.

'There's someone here to see Dorothy,' Marie-Anne said. 'Lieutenant Tobias Mitchell.'

Helen's face showed her surprise. Gloria had told her that Toby was being relocated down south and the chances of Dorothy seeing her chap were pretty hit and miss, at least until the summer.

'Send him in,' Helen said, suddenly worried. Suddenly thinking of Peter. Of Rosie. *Please don't let it be bad news.* She knew Toby had brought messages and updates about

Peter's welfare in the past – most recently on Christmas Day. She felt a terrible sense of trepidation.

'Miss Crawford!' Toby came bounding into the room, causing Winston the cat to shoot out of his basket and scamper out of the office. Toby had his cap under his arm as he strode towards her with his arm outstretched and a smile on his face.

Thank God. Relief flooded through Helen's body. *This was not a death call.*

Helen stood up to shake hands.

Looking at Toby as he reached over and took her hand, his presence filling the room, she could see why Marie-Anne was a little flushed. She'd forgotten how handsome Dorothy's fella was. Even more so in his smart officer's uniform.

'Lovely to see you, Lieutenant Mitchell.'

'Toby, please,' he said, shaking Helen's hand with gusto. 'My apologies for intruding like this. I know how busy the yard must be at the moment. Only, I've managed to snatch a few hours before I have to catch my connection back to London.' Toby's white lie about his destination was necessary as he had to keep the location of the base at RAF Tempsford top secret. The entirety of the airfield had been camouflaged so that it was not even visible from the air.

'Of course,' Helen said, looking up at the clock. It had just gone midday. 'You want to spend it with Dorothy?'

Toby smiled and Helen could see that he was used to getting his own way. He had a very boyish charm about him.

She laughed. 'How can I refuse? And on today of all days. I'll get Marie-Anne to go and fetch her.'

'No, no,' Toby insisted. 'Don't worry. I'm sure you've all got more important things to do. I'll go myself. If you can just point me in the right direction.'

As Toby strode across the yard, not for the first time he felt in awe of the woman who had captured his heart. The place was a minefield of metal and machinery. There were huge piles of chains and girders stacked randomly about the yard. Two cranes were trundling over to the dry docks, one behind the other, each with mammoth-sized metal plates swinging from their jaws. He smiled when he saw V FOR VICTORY scrawled on the side.

A group of young lads who looked like they were playing catch with a red-hot rivet stopped and stared at him as he made his way across to the nearest half-built landing craft. A young boy who looked barely out of short pants waved to him as though he were a movie star. The awe-struck lad was holding a thick chunk of chalk, which Toby knew was for marking numbers onto the metal plates to show where they were to go on the ship's hull. He had learnt much about the process of building a ship since he had started to court Dorothy.

As he approached the nearest dry basin, he raised his vision to the top decking and immediately spotted the women welders, their array of colourful headscarves and the sparkling fountains they were creating with their welds setting them apart from the flat-capped men armed with rivet guns working nearby. The women all had their masked heads down in concentration and had not seen him approach.

Slowing as he reached the scaffolding that had been erected around the body of the LCT, he wondered how he was going to catch their attention; there was the most deafening percussion of sounds all around him – drilling, hammering, the clashing and clanging of metal. He was just about to climb up a ladder leaning somewhat precariously against the staging when he saw Martha, whom he recognised because of her muscular physique, tapping Dorothy on the shoulder. He saw the shower of molten metal die as Dorothy turned to look up at Martha, pushing up her mask as she did so. Her head turned slowly as she looked at where her workmate was pointing. He saw her mouth open and knew that if it weren't for the sounds of the shipyard, he would be hearing her shriek with excitement. It was another reason he loved Dorothy – she didn't give a damn what anyone thought of her. She might well be the most gorgeous woman he'd ever met, but what attracted him to her even more than her sensational looks was her couldn't-care-less attitude.

He watched with a big smile on his face as Dorothy grabbed her haversack and made her way along a wooden platform, then down the ladder that Toby had been preparing to go up.

When she got to the bottom, she flung her arms around him and kissed him on the mouth. He kissed her back, which was difficult as he was smiling so much. Before turning to leave, he looked up at the women, who were staring down at them – all grinning from ear to ear. He focused on Rosie and mouthed, 'Peter's fine,' putting his thumb up to make sure she'd understood. He saw relief spread across her face. Toby hoped more than anything that Peter would make it back. Rosie was a strong woman – she had to be, given the life she'd led, but seeing her reaction on Christmas Day on hearing that Peter was alive, he would not like to be a witness to her reaction should he ever have to bring her different news.

Pushing away those thoughts, Toby grabbed Dorothy's hand and they both hurried back across the yard and through the main gates.

'What are you doing here?' Dorothy asked as soon as they were a hundred yards or so away from the yard and could just about hear themselves speak.

'How could I not come,' he laughed. 'It's St Valentine's Day. And it is therefore imperative that I see my girl.'

Dorothy laughed. She felt like dancing on the spot she was so happy. Even if it was in her steel-toecapped boots.

'I'm guessing,' she said, 'that you're either on your way up to Scotland or heading back to wherever it is you're based down south?'

Toby nodded. He had explained to Dorothy that he couldn't tell her much about where he was or what it was he did and she had accepted that, although she'd told him that she wanted to know everything once the war was over.

'How long have we got?' she asked as she pulled out her compact mirror from her haversack and started dabbing away dirt from her forehead. She was always left with a dirty, sweaty line where her helmet had been.

'Only a couple of hours, I'm afraid. I have to be on the fourteen-thirty train.' He pulled a grim face.

'You checked it was all right with Helen?'

'Of course,' Toby said, stopping to pull out a starched white cloth handkerchief from his trouser pocket and gently wiping away the smudges of soot and smears of dirt on her face. Her very beautiful face.

'God, you're gorgeous,' he said, giving up wiping her face clean and kissing her instead.

They stood, bodies pressed together, Toby in his immaculate khaki uniform, his fair hair Brylcreemed back into submission, Dorothy in her denim overalls ingrained with dirt and sporting a myriad of pinholes from wayward welds.

When they finally broke away, Toby untied Dorothy's headscarf, allowing her long dark brown hair to fall free.

Dorothy took her scarf back, twirled it around in the air, before grabbing Toby's hand and marching up the embankment.

'This is sooo exciting!' she said. 'Where we going?' She laughed. 'I hope it's nowhere posh, because I doubt very much they will let me through the door looking like this.'

Toby looked at the woman he had decided was the one for him. She was full of contradictions. She could be so feminine and yet she spent her days doing a man's job; she was a bit of a snob, yet had chosen a job that many looked down their noses at.

'I thought I'd take you to the salubrious eatery in the seaside resort of Roker famous for its panoramic views out to the North Sea,' he said.

Dorothy squealed with excitement. It didn't matter that Roker was no longer a seaside resort, its beaches now filled with landmines and cordoned off with barbed wire, nor that the views out to sea were often obscured by anti-blast tape and lashing rain running down the windows; she had wanted to go to the Bungalow Café with Toby for ages. It was where Tommy and Polly had gone when they had first started dating and she had thought the place incredibly romantic ever since.

'So, tell me all your news,' Toby asked as they tucked into a plate of ham, cheese and tomato sandwiches. He was sure the old woman behind the counter had given them extra ham, which he put down to the uniform.

'Mmm,' Dorothy said. 'These are lovely.' She savoured the big mouthful she had just taken. 'You have saved me from a packed lunch I was not particularly looking forward to consuming today.'

Toby chuckled as he poured their tea. 'I'm guessing it was your turn to put up your "bait"?' He'd learnt that packed lunches in these parts were called 'bait', which he found odd as where he came from it was something you used to catch fish.

'It was,' Dorothy said, 'and today was not one of my finest in the culinary department.' She took a sip of her tea.

'I don't know,' Toby said with a mischievous look in his eye, 'what will you do when you're married and you have to cook your dear, hard-working husband a decent meal every night?'

Dorothy almost choked on her sandwich. 'Well, for starters, it's *if* I get married.'

She returned his mischievous look.

'I might not be the marrying kind.'

She took another bite of her sandwich and watched Toby's reaction. He immediately laughed. 'Oh, I think you *are* the marrying kind.'

'Well, *if* I am,' Dorothy continued, 'and I do get married, it's quite simple. I will not be slaving over the oven and making my *dear, hard-working husband* a decent meal. First of all, because I will employ a cook, and secondly, because I think my ability to cook a meal – never mind a decent one – is nigh-on non-existent.'

Toby laughed. He wished he could spend the entire day – and night – with Dorothy. She made him laugh. Made him feel young and carefree. She made him forget about this abominable war, and the decisions he was having to make every day – decisions that could as easily save a man's life as send him to an early grave.

As they ate their sandwiches and drank a second pot of tea, they chatted away, Dorothy telling him all about the landing craft they were building and how different they were from the merchant ships they had worked on until now. 'Rosie has become even more of a slave-driver than she already was,' she said. 'Honestly, you'd think we were in a competition to build it in record time.' Toby guessed why Rosie was so invested in the speed in which they were being produced. Peter.

'And how's Gloria? And Jack?' he asked tentatively. He knew there was something about Jack's sudden return Dorothy wasn't telling him. The very fact she wasn't telling him meant it must be serious.

'They're good,' Dorothy said, taking another sip of tea. Dorothy had told him during the weekly phone calls he made to Mrs Kwiatkowski's that Jack had got his old job back at Crown's and that, amazingly, Hope had taken to him as though he had never been away. Dorothy had put it down partly to Hope having heard Jack's voice over the phone these past six months, but mainly to the little girl sensing how happy her mammy was to have Jack about.

'They're not getting any hassle from anyone?' Toby probed. It was obvious their affair would be viewed as scandalous, especially as Jack was married to Miriam, the daughter of the revered Mr Havelock – a man Dorothy didn't seem to rate at all, judging by the way she talked about him. Neither did she rate Miriam, for that matter, although he could understand why she didn't like Jack's estranged wife. She sounded a real she-devil – she had conned Jack into marriage and, unsurprisingly, their life together had not been a happy one.

'No, no hassle. Not yet,' Dorothy said, pushing her plate away and wiping her mouth with the paper serviette. 'But that's probably because they're keeping a low profile. At the moment hardly anyone knows. I think they're trying to keep it really low-key until Miriam files for divorce.'

'She's not already done so?' Toby asked.

Dorothy shook her head. 'She's still in Scotland.'

Toby smiled at the old woman for the bill.

'And the twins, are they well?' Toby thought what Bel and Joe had done was wonderful. There weren't many couples these days who would adopt one child, never mind twins.

'Very well,' said Dorothy. '*Very* lovable and *very* loud.'

Toby chuckled.

'And I don't think I need to ask if Angie and Quentin are still head over heels?'

'Not need at all,' Dorothy said. 'Angie tries to play it down but isn't doing a very good job.'

Toby smiled. It had been obvious to everyone – apart from Angie – that she and Quentin were made for each other, even if they were from opposite ends of the social spectrum.

'And any more news about Bobby?' Toby knew about his head injury. Reading in between the lines, he wondered if there was more to it.

'Not anything new,' Dorothy said. 'He's still being "observed".'

Toby nodded.

'And has Gloria thought any more about telling them – about Jack?' He couldn't believe it when Dorothy had told him that they didn't know their mother had divorced their father and they now had a little sister.

'She's made up her mind. She's going to tell them. I said I'd help her compose a letter, but she said it's something she has to do herself.'

'Well, at least they're stationed on the same ship, so they'll get the news together,' Toby said. He looked at Dorothy and took hold of her hand. 'You know how proud I am of you, don't you?' he asked. He meant it. Wholeheartedly. He had met a lot of women of Dorothy's background and none of them had the grit, or physical strength, to do the work she did. He had roared with laughter, though, when she'd confessed to him that she had only applied for the job because she'd fallen for some good-looking riveter who worked at Thompson's. But that was Dorothy for you. It was why he loved her. Was why he was here today – to tell her just that.

'Here you are.' The old woman handed the bill to Toby, who immediately put a few notes on the little plate, leaving a very generous tip. The woman smiled her thanks, pushed the money into the pocket of her pinny and turned to Dorothy.

'Yer work on the ships, pet?' she asked.

'Yes,' Dorothy nodded. 'I'm a welder at Thompson's.'

The old woman patted her on the back and handed her a parcel wrapped up with string. 'Take this for your squad. Hettie and I – ' she cocked her head over at the counter ' – think yer deeing a grand job. Keep it up. Deeing yer town 'n yer country proud.'

Dorothy was taken aback. She suddenly felt tears spring to her eyes. This was turning into such a special day.

'Oh, thank you, that's lovely,' she said, taking the cake. 'That's really kind.'

'Least we can dee, pet.' The old woman stuffed her hands in her pocket and gave a throaty chuckle. 'Now get yourself back to work, and you – ' she looked at Toby ' – go 'n win that war.'

Toby stood up and tipped his cap.

'I'll certainly give it my damnedest,' he said, his face showing his resolution.

As they walked back to the yard, Toby smiled to himself. There was he thinking the generous ham sandwiches had been down to his uniform. He looked at Dorothy – it was *her* uniform that had inspired.

'So, when am I going to meet your parents?' he asked.

Dorothy let out a slightly bitter laugh. 'It depends whether they can find the time. They only squeeze me in on a Sunday to ease their conscience and make sure I'm still in the land of the living.'

'Well, why don't I try and get a Sunday off sometime soon and I can come with you?' Toby looked at Dorothy. She always got tetchy when talking about her family. 'You know, we've been courting for more than a year – I think it's time I met your family, don't you?' Ideally, he would have liked to have met Dorothy's father, but Dorothy had made it quite clear she had no idea where he was.

'I *do* want you to meet my mum and Frank,' Dorothy said.

'Why do I sense a "but"?' Toby asked.

Dorothy shook her head and put a smile on her face. 'There is no "but". It'll be interesting – you meeting them.' In her mind, it was simply a necessity – something to be endured in order for her to be asked for her hand in marriage.

'Come here.' Toby pulled Dorothy towards him.

'Careful, I don't want to squash my cake.'

'I thought she said the cake was for your squad.'

Dorothy laughed. 'I might give them a sliver.'

Toby kissed her passionately.

'Dor ...' Toby looked at Dorothy, his voice serious, his eyes looking into hers, wanting to read her reaction – to see if she too felt the same. 'I wanted to tell you something. You know ... with it being Valentine's Day, and all that.'

Dorothy looked at him. 'Yes?'

'I want you to know ...' He hesitated. 'I want you to know that ... well ... that I love you.'

A smile slowly spread across Dorothy's face.

She laughed.

'I thought you'd never tell me.'

She kissed him.

'That's good,' she said, 'because I would have hated this relationship to have been one-sided.'

Toby looked at Dorothy.

'Is that your way of telling me that you love me too?'

Dorothy kissed him.

'It is.'

Toby felt a rush of relief. He hadn't been entirely sure if Dorothy really wanted to get serious. They had snatched whatever time they could together since their first date at Polly and Tommy's wedding, and they had kissed and cuddled, although that was all. He knew Dorothy wasn't seeing anyone else, but still, he wasn't totally sure if she wanted to take their courtship to the next step. Sometimes he thought he could read her like a book, other times not. Now he knew. *She loved him.* She'd told him, even if it was in a roundabout way.

Later on that evening, Helen and Matthew walked into the dining room at the Grand. She had agreed to go with Matthew on condition he did not see it as any kind of a date, despite it being Valentine's Day; it was simply because she was hungry and hadn't been anywhere nice for ages. Matthew had been pleased as punch, joking that he would take what crumbs he could. Helen had only agreed to dine at the Grand, and had not asked Matthew to change the venue, because she knew her mother wouldn't be there.

Dr Parker, meanwhile, had only booked the Grand because he believed that there was no way Helen and Matthew would be there, knowing that Helen would not risk going anywhere her mother might be. He had no idea that Miriam was still in Scotland.

When they all spotted each other, it was hard to tell whose face fell the most – Claire's, Matthew's, John's or Helen's. It would probably be classed as a draw. On seeing each other in the bar before they were seated by the maître d', they all forced expressions of pleasant surprise, saying what a coincidence it was. John asked about Miriam and was a little puzzled to hear that she was still over the border, silently cursing himself for not considering the possibility that she might not be back. The last thing he'd wanted this evening was to see Helen and Matthew together. It rankled him. He knew it shouldn't, that he and Helen were merely friends, but it did.

Helen fought hard not to show how she felt about Claire. She did not want her to gain the satisfaction of knowing how jealous Helen was – or that she didn't like her, especially as it was inevitable that their paths would eventually cross at the asylum while she was visiting her grandmother, when she would need to keep the doctor on their side.

They made polite small talk, chatting about the last time they had all seen each other at Artie's christening and what a lovely ceremony it was, and how festive and cosy it had all been in the Tatham Arms. Claire felt her hackles rise again, recalling how John and Helen had seemed so cosy chatting by the bar that day, and how she had desperately wanted to ask what it was they had been talking about, but knew it would not have been appropriate.

During their chit-chat, Matthew tried his hardest to give the impression that he and Helen were an item. He gently touched Helen's elbow and stood close enough to her to intimate that they were physically close and at ease with each other. Miriam had told him a while ago that Dr Parker had had his eye on Helen, and although the doctor had clearly chosen one of his own, Matthew was still concerned he might feel he'd made a mistake and change his mind. He needed him to believe that Helen was taken; that it was too late even if he *did* have a change of heart. He was helped enormously by Dr Eris, who brought up the lovely photograph of them both published in the *Echo*.

Dr Parker might have been convinced that Matthew and Helen were an item, but Dr Eris wasn't taken in. She was a psychologist after all. She made her living out of reading people – and she had read Matthew well, had sussed him out from first meeting him at the christening. The man wanted Helen, but Helen didn't want Matthew.

Dr Eris knew exactly what Helen wanted and she was going to make damn sure she never got it.

When the maître d' finally showed them to their reservations, both couples tried not to show just how relieved they were to be sitting at tables far enough apart that they could not overhear each other's conversations – conversations which, it had to be said, were quite bland in comparison to the thoughts swirling around in their heads.

Chapter Ten

Two weeks later

Monday 28 February

Every evening, Gloria would follow the same routine: after giving Hope her tea, she would settle down at the small dining table and set about writing her letter to Bobby and Gordon. But it was no good. Every evening, Jack would get back from work and find Gloria with a pen in her hand, a sheet of paper on the table, a frown on her forehead and several screwed-up balls of paper on the floor. Each time, Jack suggested that it might be a good idea to take Dorothy up on her offer of help with writing the letter. 'She's desperate to help. Plus, she'd be perfect – she's had a good schooling … she might be able to help you put it in a way the boys can understand,' Jack cajoled.

Finally, one evening, Gloria relented. Jack smiled and picked up Hope, who was holding aloft a scrunched-up piece of paper as though presenting him with a prized possession. Telling Jack to keep Hope entertained, Gloria retreated into the kitchen and made the tea. Chopping up onions while heating up a knob of lard in the pan, she kept thinking about her two sons, wishing she had told them everything from the off: how their father's violence had got much worse after they had left for sea, as had his drinking, but she hadn't wanted them to know for they had their own lives now. She didn't want them worrying about their mam. They'd done enough of that as bairns. She realised that now.

As she added bacon to the pan, causing a burst of ferocious hissing and spitting, she wondered if she'd told them about the escalating violence and how Vinnie had been seeing another woman for two years before Gloria had finally chucked him out, whether this would have made them more understanding, more empathetic about her present situation; whether it would have paved the way to telling them about rekindling her love affair with Jack and then, later, about Hope. If she told them now, though, it would look like an excuse, like she was justifying living in sin with a married man and their illegitimate child.

As she turned and looked into the lounge, she saw Hope sitting on Jack's lap; their little girl was sucking her thumb, immersed in a story her daddy was reading her.

Gloria forced herself to stop worrying.

She would get the letter written next week – with Dor's help. Then she'd send it off and know at least that they had heard the news from her and no one else. There were other lads from the town on their ship and she'd started to worry that when the local gossipmongers eventually got wind about her and Jack, which in time they undoubtedly would, they would beat her to it. If she told them now, she'd get ahead of the rumour mill and hopefully, by the time her boys came home when the war ended, they would have been able to digest the news and perhaps – just perhaps – find it in their hearts to forgive her for not leaving their dad sooner, when they themselves had been bairns. The guilt of not having done so had weighed heavily on her for a long time.

Chapter Eleven

Wednesday 1 March

The women were sitting in the Admiral, having realised they hadn't been out for a drink en masse for ages.

'Pearl's set a date,' Polly announced.

'What? Set a date for the wedding?' Martha asked.

'Of course *for the wedding*,' Dorothy said, rolling her eyes to the pub's beamed ceiling. 'What else would she be setting a date for?' She looked across the table at Polly. 'So, come on, when is it?'

Polly took a sip of her port and lemon, looking around the table at her workmates. How life could change. How people could change. Not so long ago, the prospect of Pearl getting married would have barely caused the bat of an eye; at most, a few mumbled, derisory comments. The faces looking at her now were expectant, happy – eager to know more. Whether Pearl liked it or not, she had become something of an accidental heroine the day she'd gone to battle with Mr Havelock and had helped them all.

'Well, she's been lucky – or should I say, Bill's been lucky, as he seems to be the one doing all the gadding about and organising. Anyway, when he went to see the registrar the other day, the person before him had just cancelled her date.' The reason being, Polly did not add, the poor woman had just had notice that her fiancé had been killed in action. 'And the day that had just become free was Saturday, April the seventh, which is—'

'The Easter weekend!' Dorothy shrieked.

'Why do I think something else exciting is happening that weekend,' Gloria said.

Angie looked at Gloria and gave her a weary nod. 'Toby's just managed to wrangle some leave that weekend.'

'And,' Dorothy said, silently clapping her hands, 'we're bullying Quentin into getting leave then as well.'

'Correction,' Angie said. '*Dorothy* is bullying Quentin. Every time he rings up, she snatches the phone off me 'n tells him we're all gannin out on Easter Saturday on a double date' – Angie widened her eyes – 'somewhere posh.'

Hannah chuckled. 'Dorothy, you're getting worse.'

'And as he's got a forty-eight-hour pass, he's going to meet *the family* on Easter Sunday.' This time it was Dorothy who widened her eyes.

'Does that mean he'll ask you to marry him then and there?' asked Martha.

'No, *silly*,' Dorothy said, 'it just gives him the green light.'

'But what happens if they don't give him the thumbs up?' Martha asked.

'Oh, they will,' Dorothy said. 'I can just imagine their relief at being able to finally get shot of me – make me someone else's responsibility.'

'I'm sure they don't really think like that,' Hannah said.

Dorothy arched an eyebrow.

'Anyway, where's the queen bee?' They all knew Dorothy was talking about Helen. 'Bet you she's got much more glamorous places to be than the Admiral.'

'I did ask her to join us,' Rosie said, 'but she's gone to see her *relative*.' Rosie was very aware that there could be no slip-ups at all with regards to Henrietta. It just needed one pair of flapping lugs to catch on to what they were talking about and the results could be disastrous.

'Ahhh,' Dorothy and Angie said in unison.

'Not the most glamorous of nights out, then,' said Polly.

'No, but I think she combines it with seeing Dr Parker,' said Gloria.

This precipitated another 'Ahh' from Dorothy and Angie.

'Right, my round,' Rosie said, standing up. 'Same again?

Everyone nodded.

'I'll come and help you,' Gloria said.

After pushing their way through the densely packed pub, Rosie shouted the order to the barman, before turning back to Gloria.

'Everything all right with Jack?' she asked.

'Yes,' Gloria nodded. 'We're good. Better still now that I've made up my mind about telling the boys everything. I'm just glad I've Dorothy coming round on Friday to help me with it – or should I say, *writing* it for me. I think that's been half the problem. Why I've left it this long.'

Rosie laughed. 'I must admit, I don't think you could have left it much later. Any longer and this war would have ended and they'd be back to celebrate with their mam … *and* their mam's fancy bit … *and* the little sister they had no idea they had.'

'Don't,' Gloria said. 'I feel bad enough as it is. The more I think about it, the more I can't believe I haven't told them before now.'

'They'll be fine,' Rosie said. 'I'm sure they'll just be happy their mam's happy – and not with you-know-who.' Even Rosie hated to call Vinnie by his name.

'And you?' Gloria asked as the barman put their drinks onto a tray. 'Are you bearing up?'

'I am,' Rosie said, paying the barman. 'Ever since Christmas I've felt …' she paused '… hopeful.' Another pause. 'As if everything's going to turn out all right. Just like it has with Charlotte.' She picked up the tray and laughed. 'Well, to an extent.'

'She still being clingy?' Gloria asked.

'Not as bad as she was, but she's still wanting to be with me all the time, or with Lily, or, ideally, with us both – at Lily's.'

Gloria chuckled as she helped make a path through the crowd of bodies back to their table. They arrived just in time to hear the end of the discussion about what the women were all going to wear to Pearl's wedding.

'A toast,' Dorothy declared, raising her glass.

'To what?' Martha asked.

'To love, of course!' Dorothy said.

'To love,' everyone chorused.

Everyone was well aware, though, that Dorothy was not thinking about Pearl and Bill when they all clinked glasses, but the love in her own life – or rather her hopes of seeing Toby on his knee and a big sparkling diamond ring in his hand in the near future.

Chapter Twelve

Two days later

Friday 3 March

Able Seaman Bobby Armstrong felt a tap on his shoulder and looked up.

'Sorry?' He turned his head so that he could hear.

'Can I see your travel papers?' the conductor asked, more loudly. He had thought the sailor sitting looking out the window was purposely ignoring him, or asleep.

'Course,' Bobby said, rifling around in his duffel bag and producing the requested documentation.

The inspector gave it a quick once-over and handed it back before moving on to a naval officer sitting further down the bus. He guessed, judging by the number of navy blue sailor suits and a couple of officer's uniforms, that a ship had just docked.

Bobby watched the inspector make his way down the aisle, scrutinising everyone's travel cards. The men from the ship he'd cadged a lift with from Iceland would have return tickets. They'd be back on deck later that evening. His, on the other hand, was one-way. He wouldn't be back on any kind of deck any time soon. Some, he knew, would have given anything to be heading home now – away from the horrors of war, back to the warm embrace of families, wives and children, but he wasn't one of them. He looked down at his travel warrant and shoved it back in his duffel bag. His life's possessions were stuffed into a two-foot-long denim bag. Seeing the edge of his medical discharge certificate, he pulled it out and looked at it. He read the words *unilateral hearing loss*. The loss of hearing in his left ear had brought about the end of his naval life.

As the bus went over a pothole, Bobby automatically grabbed the rail of the seat in front of him. Looking out into the darkness, he thought about his father. At least he would not be there to greet him when he arrived back home, although what had possessed Vinnie to sign up for active duty was beyond him. Bobby had lost count of the number of times he, Gordon and his mam had been forced to listen to Vinnie's beer-fuelled rantings about having done his duty in the First War and if there were ever another, he'd tell them exactly where they could stick their conscription form. Perhaps his father had turned over a new leaf, got a sudden bout of patriotism? Somehow, he doubted it.

Looking back down at the creased certificate, Bobby felt his fist clench in frustration as he thought about his own need to fight Jerry – and how it had been ripped away from him. If he'd just been a few feet further from the funnel when it had taken a hit, then the piece of steel that had come flying off would have skimmed past him and not smacked him on the side of the head, knocking him clean out, leaving him with a deep gash that needed a fair few stitches and a headache like no other for days on end.

The real damage, though, couldn't be seen. The first he was aware of anything serious being wrong was when he'd woken up with pus, tinged with blood, coming out of his left ear. He'd sat up and felt shooting pains in his head on top of the headache from hell. The doc had taken a look and diagnosed a middle-ear infection, and asked him if he could hear anything in that ear. Bobby had told him that he could – a shrill ringing. He hadn't liked the way the doc had looked and the way he'd told him it would be a case of 'wait and see'. He'd waited, and whenever the doctor came to see him, he'd lied outright when asked if he felt dizzy or nauseous. He'd lied again a few weeks later when the ringing finally subsided, saying he could hear fine. The doctor hadn't believed him; he was no fool. A simple test disproved Bobby's claim. He had tried to bribe the ship's doctor, who had told him sternly that *he* would pretend *his* hearing had failed.

Bobby had gone to see the captain and practically begged him to keep him on board, trying his utmost to convince him that the hearing in his left ear would come back eventually – what did doctors know? And what did it matter that he couldn't hear in one ear? He could still be a seaman – he could still do his job. But even though Bobby had argued his case as though attempting to beat the death penalty, his captain had given him his marching orders, albeit reluctantly.

'Your hearing loss could jeopardise your own safety – as well as those you're fighting alongside. You can go back home a hero, Armstrong,' the captain had told him. 'You have nothing to be ashamed of. Quite the reverse. You'll be getting medals to prove it.'

Bobby had wanted to retort that he felt no shame, nor did he give a damn about any medals, he just wanted to carry on doing what he'd been doing. He wanted to fight to the bitter end until Jerry was beaten. But it was no good, the doctor had given his final diagnosis: two months had passed and there had been no improvement whatsoever in his hearing – there was no chance it would come back now. And so, Bobby had been shipped back to dry land for a life on Civvy Street.

Bobby sat up straight in his seat. *Opportune* had played an important part in Operation Torch, patrolling the

Mediterranean and supporting the famous British naval formation, Force H. They had effectively blown the enemy out of the war and cleared the Arctic and the Atlantic for the impending invasion of Europe.

Which was why Bobby felt so angry. He felt as though he had been deprived. As though he had been put on the sidelines just as his team was about to clinch victory. He wanted to be there. He didn't care that it would be dangerous. When they had gone to war, he had accepted he might lose his life; he would have given that life if it meant Hitler and his madmen were snuffed out and their ideology wiped off the face of the planet.

Bobby put his elbow against the window and looked out. It was dark. All he could see was his own angry reflection, looking at a future he'd been denied.

When Gloria opened her front door, she took a step back on seeing Dorothy. She had seen her workmate dolled up to the nines before, but this evening she looked particularly stunning. Her long, dark brown hair, which was normally piled up and stuffed into a faded headscarf, had been washed and curled away from her face into victory rolls. She had on a stunning red dress that Gloria hadn't seen before, with a rather low-cut neckline and a nipped-in waist, which accentuated her womanly, hourglass figure.

'Dear me,' Gloria gawped, 'I think yer've surpassed yerself tonight, Dor.'

Dorothy laughed, put her hands on her hips and struck a pose as though she was just about to walk down the red carpet but had stopped to allow for the flash of the photographers' cameras.

'It is Friday night, Glor! A girl's gotta make an effort,' Dorothy said, sashaying into the flat.

Gloria knew Dorothy was going to the Ritz after she had helped her write her letter to Bobby and Gordon.

'Does Toby know you go out looking like this?' Gloria asked, closing the door behind her.

'Of course,' Dorothy said, putting her handbag and gas mask by the side of the door. 'I spoke to him just before I came out and described in great detail exactly what I was wearing.' On seeing Hope, she pulled a pantomime happy face and put her arms out. Hope immediately abandoned her dolls and stretched her arms up towards her glamorous godmother.

'How's my favourite little girl?' she said, heaving her god-daughter up onto her hip. 'Getting bigger by the day.'

Hope giggled and nodded that she was.

'Oh my goodness, I wonder what I've got in my hand-bag.' Dorothy pulled a puzzled expression.

'Sweeties!' Hope squealed.

'Of course, how could I forget,' Dorothy said in mock earnestness. 'I wonder where they are?'

'Handbag!' Hope shouted.

'Well, you better go and see if they're there,' Dorothy said, putting her back down and looking to the doorway.

Gloria watched as her daughter hurried over to Dorothy's black suede clutch purse, sat down next to it and carefully undid the gold clasp. Peering into the bag, she carefully put her little hand in and retrieved a white paper bag full of her favourite boiled candies and twists of toffees.

'Let me get the tea tray,' Gloria said. 'I've put everything we need out on the table.'

Dorothy looked over to the small dining table and saw that there were three pens and a few sheets of paper. She put her hand out to Hope. 'Shall we write to your big brother, then?' Hope held her bag of sweets to her chest, took her godmother's hand and walked over to the table.

Gloria headed for the kitchen. 'Did Quentin turn up all right?' she shouted through as Dorothy helped Hope onto the chair. She wasn't quite tall enough to do it herself, especially as one hand was gripping her weekly treasure as though her life depended on it.

'Oh, yes, bang on time. This *is* Quentin we're talking about,' Dorothy said, rolling her eyes as Gloria came back through to the main living area.

'Where's he taking her this evening?' Gloria asked, putting the tea tray down and sitting at the table.

'Meng's,' Dorothy said.

'Nice,' said Gloria. Meng's, a café by day and a restaurant by night, was known for its fine French cuisine.

'And I'm presuming you and Marie-Anne are hitting the Ritz after you've finished here?'

'Of course – Marie-Anne and a couple of her friends from school.'

'Ah,' Gloria said, pouring out their tea. Now she knew why Dorothy was so done up; she always had to be the most stunning one in the group whenever she went out.

'So,' Dorothy looked at Hope, 'are we ready?'

Hope had a bulge coming out of one of her cheeks. She nodded enthusiastically.

'What do we do when we're given such a big bag of sweeties?' Gloria looked at her daughter.

'Shhaare,' Hope said, a little spittle dribbling from the side of her mouth. She picked up the bag of sweets and offered it to Dorothy, who shook her head. 'No, thank you. It'll spoil my lipstick.' Hope smiled her gratitude. She held the bag towards her mammy, who took one and popped it into her mouth. Dorothy knew Gloria only took a sweet out of principle. She wanted her daughter, who was growing up an only child, to learn good manners.

'Right,' Dorothy picked up the pen and paper, 'I think we should begin this letter by telling brothers Bobby and Gordon all about their *sweet* little sister.' Hope giggled and took a pen and a piece of paper and started scribbling.

Dorothy looked at Gloria, who had a cup of tea in both hands and a glum expression on her face.

Just then the front door opened and Jack walked in.

'Daddy!' Hope swivelled around off her chair and ran to Jack, who picked her up and held her in the air.

As they drove along the Seaburn seafront and on to Roker, Bobby was hit by a flood of memories: the excitement of travelling by bus and then by tram to the beach with his mam and Gordon, making castles and moats, swimming in the sea, eating gritty home-made sandwiches. Their dad, thankfully, was never there. If he had been, Bobby would not be conjuring up those memories, but burying them. Vinnie had never been a family man; 'the bairns' were the woman's domain. He was the man. He worked and brought home a wage, kept food in their bellies and a roof over their heads. Only, as they got older, he hadn't even done that – most of his wages had been poured down his neck and pissed up against the wall of their local.

At least, Bobby thought as through the darkness he caught the slight shimmer of rippling waves in the distance, his father was on one of His Majesty's frigates somewhere in the North Atlantic. There'd be just him and his mam. And better still, he would not be returning to the home he'd been brought up in. His mam had written to him and Gordon, telling them she'd moved to a flat on Borough Road that was small, but cosy – and had two bedrooms. He knew she wouldn't mind him staying with her

– rather, she'd insist. It would not be for long, though. Once he found a job, he'd find his own place.

Seeing the arched outline of the Wearmouth Bridge, he sat up. It felt strange returning to Sunderland without Gordon by his side. It had been hard saying goodbye to him at the docks in Reykjavik. Much harder than he'd anticipated. He was going to miss his brother. This was the first time they'd been apart for years. Gordon had argued that Bobby should write and tell their mam that he'd been medically discharged and was coming home, but Bobby had insisted he wouldn't and had made Gordon promise not to write to their mam behind his back and warn her of his return. He hoped Gordon had kept that promise – that he'd understood just how important it was for him to return to Sunderland with as little fanfare as possible.

'Don't let me stop you,' Jack said as he put Hope down, then shrugged off his coat and hung it up on the hook by the door. 'I've been told this letter has to be off in the post tomorrow – by hook or by crook.' He smiled as he walked over to Gloria and gave her a kiss.

'Work all right?' she asked.

'Aye,' Jack said. 'All good at Thompson's?'

'Punishing, unrelenting, gruelling, monotonous,' Dorothy answered for Gloria. 'Made worse by Rosie the slave-driver.'

Jack laughed as he picked up Hope and popped her back on her chair. Gloria had mentioned Rosie's obsession with the LCT they were working on – not just the speed of the build but also the quality. He knew it paralleled her obsession with getting Peter back from France.

'So,' Jack looked at Dorothy and smiled, 'I think yer've got yer work cut out, if yer gannin out tonight, which I'm guessing yer are. Can't see yer getting so togged up just to come here.' Jack walked into the kitchen. 'I didn't know Toby was up?'

'He's not,' Gloria said, raising an eyebrow. 'Dorothy is going out with Marie-Anne and her mates. Although Dorothy has made sure that Toby is well aware of what he is missing out on.'

'Poor lad,' Jack laughed, ruffling Hope's thick black bobbed hair as she unwrapped a toffee and pushed it into her mouth.

'Got to keep them on their toes,' Dorothy said. 'I don't want him thinking I'm sat at home mooning about, waiting for him on a Friday night.'

'Heaven forbid.' Gloria looked at Jack with a mix of love and laughter in her eyes. She still felt her heart lift with joy every time he came in from work. She was sure it always would.

Jack leant over the table and put his calloused hand on the side of the teapot. 'I'll make us a fresh brew.' He gently touched Gloria's hand before heading off to the kitchen.

'OK,' Dorothy said. 'Let's get cracking.'

Hope shuffled off her chair and over to Dorothy, who picked her up and put her on her knee.

'This is going to be a joint effort,' Dorothy said, kissing the top of Hope's head and smiling across at Gloria.

Bobby jumped off the tram at Mackie's Corner at the top of Fawcett Street as he needed to stretch his legs and wanted to reacquaint himself with his hometown. The moon was large, affording a modicum of light that allowed him to make out his surroundings despite the blackout. He hadn't been back home since before the start of the war, yet it felt as though it was just yesterday. He knew that the place he'd grown up in had become one of the most heavily bombed towns in the country due to its industry, and that with housing sitting alongside shipyards, factories and collieries, missed targets meant that homes had been hit instead. He also knew that after each raid the town had licked its wounds and gone about its business again, making ships, mining coal and building engines. Walking down the street that ran through the main shopping area, he passed the grandiose town hall with its towering clock. Looking across at the blacked-out windows of Meng's restaurant, he smiled. He and Gordon had pressed their faces up against the floor-to-ceiling windows many a time to look at the wonderful, mouth-watering arrays of pastries and cakes on display.

He slowed down as he passed the cordoned-off bomb site where Binns, the town's most exclusive department store, had once been. His mam had written and told them about each bombing that had hammered the town, but seeing the shadowy outline of a huge mound of bricks and rubble where once the grand three-storey store had stood was still shocking.

Turning left at the bottom of the street, he looked across the road and was glad to see the darkened outline of the town's magnificent museum, which was thankfully still in one piece.

He quickened his pace as he walked along Borough Road towards the start of the east end. He suddenly felt a rush of boyish excitement at seeing his mam. She wrote regularly, but it had still been almost four years since he'd seen her – been able to give her a hug. He couldn't wait to see the look on her face when he knocked on her door and she saw it was him.

Chapter Thirteen

'Surprise!' Bobby dumped his coat and duffel bag by his feet on the mat at the entrance to the basement flat and put his arms out.

Gloria stood stock-still, her hand holding the front door open, looking at her eldest son. She was in complete shock.

'Mam, it's me! Bobby. Have you forgotten what your own son looks like?' He laughed, scooping her up in his arms and giving her a big bear hug, almost lifting her off the ground.

'Bobby … I can't believe it.' Gloria's voice was muffled against her son's navy blue sailor's uniform; her slippered feet just touching the floor.

Bobby put his dumbfounded mother down and then rested his hands on her shoulders and looked at her. 'You look well, Mam. Very well.' His smile was wide, and his brown eyes twinkled. This was the happiest he had felt since leaving his ship.

Gloria reached up to touch her son's cheek and promptly burst out crying.

'Oh, Mam.' Bobby wrapped his arms around her once again. 'Don't cry. You should be happy.'

'I am. I am.' Gloria was now half laughing, half crying. 'Just shocked.' She wiped the tears away with both hands. 'Are yer back for good?' She looked at his head. 'What about this head injury?'

Bobby laughed, rubbing his hand self-consciously across the top of his head; his hair was more like stubble as it had been clipped so short. 'All these questions. Can I get a nice cup of tea first? Perhaps I can even get through the door?'

As he spoke, he looked over his mam's head and spotted the most amazing-looking woman – long dark hair, fashioned like a Hollywood starlet – and the thought went through his head momentarily that she might be famous before he dismissed it. His mam had not mentioned being chummy with any movie stars. His vision dropped down to the little girl sitting on her lap. She, too, was a gem. Same dark hair, only bobbed. Same heart-shaped face. Mother and child were staring at him, looking almost as stunned as his mam. He immediately took his cap off. 'Sorry, ma'am, I didn't see you sat there.'

Gloria stepped aside so he could come into the warmth of the flat. So entranced was Bobby by this vision of unexpected beauty in a red dress, he didn't see Jack standing in the kitchen doorway.

Striding across the living area, Bobby threw out his hand. 'Glad to make your acquaintance ... ?' His deep voice rose in a question.

'Dorothy. Dorothy Williams.'

As soon as their hands touched, they both got a short, sharp electrical shock.

'Oh my God,' Dorothy laughed. 'Did you feel that?'

'I certainly did!' Bobby beamed back at her.

Sensing movement to his left, Bobby looked round and it was only then that he saw Jack.

'Sorry, mister, I didn't see you there.' Presuming the man was a neighbour or a friend, he again threw his hand out and the two men shook. Their handshakes were equally firm.

'Jack Crawford.'

'Bobby Armstrong.'

Straight away, Bobby turned his attention back to Dorothy and the little girl on her lap.

'And what's your daughter's name?'

Dorothy laughed a little too loudly, betraying her nerves. 'Well, you're right – we do actually look uncannily similar.' She flashed Gloria a look and then glanced down at Hope; a trickle of toffee-laced goo was making its way out of the corner of her mouth. 'But we're not related.'

Bobby glanced down at Dorothy's left hand and saw it was devoid of any kind of jewellery. His heart leapt. This homecoming was getting better by the second.

'This is my god-daughter,' Dorothy said. 'Hope.'

'Pleased to meet you, Hope.' And for the third time Bobby stretched out his arm and gently shook the chubby little hand of the toddler who was almost as pretty as her godmother.

'Sit down, Bobby, sit down,' Gloria said, taking him by the arm and gently pushing him onto the seat next to Dorothy and Hope. 'Let's get yer a nice cup of tea.' Gloria hurried into the kitchen. 'Are yer hungry, Bobby?' she called out. 'How about a sandwich?'

'No, Mam, a cuppa tea's just fine for the moment,' Bobby shouted back. He had been hungry, but on seeing the vision of gorgeousness in her figure-hugging red dress, his appetite had immediately vanished.

'You staying for another, Dor?'

'Eee, no, Glor, I'd best get off …'

The words were barely out of her mouth when Bobby suddenly hit his forehead with the palm of his hand. 'You're Dor! Mam's workmate at Thompson's!' Bobby looked incredulous.

Dorothy shuffled about uneasily on her chair. She was glad Hope seemed more than happy to stay sitting on her lap, sucking on her toffee and staring at the incredibly handsome man who was her brother.

'That's me.' Dorothy forced herself to sound jocular.

'Sorry to sound so surprised, you're just not what I expected.' Bobby looked up at his mam as she placed a cup of tea in front of him. He wanted to add that the Dor he'd read about in the letters Gloria had sent him and Gordon described Dorothy as a bit of a dipstick, the squad's clown – her and another girl called Angie. His mam had missed out the part about her being a real looker.

Bobby caught Dorothy looking up at Gloria and the man called Jack before she started to fold up a piece of paper on the table in front of her.

'Is this young lady having a lesson?' he asked, smiling at Hope. The little girl was totally adorable. He looked back at Dorothy. 'Mam says you're the educated one of the squad?'

Again, Dorothy forced a laugh. 'More that I read lots of trashy books.'

'So, Bobby,' Gloria sat down next to her son, putting her hand on his arm, 'tell me – what's happened? Why are you back?'

Bobby took his mam's hand in his own and squeezed it. 'I've been medically discharged.'

'Your head injury?' Jack asked. From where he had been standing, he had spotted scarring on Bobby's head behind his left ear where the hair hadn't grown back.

Bobby was aware that Jack had said something because everyone's attention had gone to him, but he hadn't heard a word. He turned his head round and tilted it slightly to the left. 'Sorry, what was that?' He looked at Jack properly for the first time. Was he the little girl's father? A bit old. Perhaps he was Dorothy's father? They had similar dark looks.

'Yer head injury,' Jack repeated. 'Is that why they've medically discharged you?'

Bobby nodded. 'Yes. Got a bash on my head and lost the hearing in my left ear.' He wanted to say more: how frustrated he was about the decision; how he'd pleaded for them to let him stay on, at least until after the planned invasion of Europe. But he didn't. He didn't want to come across as a whinger, especially in front of Dorothy.

'So, no other long-lasting injuries?' Jack pursued the point. After suffering amnesia, he had learnt how complex the brain was and how head injuries could cause problems that weren't always immediately noticeable.

'No, I've not lost any of my marbles,' Bobby laughed, knowing what Jack was intimating. 'Not that I had many to start with.'

Bobby glanced at Dorothy and smiled. He couldn't keep his eyes off her. He forced himself to take a sup of his tea, his eyes still flickering up at her.

Just then Hope suddenly got restless and wriggled off Dorothy's lap.

Smiling as she toddled past, she made a beeline for Gloria.

Bobby watched as Hope stretched out her hands, lifted her angelic little face up to Gloria and called out, 'Mammy!'

Chapter Fourteen

'Mammy?' Bobby repeated, looking confused, as Gloria got up from her chair and picked up the pretty, dark-haired little girl.

'Yes,' Gloria said, 'that's right … I'm Hope's mammy.'

She hitched Hope into a comfortable position on her hip. 'I'm so sorry, Bobby, I should have told you sooner.'

Bobby shook his head in disbelief; he didn't say anything, just sat glued to his seat at the dining table.

'And I'm Hope's father.' Jack stepped forward and put his hand on Gloria's shoulder.

Bobby looked to Dorothy as though for confirmation. She nodded.

There was a moment's silence before Gloria sat down, Hope still clinging to her like a little monkey. Dorothy got up and tried to take her, but Hope shook her head vehemently and buried her head in her mammy's bosom.

As Dorothy returned to her seat, Gloria started to speak, her voice low and even, relating to her son how, shortly after starting work at Thompson's, she had met Jack, who was working as the yard manager. They had started a relationship and not long afterwards she had unexpectedly fallen with Hope.

Bobby did not speak a word or interrupt as his mam told him that her marriage to Vinnie had been a long time dead, something, she said, both he and Gordon had probably realised when they were still at home. It had taken a while, but she had finally made it official and divorced him shortly before he was sent overseas. Gloria kept the events of the past three years as brief and to the point as possible. She omitted to mention any of the terrible violence that Vinnie had subjected her to, not wanting to sound as though she was making excuses for what had happened.

'All I can say, Bobby, is that I'm so, *so* sorry that I didn't tell you and Gordon beforehand – and that you've had to find out like this.' She attempted a smile but gave up on seeing her son's stony demeanour. 'I know I should have come clean a long time ago, but I just kept putting it off and putting it off – and then time went on 'n it got harder 'n harder … I guess I just didn't know how to tell you … I wanted it to be face to face—'

'Glor was just about to write you a letter,' Dorothy interjected.

Bobby turned and looked at Dorothy. He didn't say anything, but instead got up and started pacing up and down the living room.

'OK, just so I've got this right,' he said, his eyes darting from his mam, who was holding Hope – *his sister* – to Jack, his mam's *married, live-in-lover*.

'You started work at Thompson's – ' he exhaled ' – when you were still married to our dad.' A deep breath. 'And within a few months you'd started seeing the yard manager.' He cocked his head over at Jack, who was standing behind Gloria, his hands resting protectively on her shoulders. Jack's eyes were glued to Bobby, ready to react if he looked as though he was going to lose it. There was a good chance. He was his father's son, after all.

'A man who was also still married,' Bobby continued, glaring at Jack. 'And a few months later you were – ' he looked at Hope ' – in the family way.' Bobby was struggling not to raise his voice, something he didn't want to do,

114

not with a little one about. 'And it's now been more than three years and you never thought to tell Gordon and me during all that time?' Bobby stopped pacing and was now standing, arms akimbo, in the middle of the living room. He shook his head. 'You never even thought to tell us that you'd left Dad – never mind divorced him?'

Gloria opened her mouth, but nothing came out. There was another long silence.

Suddenly, Bobby felt as though the walls of the small flat were closing in on him.

'Sorry, Mam, but I'm gonna have to go. I need some time to let all this sink in.' He went to the doorway where he had dumped his coat and pulled it on.

'But where yer gonna stay?' Gloria fretted, standing up and handing Hope over to Jack. 'You've just got back. Stay here. Let's talk this through.'

Bobby shook his head, shot Jack another dark look and turned to leave. Grabbing his duffel bag, he opened the door and left the flat.

Dorothy looked at the table and seeing that Bobby had left his white peaked sailor's cap, she grabbed it and went after him.

When Dorothy reached the top of the stone steps that led to the Borough Road, she immediately caught sight of Bobby, his broad physique and the square shoulders of his sailor's coat just about visible in the dark of the blackout.

'Hey, Bobby, you forgot your cap!' she shouted out.

She saw him turn on hearing her voice and she hurried towards him. When she reached him, she was suddenly aware of how tall he was. He had seemed tall in the flat, but she'd put that down to the room's low ceiling as well as to Gloria being quite short, but now she was standing next to him, she realised he must have been nearly six foot.

'Thanks.' His voice was deep, serious and surly. He took his cap and put it on.

'Where're you going to go?' Dorothy asked. It was getting late and she doubted he had much money to waste on a hotel.

'Hostel ... Sally Army,' he said, looking down at Dorothy's flushed, attractive face.

Dorothy could feel the intensity of his stare.

'I know somewhere that'll have you,' she said, looking down at her wristwatch, more to avoid his stare than to see what time it was. 'Hopefully, it won't be too late.'

She started walking.

'Follow me,' she ordered, still not looking him in the eye.

Bobby did as he was told, keeping to her left as they crossed the Borough Road and walked past the Burton House Hotel pub. Two middle-aged men still wearing work overalls and flat caps bundled out the entrance, bringing with them the smell of smoke and beer. A brief snatch of sound escaped. Laughter and loud chatter. The place sounded lively.

'I know it's not really any of my business,' Dorothy said, looking up at Bobby's profile as they turned right into Tatham Street, 'but I really don't think you should be mad with your mam.'

'You're right,' Bobby said, glancing down and catching Dorothy's eye. 'It's not really any of your business.'

Dorothy stopped in her tracks and glowered at him. She wanted to tell him that, actually, it *was* her business. Gloria was more than a workmate. She was more like a mother to her than her own. She wanted to tell him that she loved and cared for Gloria. *She'd even helped deliver her baby, for God's sake.* Dorothy wanted to tell him all this and more, but she didn't.

Looking down at this angry, ravishing vision in red, Bobby suddenly realised Dorothy had nothing to keep her warm. He shrugged off his heavy three-quarter-length jacket and held it out.

'Here, put this on. It's cold,' he commanded.

Dorothy tutted. 'I'm fine. We're nearly there.' She forced herself to look him in the eye. 'I just think you should know that your mam's been through a tough time.' She started walking. 'There's a lot you don't know.'

Bobby swung his coat over his shoulder and watched Dorothy for a moment as she stomped ahead in her high-heeled shoes.

'Clearly,' Bobby said, striding to catch her up.

When they reached 34 Tatham Street, Dorothy knocked on the front door, which was, as usual, slightly ajar. Dorothy breathed a sigh of relief. The door only got bolted when everyone had gone to bed.

'Cooee!' she called out through the gap, being careful not to make too much noise. She guessed the babies would be in bed at this time and she would be everyone's least favourite person if she woke them.

'It's only me, Dorothy,' she said in a low, sing-song voice.

Seconds later she heard steps on the tiled hallway and the door was pulled wide open.

'Dorothy! Why, this is a surprise.' Agnes looked up at the sailor standing next to her. He took off his cap and dipped his head by way of a greeting.

'Come in. Come in,' Agnes commanded.

Dorothy was glad Agnes hadn't asked her to explain why she'd turned up on her doorstep, togged up to the nines on a Friday night, with a sailor boy by her side.

'I'm so sorry to come so late,' she said, stepping over the threshold and following Agnes down the hallway. Sensing no one behind her, she looked back to see Bobby was still standing on the doorstep.

'Come on!' She waved her arm impatiently.

Walking into the kitchen, Dorothy was glad there was no one else about, just Tramp and Pup who were curled up by the range. She looked at the clock. It had gone half nine.

'Everyone in bed?' she asked as Bobby appeared in the kitchen doorway.

Agnes chuckled, disappearing into the scullery and reappearing with a pot of tea. 'That's what having children does to yer.'

'I've never known the house so quiet,' Dorothy said, keeping her voice low.

'Best time of the day,' Agnes said, putting the pot of tea on the kitchen table and waving her arm towards the chairs. 'Sit down.' She looked up at Bobby. 'You're too tall to be standing about. I need to be able to see your face.'

Bobby smiled as he hung his coat on the back of the chair and he and Dorothy sat down next to each other.

'Agnes, this is Bobby – Gloria's son.' Dorothy turned to Bobby, who immediately stuck out his hand.

'Well I never.' Agnes's face broke into a genuine smile. 'Gloria's son.' She shook his hand. 'This is a surprise. I'm Agnes, pet. Agnes Elliot. I'm a friend of yer mam's.'

Bobby nodded and smiled. 'Mam's mentioned you in her letters.'

Agnes poured their tea. 'I'm guessing yer ma got a bit of a shock, you just turning up?'

'You can say that again,' Dorothy answered for Bobby. She raised her eyebrows at Agnes and took a sip of her tea. 'Which is why we're here. It's a little bit crowded in Gloria's flat and I remembered Polly saying that you might be looking to rent out the top room.'

'I am indeed,' Agnes said.

'You can have the money upfront,' Bobby said, pulling open his duffel bag in search of his wallet.

'Oh, don't be bothering with that tonight, hinny,' Agnes said. 'Besides, you might be doing a midnight flit when you hear the twins start up in the early hours.'

Bobby smiled. 'There's not a lot stops me sleeping.'

Agnes asked Bobby a few polite questions about his life in the navy, the war in general, his brother Gordon and the reason for his medical discharge. It didn't take long for her to get a take on Gloria's lad and she was pleased to see he clearly took after his mam and not his dad. He would fit in with the rest of the household.

Sensing that Agnes felt happy with her new lodger, Dorothy finished off her tea. 'Well, I better get myself off.' She stood up. 'I'll leave you to it.'

'Where're you going?' Bobby asked, as he too stood up.

Dorothy laughed but still found she couldn't look him in the eye. 'I'm going back to tell Gloria that her son, who has just disappeared out of her life as quickly as he reappeared, is now lodging with Agnes, so there's no reason to worry, as mothers are wont to do when their sons go off in a strop.'

'I'll walk you back there,' he said, ignoring the jibe and grabbing his cap.

'Don't be daft, I'll be fine,' Dorothy said, waving her hand to show her dismissal of Bobby's offer.

'No,' Bobby said. 'I'm walking you back there. It's dark and it's late.'

Dorothy huffed. 'Women are emancipated now, Bobby. We can look after ourselves. We work, we weld, we earn our own money. Times are changing.'

Bobby made a puzzled expression and touched his left ear. 'Didn't catch a word. Deaf as a post on that side.'

Dorothy rolled her eyes.

Bobby looked at Agnes. 'I won't be long.'

Putting on his cap, he stuck out his arm to show that Dorothy was to go first.

Agnes heard Dorothy repeating her diatribe word for word as she walked down the corridor and out of the house.

'And don't pull that *I'm deaf as a post* one on me,' she said as they stepped out onto Tatham Street.

Agnes saw that Bobby manoeuvred around Dorothy so that he was on her right side, next to the road. She couldn't help but watch them as they walked up the street – Dorothy in her painted-on red dress and Bobby in his smart navy uniform, his thick woollen coat flung over his shoulder. She heard Dorothy say something about Emmeline Pankhurst and *didn't he know about the suffragettes?*, then Bobby, bending his head, saying 'Pardon?'

As they moved off into the darkness, she heard Dorothy let out a half-strangled sound of pure exasperation. Agnes wandered back into the house with a smile on her face.

It was a true saying: you never knew what was just around the corner.

Chapter Fifteen

When Bobby woke at six o'clock the next morning it took him a few seconds to realise where he was. It felt alien to be in a bed that felt huge compared to the narrow bunk beds he'd slept in for years, just as it was to wake up alone, with no other bodies within arm's reach tossing and turning and snoring or shouting out in their sleep. Sardines in a can – or rather, in a ship. His sleep that night after returning to number 34 Tatham Street had been fitful, which was hardly surprising. Never in a million years would he have guessed he'd come back home to find that his mam was divorced from his dad and shacked up with another bloke – and that she'd had another child. *He and Gordon had a little sister.*

And then there was Dorothy – that crimson dress, those curves, those dark eyes like daggers and those full lips. She reminded him of a beautiful thoroughbred filly, trotting back and forth, tossing its mane and looking down its long, regal nose.

After making his bed, Bobby made his way down to the kitchen, where he left what he reckoned would be enough cash to cover a week's board and lodging. He didn't want anyone to think he expected any kind of preferential treatment simply because he was Gloria's son. He'd said as much to Agnes last night after he'd returned from walking Dorothy back to the flat and had found a sandwich and a cup of tea waiting for him on the kitchen table. Agnes had told him in her soft Irish accent that she had no intention of treating him any differently to any other lodger she might have. And, she'd added, when he'd nodded at the much appreciated supper, she would have provided sustenance to anyone who had turned up on her doorstep after a long journey. 'Especially one of our brave boys who's been risking life 'n limb for his country 'n has, thankfully, made it back home alive.' The sadness that came into her voice had reminded Bobby that his new landlady had lost a son in this war and a husband in the one before.

Quietly unbolting the front door and carefully shutting it behind him, Bobby stood for a moment looking at this part of the east end, which was to be his new home. As he walked down Tatham Street, seeing it for the first time in the early-morning light, he looked at the parallel rows of three-storey terraced houses. Smoke had started to billow out of a few of the chimneys. He caught a glimpse of an old woman in a floral nightgown pulling back a heavy black-out curtain, before his attention was diverted to a large grey cat running across the tram tracks and darting down one of the side streets. He pulled up the collar on his navy coat; it might be the start of spring, but there was still a bitter nip in the air.

Reaching the Borough Road, he looked left to his mam's flat. He still couldn't quite believe she'd not only booted their father out – finally – after all these years, but that she'd also divorced him. *Why*, he couldn't help thinking, *hadn't she done that years ago?*

Crossing the road and turning left down Norfolk Street, he thought about the man who had replaced his father. He hoped his mam hadn't jumped from the frying pan into the fire with this Jack Crawford. The name rang a bell, but then again Crawford was a common name in these parts. He'd been so distracted by Dorothy, he hadn't paid him much heed, but lying awake in bed and replaying his homecoming in his head, he'd thought more about his mam's new fella. The way he'd stood with his hands on her shoulders – was he simply being protective? Or controlling? Had his mam exchanged one nasty bastard for another? And if she had, what about Hope? Was she having to endure the same hell that he and Gordon had?

Reaching the top of Norfolk Street, he turned right down High Street East, joining a growing stream of flat-capped workers heading to the docks. The smell was strong. The salt in the air was pungent. He would guess the tide was high. Walking along Low Street and seeing the old steamer at the ferry landing, he jogged to catch it before it left. Paying Stan, the old ferryman, he walked to the side railings and looked out towards the mouth of the Wear. It was good to feel the undulating wash of the river under his feet; the slight rocking of the deck made him feel at home. His reasons for joining up might not have been driven by a deep yearning for a sailor's life, but he had grown to love it all the same, and now, as he looked out to the North Sea, he knew he was going to miss it.

Bobby knocked on the yard manager's office door. If his mam hadn't already told him and his brother in her letters about a woman called Helen Crawford, he would have presumed this was the secretary come in early to catch up on some work for her boss.

'Sorry to bother you, Miss Crawford,' Bobby said, trying not to startle her. She looked engrossed in a large draftsman's drawing that was spread across the width of her desk. There was a huge ginger cat curled up in a basket on the floor next to her chair.

'Gosh!' Helen looked up, surprised at seeing a sailor in the doorway of her office. 'You gave me quite a shock there.' She glanced up at the clock. It had just gone seven. 'No one's usually about at this time. In the yard, yes, but not here in admin.' She scrutinised the handsome seaman standing in the doorway. He looked harmless.

Bobby looked at his mam's friend and thought she had done a good job of describing her. Very beautiful, with that subtle air that seemed inherent in those who were brought up with an education and no worries about money. He'd thought it strange his mam was chummy with a woman from the moneyed middle class, but it seemed they had become quite close over the years.

'Please, come in.' Helen waved him in.

Bobby walked into the small room and stopped in his tracks as the marmalade-coloured tomcat suddenly came padding over towards him and rubbed up against his leg.

'How can I help you?' Helen was curious. Every minute of every working day at the yard might be spent building ships, but it was actually quite a rarity to see those who sailed in them in the yard.

'I'm after a job,' Bobby said, purposefully neglecting to tell her that his mother was one of her employees and a friend to boot. He wanted to get this job off his own back.

'You're no longer with the navy, I take it?' Helen asked. She noticed that every time she spoke, the sailor turned his head ever so slightly to the left.

'Medically discharged,' Bobby said, pulling out his papers from his inside pocket. 'Not that I agreed with the decision.'

'Really? And why were you medically discharged?' She didn't want to take on someone who might end up being a liability. She looked down at the creased form he had just thrust into her hand.

'Loss of hearing in my left ear,' he said.

'Ah,' Helen said. *That explained the head tilting.*

124

'I can rivet,' Bobby said. 'I did most of my apprentice-ship at Bartram's before I went to sea. I'm sure they've still got records ...'

'That must have been a good few years ago,' Helen said, guessing the strapping young man standing in front of her must be in his mid-twenties.

'It's like riding a bike,' Bobby said, quick as a flash. 'You never forget.'

Helen pulled out a packet of Pall Malls and lit one.

'And you don't think your loss of hearing will cause any problems?' Helen asked.

Bobby barked with laughter. 'I reckon most of the men who work here are stone deaf. I spent two years in a ship-yard – if I'd stayed another two, I'd guess my hearing would be worse than it is now.'

Helen smiled. There was truth in what he said. And she'd be happy to play down his compromised hearing. She didn't give a jot if the seaman standing in front of her was as deaf as a doornail, the yard was desperate for riveters – and judging by the pull of his uniform around his chest and upper arms, she was sure he would be more than capable of keeping up with the physical demands of the job.

'All right,' she said, blowing out a stream of smoke and tapping her cigarette in the ashtray. 'Let's see how you get on over the next week and we'll go from there.' She handed him back his discharge papers.

'That's all I ask for,' Bobby said. 'A chance.'

'Right,' said Helen, fishing out a contract of employment from one of her drawers. 'Fill out this form and then I'll tell you where you can get yourself kitted out with a pair of overalls – you'll want to keep that uniform pristine.' Helen would have liked to add, *For all the girls*. She was under no illusion as to why he had worn it this morning. Still, who was she to judge; you had to use what you had in this life to get what you wanted.

Bobby quickly filled out the form and handed it back to Helen, who gave him directions to the supply shed.

'Then you can get your clocking-on board from the time-keeper and head over to the quayside by the first dry basin. There's a riveters' squad there – ask for Jimmy, he'll see you all right.'

As Helen watched the former able seaman leave her office, she wished she'd asked him why he'd chosen Thompson's out of all the yards – especially as he'd started his apprenticeship at Bartram's. Looking down at the form he'd filled in, she read his name: Robert Armstrong.

That name rang a bell.

It was only when Bobby was halfway through the morning shift that it suddenly occurred to him who Helen Crawford was related to. *Of course* – he should have realised it straight away. The dark, almost jet-black hair and striking good looks should have told him, if not the surname. It explained why Helen and his mam were so close. Why she had mentioned Helen so much in her letters. He had thought it a little odd that his mam, who was poor and working-class, would be so chummy with a rich, middle-class woman who was young enough to be her daughter.

Helen was Jack Crawford's daughter. And Hope was *her* little sister too – well, half-sister, which made them all family in a strange sort of way.

He shook his head as another penny dropped. His mam had mentioned that Helen was the granddaughter of Mr Charles Havelock, which would mean that Jack was married to Mr Havelock's daughter, Miriam, who was also well known, mainly due to her birthright and getting her picture in the local rag on a regular basis.

As he saw the glowing red nub of another rivet appear through the hole in the metal plate on the hull, his rivet gun got to work, battering it with a fast succession of blows, squeezing it flat, making it a seamless part of the ship's metal skin. And as his arms and body shuddered in time with the pneumatic hammering, he thought his return home seemed to be getting more bizarre by the minute.

As the women welders headed over to the canteen, they passed Jimmy and his squad sitting by the side of the dry basin where one of the landing craft being produced by the yard was being built. They all waved over.

As they continued across the yard, Dorothy suddenly clutched Angie's arm.

'Oh. My. God!' she gasped.

'Ow, Dor, gerroff, that hurts.' Angie pulled her best mate's talon-like hand off her arm, which was already sore from a morning of vertical welds.

'It's *him*!' Dorothy declared, standing rooted to the spot.

Angie looked at the tall, well-built worker who was striding across the yard, biting into a sandwich.

'Who's *him* when he's at home?' she asked, looking at the bloke with cropped hair and a dirty face that only seemed to accentuate his chiselled looks.

'Bobby!' Dorothy said in astonishment. 'Gloria's Bobby.'

'Blimey, Dor, yer missed out the bit about him being totally gorge.' Angie had been subjected to every cough and spit of Bobby's return from the moment she'd opened her eyes that morning.

Sensing someone was looking at him, Bobby turned his head to see Dorothy and Angie stood stapled to the spot, gawping.

'Dorothy!' he called across, a wide smile on his face, his eyes dancing with delight at seeing the woman he had spent a good part of last night thinking about. He touched the top of his head in a salute.

Dorothy turned away, avoiding his gaze. Last night, after walking her home, Bobby had refused to go back and see Gloria, refused outright, said a courteous goodnight and that it had been a pleasure to make her company. *A pleasure to make her company* – what era was he living in? Back in the days of Queen Victoria? She'd said exactly that to him, which had only made him hoot with laughter as he'd turned to make his way back to the Elliots'.

As Dorothy and Angie hurried into the canteen, they both apologised for jumping the queue in their eagerness to get to Gloria.

'Did you see him?' Dorothy asked.

'Who?' Gloria asked.

'Bobby!' Dorothy hissed into her ear.

Gloria's head jolted. 'Blimey, Dor, that went right through me.'

'Bobby's *here*!' Dorothy said in disbelief. 'He's working in the yard.'

Gloria looked at Dorothy – surprise on her face, but not shock.

'Well, that's Bobby for yer,' she said. 'Not one to rest on his laurels.'

The queue shuffled along.

'But to get a job *here*. At Thompson's?' Dorothy continued to whisper into Gloria's ear.

'Dor, you can speak properly,' Gloria said. 'It's no secret he's my son. Or that he's working in the yard.' What she was a little perplexed about, though, was that Bobby had opted to work at Thompson's. She'd have thought his first port of call would have been Bartram's. Not only had he worked there as a youngster, but it was just a few minutes' walk from Tatham Street – and, moreover, it would mean he didn't have to rub shoulders with his mam every day, something she felt he'd prefer not to have to do.

'All right, Glor!' Muriel's foghorn of a voice sounded out across the head of a young girl dishing out food. 'Good to see one of yer lads back safe and sound, eh?'

Gloria smiled. 'It is, Muriel, it is.'

'How did yer knar it was him?' Angie perked up. She had been listening intently to Dor's hissing and whispering and Gloria's nonchalant responses – and now here was Muriel putting her oar in. Bobby's turning up really had thrown the cat amongst the pigeons. And as for Dor, well she had a bee in her bonnet that looked set to stay a while yet.

Muriel let out a loud burst of laughter. 'The haircut gave it away, Ange. Then the name.' She looked at Gloria. 'Good lad yer've got there.'

Dorothy let out a disbelieving gasp, which Gloria chose to ignore and Muriel didn't hear.

'Your lads all right?' Gloria asked.

Muriel put up both hands, fingers crossed on each, by way of reply. A shout from the kitchens saw her turn and disappear from view.

'Dor,' Gloria said as she grabbed some sandwiches and moved along the queue to the tea urn, 'I wanted to thank you for last night. Getting Bobby lodgings with Agnes.'

Dorothy's attention was on the young girl who was serving out the steak and vegetable stew. She was smiling at her, hoping to get more if she was nice. She was starving.

'You don't have to thank me,' Dorothy said. 'I just wish I'd been able to make him see sense. Honestly,' she dropped her voice, 'he should be clicking his heels you're with Jack and not Vinnie.'

By the time they'd all sat down at their table at the far side of the canteen, word had got round about Bobby working with Jimmy's squad.

'You all right, Glor?' Rosie asked.

'Yes, I'm fine.'

'Honestly?'

Gloria nodded.

'Didn't you know he was starting at the yard?' asked Martha.

'No, she didn't, Martha.' Dorothy poured out a cup of tea and gave it to Gloria. 'Bobby's not the most loquacious of sons.'

Angie pulled a puzzled face.

'Loquacious,' Hannah explained, 'comes from the Latin *loqui*, meaning "to speak".'

'Dorothy was saying she doesn't think Gloria's son is much of a talker,' Olly added.

'Ah,' said Angie, taking a bite of her sandwich and making a mental note to ask Quentin if he too knew Latin.

'He doesn't waste any time, does he,' Polly said. 'He must have left the house at the crack of dawn.'

'You didn't see him when you got up?' Dorothy asked.

Polly shook her head. 'We didn't even know we had a new lodger until Ma told us this morning.'

'Bobby's a grafter, that's for sure. Even when he was a boy,' said Gloria. It was clear to them all that she was incredibly proud of her son.

'Well, I know one person who's going to be cock-a-hoop about all of this,' said Rosie, taking a bite of her sandwich.

'Who?' Angie asked.

'Helen!' Martha guessed, tucking into her packed lunch.

'Why's Helen going to be cock-a-hoop about Bobby being back?' asked Angie, looking perplexed. She was still half asleep after staying up late with Quentin, kissing and

130

cuddling and chatting on the sofa in his flat downstairs; it had been so late that even Dorothy had been fast asleep when she'd tiptoed in.

'Because Helen's in desperate need of more riveters,' Martha explained.

'Which means that I'm equally cock-a-hoop,' Rosie added, 'because Helen might just stop pilfering Martha from me and I can have a full squad full-time.'

'Talk of the devil.' Dorothy nodded over to the entrance of the canteen. Everyone looked round to see Helen making her way towards them. There was a slight dimming of voices as workers became aware of her presence. It wasn't often management mingled with the hoi polloi.

'Hi.' Helen cast a look around the table at the women. She might now be accepted by them all, but she still felt nervous when she interacted with them as a group. She pulled out a spare chair and sat down.

'I've only just got to know about Bobby,' she said, scrutinising Gloria's face. She had no idea how she must be feeling.

'But you took him on?' Dorothy questioned.

'I did,' said Helen, shaking her head when Hannah pointed at the teapot. 'But I didn't realise he was Gloria's son.'

'He didn't tell yer?' Angie asked.

'No,' Helen said, looking back at Gloria. 'He just turned up, said he'd been medically discharged, that he had experience riveting and could he have a job. I kept thinking the name rang a bell. But I'm so used to you using your maiden name – ' she threw Gloria an apologetic look ' – I didn't think. It was only just now, when Marie-Anne came to see me and said it was nice of me to give your son a job, that I realised.'

'Typical Marie-Anne. Never misses a trick,' Dorothy muttered. Marie-Anne always got to know everything there was to know about a new worker – especially unmarried men in their twenties.

'Don't worry,' Gloria reassured. 'Bobby wouldn't have wanted to put you on the spot. Make you feel like yer had to give him a job.'

'Tight-lipped more like,' Dorothy sniped.

'I can't stay,' Helen said, looking at Gloria, 'but I just wanted you to know I didn't realise it was Bobby – and to check you're all right. I'm guessing it was probably a bit of a shock – and probably more than a little awkward – him turning up out of the blue?'

'Just a little!' Dorothy spluttered.

Helen looked at Dorothy and thought she seemed ready to pop.

'Dor was there last night,' Gloria explained.

Helen nodded, knowing that Dorothy usually went round to see Hope on a Friday evening.

'I'll come round after work for a cuppa and a catch-up, if that's all right?' Helen knew Bobby's arrival must have been a shock to her father as well.

'Course it is. We'll see yer later,' Gloria said, forcing a smile.

As the women started to chatter amongst themselves, Gloria could feel the guilt, which had lain dormant for a long time, start to bubble back up to the surface. Now that Bobby was back, she knew that there would be no pushing it down again.

At the end of the shift, the klaxon sounded out and the entire workforce downed tools. As it was a Saturday, no one wanted to waste any time getting home – or to the pub.

'Yer must have seen quite a bit of action?' Jimmy asked Bobby as they made their way across the yard to the time-keeper's cabin.

'A fair bit,' Bobby said. 'More so after being stationed on *Opportune*.'

'Ah, one of Thornycroft's,' said Jimmy. Thornycroft was a well-known shipyard in Southampton. 'HMS *Opportune* – an O-class destroyer ordered back in September 1939 for the First Emergency Flotilla. Commissioned in August 1942.'

Bobby smiled. His new boss, he was fast learning, had a near-on encyclopaedic knowledge of just about everything and anything to do with the maritime industry – from naval vessels to merchant shipping, going back to the days of wood and sail. It was impressive.

'Yer mam told me you were mainly in the North Atlantic,' Jimmy said.

Bobby had also learnt today that Jimmy got on well with Rosie's squad of welders and had even helped his mam move from their old house on the Ford estate to the flat on Borough Road. It seemed as though everyone, bar him and Gordon, knew his mam had left his dad.

'That's right. North Africa, the Arctic, the Atlantic,' Bobby said. 'Mainly escorting convoys.'

'And Glor said yer were in the Battle of the North Cape?' Jimmy asked, looking at Bobby. He'd been a little wary of the lad to start with – knowing who his dad was – but from what he'd picked up working alongside him today, you'd never have guessed the two were in any way related.

'I was,' Bobby said.

'What a way to bow out,' Jimmy said, 'sinking the *Scharnhorst*. The papers here were full of it.'

Bobby would have given anything not to have had to 'bow out', but didn't say so. He didn't want Jimmy, or any of the others in his squad, to feel like he didn't want to be there. It was just that he'd have preferred to be with Gordon on *Opportune*, especially as he'd heard before leaving that they were being deployed to combat German torpedo boats in preparation for the invasion of France.

'*Felix oportunitate pugnae,*' Jimmy said as they both handed in their white boards to Davey.

'"Happy at the chance of a fight",' Bobby translated with a smile. It was *Opportune*'s motto. *If only he could have had the chance of one last fight.* Still, he had to console himself with the thought that he was still a part of that fight. He mightn't be with Gordon when *Opportune* joined the air and sea attacks on northern France, but the landing craft he would be working on over the next few months would be. It was of some consolation.

'Bobby!'

Jimmy glanced over his shoulder.

Bobby hadn't heard anything, but looked at what had caught his boss's attention.

'Mad as a hatter, that one,' Jimmy warned, nodding back at Dorothy, who was hurrying towards them. Angie was trailing behind her.

'I'll leave yer to it.' He gave Bobby a pat on the back. 'Good luck.'

Bobby smiled as he stopped to wait for the pair. He'd take whatever luck was sent his way, but not for the reasons Jimmy had meant.

'The perfect end to the day,' Bobby said as Dorothy caught him up.

Dorothy ignored him, continuing instead to walk down to the ferry landing. The initial crush of workers had either headed up to their homes on the north side of the river, or caught the earlier ferry over to the south side.

'I wanted to have a word with you,' she said.

'As I did with you,' Bobby countered. They had now come to a halt on the ferry landing. Bobby looked down at Dorothy, who seemed shorter than last night, which, he realised, was because she was now wearing flat leather hobnailed boots.

'I wanted to thank you,' he said.

'What do you mean?' Dorothy snapped.

'For helping me get sorted with somewhere to stay. For getting me board and lodging with Mrs Elliot,' Bobby said.

'Everyone calls her Agnes,' Dorothy said. 'Like I said last night, we're not still living in the Dark Ages.'

Bobby barked with laughter.

'Some might beg to differ,' he said.

His comment stumped Dorothy for a moment.

'Aren't you going to introduce me to your friend,' he said, 'or is that also now not the way things are done?'

Dorothy rolled her eyes up to a clear afternoon sky, marred only by the shimmering grey of the barrage balloons.

'This is Angie,' she said simply.

Bobby wiped his dirty hand on his denim overalls and reached out to shake Angie's hand. She chuckled. 'I wouldn't worry about it being dirty.' She held up both hers, which were covered in grime, before taking his hand and shaking it.

'Nice to meet yer, Bobby,' she said, staring up at him and feeling a little disloyal to Quentin for sensing herself blush. It was hard, though. Gloria's son was very dishy.

'All aboard!' the ferryman shouted out as *W.F. Vint* butted the quayside.

'So, when're you going to go and see your mam?' Dorothy asked as they piled onto the ferry.

Bobby looked out to the river but didn't reply.

Realising he genuinely hadn't heard, Dorothy moved around so that she was on his right.

'So, when're you going to see your mam?' she repeated.

Bobby looked down at her, his eyes twinkling, before turning his attention to Angie. 'Is your friend always this bossy?'

Angie nodded and widened her eyes. 'Always.' She caught Dorothy glaring at her. 'Yer wanna live with her,' she mumbled under her breath.

'Well, Ange, if he does "wanna live with" me,' Dorothy quipped, 'he'll have to marry me first, as Bobby here is not one for living in sin.'

Her comments were followed by laughter from Bobby.

As Bobby headed off to the café Angie had recommended on High Street East, which she'd told him was run by two women called Vera and Rina, he thought about Dorothy's jibes and accusations that he had 'the mindset of an old man'. He would have liked to tell her that wasn't the case – that he was actually quite a liberal and didn't think marriage was sacrosanct; nor that a couple should stay together 'till death do us part' if they were unhappy, particularly if the wife was being battered on a regular basis. But while he certainly didn't care if a woman had a child out of wedlock, he did care about the repercussions a mother's unmarried status might have on the child. Surely his mam must realise that Hope would be branded a bastard and taunted because of it when she was older. For that reason alone, Jack should have got divorced and married his mam; for their daughter's sake, if nothing else. Which begged the question, why hadn't he? He'd certainly had long enough.

As Bobby pushed open the door to the cafeteria, he was hit by the smell of freshly baked bread, mixed with frying bacon. Angie had told him not to mind the small, round, grumpy owner – she was brusque with everyone, even those she liked. She said it was worth enduring for her famous butties and had started to say something about the cakes there, but hadn't got to finish her sentence as Dorothy had elbowed her and dragged her off home.

'What can I do yer for?' Vera asked, drying her hands on a tea towel.

'Bacon butty, please,' Bobby said, thinking Angie's description of the proprietor of the café was spot on. Looking through into the kitchen, he saw a taller, regal-looking woman who he guessed was Rina.

'Sit yerself down 'n I'll bring it over,' the old woman ordered, her attention and scowl moving to the next person in the queue.

Sitting down at a table in a corner of the café, Bobby poured himself a glass of water while he waited. His arms felt tired. He'd forgotten how intense riveting could be. He'd lost some of his fitness while he'd recovered from his head injury; it wouldn't take long to get it back, though.

Perhaps, he wondered, it was not such a bad thing that his mam and Jack weren't married. If he turned out to be another Vinnie it would make it easier, wouldn't it? Or not? He wasn't sure. Had his mam stayed with their dad because they were bound by their marital vows? He'd never been able to understand why she hadn't left him. Nor did he think he ever would.

He smiled politely as Vera plonked his plate and cup of tea in front of him. At least, he thought as he took a bite of his bacon sarnie, he would get to know more now he was working at Thompson's; it might be the second-biggest shipyard in the town, but everyone still knew each other's business, whether they wanted to or not.

Taking a big slug of perfectly brewed tea, Bobby's mind went to Hope. He was also going to make sure his little sister was safe. He'd pop in to see her every week. It was the least he could do. He would do whatever it took to save another child from going through what he and Gordon had been forced to endure. If his mam was being used as another man's punchbag, well, then, that was her prerogative – she was a grown woman and could make her own choices – but he wasn't going to let Hope suffer. No way.

Chapter Sixteen

Wednesday 8 March

'John!' Helen jumped out of the car and hurried across to Dr Parker, who was walking down the steps of the asylum. Giving him a kiss on the cheek, she stood back. 'I'm guessing you've been busy?'

'No more than usual,' he said, his heart drumming a rapid beat as it always did on seeing Helen. 'But I'm guessing *you* are, if you can't squeeze me in for a quick cuppa.'

Helen frowned. 'I've always got room to squeeze you in, John. I did ring yesterday to see if you'd be about today, but you never called back.'

'Ah, that explains it,' Dr Parker said. 'Denise must have forgotten to pass the message on. Strange, though. She's always so efficient.' He took Helen's arm. 'Well, why don't we have a little stroll around the grounds in lieu of a cup of canteen tea?'

Helen felt her body tingle as he touched her. She had on a short-sleeved blouse and she could feel the goosebumps as his fingers gently touched her skin.

'Sounds like a good swap,' she said, looking out at the perfectly manicured grounds of the asylum and feeling the start of spring on her face. 'Just what the doctor ordered.' She turned and smiled at John. *How she wished she didn't desire him so.* 'I could certainly do with some fresh air and I'm sure you could too. You're looking a little pale. Or is that too many late nights?' She smiled mischievously. 'Talking of which, how's Dr Eris?'

Dr Parker let out a loud laugh as he reluctantly let go of Helen's arm and started walking along the gravelled pathway that bordered the asylum. 'She's good. Although my pasty complexion is due to a week of night shifts.'

Helen was pleased; the green-eyed monster that always started to stomp about whenever she thought of John and Claire together – especially together late at night – was appeased.

'Which was why I've been here,' Dr Parker continued, 'to arrange a night out. I think Claire needed reassuring that it was work and not a lack of desire that has been keeping us apart.'

Helen let out fake laughter to mask the painful jab of jealousy.

'Well, I think Claire should count her blessings. Poor Polly has to do with the occasional letter, and Rosie not even that.' The words were out before she could rein them back in.

Dr Parker caught the irritation in Helen's tone, confirming what he'd thought from the start – Helen and Claire would never be the best of friends. Helen tried to make out she liked Claire, as Claire did with Helen, but it was no good – their true feelings for one another always managed to slip out and show themselves.

'How's everyone at work?' Dr Parker asked, his concern genuine.

'They're all good,' Helen said. 'Working like Trojans, I have to say – and for once it's not me being the slave-driver.'

'Rosie?' Dr Parker knew about the LCTs they were building and how important they were for Rosie – and Peter. Helen nodded. She, like Dr Parker, believed that Rosie's need to get the landing craft down the ways as quickly as possible was because she felt she was helping to fight Peter's corner. The war in Europe was escalating, with the Americans stepping up their daylight air raid attacks on Berlin.

'Gloria and Jack all right?' Dr Parker asked.

'Oh, my goodness,' Helen said, stopping in her tracks. 'No, they're not!'

'What's happened?' John's face was serious. Thoughts of Miriam or Mr Havelock executing revenge on them sprang to mind.

'Bobby's back!' Helen said. Seeing a wooden bench nearby, she walked over and sat down. Dr Parker followed.

'But I thought he was still at sea? That he was under medical supervision.'

'Not any more,' Helen said, her emerald eyes looking at John. 'He's been medically discharged. He turned up unannounced at the flat.'

'Oh dear … And I'm guessing sod's law means that he turned up when Jack was there – and Hope.'

'And Dorothy,' Helen added.

'I can imagine it was a bit … strained?' he said.

'Just a bit,' said Helen, before taking a deep breath and telling her friend all that had happened: how Bobby had turned up and not been at all happy to find his mother living in sin with a married man, and with a child born out of wedlock; how he had left but Dorothy had gone after him and taken him to Tatham Street, where Agnes had given him board and lodging; and then how he'd come to Thompson's at the crack of dawn and asked her for a job.

'He started Saturday morning and he's barely left the place since,' Helen laughed. 'He's been doing all the overtime going and when there's no more riveting to be done, or it's got too dark, he heads over to the platers' shed and gives them a hand.'

'So what happened with his head injury?'

Helen smiled, having known this would be the first question John asked her.

'Well, his medical discharge form just said "unilateral hearing loss".'

'Interesting,' said Dr Parker. 'Deafness after head injuries is more common than people think. We've had some cases here – ruptured eardrums, dislocated ossicles, or severed auditory nerves. Stops sound being transmitted to the brain.'

'Mmm,' Helen smiled. After she had helped him with Artie's birth, John seemed keen to educate her on all things medical. 'I'm not sure what it was, just that the bash on the head did it.' She paused. 'By all accounts, he's not great on talking either.'

'It's affected his speech as well?' Dr Parker asked, his interest piqued.

'No,' Helen laughed, 'I'm being facetious. He's not really chatted to Gloria since Friday, although it's not that he's *not* speaking to her full stop – he acknowledges her at work, and is pleasant enough, but that's about it.'

'Oh dear,' Dr Parker said. 'Poor Gloria. She must be very conflicted. Overjoyed at having Bobby back, but gutted there's this divide between them.'

Helen smiled at him. 'You sound like you've been taking some lessons from Dr Eris. Very insightful.'

'Just common sense really. I'm sure that's your take on it as well?'

Helen nodded. 'It's a shame that it wasn't the kind of reunion you'd expect, having not seen your son for nearly four years, but that's life, isn't it? Nothing ever turns out the way you expect?'

Dr Parker nodded. They were both quiet for a moment. Both thinking their own thoughts.

'But it's early days,' Helen said eventually, 'and at least everything's out in the open. She's written a letter to Gordon, so he should know by now. No more secrets.' Helen got up. 'Talking of which – ' she looked at her watch ' – I'd better go and see Grandmama before visiting time is over.'

'How's your dad dealing with Bobby's return – or rather, Bobby with your dad?'

'Well, they've barely spoken. Dad's not said anything, just that it's good Bobby's back and that he's all right, bar his hearing, but Gloria said Bobby gave Jack a look like the summons when he left on Friday. And Dorothy said if looks could kill, Jack would be six feet under.'

They reluctantly made their way towards the main entrance.

'Miriam still not back?'

'No.' Helen shook her head. 'It's the Grand I feel sorry for – their takings must have plummeted.'

Dr Parker smiled. He knew Helen's jokes about her mother masked her hurt that their relationship was devoid of any kind of maternal love or care.

'And the twins are doing all right?' he asked.

'Yes, they're well – Dr Billingham's popping in and checking up on them still. He doesn't have to now, but I think he enjoys going round there.'

'And our little godson is doing well?' he asked.

Helen loved it when John referred to Artie as *our* godson. 'Spoilt rotten, of course.' She smiled.

'I feel awful I've not been to see him,' he said.

Helen knew she should tell Dr Parker that he was invited to Pearl and Bill's wedding reception, but she didn't. She knew it was wrong, but she just couldn't face a rerun of Artie's christening, with the two doctors joined at the hip, Claire holding his hand, laughing and chatting with everyone, John by her side.

'Don't worry, Polly totally understands,' she said instead.

Giving him a chaste kiss on the cheek, Helen waved him goodbye and headed into the cool interior of the asylum.

Walking through the entrance area, she smiled at Genevieve, the elderly receptionist. As she hurried along the corridor towards her grandmother's room, Helen thought she'd leave it a little longer to tell John about the invite to Pearl and Bill's wedding. Hopefully, by the time she 'remembered' to invite him, it would be too late for him to get the time off.

Walking back to the Ryhope Emergency Hospital, Dr Parker wished he had asked Helen about Matthew. She would start to think it rude him not asking about her boyfriend; after all, she always asked about Claire, even if it was just to be polite. But for some reason he always avoided bringing up Matthew. It was as though he blanked him out of his mind when he was with Helen. Was the thought of them together too painful? His jealousy too unpalatable, making him push away like a plate of unwanted food any thoughts of Helen and Matthew, the glamorous Hollywood couple?

He hurried through the hospital's main gates and down the long, shingled pathway. Next time they saw each other he would ask, otherwise it was going to become a problem – the elephant in the room – and he didn't want that. Helen was his friend, they talked about everything, nothing was off-limits. They had a closeness he didn't want to lose. A friendship he did not want to forsake.

As he approached the stone steps and took them two at a time, it occurred to him that he and Helen had been through more together than most married couples had in their lifetime – a pregnancy, a miscarriage, the discovery that she had a half-sister and of her grandfather's sordid past. They had been through all this trauma together. It didn't matter that she was with someone else; John would not allow Matthew to break the very strong and special bond he had with Helen.

'Hi, Denise.' Dr Parker walked over to the reception desk in the main foyer. 'I've just bumped into Helen over at the asylum and she said she rang me yesterday to tell me she was heading over, but I didn't get a message.'

'Oh.' Denise's hand went straight to her mouth, something Dr Parker had learnt from Dr Eris meant that whatever someone was going to say next might well be a lie. 'I'm *soo* sorry, Dr Parker. I completely forgot. It was madness yesterday.' She looked down at her desk and rifled through some notelets. Her hand kept touching the corners of her mouth as though she was trying to brush crumbs away. 'I wrote it down and then completely forgot to give it to you. I'm really sorry.' She looked at Dr Parker, her face showing the sincerity of her apology.

'Don't worry,' Dr Parker said. 'None of us is perfect – thank goodness!'

'I hope it wasn't anything important?' Denise said, her pale, English-rose complexion now flushed.

'No, nothing spoilt,' Dr Parker smiled, feeling guilty for making Denise so upset and remorseful. 'I was just saying to Helen it was unusual because you are always so efficient. Please, don't fret about it.'

And with that Dr Parker walked back to theatre, his mind now back on his patients and the surgery he had scheduled in for later that afternoon.

Helen knocked gently on the door of her grandmother's room and eased it open. Henrietta was sitting where she always sat when she was expecting Helen – at her little round table in the middle of the room with a book open and two glasses of water poured out.

145

'Ah, my darling, you're late today.' It was not a reprimand, rather an observation.

'Sorry, Grandmama, but I got a little waylaid.'

'By a dashing gentleman, I hope.' Henrietta smiled, her thin lips a slash of scarlet lipstick. 'Wanting to sweep you off your feet and gallop off into the sunset.' She waved her hand in the air as she spoke, as though the gentleman and his lover were riding past her.

Helen looked at her grandmother as she sat down and was amazed at the care she took over her appearance, the same care, Henrietta had told her, she took every day, not just when she had visitors. Henrietta had shown her granddaughter her make-up: her cream rouge, blue eyeshadow, dark brown eye pencils and white face powder and puff. Helen had asked what happened when she ran out, and Henrietta had explained she simply told the nurse and she would bring her replacements. Henrietta saw nothing unusual in a nurse bringing her make-up just as she would her medication.

Helen had been keen to know more about the pills her grandmother was on, but she knew that for now this was something she could not be privy to as it would mean she would be forced to deal with Henrietta's doctor – and there was no way she wanted Dr Eris to know that she was visiting Miss Girling. She knew it was inevitable that the time would come, but she was determined to put it off for as long as possible.

'And how's my Little Match Girl?' Henrietta asked. It was the same question she always asked on her arrival. When Helen had first started to visit her grandmother, it became clear that Henrietta missed Pearl, her former scullery maid, who had visited her regularly until just before Christmas. Helen had tried to imagine the two together but failed. They must have forged a friendship of some sort, though, as Pearl had gained Henrietta's trust to such an extent that she'd dug back into a past that she, like Pearl, had very much wanted to forget.

'She's fine,' Helen said. 'Busy running the pub.'

Helen had told Pearl that she didn't have to continue coming to the asylum if she didn't want to. If Pearl felt as though she had to keep visiting just to keep the threat of Henrietta a viable one, then it was all right, she didn't have to any more. Helen had said she was happy to take the baton. The relief she had seen on Pearl's worn face was telling. She saw at that moment just how painful it must have been for her to relive the horror of her time in the Havelock house again and again, every time she visited Henrietta.

'Yer knar he won't give up, don't yer?' Pearl had said. 'As long as that man's still drawing breath, he'll be a worry.' Helen had nodded. She, too, knew that her grandfather would never give up trying to find a way out of the stranglehold he'd been put in.

'And Miriam – where's my daughter?' Henrietta asked as Helen took a sip of water. This was another question Henrietta would ask without fail whenever Helen visited.

'She's still away, Grandmama, but she'll be back soon,' Helen said, trying to sound convincing when in fact she had no idea when her mother would be back.

Helen looked at her grandmother's long taffeta skirt and touched it. 'Oh, Grandmama, I do love this skirt. The colour is amazing.'

'The hue of a ripening damson,' Henrietta said, touching it with fingernails that had been painted an identical colour.

Helen smiled. She was getting used to her grandmother's poetic descriptions, as well as her many eccentricities. 'So, what are we reading today?'

'*Persuasion*,' Henrietta declared. 'The last fully completed novel by Jane Austen, published at the end of 1817, six months after her death.'

Helen smiled. She recalled being made to read a number of Jane Austen novels at school.

'I know you probably read it when you were younger,' Henrietta said, as though reading her granddaughter's mind. 'But this time, you will enjoy it,' she said as she pushed the book towards Helen. 'You might even relate to it.' She then clapped her hands lightly and noiselessly. 'You start,' she commanded.

After half an hour of reading and discussing certain passages, their time was up.

'Wait, wait.' Henrietta got up and went over to her bedside drawer. She pulled it open and took out another copy of *Persuasion*. She carefully wrapped it in one of her colourful silk scarves and handed it over.

'How come you've got two copies, Grandmama?' Helen was worried. She had repeatedly told Henrietta that her visits were a secret – not to be discussed with anyone from the hospital, no one at all. So far, it was only Genevieve who was aware that Helen visited Miss Girling, and that was the way she wanted to keep it. 'Won't they wonder why you want two copies?'

'They think I'm mad,' she said, giving Helen a conspiratorial smile, 'mad as a hatter, they do. They think it is one of my affectations. If they don't do as I ask, I put on my face.' Henrietta put on a forlorn, deeply depressed look, which Helen thought very convincing. 'Then they give me what I want.

'Don't worry,' she added, putting her finger to her lips. It was her way of reassuring her granddaughter that she was keeping her promise not to talk about her visits.

Helen took the book and gave her grandmother a quick kiss on both rouged cheeks. Henrietta did the same to

Helen. It was their routine before they parted, and always ended with Helen reassuring Henrietta that she would see her again very soon.

Leaving the Borough Lunatic Asylum, Helen's thoughts wandered to her mother. She had now been away for over two months – much longer than she had thought she'd be, although it had to be said, Helen was glad of the break. Even though they had never spent much time together, the atmosphere when they were under the same roof was still tense. Since her mother had left on Boxing Day, Helen had had the house to herself and was enjoying the quiet and calm atmosphere. It was what she needed at the moment. It gave her the peace to think, to face up to reality and be truthful with herself. And the truth was, her trips to Ryhope were as much about John as they were about Henrietta. She was in love with him and she had to accept it. Just as she had to accept that he was with Claire. Just as she also had to remind herself that even if he wasn't with Claire, he would still not be asking her to be his wife – she was quite simply not marriage material.

'Dr Eris.' Denise waved a manicured hand over as Claire walked into the foyer.

Claire furrowed her brow questioningly as she approached the polished wooden front reception desk.

'*He knows*,' Denise whispered, her hand fiddling with one of her pearl earrings.

'*Who* knows *what*?' Dr Eris snapped.

'Dr Parker … he *knows* …'

Dr Eris felt a little nauseous. If John found out she had done a deal with Denise to block messages from Helen getting through to him, their relationship would be dead in the water. She already felt as though she was struggling

149

to keep it afloat. She'd been over the moon he'd popped in to see her about going out for dinner later on this week – then gutted to have just heard from Genevieve that he'd bumped into Helen afterwards and they had enjoyed a walk around the grounds.

And now this.

'He knows I didn't pass on a message Helen left yesterday about coming over here,' Denise said, her hands now clasped together on top of the reception desk.

'And does he think it was just *that* message – or that there have been *other* messages you've not been passing on?' Dr Eris looked around to make sure no one was about and could hear their conversation.

'Well, I think it was just this message he thought I'd forgotten to pass on – he said it had surprised him because I was so "efficient", and not to worry, there was no harm done.'

Dr Eris's body tensed in silent fury. No, there hadn't been any harm done. Far from it. John and Helen had enjoyed a lovely romantic walk in the grounds on one of the sunniest days of the year so far. They couldn't have picked a nicer day.

'Do you think he suspected anything?' Dr Eris needed to know.

Denise thought for a moment. 'I don't think so, but it's hard to tell with Dr Parker. He's always so polite and friendly.'

'Let's hope not,' Dr Eris said. The chances were John hadn't guessed. He wasn't the suspicious type. And besides which his head was always full of work – especially lately. Any free time he had was spent developing a new type of prosthesis. He was obsessed with it. He'd become more obsessed with it since his last rejection by the Ministry of War, who had informed him that they needed him there rather than on the front line. They had got wind of his research into developing more advanced artificial limbs and they'd stipulated they wanted him to continue.

The phone rang and Dr Eris waited until Denise had put the call through to one of the wards.

'Let's cut it while we're ahead,' she said.

'What? No more *not* passing on messages?'

Dr Eris nodded.

'So, I now ring and tell Dr Parker every time Miss Crawford calls?' she asked, just to make sure.

'Yes, exactly,' Dr Eris said, although it pained her to say so.

'But,' Denise hesitated, 'that doesn't mean you'll stop organising my ...' she dropped her voice '... you know, the date you promised to set up with Dr Green from the Royal?'

Denise had carried out her part of the bargain to the full: being careful to 'forget' to pass on a good percentage of Helen's messages over the past six months, certainly enough to scupper quite a number of meetings between Dr Eris's beau and the gorgeous Miss Helen Crawford. Dr Eris, on the other hand, hadn't really followed through on her side of the bargain. She'd set her up with a couple of dates, but they'd been few and far between.

'Of course I will.' Dr Eris smiled at Denise. *One more and that was her lot.* She walked away, feeling more than a little disgruntled. It looked as though she would have to figure out a new way of getting shot of Helen – once and for all.

Chapter Seventeen

Friday 10 March

When Bobby knocked on Gloria's front door, his heart leapt on seeing that it was Dorothy who answered, even if the look she was giving him was far from welcoming.

Dorothy kept her eyes on Bobby as she turned her head slightly and shouted out, 'Oh, look who's honoured us with his presence.'

Gloria came bustling out of the kitchen. 'Stop it with the snarky comments, Dor, and let him in.'

Bobby tipped an imaginary hat at Dorothy, who pulled the door wide open and stood aside.

'Hello, Mam.' Bobby stooped to give Gloria a hug and a kiss on the cheek. It wasn't quite the bear hug she'd had when he'd arrived back home last week, but she'd take what she could get. He was here, wasn't he. Even though it was with conditions. 'Come and sit down and I'll get us all a cuppa.' She waved her hand over to the table.

'And don't worry,' Dorothy added as she followed him into the flat, 'the evil Jack Crawford is nowhere to be seen.'

Bobby sighed but didn't say anything. Jack's absence had been his one stipulation to his mam when he'd caught her after work and said he'd like to come and see her at the flat and meet his little sister properly. He had also purposely asked to come on Friday, having learnt from Polly that every Friday Dorothy, and sometimes Angie, would go to see Hope before their night out at the Ritz. It explained why she had been so done up the night of his arrival.

'Ah, there she is,' Bobby said, his face lighting up on seeing his sister sitting on the rug with her dollies. He pulled out a chocolate bar from his trouser pocket. 'A little treat from your big brother Bobby.' He crouched down next to Hope, whose little face lit up. Her hands stretched out and she took the chocolate.

'Luckily, she's already had her tea,' said Dorothy.

Bobby looked up to see her towering over him, her arms folded.

'So it's OK to give her the chocolate, but check next time,' she said.

Bobby suppressed a smile. 'Roger that, ma'am.' He touched his forehead in a mock salute.

'And Gloria always makes sure Hope offers round any treats she gets, so she learns how to share.'

'*Dor!*' Gloria shouted through from the kitchen. 'Give me a hand in here, will you?'

Dorothy hesitated before doing Gloria's bidding.

Half an hour later, they had all sunk a pot of tea, Hope had consumed the entire chocolate bar, after no one had taken up the offer of a chunk, and after a brief frenzy of activity playing hide-and-seek with Bobby – quite some feat in such a small flat – she was on her last legs and struggling to keep her eyes open.

'Can I read her a bedtime story?' Bobby asked.

'*Storiee … Bobbieee,*' Hope's voice chirped up, although she was already starting to slur with tiredness.

Dorothy opened her mouth to sanction the reading of just a few pages, but Gloria managed to beat her to it. 'Course yer can. There's a stack by her cot.'

As Bobby read the story of *The Tale of Two Bad Mice*, Gloria tidied up the cups and saucers and the crumb-strewn plate that had been piled with biscuits. She was glad to see her boy still had a good appetite. Perhaps next time he'd stay for a proper meal.

Dorothy stood guard at the end of the short hallway, watching as Bobby sat next to the cot with the book open on his lap. The child's chair he was on made him look like a giant. He was good with Hope, she'd give him that.

Seeing him give Hope a goodnight kiss on the forehead, Dorothy went back into the living room.

'I'm off, Mam!' Bobby ducked his head into the kitchen. 'You take care in that yard,' he added. It was another reason he didn't like Jack. If he was any kind of man, he wouldn't let Bobby's mam work in a shipyard, of all places. 'Oh, and Mam?'

'Yes?'

'I'm gonna write Gordon a letter tonight.'

'It's all right, I've already written to him. Told him everything,' she said. She'd actually written it the night Bobby had turned up – after he'd left. Better late than never.

Bobby wondered what Gordon would make of it all – hopefully, he'd write soon and tell him.

'I'm off as well, Glor,' Dorothy said, picking up her hand-bag and gas mask. 'I need to drag Angie off that phone and out on the town.' Dorothy had told Gloria on arriving that Angie wouldn't be coming as Quentin had called, which meant that 'the whole world had to stop'. Gloria had laughed and said, 'Just as it does when Toby calls.'

'Enjoy yerselves,' Gloria said. 'See yer tomorrow.'

Dorothy pulled a face. 'One of these days we'll have a Saturday off,' she said.

'Not while Rosie's on a mission,' Gloria laughed.

Bobby waited by the open door, allowing Dorothy to leave first.

'Oh, and Glor,' Dorothy said, turning as she left, 'say hi from me to the devil incarnate – *sorry*, I mean, Jack.' She threw Bobby a stinging look. 'Send him my regards.'

After they'd both left, Gloria continued to stand in the middle of the flat, staring at the closed door, shaking her head. She'd give her son one thing – he had the patience of a saint.

Dorothy looked at Bobby as he too turned right when they reached the top of the stone steps from Gloria's flat.

'You don't have to walk me home, you know? I'm more than capable of putting one foot in front of the other.' As she spoke, she demonstrated by lifting one foot and putting it down on the pavement. She repeated the same with her other foot.

'It's how I've been brought up,' Bobby explained. 'Like Hope being taught to share, Mam taught Gordon and me that we must always walk a woman home, especially at night.' He smiled at her as they continued to walk the short distance along the Borough Road before turning right into Foyle Street. 'If you have any complaints, you're going to have to take them up with my mam.'

As they walked across the cobbles, Dorothy nearly went over on her ankle. Bobby caught her arm before she went flying. Once again, just like last week, there was a shock of static as they touched.

'Whoa, nearly,' Bobby said.

'I'm fine,' Dorothy said, yanking her arm away from him and carefully walking over to the pavement. 'What is it with you?' She rubbed her arm. 'You give me a shock every time we touch.'

Bobby laughed. 'Perhaps it's *you* that's giving *me* the shock.'

Dorothy tutted. As they approached the entrance to her flat, she eyed him. 'I just don't understand why you don't like Jack?'

Bobby looked at Dorothy. 'So, it's the Ritz tonight, is it?'

'*So*, I'm guessing your way of getting out of answering a question you deem too personal or too intrusive is to simply ignore it, or pretend you haven't heard?'

Bobby infuriated her more by simply smiling.

'Do you realise you are exploiting a disability?' she sniped.

Bobby laughed. 'Well, it's got to have some advantages.' He turned to leave. 'See you tomorrow at work.'

'Not if I see you first,' Dorothy mumbled, knowing it sounded churlish, but not caring.

'The coast clear?' Jack joked as he let himself into the flat.

Gloria walked over to him and kissed him on the lips.

'One child is fast asleep in bed. The other two have left.' Gloria smiled. 'The coast is well and truly clear.'

Jack pulled her close.

'Everything will sort itself out, you'll see,' he told her. He knew Gloria was hurt by Bobby's refusal to accept her new family in its entirety, but it had also not been as traumatic as it might have been. Bobby wanted to see his mam and be a big brother to his little sister. If his mother's new fella didn't figure in the equation, that didn't matter. He wasn't going anywhere. Nothing would ever take him away from Gloria or part him from Hope again. As long as he could be a father to Hope and hold the woman he loved in his arms every night, he could put up with just about anything.

Bobby, he was sure, would come round in time.

Jack understood how it might look. Gloria was divorced and he was still married – to one of the richest women in the town to boot. Those who didn't know him might think he was hanging in there, wanting to be taken back into his wife's arms – even more, back to a life of luxury. Just the thought of it made Jack feel ill. He would rather sleep on a bed of nails for the rest of his life than ever live under the same roof as Miriam, let alone share a bed with her.

As he watched Gloria go into the kitchen, thoughts of Miriam pushed their way into his mind. *When was she coming back from Scotland? And when was she going to serve divorce papers?* He'd have expected them to plop on the doormat well before now, especially as she clearly had undisputed grounds for a divorce: her husband had committed adultery, he had fathered a child by another woman and he was living in sin. She certainly had enough evidence, so why was she being so slow off the mark?

Chapter Eighteen

Standing with the phone receiver pressed against his ear, Miriam's brother-in-law, Angus Campbell, looked down at the glass of whisky he'd placed on a coaster next to the glossy black Bakelite phone. He hadn't touched a drop of it yet – it was to be his reward for getting through this conversation. A conversation he had put off for as long as he could. But *it was time*, as his wife Margaret had said to him last night when they were in bed. She had said it in that way of hers, soft and gentle. Not a demand or an order, simply a statement that he knew to be true.

Angus heard the ringing tone end with the click of a connection.

'*Charles Havelock speaking.*' The voice was gruff, superior and intimidating, which just about summed up his father-in-law.

'Hello, Charles … Angus here.' He looked down at the single malt and then up at the clock. He hoped the conversation would not be a long one.

'Ah, Angus, old chap, good to hear from you. Shame you couldn't make it down for Christmas, but I know how you don't like driving in the bad weather.'

Angus shook his head in disbelief. Charles had smashed his record for inserting a put-down into the conversation within a matter of seconds.

'*Bad weather* being a bit of an understatement, old man,' Angus countered. 'Three feet of snow put paid to us getting out the door, never mind on the road.' Angus knew

Charles would not like his retort, nor being referred to as an old man, but after what he'd heard about his wife's father, Angus was amazed he could bring himself to speak to him at all. The heavy snowfall had been a blessing in disguise. He and Margaret had been saved from a nightmare of a Christmas Day, according to what Miriam had told them.

'So,' Charles said. Angus could hear him blowing out smoke and guessed he was puffing away on one of his expensive cigars. 'I'm guessing you're calling about that daughter of mine. Is she ready to come back to the land of the living? She's been gone long enough.'

Angus marvelled at Charles's ability to get yet another disparaging comment into the conversation so quickly. He'd made no secret of the fact that he saw Angus's estate in one of the most beautiful parts of Scotland as some kind of backwater hamlet, stuck in the previous century.

'Well, if by *the land of the living* you mean Sunderland, old man, no, she's not ready to come back.' Angus felt a rush of anger, which was unusual for him. But this was not a normal conversation.

'What do you mean? She's been away for well over two months! She's not thinking of staying up there, is she?' Charles snapped, irritated by what he was hearing. 'She needs to get herself back down here – sort out this debacle of a marriage.'

Angus heard the clink of a glass stopper and knew Charles was pouring himself a brandy. He looked at his own untouched glass of Scotch.

'People are going to start talking. She's lucky that husband of hers is keeping a low profile – a very low profile. No one's got wind – *yet*.'

Angus heard the strike of a match and the sound of Charles puffing on his cigar.

'Bloody hell, if she'd just got the divorce papers filed before she left, it might have gone through by now.'

'There's a problem,' Angus said finally.

'What do you mean, there's a problem? She's not ill, is she?'

'Well, she is, and she isn't,' Angus said.

'Well, what is it! She either is or she isn't!'

Angus clenched his jaw.

'Miriam's a mess,' he said simply. 'She arrived on our doorstep tanked up on gin and she's been that way ever since.' Angus reckoned she must have drunk the entire contents of the bar in the first-class carriage on her train journey there, considering the state she'd turned up in.

There was silence at the other end of the phone.

'Your daughter seems to be trying to drink herself into oblivion and to be honest, Charles, she's doing a pretty good job.'

There was more deathly silence from the other end of the phone. For a second, Angus thought he'd hung up.

'Bloody hell!' Mr Havelock suddenly barked, making Angus jump. 'What's the matter with her?'

Angus felt like telling him, the *matter* was that his daughter was reeling from the fact that she had just found out her father had raped underage girls, spawning God knew how many illegitimate children, and had incarcerated his own wife in a mental institution – having lied to his own daughters, and everyone else, by telling them Henrietta was mad.

'Miriam is struggling with what she discovered on Christmas Day,' Angus said, desperately trying to keep the disgust he felt for this man out of his voice. He had promised his wife he would deal with the situation in as civil a manner as possible. This now felt easier said than done.

'All lies!' Another bark from Mr Havelock. 'A load of lies.'

Angus thought that his father-in-law actually sounded as though he believed his own words.

'Regardless,' Angus said, 'your daughter is still in a bad way and to be honest, Margaret and I are at a loss to know what to do.'

'My God! Am I going to end up with a daughter as well as a wife in the local madhouse?' Mr Havelock exhaled through his nose.

Angus felt himself stiffen. 'Not unless you decide to get Miriam sectioned as well.'

Mr Havelock said nothing and Angus wondered whether his father-in-law was seriously considering getting his daughter locked up.

'Dry her out and get her back here,' Charles said. 'I don't care how much it costs, or how you do it – just do it.'

And then the line did go dead, and Angus was left listening to the burr of the disconnect tone.

He put the receiver down, picked up his tumbler of Scotch and downed it in one.

Chapter Nineteen

Over the next two and a half weeks, every man, woman and boy at Thompson's shipyard – and the eight other shipyards dotted along the hem of the Wear – worked flat out to get ships sent down the ways. The month so far had seen the town's biggest shipyard, William Doxford & Sons, send two tank-landing craft into the river, followed by Short Brothers and Pickersgill's, who had launched one each.

The women kept up their classes in current affairs during their lunch breaks, their eagerness to hear what was happening in the world fired on by hopes of victory. The news, however, seemed to bring only death and destruction. Hundreds of British bombers hit Berlin and Essen, the Italian town of Monte Cassino was destroyed by Allied air strikes, a U-boat sunk the British corvette HMS *Asphodel* in the Atlantic Ocean, killing ninety-two of the ninety-seven men aboard, and in France, the former minister of the interior for the Vichy regime, Pierre Pucheu, was sentenced to death for treason and shot by a firing squad. Even Nature seemed bent on destruction when Mount Vesuvius erupted, killing twenty-six people and causing thousands to flee their homes.

The news back home was not particularly uplifting either. The Luftwaffe might have become strangers to the town over the past year, but the damage they'd already done was not easily fixed. Many wonderful Edwardian and Gothic structures that had been landmarks for decades had been destroyed: the grand Victoria Hall, the Winter Gardens and Binns, the town's very own Harrods, had all been either totally demolished or badly damaged. However, it was the thousands of homes that had been made uninhabitable that caused the real problem. Overcrowding was rife.

The only positive amidst all the news of doom and gloom was that Polly's worries about Tommy had abated tenfold since Gibraltar's role in the war had shifted down a gear following the successful completion of the North African campaign and the surrender of Italy. This meant that the bomb-disposal unit Tommy was a part of, whose main aim had been to remove Italian limpet mines that enemy divers had attached to the hulls of Allied ships, was pretty much redundant. The work her husband was now doing was more akin to what he had done as a dock diver before the outbreak of war: underwater repair work on ships needed to transport supplies across the Mediterranean.

During this time, Dorothy suggested that Gloria change her own day for seeing Hope to give Bobby time with his mam, so that it would be just the two of them, enabling them to repair their fractured relationship, but Gloria had insisted that Dorothy keep to her normal routine. Seeing Dorothy's puzzled look, Gloria had justified her decision by saying that it wasn't that she didn't want to patch up their differences, but she knew her eldest son needed the buffer of another person there – for the time being, anyway. 'He's struggling,' she told Dorothy. 'He mightn't show it, but underneath that happy-go-lucky, cool-as-a-cucumber act, there's turbulence.'

Dorothy, of course, didn't mind being a buffer – she'd do anything for Gloria – and if mother and son needed an intermediary, she was happy to oblige. Besides, she was certain it wouldn't be long before Bobby came round and saw sense. She'd make sure of that. Every time she walked with Bobby back to Foyle Street, she'd argue Gloria's case and berate him for treating his mam like the Wicked Witch of the West and refusing to have anything to do with Jack. 'He *is* Hope's father,' she'd say in a slightly exasperated tone into Bobby's good ear.

Dorothy had told Angie she was convinced that if she could just explain to Gloria's Neanderthal son that society's conventions had changed – that the war had altered the way people lived and getting divorced and having children out of wedlock really weren't anything to feel ashamed of – then all would be well. Bobby and Gloria would be close again and he and Jack would get on – they might possibly even be good buddies. Angie had no idea what a Neanderthal was, but knew when to keep quiet and simply nod and agree with her friend.

Helen also found herself subjected to similar tirades whenever Dorothy would drag her aside for a 'quick chat' that ended up being anything but quick. After listening, Helen would tell Dorothy that she didn't think there was anything any of them could do other than wait it out, and she was sure the situation would sort itself 'sometime soon'. To which Dorothy would huff and say, 'Let's hope *sometime* this century.'

Helen thought Jack was wise to agree to stay out of the way when Bobby paid his weekly visits to the flat, giving Gloria's son the space he needed. If Jack went up against Bobby, it would only cause ructions, which would likely make Gloria feel as though she had to choose between her son and the man she loved. And she knew her father didn't want that. It would be a recipe for disaster.

If Bobby didn't want him around for a few hours on a Friday night, her father had told her, then that was fine with him. Even if Bobby never came round to accepting him in his mother's life, then he'd deal with it. There were worse things.

Helen, though, could see that her father was becoming more impatient about when Miriam was going to file for divorce. She knew how desperate he was to make his union with Gloria legitimate. Living with her while still married to another woman did not sit comfortably on his shoulders. Not that it was something he talked about to Helen; she knew he did not want to bring his daughter onto the battlefield of his marriage.

Chapter Twenty

'I think we all deserve a pat on the back – or a bonus in our pay packets,' Jimmy said as the shipyard's entire workforce slowly made its way over to the far end of the yard to the dry basins.

'Two in one day,' Rosie smiled. She was bursting with pride. They'd managed to build two vessels bound for France in record time and they were being launched on the same day. 'It helps having a full squad,' she added, cocking her head back. They both looked behind to see the women welders walking alongside Jimmy's gang of riveters.

'With yer having Polly back?' Jimmy asked, lighting his rollie as they walked.

'That and the fact you're not nicking Martha off me all the time,' she laughed.

'I would be if Helen'd let me,' Jimmy said, deadpan, expelling smoke.

'She wouldn't dare,' Rosie said. 'I'd go spare. You've got more than your fair share now.'

They both knew Rosie was referring to the latest addition to Jimmy's squad – Bobby.

'Aye, yer right there,' Jimmy said.

'He getting on all right?' Rosie asked.

'More than all right,' said Jimmy. 'He's like a machine, he is – never stops. Driven. Can't get enough overtime. He's proving to be a real role model for the younger lads.'

Rosie glanced round to see the young rivet burner and catcher jostling each other and joking around, their young faces smeared with dirt but animated with excitement at the prospect of a launch.

'Does Bobby get on with everyone?' Rosie asked, trying not to sound like she was probing. Gloria had confided in her that she had no idea how her son was doing. During his Friday visits he was polite enough, but he still had his defences up. The time he spent at the flat was purely given over to playing with Hope – except, of course, for his verbal sparring with Dorothy.

'He's not the chattiest of blokes I've worked with,' Jimmy said, taking a string of tobacco off his lip, 'but he gets on with everyone.'

They carried on walking to the dry dock at the very end of the yard, where the first launch was to take place.

Rosie knew Gloria was over the moon that Bobby adored Hope and wanted to be a part of her life, but it was obvious to them all that she was hurt by Bobby's refusal to reconcile their differences and accept Jack as part of the family. Personally, she couldn't understand it. They were all alive – and together. They should be counting their blessings.

'How you doing, Dorothy?' Bobby asked, nudging a path through the crowd of workers all heading over to the ways.

His question was met by a dark, sidelong look from Dorothy, and a smile from Angie next to her. Dorothy walked on in silence.

'She's good,' Angie said. 'We've just been chatting about Pearl and Bill's wedding.'

Bobby smiled. He had heard all about the wedding from Bel, who had told him several times these past few weeks that she would never have guessed she would ever see her ma hitched, and that, in fact, she would not believe it until it happened.

'Are yer gannin?' Angie asked.

'I've been invited,' Bobby said. 'So, yes, I'll be there.' He looked at Dorothy, who was muttering something under her breath he couldn't make out. He followed her line of vision as she looked over at Gloria, who was chatting to Martha and the young girl from the drawing office who he knew was called Hannah.

Dorothy looked back up at him. 'Why won't you make things up properly with your mam? Today would be the perfect opportunity,' she said. 'The day of your first launch. Ships we've all been working on. Together. Men and women. *Mothers and sons.*'

Bobby laughed loudly. 'That sounds like something Churchill would say.'

They walked on.

'For God's sake, Bobby, just be nice to her!' Dorothy demanded.

'I *am* nice. You make me sound like I'm horrible to her,' Bobby defended himself.

'What? Like you are to Jack?' Dorothy hissed.

'I'm not horrible to Jack either,' Bobby said, his expression innocent.

'Actually, you're not,' Dorothy conceded. 'You're not horrible because you don't even speak to the man – *you don't get the chance to be horrible to him.*' She looked at him. 'Although, some would argue that not speaking to someone is in itself being horrible.'

Bobby shook his head and touched his ear, indicating that he couldn't hear.

Dorothy stomped round so that she was walking on his right side.

'You're being civil to your mam like she's a stranger – not like she's your mother, the person who brought you up, cared for you, loved you, who has been worried sick about you since the day war was declared.'

Bobby looked down at Dorothy. Every time he saw her, they had the same conversation. He didn't mind being castigated on a regular basis; he just wished he didn't feel like kissing her every time she opened that very loud but lovely mouth of hers.

Watching the launch of both landing craft, Rosie's physical being might well have been in a shipyard on the north-east coast of England, but her mind was somewhere on the north-west coast of France – an area she was now quite well acquainted with thanks to Charlotte getting her a map of France from the school library. They had both studied it the other night, looking at where the invasion would likely take place and wondering where Peter might be. They had chatted about the 'dress rehearsals' that were taking place on the stretches of beaches along the Devon coastline, and Rosie had explained to her little sister about the Royal Navy landing craft that all the shipyards were producing. Charlotte had, of course, taken the opportunity to quiz her big sister more about Peter, making Rosie repeat what she had already told her about how they had met and fallen in love. Charlotte never tired of listening, just as Rosie never tired of the telling. When Rosie told her again about her wedding in Guildford, how she had been married for barely two days before Peter left for the war, Charlotte had sighed, as she always did, saying, 'How sad, but *so* romantic.'

Minutes after the second landing craft hit the water, Rosie turned to her squad. 'Back to work we go!' The harder they worked, the more ships they got down the ways, the more chance they'd win this war. Which, of course, meant Peter would return.

Rosie *would* get the man she loved back. For good.

'Come on, Dor, what yer deeing?' Angie was standing with her haversack and air raid mask slung over her shoulder, hands on hips.

'Hold your horses,' Dorothy said, pretending to do up the shoelaces on her boots. 'Do you want me to go flying and break an arm and then I won't be able to work and Rosie will flip her lid?'

Dorothy looked up to see that Rosie was now standing next to Angie, looking equally impatient to be off.

'Sorry, Rosie,' Dorothy quickly added, 'I didn't see you there.' She stood up. 'And of course I know that obviously you would never flip your lid.'

'I might if you don't get a move on,' Rosie said. She liked to be the last to leave, to make sure all their machines had been switched off and their equipment put away.

'You get yourself off,' Dorothy said, throwing Angie a look. 'I've gotta go to the loo. I think I drank too much tea this afternoon. It's gone through me like water through a sieve.'

Angie frowned. Dorothy hadn't drunk any tea this afternoon. She'd said the weather was too hot.

'All right then,' Rosie said, wanting to get home, get changed and get to Lily's. The sooner her work there was done, the sooner she would be home for Charlotte. 'See you all tomorrow,' she said, having a quick last look around. Everything seemed in order. 'Have a nice evening.'

Angie waited until Rosie was out of earshot. 'What yer playing at, Dor?'

'Come on, follow me,' Dorothy commanded, tugging Angie off in the direction of the women's toilets.

'What? Yer really do need the lav?' Now Angie was totally puzzled.

'No, of course I don't. You know me, cast-iron bladder,' Dorothy said. They all had cast-iron bladders due to their reluctance to use the yard's very basic facilities. Although none of them had ever seen a rat, they'd all heard scratching sounds, which got worse the warmer the weather.

'So, what we doing?'

Angie suddenly felt herself being grabbed by the arm and propelled sideways and under the long iron neck of a resting crane.

''Ere, Dor, I'm not a rag doll, yer knar,' she said, looking askance at her friend.

'We're waiting on Bobby,' Dorothy explained. 'This has gone on too long. He needs to hear some home truths.'

'Ah, nah, Dor,' Angie wailed. 'You can't force people to dee what yer think they should be deeing.'

Dorothy shot Angie a look before focusing her attention back on the yard.

'I beg to differ,' she said defiantly.

They both watched as the yard started to clear. Dorothy knew that Bobby was usually one of the last to leave the day shift, sometimes even staying on to do a few hours with workers on the evening shift. Polly had told them that Agnes had got into the habit of putting his supper in the oven to keep warm.

'There he is,' Angie said, hopeful he wouldn't stand about chatting too long. Quentin was due to call this evening and she'd be gutted if she missed him. 'Ah, nah, he's gannin into the platers' shed.'

They stood watching and waiting for five long minutes.

'Dor, this doesn't feel right,' Angie said. 'I feel like we're spying on him.'

171

'We're not spying – we're waiting,' Dorothy said, eyes trained on the entrance to the huge prefabricated metal shed.

Another five minutes passed that felt longer still.

'Dor, I'm gonna have to gan. I'll miss Quentin's call if we hang about much longer.'

Dorothy looked at Angie's forlorn face. 'OK, let's walk over to the main gates and if he's not come by then, you can go and catch lover boy and I'll stay here.'

'Gee thanks, Dor. That's kind of you,' Angie said with undisguised sarcasm.

'I know,' Dor said as they both stepped out of the shadow of the mammoth crane. 'I'm a kind and considerate friend, I am.'

When they reached the timekeeper's cabin, it was nearly six o'clock. Dorothy shouted up at Davey to put down half five, which was the time they should have left.

'Now, we're lying as well as spying,' Angie mumbled as they walked away from the large metal gates that had been partially closed after the end of the day shift.

'No, Ange, lying would be making out we've worked an extra half-hour and we've not.'

Dorothy took a final look into the main yard before turning back to Angie. 'Go on then, go and have your verbal smooch with Quentin and I'll see you a bit later.'

'Don't forget Toby's ringing yer at seven,' Angie said, turning to leave.

'As if,' Dorothy tutted. But in truth, she was surprised to realise she actually *had* forgotten. Lately it seemed that she was thinking more about Bobby than her own beau. She was certainly seeing more of him.

'At last!' Dorothy mumbled to herself as she pushed herself up from the kerb of the embankment and wiped dirt and grit off her bottom. It was warm and she had slipped her arms out of her overalls and tied the sleeves around her waist. She had also untied her headscarf and her dark brown hair was hanging in loose, messy curls over her shoulders and down her back. She had been enjoying the feel of the early-evening sun on her skin. It wasn't often she felt anything other than scratchy denim on her body during the day. Dorothy, like all the women welders, was terrified of getting burned and scarred by spitting welds. It hurt and it was unsightly when they did get to dress up and go out.

'Bobby!' Dorothy shouted out as he took his time card off Davey and started to make his way down to the embankment.

Stopping dead in his tracks, he shielded his eyes against the sun. Seeing Dorothy walking towards him, he couldn't speak, only stare. She looked like some Greek goddess, the kind some of his shipmates had inked on their arms and chests. She looked incredibly strong, her arms toned, the muscles defined. The vest she had on looked like a man's, but what it was covering was far from manly.

'Dear me,' he finally found his voice, 'you're a sight for sore eyes.'

'And you're late!' Dorothy retorted, totally unfazed by the way he was looking at her. 'I've been waiting ages.'

Bobby gave a bark of laughter, which was part amused, part incredulous, a reaction Dorothy always seemed to provoke in him. 'I wasn't aware we had arranged a date.'

'We hadn't,' Dorothy said simply.

'That's all right,' Bobby said, still standing rooted to the spot, mesmerised by the incredibly scruffy, but also incredibly sexy woman welder standing in front of him, hands on hips, wearing a pair of leather hobnailed boots. 'I'll just add telepathic communications to my considerable list of skills.'

'Big-headedness is not an attractive quality in a man,' Dorothy scowled.

Bobby suppressed a smile. 'To what do I owe this pleasure, as it's clear it's me you've been waiting for?'

Dorothy was just about to speak when he butted in. 'No, I'm going to use my mind-reading abilities and tell you ...' he put his large, blackened hands to his temples '... you are here to speak to me about ...' a pained expression was followed by a look of enlightenment '... my mam.'

'Ten out of ten,' Dorothy said.

'Well, why don't I get us both a drink from the Admiral?' He glanced over to the pub at the bottom of the embankment. 'We can drink it by the quayside, and you can tell me exactly what it is you want to say.'

Dorothy stood for a moment. Realising she was actually really thirsty, not having drunk much all afternoon and having sweated a lot, she nodded. 'All right. I'll have a lemonade, please.'

'Lemonade it is,' he said, his eyes still on Dorothy as they walked over to the pub.

Dorothy took a long drink, then turned her head to look at Bobby. They were sitting on the edge of the wharf, between two black metal balustrades, their overall-clad legs dangling down; the seagulls were squawking above them, the murky water of the Wear gently slapping against the quayside below. Dorothy felt conscious that their bodies were almost touching.

As Bobby pulled his arms out of the top of his overalls, Dorothy leant to the side to allow him elbow room to free himself. He tied the sleeves around his waist, as Dorothy had done with hers. It was hot; the sea breeze on his skin cooling. Dorothy couldn't help but be taken aback by the sight of his tanned, very muscular arms, as well as by his array of tattoos. There was an anchor and a nautical star on one arm, a swallow on each shoulder and what looked like two cannons crossed on one of his forearms and a dagger going through a rose on the other. She forced herself not to stare.

'So, tell me,' Bobby said. 'You said you wanted to speak to me about my mam.'

'I do,' she said, a little distracted.

'And?' Bobby said, looking at her profile and thinking he would love to do a sketch of her and send it to Gordon.

'When are you going to start being nice to her – and Jack?' Dorothy turned her head and forced herself to look Bobby in the eye, something she found surprisingly hard to do.

Bobby let out a hearty laugh. 'Don't hold back, Dorothy.'

'I speak as I find,' she threw him a scathing look, 'and I find your behaviour around Gloria and Jack …' She paused, trying to find the right word. 'Distant … Distant and cold … And unfeeling.'

Bobby exhaled. He'd been back almost a month now and during that time Dorothy had repeatedly asked him the same question but in a myriad different ways. Bobby looked at her face, which was painted with smears of soot and dirt, but looked just as attractive as when he'd seen her that first night all done up to the nines.

'I think you're going to have to let it go, Dorothy. I know you think the world of Mam, and I don't want to hurt your feelings, but this is a family matter. It's something I have to sort out with my mam myself. Just the two of us.'

Dorothy sighed. Angie and Helen had said the same to her.

'I do understand that.' She tried to soften her tone. 'But the thing is, Bobby, you're not going to be able to sort it out if you and Gloria don't actually talk to each other.'

She took a deep breath.

'And also, I know when you do get round to talking, there'll be a lot Gloria won't tell you.'

Bobby narrowed his eyes. 'Like what?'

'God.' Dorothy exhaled. 'Where do I start? There's been so much happened these past few years.' She looked at Bobby, whose face was also smeared with dirt, reminding her of a soldier's camouflage. 'A *lot* since you and Gordon dilly-dallied off and left home.'

'We didn't just *dilly-dally* off,' Bobby said, beating back a swell of anger. He had a sudden flash of the two of them making their way to the navy recruitment office. Their father had just smashed every piece of crockery in the house. It had been the straw that broke the camel's back.

'Your mam's been through a tough time since you and Gordon left – a really tough time,' Dorothy said.

Bobby wanted to say that she had been through a tough time before they'd left – their father had made sure of that.

'As I know she had been before you joined up,' Dorothy added, reading his thoughts. When Dorothy had seen the bruises around Gloria's neck for the first time shortly after they'd all started at the yard, she'd known that they had not been the first, nor would they be the last.

'I bet you didn't know your dad put her in the hospital, nearly killed her – would have if Helen hadn't gone at him with a shovel,' Dorothy said.

Bobby felt himself tense. 'When was that?' He forced the words through gritted teeth.

'When he found out Hope wasn't his,' Dorothy said.

'Was he still living with Mam?'

'No, she'd sent him packing well before that.' Dorothy let out a bitter laugh. 'This was when he was living in sin with his bit on the side in Grindon. A woman, I hasten to add, he'd been seeing behind your mam's back for two years.'

Bobby wasn't surprised. While he was still at home, he had been sure his dad was off with other women.

'So, I'm guessing Mam was all right?' Bobby asked. 'No serious injuries?'

'They had to keep her in hospital overnight,' Dorothy said.

Bobby clenched his fists. If his father were here now, he'd knock the living daylights out of him.

Dorothy saw the change in Bobby's face; her eyes dropped down to his balled fists.

'I know, it makes me so mad even now just thinking about it,' she empathised.

'That must have been shortly before he signed up for the navy?' Bobby asked.

'Yeah – signed up with one hand holding a pen, the other behind his back.'

'Meaning?'

'Meaning, Rosie's husband, well, he wasn't her husband then, but anyway, he sorted it out.'

'How come?'

'I don't know the exact details.' Dorothy dropped her voice even though there was no one else around to hear. 'But at the time he was working for the Borough Police – and let's just say, he went to see Vinnie in the cells and the next thing we knew, your dad was getting on a train to Portsmouth not only having signed up, but having also signed his divorce papers.'

Bobby's eyes widened. 'Where's this Peter now? I think I'd like to shake his hand and buy him a drink.'

'He's not here any more.'

'Dead?'

'No, God, I hope not – for Rosie's sake. No, he's somewhere – but no one's meant to know where. I shouldn't really even be saying anything at all – you know what they say, "Careless talk costs lives".'

'I understand,' Bobby said.

'But let's just say his mother was French,' Dorothy said conspiratorially.

Bobby nodded. Now he understood why he'd not heard much mention of Peter, and why Rosie had been pushing everyone extra hard of late.

'It's not been all doom and gloom, though,' said Dorothy. 'There's been two good things – no, *three* good things that's happened to your mam since you and Gordon left home.'

'Go on.' Bobby finished his lemonade and put his glass down by his side.

'First off, she came to work at Thompson's and secondly, she met me and the rest of the squad.'

Bobby smiled. 'Big-headedness is not an attractive quality in a woman.'

Dorothy ignored him. 'And thirdly, she was reunited with Jack—'

'What do you mean, "reunited"?' Bobby asked.

Dorothy rolled her eyes to the still, blue skies above. 'Don't you know anything?'

'Obviously not,' said Bobby, putting his hands behind him and leaning back. 'Tell me more.'

Dorothy had to twist around a little to look at him. She felt the sun on the side of her face and allowed herself to relax. For an insane moment she had a sudden urge to lay her head on his broad chest.

'Jack and your mam ...' Dorothy forced herself to concentrate '... used to be love's young dream, before manipulative Miriam came along.'

Bobby angled his head slightly to the left to hear better, but also to take in the entire enticing vision of the storyteller. He watched as Dorothy turned and crossed her legs so that she was facing him, and he listened as she related to him the story of how Gloria and Jack were 'star-crossed lovers' who had been parted as childhood sweethearts, but finally reunited after being separated for decades.

Bobby knew that Dorothy was giving the tale plenty of topspin, and it was also clear she was determined that his mam's love story, like the movies he knew she liked to go and see, would have a happy ending.

'It really is Shakespearean,' Dorothy said, enjoying telling her tale with full theatrics, even if she did only have an audience of one. 'When Jack finally makes the journey home from America – over the moon that he is finally returning to the woman he loves – and is about to learn that he has a newly born baby daughter, the ship he's travelling on is torpedoed and he nearly ends up dead at the bottom of the ocean.'

Bobby's eyes kept straying to Dorothy's mouth, making him wonder what it would be like to kiss her.

'Amazingly, he's rescued and survives,' Dorothy continued, her eyes widening. 'But he falls into a coma, and for weeks on end it's touch and go – until one day he wakes up.' Dorothy raised her arms into the sky as though praising the gods above. 'He is alive and well. Apart from one major hiccup – he can't remember a thing! And so he ends up going back to live with Miriam!'

Bobby had heard bits and pieces about Jack from Jimmy and some of the other workers. He had a reputation as a fair manager, a decent bloke, who'd been part of Churchill's British shipbuilding mission to the United States and had been instrumental in educating the Americans on how to mass-produce the more efficient and economic Liberty ships. Bobby had listened carefully to what people had to say – and the way they had said it – and no one, as far as he could tell, had a bad word to say about his mam's new bloke. Bobby, though, was still wary. His own father had put on a good act outside the home. There were plenty of people who thought Vinnie was a decent chap – he was a veteran of the First War, no less – but it'd been a very different story behind closed doors.

'If Jack's such an all-round Mr Nice Guy,' Bobby said, 'why is it he's not divorced from his wife?' He eyed Dorothy. 'Nothing to do with the fact she's loaded to the hilt, is it? And he doesn't want to go back to a life of poverty?'

'Oh, Bobby, you really have no idea – no idea at all.' Dorothy's laugh was deep and held no mirth. 'The reason Jack's still tied to that vile woman is the same reason he's been stuck on the Clyde for two whole years, unable to come back and see his own daughter and the woman he loves.'

Bobby frowned. 'I don't understand.'

'Exactly. That's the point I've been trying to get you to understand since you turned up.' Dorothy felt a hint of victory. 'There's a lot you don't understand.'

'Then tell me.'

Dorothy felt herself deflate. 'I can't.' She put her hair behind her ears. 'All I can tell you is that Jack and Gloria did not see each other once over those two years because of what might happen to some people they care about.'

Bobby rubbed his hand across the top of his head, a habit Dorothy had noticed he did when he felt flummoxed or agitated.

'I know it's confusing, but I can't tell you any more because, well, I just can't – I'm sworn to secrecy.'

Bobby sat up straight, brushing his hands free of dirt and putting on a look of disbelief at the idea that Dorothy could keep a secret.

'But what I can say is that Gloria's had to cope with a lot on her own,' she added.

'She had you lot,' Bobby said.

'That's nice of you to say,' Dorothy said with sincerity. 'We all try and be there for each other. But it proves the point that I've been trying to make since you came back: your mam's a lovely, kind-hearted person who's made sacrifices for the well-being of others – has put her own love on hold so that people she knows and cares about don't suffer.'

Bobby didn't say anything but looked out across the Wear to the south docks, his face serious and pensive. Dorothy wanted to ask what he was thinking, but something told her he wouldn't tell her even if she did. She finished the rest of her lemonade and got up. 'I have to use the pub's facilities.'

Bobby stood up, slid his arms back into the top of his overalls, picked up his empty glass and took Dorothy's off her. 'OK, I'll pop these back and you can continue filling me in about all the things I don't know on the way back home.'

Dorothy didn't need any encouragement and chatted away quite happily as they got the ferry back over to the south side. She took particular pleasure in relating Hope's birth to Bobby and how it had really been her and Angie who had been the stand-in midwives, although she had forced Angie to cut the cord. Bobby chuckled away, again a little unsure about how much of the story was exaggeration and how much true. 'And that's how I earned my stripes as Hope's godmother,' she said.

As they walked up Low Street, Dorothy relayed the drama of Hope's christening, when Jack had turned up with Arthur, Tommy's grandfather. Bobby knew who he was as Polly and Agnes often mentioned him.

'They were both dripping wet, and poor Arthur looked like he was going to breathe his last,' Dorothy said. 'But when Jack walked to the font and took Hope in his arms, it was like father and daughter were mesmerised by each other. It felt really special.'

For a while, they walked down Norfolk Street in comfortable silence. Dorothy had enjoyed her storytelling and Bobby had enjoyed listening.

'Just out of interest,' she said as they started down Foyle Street, 'your tattoos?' They crossed the road. 'I know that the star means a sailor will always find his way home, and that an anchor is something to do with crossing the Atlantic, but I'm never sure about the swallows – something about distance sailed?'

'That's right,' Bobby smiled. 'Five thousand nautical miles ... Do you know what the crossed cannons and the rose and dagger mean? They're always the ones to confuse.'

'I'm guessing they're something to do with war or fighting?' Dorothy said.

'That's right,' Bobby said. 'The cannons represent military naval service. And the rose and dagger mean a sailor is loyal and willing to fight anything, even something as sweet and beautiful as a rose.'

Dorothy didn't say anything.

'You haven't been out with any sailors before?' he asked, a cheeky glint in his eye.

'Of course I have,' Dorothy said in her best hoity-toity voice. She returned his look of mischievousness. 'But I haven't had the pleasure of seeing them with their tops off.'

Bobby barked with laughter. 'You're certainly a rare one, Dorothy. I'll give you that much.'

By now they had reached the steps to the Georgian terraced house that had been converted into apartments. He caught the twitch of a curtain at the window of the ground-floor flat.

'Thanks, Dorothy,' he said, his tone genuine.

'What for?'

'For everything you've told me.'

'Oh, you don't have to thank me,' Dorothy said in all sincerity. 'I didn't do it for you – I did it for Gloria. She's been like a mother to me – has been to all us women welders, actually.'

Dorothy looked at Bobby and expected to see pride that his mother had been such a pillar of strength and support, as well as loving and caring, but she didn't. Instead, she caught a look she'd seen before when they'd chatted about Gloria; it was a look she couldn't read.

'So, does that mean you'll be all right with your mam now – and with Jack?' Dorothy asked in earnest. 'Now that you know everything?'

'Oh, Dorothy.' Bobby smiled as he sighed. 'You are a one for a happy-ever-after ending, aren't you?'

'Of course,' Dorothy said. 'What other kind of ending would anyone want?'

Bobby didn't reply, but tipped an imaginary cap and watched as she let herself in the front door and waved him goodbye.

'Dor! Where have you been? We were just starting to get worried about you, weren't we, Mrs Kwiatkowski?'

The old woman nodded as she headed over to put the kettle on, although as soon as she had seen Dorothy and the tall, strapping lad walking up the cobbles, she had known she was fine – more than fine.

'And yer've missed Toby's phone call!' Angie said in disbelief.

'Oh my God! I completely forgot,' said Dorothy. 'I just presumed I'd be back in time, but Bobby and I ended up having a lemonade and then I got all carried away telling him about Gloria and Jack and Hope – and everything that's happened since we all started at the yard.'

'Everything?' Angie frowned, thinking of all the secrets it was imperative they kept.

'No, not *everything*,' Dorothy frowned back.

'Well, that's a relief at least,' said Angie. 'So, what about Toby? When yer gonna speak to him?'

'Why don't you call him back now?' Mrs Kwiatkowski suggested.

Dorothy fought back a wave of guilt that she had missed Toby's phone call – and that it was because of another bloke.

'You sure?' Dorothy said, going over and hugging the old woman. 'You're the best. I'll make it quick, and I'll pay you back, of course.'

'He sounded gutted when I said yer weren't back from work,' Angie said. 'He tried to make a joke of it 'n said there must be something "dreadfully amiss if you and my girl have been apart for more than five minutes".' Angie had just about perfected what she called an 'upper-crust accent' due to the amount of time she spent chatting to Quentin.

Dorothy laughed. 'Sounds like Toby.'

She walked over to the phone.

'But it's been worth it … It's been a long haul, and boy oh boy is Bobby as stubborn as a mule, but I've broken him. Wait until I tell Toby that I've finally made him see sense. Shown him the error of his ways,' Dorothy shouted over her shoulder.

'I'm sure Toby's gonna be over the moon,' Angie said, deadpan.

Angie took Mrs Kwiatkowski's arm as they both headed out of the kitchen to give Dorothy some privacy for her call to Toby.

'He will be!' Dorothy said, picking up the receiver and starting to dial.

Angie and Mrs Kwiatkowski looked at each other, both shaking their heads. Neither of them needed to say what they were thinking.

Chapter Twenty-One

France

Peter sat on a wooden chair in the kitchen of a large farm-house, just outside Caen, that had been taken over by a small group of *maquisards*, a rural band of fighters in the French Resistance. The Tempest circuit, which Peter headed, had moved to the new base at the beginning of the year. He had managed to keep intact his circuit of a radio operator, whose job it was to intercept and decode messages, a liaison officer, who met with local resistance fighters, and a courier, who relayed messages and information. No mean feat, as many *réseaux* had been infiltrated and their members captured or killed: a treacherous situation, much like his former circuit White Light. Peter worried, though, that their luck was running out and prayed it would last just that little bit longer, as the next couple of months were going to be the most dangerous – as well as the most important – of their time behind enemy lines.

That evening Peter had suggested to his men that now might be a good time to write letters to their loved ones in the event of their death. It was not widely known, but it was common practice in wartime for soldiers to write a 'last letter', especially before going into battle. The hope being that a final few words from a loved one might ease the burden of their loss, or at least gift them something to remember them by.

For Peter and his circuit, there was no sugar-coating the issue. They were planning a number of clandestine operations, mainly the sabotage of primary targets, but also the reconnaissance of strategic areas, having been sent colour-coded messages from London. 'Green', 'Black', 'Violet' and 'Blue' were orders to derail French train tracks, blow up fuel depots and take out phone and power lines in the vicinity.

Peter looked at his watch. It was gone eleven. He was glad he had the kitchen to himself. Arron, his radio operator, was in a small room at the back of the house waiting for a message from headquarters. Phillip, the courier, who had been on the move for the past two days, was already in bed, exhausted, having had very little sleep. And Francis, the liaison officer, was in his room, no doubt doing the same as Peter.

Putting pen to paper, Peter consciously put all thoughts of war aside and instead focused on those of love – on what he wanted to say to the woman he adored – the words that might be his last to her.

Taking a sip of strong French coffee, which he was now accustomed to drinking from a small bowl, he looked into the dying embers of the fire and pictured Rosie asleep in their bed. He looked at the blank sheet of paper. There was so much he wanted to ask her. What was she thinking? Feeling? How was Charlotte? Work? Lily's? Toby had sent the occasional message when he could, simply relaying that Rosie was well – and at the end of last year he'd sent a brief, coded communication that Charlotte was back living at home. *That must have opened up a can of worms.* How he wished he'd been there to help Rosie. Had Charlie found out about her sister's 'other life'? About Lily's? Her uncle Raymond? So many questions.

He'd been told his identity would most likely be compromised after this latest operation, which meant that if he made it out alive, he was heading home. Suddenly, the thought of being with Rosie in the bed in which he had imagined her sleeping flashed across his mind's eye; it was so real that he could almost feel their bodies next to each other, holding each other; he was breathing in her smell, feeling her blonde hair against his face. The last time they had been together they had made love; afterwards, neither had been able to sleep, their time together too precious.

Peter looked at the blank sheet of paper again and as he let his mind wander, he imagined himself waking Rosie up, kissing her softly and talking to her. As he did so, he wrote exactly what he would say to her if she were, in fact, there, sitting up in their bed, looking at him and listening.

He continued writing for the next hour, his make-believe world only broken once, when Arron came in and relayed a decoded message explaining that when the first three lines of Verlaine's 'Chanson d'automne' were read out on *Radio Londres*, it meant that the invasion of the north coast would take place within two weeks. There had been rumours that the attack was to happen at Easter, in just over a week's time, but those had been scorched, and now it seemed more than likely it would be May, possibly the beginning of June. No one knew for sure. Even those giving the orders weren't a hundred percent. Much was dependent on the weather and the tides.

By the time he had finished writing, Peter was missing Rosie more than he had ever done before. What he wouldn't give to be with her now – especially if it was to be his last time. He refused to castigate himself for thinking such thoughts for he had to be practical and face up to the reality that he and his men might not make it back to their homeland. But if they didn't, there was no doubt in his mind that the sacrifice would have been worth it, for the next few months would decide the fate of the war – and thereby, the fate of humanity.

Chapter Twenty-Two

Friday 31 March

'Knock, knock!' Marie-Anne said as she walked through the open doorway of Helen's office carrying a tea tray.

'Thanks, Marie-Anne. You know you can always get one of the office juniors to do the tea?'

'That's all right, Miss Crawford. It's no bother at all.' Marie-Anne *had*, in fact, got the office junior to make the tea – only she'd taken the tray off her and brought it to Helen herself. 'Did you hear about the bomber coming down near Ryhope pit last night – well, early hours, by the sounds of it?'

'No, what happened? Was anyone hurt?' Helen immediately thought of Dr Parker.

'It was one of our own – a Halifax. The pilot died, and some poor bloke on his way to work at the colliery got hit by debris and died.'

'Goodness, that's terrible. But that was it, no one else was hurt?' Helen needed reassurance.

'I think three of the crew were injured, but I didn't hear of any others,' Marie-Anne said, turning to go. She knew Helen would want shot of her so she could ring the Ryhope Emergency Hospital. She wouldn't rest until she knew that Dr Parker was alive and well.

'Thanks, Marie-Anne. Will you shut the door on the way out?' She smiled. Marie-Anne was already doing it.

Grabbing her cigarettes, Helen dialled the hospital. God only knew how Rosie, Polly and Gloria managed to keep sane worrying about the men they loved.

'Hi, Denise,' Helen said, pausing to light a cigarette.

'Ah, Miss Crawford, how are you?'

'I'm good, thank you, Denise.' Helen blew out smoke. 'I'm sure you can guess why I'm calling.'

'I can,' Denise said, 'and I can assure you that Dr Parker is well. Let me see if I can put you straight through. He should be on the ward now.'

Helen listened to a succession of clicking noises before she heard John's voice.

'Helen, wait there, I'm just going to put you through to the office so the whole ward doesn't hear our conversation.' Helen heard men's voices in the background, which she guessed were John's 'new recruits'. She could tell they were giving John gyp after hearing that there was a woman on the phone. The spirit of the men John treated never ceased to amaze her. There was a click, followed by dead air, before another click.

'I'm back,' he said.

'I'm so glad I managed to get through to you,' Helen said. 'Denise is being very helpful of late.'

'I know,' Dr Parker said. 'I think it's been since her "forgetfulness" the other day.'

'I think she might have been *forgetful* a few times before.' Helen took a drag on her cigarette. 'Maybe her mind's been elsewhere. Maybe she's *in love*.'

Dr Parker chuckled, although there might have been some truth in Helen's diagnosis. He had heard on the hospital grapevine that Denise had been on a few dates with a doctor from the Royal.

'Marie-Anne just told me the awful news about last night's crash,' Helen said, her tone now sombre.

'I know. Awful. Tragic. But thank goodness the pilot managed to avoid the miners' cottages and crash-land on the colliery instead, otherwise it would have been much worse.'

'Where was he going – or coming from?' Helen asked.

'From what I've heard, the plane got damaged en route to Nuremberg, just about managed to limp back, but deviated off course, ran out of fuel and had to make an emergency landing.'

They were both quiet for a moment, thinking of all the families that might have died if the pilot hadn't managed to avoid the rows of houses next to the village's coal mine.

'Everything all right at your end?' Dr Parker asked. As always, his concern was genuine.

'Yes, yes,' Helen said. 'Well, actually, I've got an apology to make.'

'Why's that?'

'I should have told you earlier, but I just completely forgot. You've been invited to Pearl and Bill's wedding reception. Bel asked me to invite you when I was round there the other week – and then it just totally slipped my mind.'

'That's understandable, you've got a lot going on, what with work and everything ...' Dr Parker's thoughts automatically went to Matthew.

'That's very forgiving of you, John, but the thing is, I really do have to apologise as the wedding's next Saturday,' Helen said, guiltily.

'What – a week on Saturday?'

'Yes, but don't worry if you can't make it. I'm sure Pearl and Bill won't mind in the least.'

'No, it'll be a perfect chance for me to see our godson. You know, I've not seen him since his christening?'

'Oh, I wouldn't worry, Polly understands. She knows what you do is really important and that you barely step over the hospital boundaries these days,' Helen said. *Not unless it's to take Claire to some fancy restaurant in town.*

'No, I'll definitely come,' Dr Parker said. Helen could hear pages being turned. 'I'm just checking the rota and I've got that Saturday off, so I won't even have to twist any arms.'

'Oh, all right.' Helen tried to sound chirpy. 'You're sure Claire will want to come? It won't be particularly fancy. The usual knees-up at the Tatham.'

'I'm sure that won't put Claire off. And I can always take her somewhere more *fancy* afterwards if she wants.' He wasn't going to pretend that Claire would be clicking her heels at the prospect of spending Easter Saturday in the east end. Taking her to the Palatine afterwards would even the score.

'Everyone else all right?' Dr Parker asked.

'Yes, all good here. Busy. Getting ready for our nation's very own big day. Did you see they've been appealing for lorry drivers for the second front?' Helen asked.

'I did – you're not thinking of applying?' Dr Parker asked, half joking.

'No,' Helen laughed. 'But I did tell Gloria to make sure Rosie didn't read about it for fear of her running off and signing up.'

'Can she drive?'

'No, but I'm sure that wouldn't stop her.' Helen's laughter was sad.

'She still working like a trooper?'

'Oh yes, she's very determined. Mind you, everyone is. It's in the air. That sense of anticipation. A kind of nervous excitement.'

'It's been a bit like that here. We've been told to make sure we're prepared. To free up as many spare beds as possible.'

193

Dr Parker wasn't sure how much they should be chatting about the impending push to reclaim Europe and changed the subject.

'Are all the women at the yard all right?' He paused. 'Gloria?'

'Oh, well … yes … yes and no.' She sighed. 'I do feel for her and Dad – they finally get to be together and then there's this awkwardness with Bobby.'

'Anything happened?'

'No, but that's just it – it's the underlying tension, what's left unsaid.' Another sigh. 'Although Dorothy reckons that she's talked Bobby round.'

'But you're not quite so sure?'

'I really hope she has,' Helen said, 'but I have my reservations. I think this goes deeper.'

'How so?'

'I'm not sure, just a feeling,' Helen mused.

'And are Gloria and Jack coping with it all right?' Dr Parker asked.

'Yes, they're both pretty hardy. And they think it's sweet what Dorothy's doing. They know that it doesn't matter what they say, they won't stop her in her determination to see them all become one big happy family.'

'I suppose there's no harm in trying,' said Dr Parker.

'Well, she'll find out tonight if she's succeeded or not,' Helen said. 'She popped in before the start of the shift to tell me she can't wait to see Gloria's face when Bobby goes round there tonight.'

'So, she's not told Gloria that she reckons she's talked Bobby round?'

'Nope,' Helen said. 'Apparently, it's going to be a surprise.'

*

194

At seven o'clock that evening, three days after their tête-à-tête by the banks of the Wear, Dorothy left Gloria's flat with Bobby, having spent the last hour with Hope. She was spitting feathers.

'I cannot believe you, Bobby!' she hissed as soon as Gloria had said her goodbyes and shut the door.

'Why?' Bobby asked, putting his hand out for Dorothy to go first.

She gave him a look of fury before she stomped up the stone steps.

'Because,' she said, turning when she got to the top and looking daggers at him, 'everything's meant to be all right now.'

'How come?' he asked, automatically stepping round to her left so that he was walking by the side of the road.

'How come?' Dorothy forced herself not to scream the words. 'Because we chatted about it on Tuesday night? Outside the Admiral? Remember?'

Bobby laughed. 'Yes, I remember.'

'So?' Dorothy demanded.

'I don't know what you expected, Dorothy,' Bobby said as they turned into Foyle Street.

'I expected ...' Dorothy gasped '... that you would be fine with your mam now – normal, loving.'

When they reached her flat, Dorothy turned and looked at Bobby.

'I'm so very disappointed.'

Bobby looked at Dorothy and thought he'd never seen anyone look so beautiful and yet so sad. He wished he could make her happy, but he couldn't. What she wanted of him had to come from the heart. It had to be true. And at the moment there was a part of his heart that felt very stony, very cold and unfeeling, and there was nothing he could do about it. He'd tried to make himself feel different, like Dorothy wanted, but he couldn't.

He stood with a heavy heart and watched as she gave him one final, hate-filled glare before letting herself in and slamming the door behind her.

Chapter Twenty-Three

Good Friday

Friday 7 April

For the first time since the war began, the children of Sunderland gathered in the town centre for a Good Friday celebration. Bel and Joe took Lucille and the twins, and Polly and Gloria, who had taken a rare day off work, took Artie and Hope. Thousands of Sunday-school children sang hymns, after which they all left in a procession that led them back to their various churches. Polly then took Artie to visit his great granddad's grave, where she told him all about his namesake, and also about his uncle Teddy, whose grave they couldn't visit as it was on the other side of the world in a place called Sidi Barrani. As they made their way back home, her voice lifted as she told her sleepy little baby boy all about his daddy, whom he would be seeing soon. Hopefully.

Hannah, Rina and Olly enjoyed a different religious celebration as it was the start of the Jewish Passover, which officially began at sunset, but the preparations had started earlier in the day. For the first time, Olly mentioned to Hannah's rabbi his desire to convert. The rabbi had smiled and said he would teach him all about Judaism, after which, if he still felt the same, they could talk further.

Following the afternoon shift at the Tatham, Pearl hurried off to West Lawn. She had given in to Vivian's bullying that she be allowed to cut and dye Pearl's hair. It also meant that Pearl would be able to see Maisie in her home environment – a place she had only visited once before, just hours before the showdown with Charles Havelock on Christmas Day. Pearl would never judge her daughter for the work she did, but she had been pleased when Maisie had confided that Lily had given them the go-ahead to develop the Gentlemen's Club and the 'escorting' side of the business.

En route to the bordello, Pearl took the opportunity to pop in to see Gracie's parents, Mr and Mrs Evans. Since she had first gone to see them both at Christmas, she had visited them regularly. They had been disappointed to hear that Bel had decided not to bring Charles Havelock to justice, but they had agreed that at least something good had come of it all. Every time Pearl visited them thereafter, they would remind her that they were prepared to help in any way, if and when needed. The couple's hatred for the man who, they said, might as well have put the noose around their daughter's neck himself, was very much alive and it easily matched Pearl's hatred for the man who had changed the course of her life.

Meanwhile, Helen was spending time with her grandmother, having let the office workers leave work early as today would have been classed as a common-law holiday, were they not at war.

'You haven't that glow about you today,' Henrietta commented as Helen sat down to read another chapter of *Persuasion*. 'Which means,' she added as she poured them both a glass of water, which she liked to pretend was her Russian vodka, 'you didn't see your doctor friend before you came here.' Helen smiled and told her grandmama that she was indeed right, but she would be seeing him tomorrow at the wedding of Henrietta's 'Little Match Girl'. Helen had told her grandmother about Pearl's upcoming nuptials, and Henrietta had declared how fabulous it would be if she were able to attend. Something, Helen thought, Pearl might not be so keen on, even if Henrietta was allowed out.

At the same time that Helen was visiting her grandmother, Bobby was heading off to see their little sister. On arrival he was gutted to find that Dorothy wasn't there. Gloria told him that she was staying in and washing her hair in anticipation of a hectic weekend. Dorothy had made it known to anyone who would listen that this was a particularly important couple of days as not only was there a wedding to attend, but she was taking Toby to meet her parents. Gloria didn't have to say it, but the inference was clear. If Toby wanted to meet Mr and Mrs Williams, it could only mean one thing – marriage was on the cards. Dorothy's prediction at the start of the year was coming true, although Gloria couldn't help but wonder if this was still what Dorothy really wanted. There was undeniable chemistry between her and her son. Just looking at Bobby now and seeing the fleeting look of deep disappointment on his face, it was clear that her eldest had been struck by Cupid's arrow. She felt for him. And Toby. Someone was going to end up with a broken heart. The path to true love was never an easy one, as she knew only too well.

Gloria would have loved to talk to her son about this, as well as what was causing the tension between them, instead of the usual superficial chit-chat she'd had to endure since his return. She had an idea of what really lay beneath the surface of Bobby's suppressed ire towards her, which she believed didn't concern her living arrangements, regardless of how scandalous they might be. But much as she wanted to give Bobby the opportunity to air his grievances and tell her what was really bothering him, she knew now wasn't the right time. Her son was distracted by a love that looked destined to be unrequited. She would have to wait and hope that in the meantime the frostiness Bobby felt towards her – and Jack – might start to thaw.

Chapter Twenty-Four

Saturday 8 April

Rosie looked around the small registry office as people started to make their way in from the main foyer to take their seats. The room was small and felt smaller still due to the dark wooden panelling on the walls, but the windows were open, which was allowing in a fresh breeze. The last time she'd been here was for Bel's wedding to Joe. She smiled to herself. She would never have guessed back then that the next time she'd be here would be for Pearl's wedding – Bel's ma was the last person she'd have believed would be getting married. It was another example, Rosie thought, of how unpredictable life could be.

Charlotte shuffled as she straightened her new summer dress, fighting the urge to rub her eyes. She managed to stop herself. Rosie had allowed her to put on some mascara and a smudge of blue eyeshadow and she did not want to end up looking like a panda. She was sitting in between the two people she loved and adored more than anyone else in the world – Rosie and Lily. Looking at them both, she saw that Rosie had on the minimum of make-up, just enough to hide the smattering of facial scars their uncle had left her with, whereas Lily had, as usual, plastered enough on for all three of them.

'Is Miss Crawford not coming with Mr Dishy?' Charlotte asked.

Rosie looked at her. It hadn't escaped her notice that her not-so-little sister had started to show an interest in the opposite sex. She'd learnt from Lily that a group of boys from a school nearby were walking Charlotte and some of her friends part of the way home. Rosie had felt a little put out that Charlie had confided in Lily about the boys and not her. Sitting back, she sighed. If Pearl's wedding was a turn-up for the books, then it was trumped by the fact that Lily – the madam of a bordello – had become a surrogate mother to her little sister. The world really had become topsy-turvy.

'Bill looks nervous,' Charlotte said.

Bill, it had to be said, was indeed looking tense, as well as uncomfortable, in a hired black suit that was a fraction too small for him, causing him to tug at the cuffs every now and again. He was standing by the registrar's large, polished cherry-wood desk and was chatting to Joe, his best man.

'He has good reason to be,' Lily chuckled, causing Rosie to give her a 'be-on-your-best-behaviour-or-else' scowl.

George, who was sitting next to Lily, was also wearing a black suit, only his had been tailor-made to fit and did not feel uncomfortable. Leaning forward in his seat with both hands on top of his ornately carved walking stick, he was mulling over a conversation he'd had the previous evening with the Brigadier about the state of play on the other side of the Channel. Tactics of military deception were presently being employed with the aim of misleading the Germans about the date and location of the Allied landings. Peter and his circuit would likely be part of the spreading of any misinformation, as well as preparing acts of sabotage for when the invasion was imminent. Rosie's husband was well and truly in the thick of it. Looking at Rosie, he could see that she was tired. She was working herself into the ground, convinced that by doing so it would help to bring about a victory that would see her husband return to her. He hoped to God all her hard work and extra hours made her wish come true. He dreaded the state she'd be in if Peter did not come back.

'Look! Here's Gloria and Hope,' Charlotte said, waving them over.

Gloria saw them and made her way over. Hope was toddling by her side, holding her mammy's hand and looking as sweet as pie in a vibrant yellow dress that had once belonged to Lucille. Rosie, Charlotte, Lily and George turned in their seats to welcome them as they manoeuvred themselves into the row behind. None of them asked where Jack was as they knew Gloria thought it was still too early for them to be seen out in public as a family, especially as divorce proceedings hadn't even been instigated. Jack was to meet them all at the Tatham as this was the only place Gloria felt as though they could be seen together, although she'd told Jack to refrain from showing her any kind of affection.

'The bride hasn't legged it then?' Gloria said as she lifted Hope onto the chair next to her.

Rosie laughed. 'As far as I'm aware, she's still in the building.'

'She'll have Kate chasing after her if she does get cold feet,' Lily said, smiling down at Hope. 'She was up all night doing her headpiece.' They all knew Kate wanted to become as well known for her millinery as for her seamstress skills.

George lifted his trilby at Gloria and smiled at Hope, who was staring up at Lily's orange hair, piled high into an extravagant updo.

'Dorothy and Angie!' Charlotte exclaimed. 'With Toby and Quentin!'

Rosie felt her heart thump, as it always did when she saw Toby.

Dorothy waved over as they took their seats on the other side of the aisle. Toby tipped his peaked officer's cap and put his thumb up, which these days was their personal code for 'Peter's fine.' In reality, it meant that Toby simply hadn't heard otherwise.

'Dorothy looks stunning,' Charlotte said.

Rosie looked across and seeing Dorothy in a clinging red dress, she was catapulted back to her own wedding – she had worn a similar red dress, which had raised eyebrows. It had been her Christmas present from Kate and she had worn it simply because she had nothing else. When she had gone to see Peter after he'd sent her a telegram and a travel warrant, she'd had no idea she'd end up getting married.

Suddenly, they all heard the door open and a baby start to cry. They turned to see Polly with Artie in her arms, unhappy at having been taken out of his cosy pram. On seeing the rows of faces that had naturally turned in his direction, most of which were smiling, his wailing stopped as quickly as it had started. Polly breathed a sigh of relief and sat down in the back row, ready for a quick exit should Artie decide his lungs needed exercising again.

Following in Polly and Artie's wake were Agnes, who was wearing her best black dress, Dr Billingham and the Elliots' next-door neighbour, Beryl, who was in particularly good spirits as she had just received a letter courtesy of the Foreign Office informing her that her POW husband was well, and that she'd soon be able to send letters and food parcels.

Behind them came Hannah, Olly and Martha, who had just been to the café, helping Vera and Rina make the last of the sandwiches for the reception. Vivian appeared next, looking as always like a replica of Mae West with her dyed blonde hair, and wearing a vibrant peacock-blue cotton dress that would have been relatively conservative were it not for the plunging neckline. She hurried through the door and down the side of the room, taking a seat next to George. She had just touched up the bride's coiffure and was pleased with her handiwork. Seconds later, she was followed by Kate, who had also just finished giving the bride's dress a quick checking over and making some minor adjustments to Pearl's headpiece.

As the 'Wedding March' started up, everyone fell silent. The record, which had just been put on the gramophone by one of the clerical staff sitting at a small table at the back of the room, was the only music to be played at the ceremony. Pearl had said she wanted a no-frills affair, no readings or 'anything fancy', with just family and close friends. Pearl still couldn't quite believe she was getting married and was as nervous as hell. She wanted it over and done with as soon as possible and to get back to where she felt at home – in the Tatham with a drink in one hand and a fag in the other. The registrar was more than happy to abide by Pearl's wishes, especially as the list of soldiers, sailors and airmen wanting to marry their sweethearts before leaving for the beaches of northern France was growing by the day.

With the music announcing that the ceremony was now under way, the dozen or so guests all turned to see Lucille, looking adorable in an ivory dress and gripping a small wicker basket of petals, walk into the room. There were a few 'Aahs' and chairs scratching on the parquet flooring as people twisted around for a better view.

Pearl followed through the large oak doors. She was wearing a powder-blue dress with a floral print that was floaty and feminine; Kate had made it out of a long evening dress one of her more well-heeled patrons had given her. Vivian had also done a sterling job making sure Pearl's hair looked classy, not brassy. Kate's delicate gold headpiece, a veritable work of art made with a selection of glass-effect leaves and flowers, blended in perfectly with Pearl's swirling updo, loose strands of hair having been teased free to frame her face. Her make-up had been applied artfully by Maisie and not shovelled on as it was normally. For once, Pearl wasn't mutton dressed as lamb.

'Quite a transformation,' Lily said under her breath.

'Kate never fails,' Rosie whispered.

The guests looked as Pearl was followed by her two daughters, Bel and Maisie, both looking gorgeous in cream-coloured summer dresses that complemented their complexions. This was exactly the wedding Pearl wanted – her two girls and her granddaughter close by, and just a handful of guests – for this day was as much about celebrating her family as it was about her marriage to Bill.

It was something her soon-to-be husband was aware of and didn't mind. If anything, it made him love her even more. If that were possible.

After reaching the registrar's table, where the groom and the best man were also standing, Pearl handed Lucille her wedding bouquet, gave her a kiss on top of her head and ushered her towards Bel and Maisie, who were taking their seats at the front.

Bill bent and gave his bride a quick kiss as the music stopped and the congregation fell silent.

As the ceremony got under way, Rosie sat back, breathed in the smell of old wooden furniture and listened to the words being spoken by the registrar. She cast her mind back to her own wedding. It had been in a completely different town, three hundred miles down south, and had taken place in the dead of winter, but it felt remarkably similar. Like Pearl and Bill's wedding, hers had been short and sweet, mainly because Peter had only just managed to get a special licence and they'd been lucky to be squeezed in; like Peter, many of the husbands-to-be were in the forces and desperate to marry their loved ones before they went back to war.

Rosie watched as the registrar addressed Pearl and Bill, who were standing in front of his desk. Pearl started to fidget with her dress and Bill took her hand and squeezed it. They continued holding hands throughout.

'Will you, Pearl Hardwick, take this man, William David Lawson, as your lawfully wedded husband, to have and to hold from this day forward, for better, for worse, for richer, for poorer, in sickness and in health, to love and to cherish till death do you part?' The clear, confident voice of the registrar sounded out.

'I do,' Pearl said, her voice uncharacteristically shaky.

Rosie suddenly felt unusually emotional and found herself blinking back tears. For a moment she felt herself back in the registry office in Guildford, looking into Peter's serious blue eyes. Her wedding day had been full of conflicting emotions: happiness that she was marrying the man she loved – the only man she had ever loved – but also sadness that the man she was agreeing to marry might make her a widow for longer than he would make her a wife.

A tear escaped and Rosie brushed it away quickly. Peter had survived this long. He would get through this last battle alive. *He had to.* She would never admit it to anyone – it would seem so weak, and she had tried so hard to be so brave her whole life – but when it came to Peter, she knew his death would be the only battering from which she would not be able to get up.

Charlotte saw that her sister was becoming emotional and was shocked. Rosie was not the sentimental type. She nudged Lily and cocked her head towards her big sister.

Leaning forward, Lily briefly touched Rosie's hand. 'You all right?'

Rosie nodded, taking a deep breath and touching her wedding band, an 18-carat gold ring that Peter had bought on the morning of their wedding from the jewellers next to their hotel. She looked up to see that Bill was putting a shiny new gold ring on Pearl's hand.

'I now pronounce you man and wife,' the registrar declared.

He paused, before adding, 'You may now kiss the bride.'

It was at that exact moment that Artie chose to burst out crying, causing all the guests to burst out laughing and giving Bill the opportunity to wrap his arms around his new wife and give her a kiss on the lips. She kissed him back, though it was just a quick one. She looked embarrassed; she was not one for such public displays of affection. Rosie remembered the awkwardness she too had felt at this part of her marriage ceremony.

Bel and Maisie stepped forward to sign the green ledger spread out on the registrar's desk, and Lucille squashed herself in between her mammy and her aunty to see what was going on. Rosie remembered the two strangers, both clerical workers at the registry office, who had been asked to witness her marriage to Peter. After the short ceremony, the pair had made an impromptu reappearance when she and Peter had walked out of the main building and had showered them with confetti. The woman had surprised Rosie by giving her a hug. She would never forget the words she had whispered in her ear: 'May it be long and happy!' Rosie knew her marriage with Peter would be a happy one – but she could only hope and pray that it would be a long one.

*

207

When Pearl and Bill walked out of the registry office, they were met by a chorus of 'Congratulations!' Polly had managed to buy a couple of packets of confetti from the shop Charlotte had discovered near the Grand when she'd been helping Bel organise Polly's wedding. When the happy couple reached the bottom steps, Joe put Lucille on his shoulders and she sprinkled the petals from her basket over the newly-weds. The ones that fell on Pearl's head-piece stayed there, giving Kate an idea for another, more elaborate floral-themed one.

As they all started to make their way to the Tatham, George offered to take them there in his MG, as he had Bel and Joe for her wedding and Polly and Tommy for theirs, but Pearl declined, repeating her mantra of 'no fuss, no frills'.

'Eee, I have to say, I'm not half glad that's all over 'n done with,' Pearl said to Bill as they turned left at the bottom of John Street and crossed over Borough Road. Bill had a big smile on his face as he shook off his jacket and started rolling up his sleeves.

'I'll second that, Mrs Lawson,' he said

Pearl looked momentarily puzzled before letting out a loud laugh.

'*Mrs Lawson*! I wondered who yer were talking to then!' She continued chuckling, which was, in part, relief that the registration of their marriage had been endured and was now, thankfully, over.

'*Mrs Lawson*,' she repeated. 'That's gonna take some getting used to ... Been a Hardwick my whole life.'

'And now you'll be a Lawson for the rest of your life,' Bill said, putting his arm around her shoulders and pulling her close.

It only took a few minutes for them all to make their way along Borough Road and then right down Tatham Street.

When they reached the front door of the pub, Bill stepped aside, waving everyone in.

'Get yourselves in and get a drink. We'll be in in a minute.'

Bel and Maisie passed their ma and gave Bill a questioning look as Lucille pulled her aunty Maisie's hand, her other still carrying her basket, which was empty of petals but now contained her grandma's blue wedding bouquet.

'Why're we waiting out here?' Pearl asked. 'I'm choking for a drink and it's not 'cos I'm thirsty.'

'I've got you a wedding present,' he said.

'Ah, yer soft bugger. I didn't knar we had to buy each other presents as well as marry each other.'

Bill laughed.

'You don't. But I wanted to give you something that I think you're going to really like.'

He pointed to the sign above the door.

'You are now not only Mrs Pearl Lawson, but the joint licensee of the Tatham Arms.'

Pearl looked at the newly inscribed wooden panel above the main entrance. And sure enough, there it was:

Mr William Lawson & Mrs Pearl Lawson, licensed to sell beer, wine and spirits for consumption on the premises.

Pearl's chin almost touched the pavement.

'Ah, Bill,' she said, clearly taken aback. 'I dinnit knar what to say.' She kept looking at the gilt-painted lettering on the sign. 'I think yer might have made me the happiest woman on this planet.'

Bill looked at Pearl. She was smiling like the Cheshire cat.

'And you, my dear, have just made me the happiest man on the planet, so I guess we're even.' He kissed her and she kissed him back, because she wanted to, and because she thought she might blubber if she didn't.

'Now, shall we go and get that drink, Mrs Lawson?' Bill asked.

'Mrs Lawson, *Licensee of the Tatham Arms*, dinnit forget,' Pearl said as she walked into the pub. Her pub. Their pub.

Chapter Twenty-Five

Bill clinked the side of his glass with his spoon, forcing the guests to quieten down.

'You all know I'm not one for speeches, so I'm just going to keep this really brief,' he said.

'Thank Gawd for that!' someone heckled.

'I want to say thank you to everyone for coming and helping us celebrate – and to point out that there is no free bar!' he laughed.

There were a few boos.

'Although everyone's first drink is on the house—'

This was followed by a robust chorus of 'Hurrah!'

'So, before the stampede, I just want to raise a toast to my new wife, Mrs Pearl Lawson.'

Everyone's attention went to Pearl, who looked as though she wanted the ground to swallow her up.

'It's quite simple, Pearl ...' Bill turned to look at his bride '... I love you to pieces.'

Bill lifted his glass and took a sip.

Everyone followed suit.

'And just one more thing before I get back to where I belong – behind the bar,' he chuckled. 'Pearl's granddaughter Lucille is going to throw the bouquet, so, ladies, either make a run for it now, or keep your eye on the ball – or should I say, the bouquet.'

All the young unmarried women had known that Lucille was to do the honours as Pearl had not wanted to cause a commotion outside the registry office, so they had positioned themselves within catching distance. Dorothy and Angie were, naturally, amongst the dozen or so hopefuls.

'God, look at him!' Dorothy hissed into Angie's ear.

'Who?' Angie said as she followed Dorothy's angry stare over to where Bobby was chatting to Matthew's secretary, Dahlia, nicknamed the 'Swedish seductress' by Marie-Anne, who had invited her as her companion in the hope that she might pick up some tips.

'*Bobby*, of course,' Dorothy said. 'Look at him! Happy as Larry, chatting up Dahlia.'

Angela saw that Bobby and Dahlia were indeed both happy and chatting away to each other.

'Actually, they look well suited,' Angie said, returning her attention to the ritual of the throwing of the bouquet.

'What makes you say that?' Dorothy snapped. She wished it didn't bother her, but it did. She didn't know why, but seeing them together irked her.

'Dunno,' Angie said, her focus firmly on Joe and Lucille. Joe had stepped forward so that he was standing in front of the bar. He nodded down at Lucille, who was clutching the hand-tied flowers. She nodded back, her face serious.

'What? Because they're both just about the same height?' Dorothy persevered.

Angie glanced back over at Bobby and Dahlia. It was true. Dahlia was almost the same height as Bobby, but then Angie noticed she was wearing a pair of gorgeous, high-heeled shoes.

'I suppose so,' she said. 'And because they're both very good-looking. He's tall, dark 'n scrummy. She's all blonde, blue-eyed 'n leggy.'

Dorothy inspected them both. There was no denying it, they *were* a good-looking couple.

Angie watched Joe and Lucille and thought they reminded her of two circus performers getting ready to do their trick.

'I've got a good mind to go over there and tell Dahlia to steer well clear.' Dorothy was speaking into Angie's ear, but her eyes were still glued to Bobby and Dahlia.

Angie watched as Joe stepped forward and put Lucille on his shoulders. He then slowly turned around so that they both had their backs to the hopeful brides-to-be.

'Tell her that he's a cold-hearted, stubborn, selfish man and she should avoid him like the plague.'

'I don't think Dahlia's that bothered about his personality, Dor,' Angie said, looking across to see that Dahlia had moved a little closer to Bobby and was whispering something into his good ear. She quickly turned her attention back to Lucille, who was slowly raising the bouquet above her head.

'Well,' Dorothy said, watching as Bobby said something back to Dahlia, making her laugh and toss her long, corn-coloured hair back at the same time, 'I'd better tell her, his body's covered in ink.'

'What? He's got lots of tattoos?' Angie asked, eyes still focused on the wedding posy. It was a lovely, home-made tie of flowers, which she knew had been picked from Albert's allotment.

'Yes! *Tattoos*,' Dorothy said, watching as Bobby rubbed his hand on his head, giving Dahlia a half-smile.

'How do you know he's covered in tattoos?' Angie suddenly said, turning her head and looking at her friend. 'You never told me that before.'

'*And here goes!*' Bill shouted out, raising his glass in the air. '*One ... two ... three!*' Knowing that was her signal, Lucille threw the bouquet back with all her might, high up into the air. Dorothy was just about to explain to Angie how it was that she had seen Bobby without some of his clothes on and therefore knew he had tattoos, when all of a sudden there was a loud cheer and she felt something soft hit her in the side of the face. Looking down, she saw a small bunch of wild flowers, tied with a blue ribbon, on the floor of the pub by her feet.

Angie sighed and bent down. Picking them up, she held them aloft to show the expectant crowd of wedding guests that the flowers might not have been caught as tradition dictated, but at least they, along with the hope of a future marriage, had been rescued from being trampled underfoot.

'Thanks for being my escort – again,' Helen said as she and Matthew entered the Tatham.

'My pleasure, as always,' said Matthew, pulling open the door that led into the bar. As he did so, they were both hit by a blast of warm, smoky air and an atmosphere that could only be described as full of revelry.

'Actually, you were *properly* invited by Pearl,' Helen added. 'She likes you.' It was true. Pearl had told Bel to tell Helen that her 'usual fella' was also invited to the reception.

Helen caught sight of the bride over a sea of heads. She was surprised to see Pearl behind the bar, serving her guests. She turned her head to continue speaking to Matthew. 'Or should I say, I think she liked the generous sum you left behind the bar after Artie's christening.'

Matthew laughed. 'Don't worry. I have come armed with a bulging wallet.'

'And I have come armed with a present that will be equally welcome,' she said as she fought her way to the bar.

Seeing Helen and Matthew, Bill quickly finished serving and went over to put his hand out. 'Glad you could both make it.' He actually felt incredibly guilty at seeing Helen. He had wanted to invite her to the registry office, as not only was she Bel's niece, but she had given Bel the report that had gone some way to proving her paternity. Regardless, Pearl had told Bel that she would not have a Havelock at her wedding, but to relay to Helen that she was more than welcome to come to the reception, along with the good-looking, dark-haired bloke she'd brought to the christening. Seeing Helen here today with her chap, Bill was glad she did not seem to be holding any kind of a grudge. *Far from it.* His eyes nearly popped out when she put a bottle of single malt on the bar.

'Your wedding present,' said Helen. 'Congratulations, Mr and Mrs Lawson.'

She smiled at the looks on Bill and Pearl's faces. It had been one of the best bottles of Scotch stocked in the town's top wine and spirit merchants, J.W. Cameron & Co. She had gone there because her grandmother had told her about the place, which was where she used to buy what she called her 'Russian water'.

'I didn't think you'd be working today,' she said.

'Yer obviously didn't see the new sign above the front door,' said Pearl.

Helen looked at Matthew. He, too, had a puzzled expression on his face.

'Mrs Lawson here,' explained Bill, looking proudly at his new wife, 'is now joint licensee of this revered establishment.'

'Well, double congratulations!' said Helen.

'I reckon that means double the drinks,' said Matthew, getting out his wallet and handing Pearl a note.

'Cheers, pet,' Pearl said. 'I'll save mine for later. Can't have the new proprietor tipsy on her first day, can we?'

Helen thought you could have knocked her over with a feather. *Pearl behind the bar and not drinking.* Bill could probably have saved himself a lot of money if he'd done this the moment he'd taken Pearl on as a barmaid.

As Matthew ordered their drinks, Helen smiled. She would guess that Pearl was just as ecstatic about her wedding present as she was about her nuptials.

Dorothy was chatting to Toby, but was only half concentrating. Bobby had just brushed past her and was now standing a few feet away, next to Pearl, who was taking a fag break and sitting on the other side of the bar. By the looks of it he was congratulating her, bending over and giving her a kiss on the cheek. Cocking her head and blocking out Toby's voice, she could just about hear Bobby thanking Pearl for inviting him to the wedding and apologising for not making it to the actual ceremony as he had been needed at the yard. She couldn't believe it when Pearl smiled and patted him on his shoulder, telling him that she didn't mind one bit, and he'd come for the best part – 'a bit of grub 'n a few jars'. *She was even offering him one of her cigarettes.*

'Honestly!' Dorothy said to Toby out of the corner of her mouth.

'What's up?' Toby asked, knowing Dorothy's attention had been elsewhere, not that this perturbed him. It was one of her quirks; whenever they were out, she'd always have an eye or an ear on something that was happening in their vicinity. He'd often thought she'd have made a good agent. She never missed a trick.

'Nothing,' she said, as her eyes flickered across to see Bill walking over and shaking hands with Bobby.

'Dor, what's got your goat?' Toby persevered.

'Oh, it's just Bobby,' Dorothy said, forcing herself to focus on her beau again.

'Ah, no surprises there,' he said, looking across as Bobby waved a note at the barmaid and pointed towards the newly-weds to show he wanted to buy them a drink.

'He's got his feet well and truly under the table,' Dorothy said.

'Well, I'm guessing this is his local if he just lives across the road?' Toby said, trying to cool Dorothy's growing irritation. Every time she started on about Bobby, she got more and more vexed.

'Not just here,' Dorothy groused. 'Everywhere. Agnes always leaves a bit of supper out for when he gets in, Polly really likes him because he was in the navy like Tommy, Joe gets on with him because they both worked at Bartram's when they were young, and Bel likes him because she likes everyone since she adopted the twins. Everyone thinks butter wouldn't melt in his mouth, when the truth is, he's a cold, hard-hearted man who's making his mother unhappy.'

Toby looked across to see Gloria laughing at something Agnes was saying. 'I'm sure Gloria's all right. He'll come round. He probably just needs to get used to the situation.'

Dorothy scowled. *'Et tu, Brute?'*

Toby laughed. 'Forget Gloria and Bobby – let's talk about tomorrow.' It had been agreed that Dorothy would take Toby to meet her parents in the morning. 'You're sure they don't think it's rude that I can't stay for Sunday lunch? They understand I have to go back down south?'

'Of course they'll understand,' Dorothy said. Secretly, she was over the moon that Toby couldn't stay for lunch; she couldn't think of anything worse than sitting round the table with her mother, stepfather and four siblings, making polite conversation. 'In fact, you could tell a little white lie and say you've got to leave that bit earlier so we only have to be sociable for an hour at the most – and then me and you can go somewhere posh for a bite to eat.'

'Sounds like a plan,' Toby said.

*

217

Dr Eris forced a smile as Dr Parker opened the door to the lounge bar. It was her fault they were running late. Their tardiness had been orchestrated so as to spend as little time as possible at the wretched wedding reception. Still, she thanked her lucky stars they hadn't been expected to attend the actual ceremony – in a *registry office*, of all places.

Stepping into the crowded pub, she immediately came face to face with Helen. *Typical.* The last person she wanted to see was the first person she bumped into.

'Ah, Helen! Lovely to see you.' Dr Eris embraced the woman she despised and gave her an air kiss.

Helen forced herself to smile at the woman she loathed. 'Claire, how are you? Lovely to see you. And so good you could make it. John says you're all working round the clock?'

Dr Eris felt herself bristle at the reminder that the woman who could give most Hollywood sex sirens a run for their money was friends with the man she planned on marrying. As soon as possible. 'Well, he'd be right there. John's lot are overrun with war casualties, and at the asylum we are seeing quite a substantial increase in the wounds to men's minds.' She lowered her voice. 'Not that we're meant to broadcast the fact, but I know you are very discreet.'

Helen nodded, feeling that Dr Eris was leading up to something else. Something unrelated to the bodies or minds of their patients. Glancing at Matthew and John, who were standing next to them, she caught the word 'Bucharest' and knew they were engaging in war talk. Earlier on in the week the papers had been full of reports about the bombing of the Romanian capital, which had had limited success and had led to the deaths of thousands of civilians living near the railroads they were targeting.

'So, tell me,' said Claire, drawing Helen's attention back to their own conversation, 'I believe there is another reason you have become somewhat of a regular visitor to Ryhope – apart from seeing John, of course.'

'You might be right,' Helen said, tentatively. She was reluctant to tell Claire anything until she was aware of exactly what she knew.

'You're sounding very mysterious,' said Claire, a twinkle in her eye. 'Would I be overstepping the mark in asking who it is you are visiting?'

'Oh, it's a very old and very distant relative,' Helen said, looking over Claire's shoulder, desperate for a distraction and overjoyed to see Polly come into view with Artie on her hip.

'Oh, look!' she said, loud enough to stop John and Matthew chatting. 'Here's Polly – with Artie!'

'Excellent!' said Dr Parker, glad of the excuse to break away from Matthew. The man was annoyingly perfect. 'I'd best say hello to my godson – my, hasn't he grown!'

'Stay here,' said Helen, desperate to extract herself from any more probing questions from Claire. 'I shall bring mother and son over and we can all "ooh and aah" to our heart's content.' And with that Helen put down her drink and squeezed her way through the busy pub to fetch Polly and Artie.

As she watched Helen weaving her way through the wedding guests, waving at Polly to get her attention, Claire's mind started to whirr as she thought again about Helen's regular visits to Ryhope. *Very old and very distant.* Miss Girling wasn't that old. She might be in her sixties, but she looked well for her age, more like fifty. And distant? Perhaps. Perhaps not. When Denise had told her about John pulling her up on her failure to pass on Helen's message, it had put paid to her attempts at scuppering the frequency of Helen and John's cosy little get-togethers in the canteen. She had been forced to look at other ways to keep the pair apart, which had led her to think not only about how she could limit the regularity of their rendezvous, but about how to take Helen out of the game altogether. She'd realised that she needed to find some kind of leverage that she could use to force Helen to cool her friendship with John; she'd need to do some digging, but she was confident she would find something. Everyone had secrets. Her work had taught her that. And that was when she had thought about Helen's visits to the asylum. She'd been so focused on Helen's friendship with John that she hadn't looked beyond that; she hadn't looked at who it was that was bringing her to the asylum in the first place. Who it was that Helen was visiting.

It hadn't taken much to find out. A quick chat to Genevieve and she'd learnt that Helen had turned up fairly late on Christmas Day to see Miss Henrietta Girling. *One of her own patients.* How was that for a coincidence? And it was strange that Henrietta hadn't mentioned it. When she'd gone back over Miss Girling's doorstep of a file, she could have kicked herself for not making the connection earlier. The stuck-up, blonde, skinny-as-a-rake woman who had been a relatively frequent visitor until the start of this year was none other than Helen's mother. Miriam Crawford. She'd only met the woman a few times since she'd started working at the asylum, so she supposed she could be forgiven for not realising, especially as Helen looked nothing like her mother.

Seeing Helen returning with Polly and the wretched baby in tow, she felt more than ever that Helen was hiding something. Otherwise why hadn't she told her before that Miss Girling was a relative – even if she was a 'distant' one? Helen must know that she was Miss Girling's doctor. Miriam must have mentioned to her daughter that their mad great-aunty in the asylum had a female doctor – that alone would have told Helen. There were no other women psychologists, or women doctors of any kind for that matter, at the asylum.

And John – he must have known that Helen was visiting Miss Girling and yet he hadn't mentioned it to her. Mind you, that was John: the height of professionalism; never one to break a confidence.

Dr Eris smiled as Polly finally made it through the throng of east-enders. She saw Helen head off to speak to a group of women who Claire knew worked as welders. Matthew was making a beeline for the bar. God, she couldn't wait to get out of this smelly, smoky, spit-and-sawdust pub. She glanced down at her watch and worked out how much longer she would have to endure this wedding reception before she could hold John to his promise of a meal at the Palatine.

As Polly reached them, Dr Eris plastered a look of adoration on her face and a wide smile.

'Isn't he gorgeous?' she purred. The upside of being a psychologist was that you learnt how to lie – and lie well. Which brought her back to Helen and her visits to Henrietta. She was pretty sure Helen was lying about something – she just didn't know what. Not yet, anyway. But she'd find out – of that she was sure.

After chatting to the guests, Helen and Matthew found a seat and sat down.

Jack came over to say hello to his daughter and the man he had been told was simply a friend – and not, as it looked to him, a potential suitor.

Although Jack hated to bring Miriam into any conversation, he broke one of his cardinal rules and asked Helen if she had heard anything from her mother of late.

'I rang Aunty Margaret the other day,' Helen said, 'asked her if Mother had decided to move in with them permanently, which she didn't seem to find amusing.'

Jack raised his eyebrows. *I'll bet she didn't.*

'So, she didn't give any indication about when she was coming back?'

Helen knew her father must be champing at the bit to get the divorce all done and dusted.

'I'm afraid she didn't,' Helen said. 'I'll push for more information next time I call.'

'No, don't do that. I can always call her,' Jack said.

Helen gave a bitter laugh.

'Yes, Dad, as if Mother's *really* going to speak to you.'

Once everyone had settled and enjoyed a few drinks, Pearl told Geraldine that now would be the perfect time to put out the buffet. Geraldine forced a smile and disappeared out the back. She had to be nice to Pearl, it was her wedding after all, but since hearing the news that the bride was now also joint licensee, she was dreading the new regime that would surely come into being over the next few weeks.

Seeing Geraldine reappear from the back with a tray of sandwiches, Rina and Vera bustled over to help.

'Food,' Rina said, 'is all about the presentation.'

'And about having the ingredients to make it,' Vera huffed, even though they had done well with this particular spread. Not only had Maisie got hold of a cooked joint of gammon, which had been used in the sandwiches, but Rina had brought some rugelach – spiral-shaped pastries laced with sugar, raisins and ground nuts – which she'd made for the occasion.

Most of the guests were now sitting around the pub tables anticipating the start of the buffet. The occasional waft of freshly made sandwiches and home-made pies had whetted everyone's appetite whenever any of the bar staff had gone out the back.

Helen, Matthew, Rosie and Charlotte were sitting round one of the tables. Charlotte still found Helen rather scary, but was over the moon to be so near the gorgeous Matthew Royce. Charlotte thought he looked like Clark Gable minus the pencil moustache.

'Not that I want to bring work up on such a jolly occasion,' Matthew said to Helen as he watched the food being carried out and carefully laid out along the bar, 'but have you heard about the Studland Bay fiasco?'

Helen and Rosie nodded solemnly. Word had gone round that on Tuesday a trial run of Duplex Drive amphibious landing tanks had run into difficulty, six of them sinking when conditions were affected by a sudden change in the weather and wind velocity.

'At least we know the tanks shouldn't be unloaded too far away from the beach,' Helen said. 'They'll need to be released in shallower water.'

All their minds were on the LCTs that their yard, and all the town's other shipyards, were producing. Austin's had launched the most recent LCT just yesterday.

'I suppose it's a good thing they found out now rather than on the day of the invasion,' Rosie said.

None of them mentioned the six men whose lives had been lost in the learning. They were at a wedding, after all, and had a teenager hanging on their every word to boot.

After the buffet had been reduced to a pile of crumbs, the clear-up got underway. Geraldine was relieved to see that as arranged, the two young girls from down the road had turned up to do all the clearing-up and washing-up. Looking at the pile of dirty plates, there was barely a crust left to chuck out for the birds. A good job she had put herself a plate aside for later.

As the bar was given one last wipe down, the guests started to head over to order more drinks. Spotting John, Helen excused herself and went to see him.

'I saw you managed to have a catch-up with Dad,' she said, sidling up to him as he waited by the bar.

Dr Parker turned round and smiled. Helen's beauty and those emerald eyes never failed to take his breath away.

'Yes, yes, he seems very well, doesn't he?' he said. 'I can't believe it's been over two years since it was doubtful whether or not he was going to come out of his coma, never mind make a full recovery.'

Helen nodded, thinking back to that time. It had been when she and John had first met each other.

'I told him I'd still like to write a paper on his case when the war's over. There's still so little known about retrograde amnesia.'

Helen laughed. 'John, you're always thinking of work.' She looked across at Polly, who was handing Artie to Bel. 'So, did you enjoy your time with our godson? You and Claire looked like you were having a good coo over him.' Helen tried to keep any jealousy she'd felt on seeing them looking quite the cosy couple out of her tone.

'Yes, yes,' Dr Parker said. 'I had to apologise to Polly for being an absent godfather. It's shameful I've not seen him since the christening.'

Helen laughed. 'You're far too conscientious, John. I'm sure Polly does not mind at all. She knows you're saving lives and limbs.' As she spoke, her vision strayed to Major Black in his wheelchair. He had lost both limbs in the First War. He was puffing away on a large torpedo-shaped cigar and was in deep conversation with Agnes and Dr Billingham.

'Besides,' Helen said, 'Artie's other godfather is doing a sterling job.' She raised her eyebrows. 'He's becoming quite a fixture at the Elliots'.'

'Really?' John said, looking over at Dr Billingham and giving him a wave. He knew it must be hard for Helen to regularly see the man who had saved her life but had been unable to do the same for the baby she'd been carrying.

Helen lowered her voice. 'I'm not sure whether it's Agnes or the lovely food she keeps serving every time he turns up that has him making regular trips into the east end. But judging by how she's dressed today, and the fact she let Vivian loose on her hair this morning before she did Pearl's, I think I know what I'd be putting my money on.'

'Looks like love is in the air all round,' Dr Parker said, looking across at the next table to see Angie and Quentin chatting away. They looked as besotted with each other as when he had seen them at the Palatine on Christmas Eve.

'I think you're right,' she agreed.

Hearing Dorothy laugh, they both looked across to see her leaning into Toby, who was putting his arm around her and pulling her close.

'And if Dorothy gets her way, there'll be a ring on her finger in the not too distant future.'

'And then there's you and Matthew,' Dr Parker said. The words were out before he could stop them. He'd had more to drink than usual, which appeared to have had the effect of stripping him of his usual inhibitions.

Helen spluttered. 'What do you mean by that?' Her face was a mix of amusement and incredulity.

'Well, I saw you were both in the *Echo* again the other day,' Dr Parker said, immediately feeling a little embarrassed he'd brought up the subject. *Damn that last pint.*

'Yes,' Helen said, brow furrowed, 'the one taken at the launch at Pickersgill's last Friday?'

'That's the one.' *Ah well, in for a penny, in for a pound.* 'I'm just waiting to see both your names in the Announcements section, although I hope you tell me before I have to read it there first.'

Helen looked at Dr Parker as though he was crazy. 'What on earth are you talking about, John?'

'Well, you know, if Matthew were to propose to you—'

Helen hooted with laughter. 'Well, I think we might have to start courting first. And I can't see that *ever* happening.'

'What?' Dr Parker had been of the firm belief that Helen and Matthew had been an item since Artie's birth in September, if not before then. 'You're not courting?'

'No, we most certainly are not.' Helen said it in such a way that it was clear she was telling the truth; not that she'd have any reason to lie.

Again, Helen laughed. 'I'm amazed you'd think that, John.' She lowered her voice and quickly looked around to make sure Matthew was still sitting at the table with Rosie and a lovestruck Charlotte and was not able to hear their conversation. She mightn't want to date Matthew, but she also didn't want to hurt his feelings. 'You know me so well and yet you think I'd be with someone like Matthew?'

'Well,' John started to defend himself, when actually he felt like rejoicing, 'it's not such a stretch of the imagination. He's not exactly a bad catch. Tall, dark and handsome, and even if he is a widower, he's still relatively young ... comes from a good background ...'

Helen looked at John and thought he was right. She understood why he would think that because he had no idea her heart was still yearning for someone else – for *him*.

'Now you're starting to sound like some society matchmaker,' Helen chuckled. She looked around the room again and saw that Matthew had got up and was introducing himself to Bobby, no doubt interested to see who his secretary had her eye on. He had told her that Dahlia was single and that she had hinted to him on occasion that it was something she was keen on changing.

Helen turned her attention back to John. She hadn't eaten much and the vodka and soda she'd drunk had gone to her head a little. Suddenly, she had a fantasy of stepping forward a little so that their bodies were touching and kissing him gently on the lips. She instantly reprimanded herself.

'But even if Matthew and I were courting,' Helen said, taking another sip of her drink, 'I doubt very much he'd be dropping down on bended knee.'

'Why on earth not?' Now it was Dr Parker's turn to sound incredulous. 'Most men would be queuing up to walk you down the aisle.'

'Perhaps,' Helen said, again dropping her voice, 'but not if they knew the whole truth.'

'The whole truth about what?' Dr Parker was totally perplexed.

'About my life,' Helen whispered. 'About all the things that have happened.' She looked at John. 'You know, men expect their brides to be married in white. To be *virtuous*.'

Dr Parker hooted with laughter. 'Really, Helen, you do amaze me. You're one of the most progressive women I know and here you are expounding an ideology I would have thought you wouldn't give the time of day to.'

'What, you don't agree with it?'

'Of course I don't agree with it. Honestly, Helen, I really would have thought *you* would know *me* better than that. It shouldn't matter about any of those things. What matters is that you love each other and want to be with each other for the rest of your lives. It doesn't matter one jot what has happened in either of your lives beforehand.'

Helen couldn't believe what she was hearing.

'Really? That's what you *really* think?'

'Of course,' Dr Parker said.

'With regard to your own life, as well as to other people's?' Helen persisted. She still couldn't quite believe that she had got it so wrong for so long.

'Of course about *my own life*.' He looked at Helen and furrowed his brow. 'As if I'm going to say it's fine for other men, but not for me.' His laughter this time was laced with exasperation.

'You are the most complex woman I've ever known,' he said, shaking his head.

Helen was looking at John, desperately wanting to say so many things to him, to tell him that she'd been in love with him for so long and still was, that the only reason she hadn't told him was because she thought he'd never consider dating her because of her past.

But she knew she couldn't.

John was here with his girlfriend. It would be inappropriate and undignified and quite frankly, embarrassing.

'You two look as though you're having a rather interesting – and might I say, very *animated* – conversation.'

Helen heard Claire's soft, lilting voice before she saw her. She looked round and desperately tried to think up a convincing lie. Seeing Toby talking to Dorothy, she dropped her voice. 'Just chatting about one of the workers, who, it's looking likely, might well be getting engaged.'

Helen looked at Claire, who flashed John a look. It was a look which hinted that Dorothy might not be the only person expecting a marriage proposal in the near future.

As the late afternoon turned into early evening, some of the older guests, and those with children, started to say their farewells. Seeing Kate chatting to Pearl at the bar, Rosie knew she would be telling Pearl that she was leaving and that the dress was for keeps, but if she wanted it looking after until she wore it again, she would love to use it as the Maison Nouvelle's new window display, along with the headpiece. Rosie found it curious that the pair got on. Rosie wondered if it was because they had both spent much of their lives on the wrong side of the tracks.

Shortly after Kate's departure, Agnes and Beryl left to relieve Beryl's daughters, Audrey and Iris, of their child-minding duties. They were followed by Dr Billingham and then Mr Clement, the photographer, and his wife and three daughters. Georgina Pickering, who'd become close to the women after being introduced to them by Rosie, left with the Clements. Georgina was now scraping a meagre living reporting and taking photographs for the local paper, having vowed to herself that she would not go back to doing private investigations; the guilt of the work she had done for Miriam still weighed heavily on her and she worried the women would discover that it was she who had found out their secrets and handed the information over to their nemesis. Today, she had enjoyed picking Mr Clement's brain on all things photography related, and having done so, was eager to get back home to check on her father, who had not been well enough to attend the celebrations; nor had he had the inclination, but he was happy to hear about the event second-hand from his daughter.

Mr and Mrs Perkins left with Martha, followed by Vera and Rina, who had been complimented many times over for the spread they had magicked up despite the restrictions of rationing. Rina had mentioned Vera's café on High Street East in passing to those she didn't know, saying that it would be lovely to see them there in the future. Vera listened as Rina did an excellent job of drumming up business, making people's mouths water with her descriptions of the special Jewish pastries she made, as well as the more traditional cakes Vera baked, which 'taste like they used to before the war'. Feeling a little tipsy on port, Vera had nearly told Rina how glad she was that she had taken her on two years ago, but not wanting to spoil her reputation as a curmudgeonly old woman, she'd refrained.

Bel was desperate to get back to the twins but had stayed longer, knowing how much it meant to her ma that she had her family around her. It wasn't often that she, Maisie and her ma were together. Maisie and Bel had given the bride and groom a rather unconventional wedding gift by ensuring that Ronald, who was Pearl's former drinking and poker-playing buddy and amorous pursuer, did not turn up to partake in the celebrations. It had been easily enough done by exchanging booze and fags for the promise of a no-show. Bel and Joe finally left when George returned in his MG to pick up Maisie and Vivian, having already taken Lily back to the bordello first.

Pearl waved them all off on the doorstep of the Tatham and stayed there for a moment, enjoying the quietness of the evening and thinking that today hadn't been a bad one. Not bad at all.

Gloria had left earlier with Hope, who had exhausted herself playing with Lucille; the pair had spent most of the time running up and down the hallway that led from the front of the pub to the back. Jack had followed shortly afterwards.

The women welders had naturally gravitated into a group by the bar and were chatting away. Toby and Quentin were talking with Olly, whom they knew a little, and were surprised at how well they all got on.

Dorothy, naturally, was holding court, making Rosie, Polly, Hannah, Charlotte and Angie either chuckle, tsk or roll their eyes in despair.

Bobby was sitting at a table with Dahlia and Marie-Anne and a lad called Hector who was one of Joe's Home Guard unit.

'Same again, everyone?' he asked, standing up.

'Yes, please, Bobby.' Dahlia gave a Bobby a smile, making a point of crossing her long, very slender legs, causing her dress to slide up.

'Cheers, mate,' said Hector. 'My shout next.'

'Thanks, Bobby,' said Marie-Anne. 'You know, you're so much nicer than I expected.' She put her hand to her mouth.

Bobby let out a bellow of laughter. 'No guesses who you've been chatting to.' He looked over at Dorothy, who was regaling her friends with a story that was making them all chuckle.

He walked over to the bar and ordered sherry for the women, a pint for Hector and a shandy for himself. Angie had now taken over the story, which he had ascertained was about how she and Dorothy had come to be friends and which involved some bloke called Eddie the riveter who had been seeing another woman behind Dorothy's back. Bobby thought Eddie the biggest fool on the planet. He continued to eavesdrop and heard that the other woman was Angie.

'I'll never forget as long as I live,' Angie regaled, 'sitting with Eddie and his mates, and this strange woman wearing overalls comes over as if she's gonna give him a pint, 'n she says, "This one's for free, like all the others you've had out of me." And then she pours the whole lot over his head. Eee, I couldn't believe it! And then she turns to me and says, "If I were you, I'd keep my legs and purse shut with this one. Trust me. No good will come of it."'

Bobby had to stop himself smiling as all the women started hooting with laughter remembering that day in the Admiral.

'I thought to myself,' Angie said, looking at her best mate, 'sod Eddie, I want to be with that mad cow – and all her mates she's drinking with. They look a right lot!'

Bobby couldn't help but feel the same now.

He was just paying for the drinks when he felt someone bump into him.

It was Toby.

'Sorry there, old chap.'

'No worries,' Bobby said, 'good to meet you. I've heard a lot about you from Dorothy.' This was a little bit of an exaggeration as Dorothy hadn't exactly chatted to him directly about Toby, but he had picked up bits and pieces from what she had told Gloria during their Friday nights with Hope.

'All good, I hope?' Toby said, putting out his hand.

The two men shook.

'Dorothy tells me you were on HMS *Opportune*?'

Bobby nodded and seeing Geraldine putting the drinks he'd ordered on a tray, he handed over a note and told her to keep the change. The girl had been run ragged all day and looked ready to drop.

'And Dorothy tells me that you're with the War Office?' Bobby asked.

Toby nodded.

There was a moment's awkwardness.

'Well, nice to meet you, Toby. You're a very lucky chap.' He nodded over to Dorothy, who had just noticed the two chatting and did not look pleased.

Toby chuckled. 'And you too, old chap.' He flicked a look over to Dahlia, who had her compact out and was reapplying her lipstick.

Bobby smiled and picked up his tray of drinks. Toby turned to the bar and ordered a round from Geraldine, who had perked up after her generous tip.

Bobby glanced over at Dorothy. She was still giving him a look like thunder, which he returned with the slightest of winks, knowing it would infuriate her.

As he walked back to Dahlia, he caught her looking at Matthew. It would seem they were using each other to make the true objects of their affections jealous. Unfortunately, looking at the way Matthew was talking with Helen, and Dorothy with Toby, neither he nor Dahlia was having much success.

Seeing Toby putting his arm around Dorothy's waist, Bobby felt a stab of jealousy. Still, he wasn't one to give up. Dorothy might well be on the verge of being proposed to, but it hadn't happened yet.

He felt there was a shred of hope. Dorothy was passionate about him, that much was obvious – just not in a good way. What he had to work out now was how to turn that round before it was too late.

When Helen went to bed that night, she tried to read another chapter of *Persuasion*, but just couldn't concentrate. All she could think about was her conversation with John. It was all she'd been able to think about since their talk at the Tatham. Every time she thought about John's words, she felt a searing excitement. Why had they never discussed this before? Why had she just assumed he wanted a bride who was as pure as the driven snow? Helen gave up on reading and switched off the light. All she'd been able to hear since she'd fallen for John was her mother's voice telling her she was 'sullied' and 'spoiled goods'. *And she had believed her.* She'd been brainwashed. But today she had found out that John didn't think like this at all! He clearly didn't give two hoots whether the woman he married was 'virtuous' or not. For John it was all about love. He was a true romantic.

If that was the case, and if he was attracted to her, as she suspected he was, an attraction she'd thought he had fought because he would never be able to make an honest woman of her, then …

Helen's heart started pounding as she considered the possibilities.

But then her elation was felled by thoughts of Dr Eris.

John was with Claire.

They were serious.

He was a romantic.

Therefore, if John was with Claire, he must be in love with her. Mustn't he?

When John and Claire got back to Ryhope, they were caught by Genevieve as they came through the main entrance.

'Dr Parker?'

'Yes, Genevieve?'

'Dr Jameson has just rung asking for your advice on something or other. He sounded a little fraught, I have to say. I asked him if it could wait until morning, but he insisted that as soon as I saw you return I had to "plead with you" to go and see him on the ward. His words, not mine.'

Dr Eris had a shooting vision of snapping the junior doctor's bloody neck. John had just treated her to a very romantic meal at the Palatine, which had gone some way to making up for having to endure spending their day off in a smoky east-end pub. Next she had planned a night of seduction.

'That's all right, Genevieve, don't worry,' Dr Parker said. 'Call through to the ward and tell him I'll be there in ten.'

'Come on, then,' Dr Eris sighed, then smiled, doing a good job of hiding her anger and frustration. 'I'll see you off.' She took his arm and they went out into the fresh night air and kissed each other goodnight.

Heading back into the asylum and to her quarters in the West Wing, Claire realised the clock was ticking and she really needed to cement her relationship with John, especially having heard that he now knew Helen and Matthew were not an item. That really was a spanner in the works.

She was pretty sure that Helen was still after John and that John was still blissfully ignorant of the fact – but for how long? Helen's visits to the asylum meant she was seeing more of the man Claire fully intended to marry. Her misdirection of Helen's calls courtesy of Denise had only worked for so long. Now Helen was back and seeing more of John than ever before, thanks to her mother's great-aunty. Which begged the question: why hadn't Helen visited before, especially as it provided the perfect excuse to meet up with John? It just didn't make sense. Something smelled off. She'd get to the bottom of it. Get herself a bargaining chip before John's friendship with Helen turned into anything more. She was determined she was not going to suffer the same fate twice and have the man she wanted to marry snatched from under her nose. Never again. She really did not want to have to resort to playing the oldest trick in the book in order to get a ring on her finger, especially as she had no burning desire to have a baby. That could only be a last resort. There had to be another way.

She just needed to find it.

Dr Parker hurried off into the darkness. He didn't need a torch as he knew the way from the asylum to the Ryhope with a blindfold on if need be, although walking in the blackout was pretty much akin to that. Striding along the narrow country lane that provided a short cut back to the military hospital, Dr Parker berated himself every step of the way, telling himself to stop feeling happy – elated even – because Helen and Matthew Royce were not courting, as he had firmly believed.

Thank goodness Dr Jameson had called. He'd have to stop himself giving him a slap on the back and thanking him for being an overly anxious, verging on the neurotic, newly qualified doctor and calling him away from his date this evening. He had been thinking of ways to cry off staying over at Claire's tonight. Ever since Helen had told him that she wasn't seeing Matthew, all he'd wanted was some time to think. He'd taken Claire to the Palatine and they'd had a perfectly lovely evening, but if he was honest with himself, what had led to his good humour was Helen's revelation.

Dr Parker climbed over a stile and into the grounds of the hospital. He realised with a sinking heart that here he was again, obsessing about Helen even though he had resolved to stop doing so after the madness of last September, when a flurry of dreams about her had compelled him to go and declare his feelings. He'd never got a chance to ask her if she loved him, as his dreams had made him believe, because Artie had decided to come into the world a little earlier than anticipated; then, afterwards, when he'd again been about to declare his undying love, Matthew had bumped and barged between them and kissed Helen right in front of him. No wonder he'd thought they were an item. But looking back, that kiss could just as easily be interpreted as a show of friendship as much as it could a lover's exchange. He'd firmly believed Helen and Matthew were a couple, but he'd been wrong. *God, if only he'd known that then.*

As he walked onto the gravel path that led to the hospital entrance, a thought suddenly occurred to him. *Perhaps his dream really had been true?*

Dr Parker slapped himself on the head, as though to bring himself to his senses. What was he doing, running headlong towards the rabbit hole of insanity? He'd done this before; he could not do it again. Helen was a friend. A good friend. They had recognised their friendship and how special it was at Artie's christening. And even if she wasn't with Matthew, that did not automatically mean she wanted to be with him. He had to accept their relationship was platonic. He could not give over his whole life to moping after her. After the debacle of the dream, he had told himself to man up and have an adult relationship, not fritter his life away like some sad knight of old mourning for ever a love that never was.

Besides which, he had a girlfriend already. *Claire.* Whom he adored. Found attractive. Was intimate with. Whom he loved. Didn't he?

Oh, dear God! *Get a grip, man.*

Claire was the woman he was with. The one he would marry. Wasn't she?

Chapter Twenty-Six

Easter Sunday

9 April

Dorothy watched from the top of the stone steps as Toby's Austin 8 turned into Foyle Street and drove slowly up the cobbles, pulling into the side of the road outside the main entrance to the flats. As always, Toby was punctual, and for a change Dorothy was also ready on time; the pair had agreed that not only was it necessary for Toby to make a good impression, but they also didn't want to waste a minute of the remaining time they had together afterwards.

As soon as she saw the top of Toby's head appear from the driver's side of the car, she shouted out, 'One year, four months and two weeks!'

'How long?' Toby slammed the car door and put his hand to his ear.

'One year, four months and two weeks,' Dorothy repeated. It was their little ritual. Every time they were together, Dorothy would tell Toby the exact time they'd been courting. Unfortunately, the number of times they had been out on actual dates could be counted on two hands.

As soon as she knew she had Toby's full attention, Dorothy struck a pose – one hand on her hip, the other holding her clutch bag, one leg slightly in front of the other, her body angled sideways. The black dress she had on revealed nothing but hinted at everything. Toby let out a long, slow whistle.

'Well, it has to be said, I'm one lucky man.' He kept his eyes glued to her as he took the stone steps two at a time.

'Come here,' he said, pulling her towards him and kissing her, feeling the sun on his face and breathing in the smell of freshly soaped skin and the fragrance of her perfume.

'That was a lovely night last night,' he said, nuzzling her ear. And it would be lovelier still when they were married. Dorothy might well have an unconventional job for a woman, but when it came to her sexual mores, she was, surprisingly, very traditional – and even though she was no prude, she was adamant about saving herself for marriage.

'So, are you all set?' Dorothy asked as Toby put his elbow out. Dorothy grabbed her boxed gas mask, which she had put on the ground so as not to ruin her posturing, and the pair walked down the steps.

'I am indeed!' Toby said, opening the passenger door.

Dorothy bent her knees slightly and slid her shapely derrière in first, keeping her knees pressed together as she lifted her legs into the footwell. Toby watched the whole process and wondered if Dorothy endeavoured to be as demure as possible in her free time in order to make up for the amount of hours she spent at work, in oil-ingrained overalls and covered in dirt.

Dorothy turned and looked at the back seat, which was full of presents for her family.

'Buying everyone's affections?' she smiled.

'Of course,' Toby laughed. 'I managed to get dolls for the three eldest and a cuddly lion for the little one, as well as chocolate that I acquired from the officers' mess.'

'Well done! But this must have cost you a small fortune,' Dorothy said.

Toby chuckled. He wanted to say that it would be worth every penny, provided she said 'Yes' when he popped the question. The thought of it never failed to excite and also unnerve him a little. He was pretty sure Dorothy would say yes – but you never knew. Sometimes he could read Dorothy like a book, other times not. Or was that just her being a woman? The day of the proposal, though, was still a little while off. He had to get today out of the way, and then it would be back down south until they secured the second front – after that he'd be sprinting to the nearest jewellers and buying Dorothy the biggest diamond ring he could afford.

'And I got a Simnel cake for your mother which I ordered from Vera's, although she did warn me that it might be a little sparse on the dried fruit, for which, she pointed out, two people were to blame: Rina, who she said had raided her supply for her rugelach—'

'Which, it has to be said, were well worth it.'

'Agreed ... And the second culprit,' Toby continued, 'was Jerry – so me and my men better get a move on and get shot of the lot of them so she could show off her cake-making skills to the full.'

'Sounds like Vera,' Dorothy laughed. 'Not known for her gentility or her modesty.'

Dorothy smoothed down her dress and then waved her hand to show it was time to get going.

Toby leant across and kissed her before starting up the engine.

'A heads-up,' Dorothy said. 'If Mum likes you, she'll put her hand on your arm and insist you call her June.'

'Good to know,' Toby said, pulling away from the kerb.

'And,' Dorothy said, 'when my mother asks, "Tell me, Toby, my dear, where did you meet my daughter?", you will not tell her that we met in a *bordello* and you thought I was a *call girl*!'

Toby laughed as he turned right into Borough Road.

'And that I told Madam Lily, when she suggested that I might want to stay and enjoy the company of one of her girls to tide me over the Christmas festivities, that it was you *and only you* I wanted,' Toby said, throwing Dorothy a look of love.

They drove in silence for a moment, passing the museum and turning left up Burdon Road, where the bomb damage in the adjoining park was still visible. Seeing it subdued them both. Reaching Ryhope Road, Toby looked across at Dorothy, who was staring out of the window.

'So, your real father's definitely not about?' he asked.

Dorothy swung her head round to look at him.

'No, definitely not,' she snapped. Aware of her sharpness, she joked, 'Isn't one meeting of the parents enough? Surely you wouldn't want to do it all over again?'

Toby didn't reply, but instead asked, 'You've never had the urge to track him down?'

'Nope,' Dorothy said. 'He can be dead for all I care. I'm quite happy never to set eyes on him ever again. As far as I'm concerned, it's a case of good riddance to bad rubbish.'

'Because?' Toby pushed. This was the most Dorothy had ever said about her father.

'Because ...' Dorothy hesitated '... because of what he did to Mum.'

Taking his foot off the accelerator, Toby pulled up outside the town's synagogue, admired for its colourful mix of Byzantine revival and art deco styles. He kept the engine idling and turned to Dorothy, who had dramatically splayed out her arms and raised her palms upwards, showing her confusion as to why they had stopped.

241

On the few occasions the subject of her father had been broached, Dorothy had always changed the subject. Toby suspected her reticence to discuss him was because the man hadn't been the nicest of chaps, but wasn't sure. Dorothy had never given him any indication either way.

'Would I be right in interpreting that as meaning your father was an unkind man?'

Dorothy's laugh was hard. 'That's one way of putting it. Yes, he was unkind – unkind, uncaring, unloving – but worst of all he was vile with his mouth, and violent with his hands.'

Of course. Why hadn't he realised it before?

'That's awful to hear,' Toby said, taking hold of Dorothy's hand. 'Why haven't you mentioned this before?' He looked at the woman he loved and couldn't imagine anyone being in any way cruel towards her – let alone harming her. 'Did he hurt *you* – as well as your mother?' he demanded, feeling untold anger towards the man who, until this moment, he had secretly been keen on meeting.

Dorothy looked at Toby. His eyes shone with love and care. She wished she could soften her heart a little when it came to discussing her family, but she couldn't.

'Toby, I love that you care so much and are the complete antithesis of the man who raised me for the first part of my life, but honestly, it's all in the past now. I consider myself lucky that he only took his temper out on my mum and not me. And I also consider myself doubly lucky that Mum had the gumption to leave him.' She looked out of the window at the coloured-glass windows of the synagogue, which were glinting in the mid-morning sun.

'It's why I get so angry about Bobby,' she said.

Toby felt himself wilt a little, hearing the man's name, which of late always seemed to weave its way into their time together.

242

'I'm not sure how that situation relates to your own?'

'Because *his* father was also violent to *his* mother and he should be thankful that Gloria's not with him any more and doubly thankful she's with a really lovely, decent bloke.'

Toby had spent time chatting to Jack at the wedding reception yesterday and had to agree with Dorothy's description of him.

'But Bobby's not thankful – not thankful at all,' Dorothy complained. 'And he bloody well should be.' She could feel herself getting irate and took a deep breath. 'Come on, or we'll run out of time and you won't be able to treat me to lunch at Meng's.' She was aware of the fact she was talking about Bobby again, and that it must be getting tiresome for Toby. She wouldn't like it if the shoe was on the other foot.

Toby put the car into first gear and pulled away. As they drove the rest of the way, Dorothy fought back the memories of her childhood she normally kept in check. Images of her mother's bruised wrists, which she'd tried to hide with her long-sleeved blouses, snuck to the fore, as well as those of the purple contusions and welts she'd caught sight of when she'd occasionally see her mother in a nightie.

As Toby pulled up outside the family home, Dorothy's mind wandered to Gloria and how shocked she had been to learn that her workmate, who seemed so strong and self-assured, was also the recipient of her husband's anger and frustrations. It was why she had always felt close to Gloria – despite the differences in their age and class.

Toby switched off the engine and they both got out of the car, leaning back in to retrieve the presents.

Was that also why, fight it as she may, she felt a perverse closeness to Bobby – a strange kind of bond? Because they had both witnessed the suffering of their mothers?

As they walked up the stone steps to the front door, Dorothy forced away all thoughts of her father and Gloria and

Bobby and turned to the man she would marry, giving him her most dazzling smile.

'What is it you say? Into the fray?' She kissed Toby quickly on the lips and whispered, 'Good luck. I think you're going to need it.'

When Dorothy wished him good luck, Toby had thought she was being her usual over-the-top self, but he was soon proved wrong. The moment they stepped over the threshold, he entered a world of chaos. He was greeted by four young girls all screaming with excitement as they were handed their presents, all demanding Toby's attention and asking him question after question: *What did the various colourful stripes on his uniform mean? Could they try his cap on? Had he killed anyone?* It was a never-ending stream, and then there was Dorothy's mother, who was a lovely woman but who seemed incapable of holding down a conversation. She would ask him a question or he would her, as she poured another cup of tea, and then one or other of the girls would tug her skirt or start fighting and by the time her attention was back on her guest they had both forgotten what it was they were talking about.

Dorothy's stepfather was affable enough. He liked to speak about himself, and Toby learnt that he was high up on the board of a company that owned a number of collieries in the north-east. His accent told Toby he had been privately educated, as did his innate confidence. They chatted about the government's move to allow those who were eighteen years old and older to opt to do coal-mining work rather than go to war, and how the coal ration had been dropped to four hundredweight per month. Toby had not been able to stop his vision flickering towards the fireplace in the dining room, which was stacked up, with a full scuttle to the side.

If Toby was honest, he didn't take to the man. He hadn't picked up anything untoward or nasty, not a hint of any likeness to his predecessor, but he just left Toby feeling neither wanted nor unwanted. He could totally understand why Dorothy did not seem to have any kind of feeling for him. Still, it was a happy atmosphere – despite both parents' comments showing their disapproval of the war work Dorothy had chosen to do.

Mrs Williams, or June as she had insisted he call her, was obviously devoted to her girls, if not also run ragged by them; each one clearly had her wrapped around their little finger. Dorothy was more or less ignored for the duration, which enlightened Toby further and explained why she was such an attention-seeker. Toby guessed that as much as June might want to be a mother to her eldest daughter, she simply didn't have the energy. The needs of her younger children usurped any claim Dorothy might have on her time and attention.

As they got up to leave, Toby found himself on his own with Mr Williams, who had not been as keen as his wife to disclose his first name. The room suddenly became quiet and it was only then that Toby realised June and her five daughters had disappeared.

'You know Dorothy's not mine, I take it?' he asked Toby.

'I do indeed, Mr Williams,' said Toby, holding his cap against his uniform, which the hotel laundry had pressed for him this morning.

'And I'm sure I don't need to tell you that Dorothy is very much her own woman.'

Toby nodded.

'And as I'm sure you've guessed, Mrs Williams and I were not at all happy about her taking rooms in town with the coal miner's daughter, but she went ahead and did it anyway.'

The smile faded from Toby's face. He did not like the slight nuance in Mr Williams's tone when he referred to Angie, nor that he did not mention her by name.

'So, if your intentions are as I believe them to be, then Dorothy will do what she likes regardless of what her mother or I might say.'

Toby continued to stand shoulders back, one hand by his side, the other holding his cap.

'But for what it's worth, I have to say we are both beyond relieved that Dorothy has not brought some ship-yard worker to our doorstep, and despite the people she is clearly mixing with down at that yard, has somehow managed to find herself a suitable match.'

Toby would have given anything to tell this stuffy, pretentious man that his stepdaughter had met her 'suitable match' in a bordello, only half a mile from where they were now standing.

Toby waited a few beats until he was sure Mr Williams had finished his spiel and then put out his hand. 'That's good. Good to hear, Mr Williams,' he said.

The two men exchanged a firm handshake. There was something about it that made Toby feel uncomfortable, as though they had just agreed some kind of business deal, rather than made a simple gesture of farewell. The rebellious part of him wanted to explain that he hadn't come here seeking permission to marry his stepdaughter, but as a politeness before he asked the only person he should be asking – Dorothy.

As he walked back into the hallway to say goodbye to the rest of the family, Toby thought of his own parents. He knew they'd love Dorothy to bits and that she would love them. His mother and father were, thankfully, totally non-judgemental and unprejudiced. He'd told them all about Dorothy and they had been genuinely excited about meeting her; his mother, in particular, was in awe that any woman – never mind one from a well-to-do background – would choose to work in a shipyard.

What a shame Dorothy's own family did not feel the same.

Chapter Twenty-Seven

For the rest of April, preparations for the invasion of Europe continued – both covertly and overtly. At home and abroad. In the biggest shipbuilding town in the world, there was at least one launch a week, sometimes two. Mr Havelock would regularly make an appearance, making sure his photograph appeared in the local paper. Helen would ring ahead if she was expected to attend, and if she got wind that her grandfather was to be there, she had a well-rehearsed lie that served as a believable excuse.

Short Brothers launched *Empire Pendennis*, Doxford's *Welsh Prince* and *Trevose*, Bartram's *Stanrealm* and Pickersgill's another LCT before the month was out. The need to get all types of vessels down the ways as quickly as possible had never seemed as strong as it did now. The whole country could not fail but be spurred on by the number of U-boats and Japanese destroyers that were either torpedoed or bombed by Allied forces, with the number of losses at the hands of the Axis minimal in comparison. The tally proved the Battle of the Atlantic was well on its way to being won.

A similar picture was also emerging with the number of air raids being carried out on Germany and other occupied territories, including a carpet-bombing of the Yugoslavian capital of Belgrade and air raids on Romania taking place for the first time from bases in Italy. On Hitler's fifty-fifth birthday on 20 April, the RAF gifted him 4,500 tons of bombs, which were dropped on the Fatherland, setting a new record for a single air raid.

In South East Asia, the tide of war was also turning, with the Japanese making a gradual retreat from India back into Burma. The Russians, meanwhile, were making headway in Ukraine, liberating large parts of the country, as well as in Crimea, where the Germans were being forced to withdraw their troops.

Polly added to the good news when she read the women welders her most recent letter from Tommy, which told of the first lot of repatriates – more than a thousand – arriving back in Gibraltar. Four years had passed since more than ten thousand men, women and children had been evacuated to London, Jamaica and Madeira. It was now deemed safe enough for them to return, which added to the anticipation that victory was on the horizon. A sense that was further bolstered as the country was flooded with hundreds of thousands of American troops, most of whom were housed in temporary camps in the south-west of England.

'Oversexed, overpaid and over here!' Dorothy whooped with laughter.

'Dinnit get too excited, Dor,' Angie jibed. 'They might be *over here*, but they're not *up here*.'

Dorothy pulled a clown's sad face.

'I don't know why you're pulling a face,' Gloria said, 'you've got Toby, haven't yer?'

'Yeah,' Angie laughed. 'One not enough?'

'No harm in looking, is there?' Dorothy said, putting on her hoity-toity voice.

Rosie, Gloria and Polly looked at each other and shook their heads, although they too were smiling – not at the thought of all those young Americans, but because of a rising sense of triumph, for the accumulation of such a huge number of troops could only increase the odds that the war would be won and the men they loved would finally come home.

It was because of the need to do their bit that the women's personal lives were increasingly put on the back burner thanks to overtime and Rosie's gentle but persistent cajoling to work just that bit harder and that bit longer.

Rosie's work at the bordello suffered, but Lily didn't make a big deal of it. She understood why – and that it would not be permanent. Charlotte used her sister's preoccupation with work as an excuse to argue her case for being able to go to Lily's after school. Knowing the stress Rosie was putting herself under in her determination to have some input in bringing her husband home, Lily took the reins and explained to Charlotte that as she was still only fifteen years old, she could not risk having her at the bordello during its hours of business. Perhaps, she said, they would review the situation when Charlotte was sixteen in the summer. It brought Rosie a temporary reprieve, for which she was thankful.

A song called 'It's Love-Love-Love' recorded by Guy Lombardo and his orchestra topped the Billboard singles chart in the States and was becoming hugely popular in Britain. Helen couldn't get the catchy little ditty out of her head and it seemed to repeat in a loop, especially when she was driving along the coast road to Ryhope to rendezvous with John and, of course, visit Henrietta. It was the highlight of her week and about the only socialising she did, apart from her visits to see Hope, which she tended to do on Sundays as it meant that she could also spend time with her father and Gloria.

The conversation she'd had with John at Pearl's reception kept playing over in her mind until she could repeat what he had said to her verbatim. He was not concerned with adhering to the social norms expected of their class. He would consider courting – marrying – a woman like herself, a woman who many might think, as her own mother did, had tarnished herself and her reputation by sleeping with another man before wedlock, and worse still, by falling pregnant. This, Helen repeatedly told herself, was not something that concerned John, for he was driven by the heart and not society's conventions.

The only problem, though – the rather glaringly obvious fly in the ointment – was that if this was how John felt, and what he believed, then his feelings for Claire must be purely those of love. He must be *in love* with Claire. Otherwise why would he be with her?

And that was when Helen's heart would once again sink and she would fall into a troubled sleep, invariably suffering the same frustrating dream of running but not going anywhere. Perhaps her dreams were telling her that she was pursuing something she could never attain? Of course they were. But she couldn't help herself and so she kept running – in her dreams – towards a love that could never be, certainly not while he was with another woman.

Dorothy continued to go to Gloria's on Friday nights to see Hope and to be a buffer between Bobby and his mam. It was something Gloria wanted as much as Bobby did, although for different reasons. Bobby had a feeling his mam knew the real cause of his acrimony and, like her son, was avoiding having to talk about it.

Dorothy still believed Bobby's stubbornness was due to Gloria's domestic situation, and so she continued to drop scathing comments into her conversations with him when he walked her home. He picked up some of the comments if Dorothy remembered to speak to his hearing side, but some he didn't, though it didn't matter as he often found himself unable to take in what she was saying anyway. The way she talked, her animated expressions, the many different ways she managed to scowl, never failed to distract him.

He'd imagine kissing the smooth skin on her neck when she twisted her long hair into a ponytail, only to let it go again so that it unfurled down her back. He tried to put a stop to his growing infatuation, but it was no good and was made all the more difficult because he saw her every day at work.

His squad often worked alongside the women welders. It took all of his willpower to stop grabbing hold of her and kissing her. He always persuaded Jimmy and the rest of his squad to go to the canteen when the women went, or to stay put when they ate their packed lunches by the quayside, not far from where the dock divers worked. His letters to Gordon were full of Dorothy and his work at the yard, but contained little about their mam and her new man, although he always mentioned Hope; he loved their little sister unreservedly.

Seeing his mam at work and every Friday night, Bobby wished he could make himself behave in the way he knew he should, but he couldn't lie or fake what he felt. Just as he couldn't hide his feelings for Dorothy. The irony was, he knew that if he could just bury the hatchet with his mam, then this might pave the way to softening Dorothy's heart – make her see that she should be with him and no one else – but he still couldn't pretend.

He had taken Dahlia out a few times after they had met at Pearl's wedding reception, but he had ended up talking about Dorothy, and Dahlia had ended up talking about her boss, Matthew Royce. He didn't know whose situation was worse: his for falling for a woman who not only hated him but was on the verge of getting engaged to another man – and a perfectly nice one at that – or Dahlia's, for loving a man who would only ever consider taking her as a lover, never a wife.

*

Dorothy and Angie had both accepted it was unlikely that they would be seeing much of Toby and Quentin until after the invasion of Europe, when it was hoped the war might end. They took some solace in having been able to spend Easter with their beaux, and they would often remind themselves, when they were on their own, that they were lucky their fellas were fighting the war on this side of the Channel. Neither would have liked to swap places with Polly, Gloria or Rosie. They were pretty sure Tommy's work wasn't quite as safe as he liked to make out in his letters to Polly, and it sounded like HMS *Opportune*, the ship Gordon was stationed on, would be called upon when the invasion of France finally got going. But most of all, they would not like to be in Rosie's shoes – not one bit. Peter really was on the very precipice of danger.

Chapter Twenty-Eight

RAF Harrington, Northamptonshire

Saturday 29 April

Toby walked over to one of the filing cabinets in his office at the new base at RAF Harrington. The airbase was ideal for *Carpetbagger* operations, as it was near enough to RAF Tempsford for liaison, and not too far from the main supply bases at Cheddington in Buckinghamshire and Holme in Cambridgeshire. Toby poured out two glasses of Scotch and gave one to his sergeant.

They clinked glasses.

'To the poor sods,' Toby said, his face grim.

'Aye, may they rest in peace,' Sergeant MacLeod added.

The two men each took a large mouthful, hoping the burning amber liquid would give them a little respite from the terrible news that had just come through: hundreds of American soldiers had died whilst carrying out a large-scale military practice assault, a rehearsal for the planned invasion of Normandy. The exercise, code-named Operation Tiger, had taken place over the last few days at Slapton Sands in Devon, and had been an unmitigated disaster.

Earlier, coordination and communication problems had led to deaths from friendly fire, but then yesterday an Allied convoy of eight US landing craft on their way to shore were attacked by nine German E-boats, resulting in the sinking of two of the LTCs.

An initial count of the dead was over seven hundred, with around another two hundred injured.

'What a bloody mess!' Toby spat the words out.

Sergeant MacLeod shook his head in disbelief at what he'd just heard.

'Obviously, it's been buried,' Toby said. 'There's no way this can become public knowledge.' He had been told this by his SOE superior, who had passed on the information an hour earlier.

'Och aye, nee way,' the sergeant nodded.

'All of the survivors have been sworn to secrecy. They're worried about potential leaks.'

'Aye. Never mind the embarrassment.'

They were quiet for a moment.

'And to make matters worse, it sounds like they hadn't had the proper training.' Toby's eyes widened. 'They didn't even know how to put their life jackets on properly.'

'Unbelievable,' Sergeant MacLeod said, shaking his head again in disbelief.

Toby took a sip of his drink. 'Which is why so many of the poor sods died. Drowned or died of hypothermia while they were waiting to be rescued … HMS *Opportune* did manage to engage – good job she was there.'

'Aye, good job, but a shame she couldn't get the bastards,' Sergeant MacLeod said through pursed lips.

The men spoke about the repercussions of the disastrous operation, how the Axis powers would know they were nearly ready to invade, never mind the loss of the tank landing craft. Shockingly, ten American officers from the 1st Engineer Special Brigade, who had sensitive information and top-secret knowledge of the invasion, were missing. There was talk of calling off the invasion until the bodies of all ten were found, as well as any papers they might have been carrying.

'Bloody hell,' Sergeant MacLeod muttered, lighting up a cigarette.

The two men carried on talking for a good while until, finally, exhausted by talk of warmongering and death – especially lives that need not have been lost – the subject turned, as it customarily did, to matters of the heart.

'Are yer gonna pop the questions to ya sweetheart then?' Sergeant MacLeod asked.

Toby nodded. 'I was going to hang fire until this damned war's won, but after everything that's happened today, well, it just makes me think, why wait?'

'Will ya be able to get up there any time soon?'

'God only knows,' Toby said, taking another swig of his whisky. 'But the first chance I get, I'm off.'

'She's definitely the girl for you then?'

'Oh, yes, she's one in a million, she really is.' Toby smiled for the first time since he'd taken the call and been told the news. 'You not got anyone waiting for you at home?'

Sergeant MacLeod shook his head. 'But that's not to say I haven't my eye on someone here,' he said, his face breaking into a smile.

Toby looked at his sergeant and had a good idea it was their secretary, Miss Sterling, but he knew his sergeant would never admit it until his affections had, hopefully, been returned.

They both drank in silence. It was late, which didn't necessarily mean it was quiet on the base. Many of their drops happened at night to avoid detection, so the place was often a hive of activity into the early hours. Tonight, though, the moon was waning and so most had either taken to their beds to catch up on some sleep, or had slipped into town for a few drinks and a Saturday-night dance at the local village hall.

When both their glasses were empty, Toby sloshed another generous amount into each before screwing the top back on and pulling out his drawer to put it away, hoping that next time he got it out, it would be for celebratory reasons.

As he laid it flat, he saw the pile of envelopes that had arrived the previous week. An agent returning from a reconnaissance of the beaches that stretched along the Normandy coast had brought them back along with some invaluable intelligence and photographs. Toby took a sip of his whisky and shut the drawer, saying a silent prayer that Peter's letter, as well as all those from other operatives in the occupied zone, would never see the light of day.

Chapter Twenty-Nine

The month of May heralded the fourth anniversary of the Home Guard, which was celebrated the length and breadth of the country. The biggest parade took place in Hyde Park, during which the King took the salute.

A more modest affair was held at Whitburn village, and among the cheering crowds were Rosie, Charlotte and Kate. The trio had agreed to a rare day out together, not just because they wanted to wave and show their appreciation of those who had spent the past four years defending the home front, but because it provided an excuse for them to revisit the place where they had grown up.

They made a point of standing outside the old fishermen's cottages, which had been the earliest casualty of the war when the first bombs dropped on the town and its periphery. That had been back in August 1940, shortly after Rosie had been given her squad of women welders.

Looking at her old family home now, as she, Charlotte and Kate found themselves a gap where they could stand comfortably and watch the parade, Rosie saw that the damage had been repaired and the cottages that had taken a hit rebuilt. She smiled to herself, thinking how glad she was that the little terrace had survived. It occurred to her now that she no longer felt the shadow of the past looming over her. It had gone. And with that thought came an incredible lightness of being.

She glanced at Charlotte and smiled. She looked happy. A little emotional perhaps, but that was likely because she and Kate had been exchanging stories from when they were young, each recalling their own days of innocence before their childhoods had been snatched away from them prematurely by the death of parents they adored and who adored them back.

'You OK?' she asked.

Charlotte nodded and then did something she had done only a few times before – it was something she had done while they had watched their parents being lowered into the ground – she took hold of her big sister's hand and kept hold of it.

Rosie glanced at Kate, looking *très chic* in a simple black cotton dress and low-heeled Mary Jane shoes. She looked as if she should be sitting in a Parisian café drinking coffee and nibbling a croissant while discussing the latest fashion trends.

Imagining Kate in the French capital, Rosie's thoughts went to Peter. She knew he had been in Paris during his first stint behind enemy lines. *Where was he now? What was he doing?* Part of her didn't want to know. Just as long as he made it through these next few weeks, months – however long it took for the Allies to claim back Europe. Rosie put her hand on her heart; she could feel it beating at a rapid rate. She was being hit by these waves of nervousness more frequently of late, which she told herself was understandable. She imagined athletes feeling the same at the approach of a big race. Only they weren't risking death if they lost – nor would they have to sacrifice their lives to win, for that matter.

Rosie stopped her train of thoughts in its track. She had promised herself she would be positive. Peter was going to make it. She could not even consider the alternative.

The crowd cheered as the end of the parade passed them.

'It's a shame we can't walk on the beach,' Charlotte said, breaking Rosie's reverie.

Rosie looked at the concrete pillboxes, gun batteries and rolls of barbed wire dotted along the coastline to cordon off beaches now peppered with landmines in case of invasion, something that was now believed to be highly unlikely. There was no denying Hitler was on the back foot. It was just a matter of how long it would take to make him topple over.

'We'll come back when the war's over,' Rosie said. 'We can go winkle picking like we used to.'

Rosie looked at Kate, who was making a face, and laughed.

'Somehow, Kate, I don't think that was something you and your mam used to do!'

Kate shook her head. 'I think I inherited her dislike of all things that come out of the sea.'

As they started walking along the coastal road towards Seaburn, Rosie realised that they had all come a long way since they had been children living here in this quaint, unspoilt coastal town. Coming here today had been a monumental step forward for Kate, who rarely ventured anywhere other than the walk from the bordello to the Maison Nouvelle and back again. The life she had endured after she had left Whitburn as a child had left its mark – wounds that were reopened whenever she saw one of the nuns on the street, or when they occasionally came into the shop collecting for charity

Perhaps, Rosie mused, today was as much about facing their ghosts – ghosts it was time to leave behind – as it was a celebration of the town's civil defence. It was time for the past to stop dragging at their heels so that they could walk freely into a new and exciting future.

A future, Rosie hoped and prayed, that would also include her husband.

*

260

The rest of the month for Rosie and her squad passed in a blur of sparkling welds, sweat and a growing obsession with what was happening in the news. The Battle of Monte Cassino finally ended in an Allied victory, but it came at the cost of tens of thousands of casualties on both sides. A large number of Chinese troops invaded northern Burma, the entirety of Crimea came under Soviet control, and the Japanese retreated from Imphal with heavy losses. But it was the news of a number of bombs being dropped on the Continent and, in particular, on key targets in France, that grabbed the women's attention – it was a sign that the assault on Fortress Europe was about to take place.

Behind closed doors, a report informed those high up in the chain of command that the bodies of the ten missing Americans had been found during the clear-up, or rather the cover-up, of the disastrous Operation Tiger. Knowing for sure that the men had not been captured and that they had died along with the top-secret information to which they'd been privy, meant the planned assault on northern France was back on track.

Meanwhile, the shipyards of Sunderland kept sending ships down the ways. Laing's cheered the launch of the tanker *Empire Salisbury*, Crown's the *Empire Nicholas*, a tug to be used by Admiralty in Japan, Pickersgill's another much-needed LCT and Austin's the collier *Rogate*, while the Shipbuilding Corporation christened the *Empire Tudor*.

After Thompson's launched the cargo liner *Empire Dynasty*, Dorothy persuaded the women to go on a rare night out to Black's Regal Theatre to see the dark melodrama *The Letter*, starring Bette Davis and Herbert Marshall. She also tried to cajole everyone into taking part in some of the 'Holiday at Home' events, which included an open-air dance at Barnes Park and a Sunderland Drama Club performance of *Danger Point*, but the response was lacklustre.

Angie gawked at the thought of having to go dancing twice in a week. Artie gave Polly the perfect excuse not to go, and Gloria said what they were all thinking – that for her a holiday at home meant just that: 'Sitting with my feet up and a nice cuppa in my hands, on my own sofa in my own home.'

Lily and George went to a property sale at the Palatine and purchased a house in Bramwell Road. It was their first real step towards legitimacy. Rosie was over the moon when they asked her to take control of the property since Lily was not, in her own words, 'landlady material' and George was too much of a 'soft touch'.

Helen continued visiting Henrietta – and John – during her weekly visits to Ryhope, just as Dr Eris continued her quest to get Dr Parker to put a ring on her finger. She had decided to take her foot off the accelerator and apply a little reverse psychology to achieve her aim. It had been a bit of a gamble, as it was the opposite of what she really wanted to do, but her instincts told her to ease off and it'd had the desired results. John had become keener to see her and for them to spend whatever free time they had together.

She had been helped by the fact that Dr Parker's frustrations at the powers that be for continuing to refuse to let him work with medics on the front line had lessened. They had talked about it and he had admitted that his ability to let it go was because of the anticipated invasion of France and the need to have doctors on this side of the Channel. He was also making headway in his research into improvements to prosthetics, which she found boring in the extreme, but she put on a show of rapt interest that must have been convincing as John confessed to her one evening how much he enjoyed being able to chat about it to someone who was genuinely interested. Better that he was sharing his advancements with her than anyone else – particularly Helen Crawford. Claire still needed to work out how to get shot of her. Her intuition told her the answer lay with Miriam's great-aunty, Miss Henrietta Girling, and she resolved to keep on digging.

At the Elliot household, Agnes was enjoying having a house full of children, especially the twins, as they brought back memories of Joe and Teddy when they had been babies. Thinking about Teddy always made her sad, but she knew that was natural. There were times when her mind played tricks on her and she thought he was still alive, still somewhere in North Africa, and that he would be walking through the front door when the war ended. It was why she understood Dr Billingham and how a part of his brain still refused to accept that his daughter, Mary, was dead.

Bobby was now a permanent fixture at number 34 Tatham Street, and much liked by all those living there. The money he paid Agnes for his board and lodgings was a bonus. Bel enjoyed jibing him about his two admirers, Iris and Audrey, who seemed to find any excuse to pop round when Bobby was back from work and they themselves had finished their shifts at the GPO.

Everyone knew, of course, about the unresolved tension between Bobby and Gloria, but no one interfered, the general consensus being that it was a family matter.

A view shared by everyone, that is, apart from Dorothy.

Chapter Thirty

Friday 2 June

'I can come with yer to see Hope,' Angie said. 'Quentin's not calling until after work tomorrow.'

'No, there's no need,' Dorothy said. She was perched in front of her dressing table, putting on a fresh layer of lipstick. 'I'm not going to stay long. I'm just nipping round there with Hope's sweeties and then leaving.'

Angie sat on Dorothy's bed and watched her in the oval mirror. 'What's up? You've got a face like a slapped backside.'

Dorothy huffed and turned around to face her friend.

'I've made a decision,' she said. 'I'm not going to be a buffer for Gloria and Bobby any more. It's making me too angry every time I go round there and see Bobby playing the perfect big brother to Hope and all the while practically ignoring Gloria. And Jack having to stay away just because Mr Self-Righteous doesn't want him there.'

'But it sounds like Jack wouldn't be there anyway. He works late just about every evening. Glor says he doesn't get back until after nine most nights,' Angie said.

Dorothy stood up and straightened her dress.

'Well, regardless—'

'I think Glor will be disappointed,' Angie said. 'She's always saying how Hope loves it when you and Bobby go round. Says yer both have her running around the flat, screaming with laughter. Playing hide-'n-seek. Gives her a

264

night off 'n a chance to cook something half decent while yer both keep Hope entertained.'

Angie was surprised when Dorothy didn't bat back a reply but just stood up.

'You're not going to the Ritz dressed like that, are you?' Dorothy looked at Angie, who had swapped her overalls for an old summer dress.

'I thought we might have a night off,' Angie said tentatively.

'No chance,' said Dorothy. 'We're not old maids yet.' She walked out of the room. 'I won't be long, so you better be ready to go when I get back.'

Dorothy thought she heard Angie sigh loudly, but she ignored it, grabbed her handbag and gas mask, then hurried out of the flat, down the stairs and out the front door.

It took her all of three minutes before she was outside the entrance to Gloria's flat. Taking a deep breath, she knocked on the front door. Bobby answered as usual, opening it wide and welcoming her in with the sweep of an arm.

'I won't be staying tonight, Bobby,' Dorothy said, looking behind him to see Hope pulling herself up from the clippy mat.

'Dorrie!' It was her pet name for Dorothy. Three syllables were still rather a mouthful.

Dorothy pulled out a bag of sweets from her handbag.

'Hi, gorgeous girl, I wonder who these are for?' She pulled a puzzled expression.

Hope giggled and stabbed a finger to her chest.

'Me! Me! Me!' she answered.

Dorothy smiled and handed the bag to Hope, who had a quick nose at the contents before looking back up at her godmother. 'Thank you.'

'You're welcome.'

Hope offered the bag up to Dorothy and then to Bobby. They shook their heads, both re-enacting the scene they played every week.

'Mammy! Mammy!' Hope ran into the kitchen. '*Sweeet-ieees.*'

'I'm not stopping,' Dorothy said, smoothing down her skirt and giving Bobby what she hoped was her most scornful of looks. 'I've just popped by to give Hope her weekly hit of sugar.'

'What? Yer not staying?' Gloria asked, coming out of the kitchen with a twist of toffee in her hand.

'Dorrie play!' Hope demanded, going over and grabbing Dorothy's hand. She started tugging her towards her dollies.

'Ah, honey pie, Dorrie can't – not tonight,' Dorothy said apologetically, cupping her god-daughter's cherubic face in her hands and kissing the top of her head.

Hope pulled a sad face.

'You off out tonight?' Gloria asked.

'I am, Glor,' Dorothy said, 'but that's not the reason I'm not staying.'

'Why's that?' Gloria was perplexed as well as disappointed.

'I've decided that I'm not going to be a "buffer" any more,' Dorothy said, her voice chirpy, but her face betraying her tone. She was staring at Bobby. 'For starters, I'm too angry.' Again, the chirpy voice. She looked at Hope and smiled. She didn't want her god-daughter to pick up on any kind of upset or anger. She watched as Bobby played along with the charade and smiled down at his little sister.

'So, I thought it best off to skip tonight,' Dorothy explained, 'but I didn't want my little chickpea to miss out on her sweeties.' She again put on a smile for Hope, who seemed unsure about the faux-jolly behaviour of her god-mother and her big brother.

Bobby tried his hardest not to look crestfallen, as did Gloria.

'Oh, all right,' Gloria said. 'See yer tomorrow at work then.'

Dorothy again manufactured a smile.

'Yes, see you tomorrow,' she said, directing her words at Gloria and ignoring Bobby.

As she turned and left the flat, her face fell. She hurried up the stairs so neither Gloria nor Bobby could see her true feelings. Why did she feel so awful? *Bloody Bobby.* It was all his fault. They could all be having a really lovely time if only he'd make it up with his mam.

As she walked back to her own flat, her pace naturally slowed as she imagined what it would be like if Bobby did as she wished and sorted out his differences with Gloria. She was in no doubt they *would* have a lovely time – just the thought of it lifted her spirits. She crossed the road. Just as the thought of it also left her feeling conflicted. *Would it be right to enjoy Bobby's company when she and Toby were courting?* Especially as she was on the cusp of becoming Toby's fiancée. *Were her feelings of anger towards Bobby masking something more?*

Reaching the steps up to her flat, Dorothy shook her head. She was overthinking the whole situation, getting confused because she was spending so much time with Bobby. She saw him nearly every day – on the ferry in the morning, and they worked within spitting distance of each other at the yard. That was besides being with him and Hope every Friday.

Well, at least that had now been knocked on the head.

Letting herself into the main hallway, Dorothy tried to gee herself up in anticipation of a night at the Ritz with

Angie. Trudging to the top of the stairs, she sighed. It was no good. She still felt as flat as a pancake.

'So,' Henrietta asked once Helen had sat down and they were both taking sips of their fake Russian vodka, 'how is dear John?' A mischievous smile played on her lips.

Helen eyed her grandmother. She really was much more astute than anyone would think. 'He's fine, Grandmama.'

'It would be good to meet him one day,' Henrietta said, her voice hopeful.

'It would,' Helen said. 'But not at the moment. We still have to keep our little secret, don't we?' she said. She looked at Henrietta, who had started to fuss about with her skirt, making sure it was in a perfect swirl around her chair.

'Do you remember what our secret is?' Helen asked tentatively. It was a question she always asked when she visited as a way of reminding her grandmother that their real relationship must be kept strictly confidential.

'Yes, yes, my dear, I remember,' she said.

Helen raised her eyebrows, showing she wanted more information.

'I can't let anyone know who I really am,' Henrietta said off pat, sitting up straight and checking that both jade earrings were still there; it was another of her grandmother's quirks. 'Or who I am to you.'

She paused.

'You know, darling, I've been doing the same for your mama for years – I'm well versed in the art of deception.' She let out a tinkle of laughter.

Helen forced a smile. How she hated to be compared to her mother in any shape or form.

'Good,' she said simply, pulling out her copy of *Persuasion* from her handbag and opening it up.

Henrietta placed her pale, blue-veined hands elegantly on top of her own copy of the Jane Austen classic. Helen knew this meant her grandmother was in the mood to chat rather than read, which suited her fine; she always found it hard to concentrate after she'd met with John.

'Did you know that it was George Thomas Hine who designed this asylum – this one as well as several others in the country?'

Helen shook her head.

'And it was built over the first five years of the 1890s. It is a prime example of what is known as a compact arrow echelon plan.' Henrietta recited the words as though reading them from a book. 'But what is really interesting is that in his time Mr Hine was a progressive. He wanted his designs to help the patients, so, in the case of this particular asylum, he built it on a hill so that those inside could see life beyond their present – to see hope beyond the walls behind which they were incarcerated.'

'That's really fascinating. This Mr Hine sounds like he was a good man.' Helen looked at her grandmother, thinking how the asylum had become Henrietta's world.

'Do you think you might like to leave this place sometime in the future?' she probed tentatively. It was something she had wanted to put to her grandmother for a while.

Helen watched as Henrietta's face changed and became sombre. She took a sip of water and placed it carefully back on the coaster. She did not like the tumbler to have any contact with the tabletop.

'No, my dear,' Henrietta said.

Helen saw a terrible sadness in her grandmother's big brown eyes. She had never seen her look so sad, or so serious.

'Can I ask why not?' Helen enquired, leaning forward a little, concentrating on her grandma's very pretty, albeit heavily made-up face.

'I have to stay here. It's my punishment,' Henrietta said simply.

'Punishment for what?' Helen asked, perturbed.

Suddenly the bell rang out for the end of visiting hours, making Helen jump.

'Punishment for what?' she repeated. She had to know before she left.

'For being so stupid,' Henrietta said, her lips pursed. 'I should have known. Should have known what he was doing. But I was stupid. Stupid. Stupid. Stupid.'

Helen knew her grandmother was talking about her grandfather; it was a subject they tended not to touch upon. Seeing how upset Henrietta was becoming, she took her hand and could feel it shaking.

'You're not stupid, Grandmama. Don't get upset.' She sucked back her anger. 'It's him that needs punishing.'

The bell rang again.

Helen stood up. She could have cried. But she didn't. Instead, she got up and put her arms around her grandmother and hugged her tightly.

Dr Parker sat on the wooden bench outside the asylum. It was late and dark. He had just dropped off one of his patients – a wounded soldier whom he believed to be suffering from something akin to shell shock. The poor soul had not slept since he came in, but worse still, he had not said a single word. Claire had agreed he was suffering from what was now being referred to as 'post-concussional syndrome'.

Claire had told John that she'd meet him for a walk in the grounds once she'd got her new patient settled in and John had told her not to worry how long she was. He'd finished his shift and was happy to sit outside and enjoy the peace and quiet. It had been a frantic day.

Watching Claire as she dealt with the young army private, he had been filled with admiration. She was such an amazing woman – so empathetic and kind. And they gelled together so well. She was even as passionate about improving prosthetics as he was – well, almost. And there was no doubting that the physical attraction was there.

And yet still Helen was not far from his thoughts. He'd seen her earlier on this evening for their usual catch-up before her visit with Henrietta and as always the time had flown and he'd been left with the feeling that they hadn't had long enough. Saying farewell to Helen always felt such a wrench. They hadn't mentioned the conversation they'd had about love and marriage since the day of Pearl's wedding almost two months ago, but it was still playing heavily on his mind. Helen had obviously believed he was of the opinion that a woman should walk down the aisle in white, which had got him thinking: if Helen *had* harboured feelings for him in the past, she would never have allowed herself to make him aware of how she felt, believing he would not want to court a woman who was 'sullied', to quote that awful mother of hers. *Did Helen have feelings for him that weren't purely platonic?* Or was he simply reading far too much into the situation and it was his way of allowing himself to hang on to his delusion that Helen might reciprocate his feelings?

One thing was clear: he needed to know either way before he asked for Claire's hand in marriage. It was the only way forward. The only way to move on with his life. He just had to pick the right time. And it had to be soon.

Gloria felt the brush of lips on hers and opened her eyes to see Jack smiling down at her.

'Sorry I'm late,' he said. 'We had a few problems at the yard to deal with.'

Gloria pushed herself up from the settee. The last thing she remembered was listening to the news on the BBC Home Service.

'Nothing serious, I hope?' Gloria said.

'There was an accident at the yard.' Seeing the look on Gloria's face, he quickly added, 'Not fatal – thank God.'

'What happened?' Gloria sat up.

'One of the platers' helpers sliced the tip of his thumb clean off.'

Gloria grimaced. During her time at the yard she had seen a surprising number of similar accidents.

'Is he all right?'

'There was a lot of blood, but he'll live. One of the men took him to the Royal. I'm guessing stitches and a week or so off work. I'll hear tomorrow how he's got on.'

'Let me make a nice cuppa.' Gloria started to get up.

'No, stay there, I'll get it. I'll just pop my head in and say goodnight to cheeky chops. She been all right?'

'She's been a dream,' Gloria said, 'but then it *is* Friday, which is spoil-Hope-rotten night.'

Jack smiled as he looked down to see a solitary toffee in the middle of the table beside a piece of paper with a scrawl of orange crayon on it, which he guessed indicated the lone offering was his.

'Although her fairy godmother didn't stop this evening.' Gloria raised her eyebrows.

'Really?' Jack asked, popping the toffee in his mouth.

'She says she's not going to be a buffer between me and Bobby any more.'

'Good for her,' he said through a mouthful of toffee. ''Bout time you two sorted yourselves out.'

'I know, yer right,' said Gloria. She knew she should be more proactive and force the issue with Bobby to clear the air, but she kept finding excuses not to.

After checking on Hope, who was fast asleep, Jack came back into the living area to find Gloria had gone into the kitchen to make the tea. He went in, put his arms around her and kissed her.

'Yer do know the way to a man's heart.' He kissed her again and smiled.

'Well, yer easily pleased if a simple cuppa does the trick,' Gloria laughed.

They took their cups and saucers and settled back in the lounge on the sofa.

'There was also another reason I was late back,' Jack said, taking a sup of his tea.

Gloria eyed him.

'I rang Angus and asked to speak to Miriam,' he said.

'Really?' Gloria was surprised. She knew Jack was getting irritated by the lack of any kind of communication from his wife – but she hadn't thought he'd ring her. He could barely say her name, never mind speak to her in person.

'I've waited long enough for this bloody divorce to come through.'

'And did yer speak to her? Or should I say, *would she speak to you*?'

Jack let out a sigh. 'No, I didn't. Apparently, she's having an extended break at some kind of health spa and they're not sure when she's due back.'

'And do you think that was the truth?' Gloria asked. 'Do they have health spas in Scotland? And if they do, would they be open? In the middle of a world war?'

Jack put his cup and saucer down on the coffee table and looked at the woman he couldn't wait to make his wife.

'Now you've put it like that, I'm not sure.' He eyed Gloria. 'You are one suspicious woman.'

'Only when it comes to Miriam,' she said. 'I just don't trust that woman as far as I could throw her.'

Chapter Thirty-One

Monday 5 June

Peter was sitting at the kitchen table with his radio operator and courier, as well as three soldiers from the French Resistance. They were all sipping coffee, buoyed up at having just heard that Rome had fallen to the Allies. Their talk had turned to the new provisional French government, and the daily bombings of gun batteries now taking place along the Normandy coastline and the Cherbourg peninsula. It was clear the invasion was imminent.

Perhaps because of this, Peter had been feeling particularly reflective, thinking back to his initial training at Wanborough. He'd really had no idea when Toby had recruited him to work for the SOE that his life would change so completely. Looking back at that time was like viewing another life. Another existence. Back then, he'd believed his work as a detective sergeant for the Borough Police – his dealings with a vast array of shady characters, ruthless career criminals and those who abused others for their own satisfaction – had taught him just about all there was to know about life. That and the slow death of his first wife, of course. He'd thought he'd experienced for himself how cruel life could be. Nothing, though, could have prepared him for what he had seen since he'd been dropped behind enemy lines.

He hoped that the lives of those he knew from both the SOE and the French Resistance, with whom he and his unit had worked so closely, had not been sacrificed in vain, and that they could one day be hailed as the heroes and heroines they truly were. And he hoped if his own life were also given over to the cause, its loss would be compensated for by victory.

Seeing that it was just a few minutes before eight thirty, Peter leant over and switched on the wireless. The room immediately fell silent as they waited to hear the dulcet tones of Franck Bauer, one of the recognisable voices of the London-based radio station that broadcast in French to Nazi-occupied France. Operated by the Free French, its aim was to counter German propaganda broadcasts and send coded messages.

One of Peter's men, Jacques, stood up and went over to the window, moving the wooden shutters slightly to check for any unwanted visitors. It was illegal to listen to *Radio Londres* – anyone caught would be punished with a fine and a prison sentence or sent to a concentration camp. The populace had become very wary of *la Milice*, the ruthless Vichy French militia who were known for snooping at doors to catch people tuning into broadcasts. The kitchen was so quiet you could hear a pin drop. A sense of expectation hung heavy in the air. Four days earlier, they had listened to the opening lines of Paul Verlaine's poem *'Chanson d'automne'*: *'Les sanglots longs/ Des violons/ De l'automne'* – 'The long sobs/ Of violins/ Of autumn'. The melodic, undulating words had been read out to listeners not for literary appreciation, but rather to tell the agents and the French Resistance that the invasion of Europe was to start within the fortnight. The next set of lines would be read out within forty-eight hours of the start of what the French were calling *'Jour J'*.

Peter looked around the table. All eyes were on the radio, straining to catch every word through the crackling interference. The broadcast started as it did every evening with the opening four notes of Beethoven's Fifth Symphony, sounding out V for victory in Morse code, followed by *'Ici Londres! Les Français parlent aux Français.'* 'This is London! The French speaking to the French.'

One of the Resistance fighters, a handsome young man called Louis with a mop of thick blond hair, stood up. His chair scraped back on the worn flagstones just as the words *'Blessent mon cœur/ D'une langueur/ Monotone'* – 'Wound my heart with a monotonous languor' – fought their way through the static. On hearing the second half of the melancholic poem's opening stanza, the men turned to look at each other. This was their call to action.

'C'est l'heure,' said Peter, standing up and grabbing his coat from the back of his chair. The time had come to put into action their planned sabotage operations, the aim of which was to impair the Germans' ability to send reinforcements. Their first task was to cut through one of the main railway tracks, then they were to disrupt telephone and power lines covering part of the north-west coast. Afterwards, they were to head to a small crossroads town called Sainte-Mère-Église. Peter's circuit knew that it was the Allies' intention to free the town from Nazi occupation due to its geographical importance. Having control of it would allow a clear thoroughfare for troops going from north to south.

Peter grabbed his heavy haversack which had been placed by the front door.

'Allons-y.'

Toby was sitting at his desk in his office at RAF Harrington, reading a copy of a letter from General Dwight D. Eisenhower, Supreme Commander of the Allied Expeditionary Force. That evening, 175,000 copies of the letter had been distributed to all those men getting ready to take back Europe from the deathly grip of a madman.

> *You are about to embark upon the Great Crusade, toward which we have striven these many months. The eyes of the world are upon you. The hopes and prayers of liberty-loving people everywhere march with you. In company with our brave Allies and brothers-in-arms on other Fronts, you will bring about the destruction of the German war machine, the elimination of Nazi tyranny over the oppressed peoples of Europe, and security for ourselves in a free world.*
>
> *Your task will not be an easy one. Your enemy is well trained, well equipped and battle-hardened. He will fight savagely.*

Toby sighed. This much was true and had been well proven.

> *But this is the year 1944! Much has happened since the Nazi triumphs of 1940–41. The United Nations have inflicted upon the Germans great defeats, in open battle, man-to-man. Our air offensive has seriously reduced their strength in the air and their capacity to wage war on the ground. Our Home Fronts have given us an overwhelming superiority in weapons and munitions of war, and placed at our disposal great reserves of trained fighting men. The tide has turned! The free men of the world are marching together to Victory!*
>
> *I have full confidence in your courage, devotion to duty and skill in battle. We will accept nothing less than full Victory!*
>
> *Good luck! And let us all beseech the blessing of Almighty God upon this great and noble undertaking.*

Toby sat back. They were stirring words. The men he knew were all, without a shadow of a doubt, courageous, devoted and skilled. He wished he could show this letter to Peter and the rest of the agents fighting behind enemy lines. It would give them a boost – remind them that they were not alone, that they might have to fight in isolation from the rest of their brothers-in-arms, but they were part of a team, part of the Allied forces. But most of all, he wanted them to know that they were all rooting – as well as praying – for them.

Toby looked at his watch and got up from his chair. It was time to see the operational group, a team of around thirty men who were about to board Douglas C-47 Dakotas that would land in occupied territory and provide reinforcements for SOE circuits and Resistance groups. The Dakotas would then bring back shot-down aircrew, wounded operatives and Resistance fighters for debriefing in London.

The bodies of those who had died for their country, though, would have to remain on the other side of the Channel.

Just before midnight a complex system called 'Movement Control' was activated to ensure that those about to go into battle, as well as the tanks and trucks that were to go with them, left on schedule from twenty designated departure points. Some men had been on board their vessels for the past week, waiting for the signal to depart.

Minesweepers began clearing lanes while the ships gathered at a meeting point, nicknamed 'Piccadilly Circus', south-east of the Isle of Wight, where they assembled into convoys to cross the Channel.

HMS *Opportune* started patrolling the eastern stretches of the English Channel, guarding against a German naval attack.

Meanwhile, a thousand bombers left to attack the coastal defences. Five thousand tons of bombs were expected to be dropped on German gun batteries on the Normandy coast. They were followed by 1,200 aircraft transporting three airborne divisions to their drop zones behind enemy lines.

At 05:45, a preliminary naval bombardment began from five battleships, twenty cruisers, sixty-five destroyers and two monitors.

At around 06:30, infantry arrived on the beaches, some 132,000 men having been transported by sea and a further 24,000 by air.

D-Day, the largest amphibious military operation in history, had begun.

Chapter Thirty-Two

Tuesday 6 June

'We've just got a late edition!' Dorothy pushed her way through the busy pub with Angie in tow.

'Watch yerself!' one of the caulkers shouted over his shoulder as Dorothy caused him to spill some of his pint when she accidently nudged him.

'Careful, Dor!' Angie hissed. 'We'll get lynched if yer bash into anyone else.'

They reached the table the rest of the women had commandeered. They had headed straight to the Admiral after the end of their shift while Dorothy and Angie had gone to get a newspaper. At lunchtime, word had started to spread through the yard and the canteen that British and American forces had landed on five beaches along the northwest coast of France. Muriel told them she'd heard on the wireless she kept in the kitchen that troops had landed on the Normandy coast and that it was official – the opening of a second front against Nazi Germany had finally happened.

'Blimey!' Angie said when they reached the women. 'We nearly had a scrap over the last copy.'

The women chuckled on seeing Angie's and Dorothy's serious faces.

Hannah shuffled her stool nearer to Martha and patted the two free ones next to her.

Angie flumped down, followed by Dorothy.

Gloria pushed their drinks in front of them.

'Thanks, Glor,' Angie said, taking a sip of her port and lemon.

Dorothy looked around at the women and raised her glass.

'To Peter!'

They all looked at Rosie.

'And to Gordon!' Martha said.

Everyone's attention went to Gloria.

'And to Tommy!' Hannah said.

They all smiled at Polly.

There was a mass clinking of glasses.

'And,' Angie said, looking at Hannah, 'to getting yer mam 'n dad back.'

The women looked at Hannah, whose smile was sad. She hadn't talked much about her parents of late, which they thought might be because of the increasing number of reports making it into the news of the sickening atrocities being committed at Auschwitz and other Nazi death camps.

Dorothy shook out the newspaper she was holding and spread it out in front of her. She was not the only shipyard worker reading a paper. The pub was full of workers doing likewise. It was clear the whole town felt part of what was presently happening on the other side of the Channel. Not surprisingly – they had, after all, built the vessels that had taken troops and tanks to the starting line of what everyone hoped would mark the beginning of the end.

Dorothy took a sip of her drink and then cleared her throat.

'"Deliverance day has dawned. D-Day begins with the landing of 155,000 Allied troops on the beaches of Normandy, France."' She read down. '"Allied soldiers break through the Atlantic Wall."'

'What exactly *is* the Atlantic Wall?' Martha asked.

'Hitler built coastal defences all the way from Norway, along the Belgian and French coastlines to the Spanish border,' Hannah explained.

'"Breathtaking details,"' Dorothy continued, '"of the mighty effort now being put out by the forces of the United Nations were revealed in the House of Commons today by the Prime Minister Mr Winston Churchill."' Dorothy again looked at her workmates to ensure they were paying attention. They were listening intently.

'"In a brief statement, in which MPs literally hung on his every word, Mr Churchill, who was greeted with tremendous enthusiasm, spoke slowly and deliberately."'

Dorothy put her hand on her hip and mimicked smoking a cigar.

'"Reports are coming in in rapid succession. So far the commanders who are engaged report that everything is proceeding according to plan. And what a plan! This vast operation is undoubtedly the most complicated and difficult that has ever occurred ... "'

Dorothy scanned the article.

'"Nothing that equipment, science or forethought could do has been neglected, and the whole process of opening this great new front will be pursued with the utmost resolution both by the commanders and by the United States and British Governments whom they serve ... "'

She paused again.

'"During the night and the early hours of this morning the first of the series of landings in force upon the European continent has taken place. In this case the liberating assault fell upon the coast of France. An immense Armada of upwards of four thousand vessels, together with several thousand smaller craft—"' Dorothy broke off and looked up at her audience. '*Like the ones made in J.L. Thompson and Sons.*'

Martha's face lit up. 'Does it really say that?'

Dorothy hooted with laughter.

'She's being silly,' Rosie said, looking up. 'Go on, Dorothy. Just read what it says. No improvising.'

Dorothy read the next headline: '"Mass airborne landings have been effected behind the enemy lines."'

Everyone looked at Rosie. Nobody said anything. No one had to. Those men being parachuted in would be helped by agents like Peter.

'"Frenchmen are warned."' Dorothy again looked at Rosie, then back at the paper. She cleared her throat. '"Allied bombers roaring over at dawn gave British people the first hint that big events were under way. Almost simultaneously the BBC's French transmission began to warn French people to get away from coastal areas and to avoid road, railways and bridges."'

'Why's that?' Martha asked.

'Because they'll be targets,' Rosie explained, her knee jiggling up and down. 'To stop Jerry in their tracks.' She looked at Dorothy. 'Go on.'

'This bit's been printed in bold,' Dorothy continued. '"Latest German claims are that at least four Anglo-American parachute and airborne divisions are engaged, that the airborne landings in Normandy have been made in great depth and that a *big Allied warship* has been set on fire."' Dorothy suddenly stopped reading, wishing she could take back her words.

Everyone looked at Gloria.

'It doesn't say which warship?' Gloria asked, her face ashen.

Dorothy looked down and scanned the article. 'No, sorry, Glor, it doesn't.'

'It won't be *Opportune*,' said Rosie.

'It probably won't be any warship,' said Hannah. 'If the information is coming from the Germans, it's most likely propaganda.'

'Yeah,' Angie said angrily, 'they shouldn't even be printing what Jerry says.'

Rosie stood up. 'My round, I think.'

'I'll give yer a hand,' Gloria said, pushing her stool back.

'You all right?' Rosie asked when they reached the bar.

'No,' said Gloria.

Rosie squeezed her arm. There was nothing she could say.

'You?' Gloria asked.

'No,' said Rosie, causing them both to laugh – laughter that was wholly without mirth and tinged with more than a hint of hysteria.

As Peter and the two Resistance fighters, Jacques and Louis, walked through Sainte-Mère-Église, they passed soldiers standing smoking or waiting by the side of the road, guns to hand should there be a counter-attack. The village, which he was sure had once been pretty, was now a wreck. The remains of buildings stood with their innards showing. Dead bodies were still lying in the street. Casualties were being hauled onto stretchers. Trucks trundled down the street. Peter saw a Sherman tank that had been blasted and now had two holes in its side the size of Christmas puddings. A few stray dogs were rifling through a demolished building; a sign poking out of the debris showed it had once been a *boucherie* – a butcher's shop. An old woman dressed from head to toe in black hurried down a side street.

Peter, Jacques and Louis edged their way round a group of American soldiers who had stopped to chat to a gathering of jubilant young *garçons* and were handing them chewing gum. Peter smiled at them. The town, which had been occupied by German soldiers since 1940, had been liberated and it was clear by the looks on their faces that the local people were as happy as they were grateful to the soldiers of the 505th Parachute Infantry Regiment.

Peter heard one of the young lads excitedly telling the paratroopers that 'A big plane, all lights ablaze, flew right over the treetops!' The young boy was demonstrating with his arms in the air. Seeing the soldiers' puzzled expression, Peter stopped and translated while Jacques and Louis rested on a nearby wall.

'"And the plane, it was followed by others. They came in great waves. Almost silent! It was like a giant shadow covering the earth."' Peter continued to translate, thinking that the boy was quite the storyteller. '"Suddenly, what looked like huge confetti came out of the bottom of the plane and fell quickly to earth."' Peter stopped as the boy paused for dramatic effect, before pointing at the American soldiers. '"Paratroopers!"'

Everyone laughed as the soldiers gave them more sticks of gum, ruffled the young boy's hair and told them all to 'scram'.

Peter chatted for a little while to the airmen, who told him that it had not been the easiest of victories due to what they said was 'a bad drop' in the early hours of the morning. A house just off the main square had caught fire – they had guessed probably due to a flare sent down by a pathfinder aircraft. The fire had become a blazing inferno, illuminating the sky and making the paratroopers who were descending easy targets. As a result they'd suffered heavy casualties; some were cruelly sucked into the fire and others had been forced to land in the middle of the town. They'd been sitting ducks for the hundred or so German soldiers desperately trying to keep command of the town. Many paratroopers had been left hanging from trees and utility poles and were shot before they could be cut loose. One man had actually got stuck on the church spire, but, miraculously, had lived to tell the tale.

Walking further on, Peter saw that the unit's colours had been raised in front of the town hall, although it was clear that the taking of this town was still precarious and there was an expectation that they might well have to fight off sporadic counter-attacks from Jerry.

Looking across at Jacques and Louis, Peter could see they were both exhausted, as was he. None of them had slept, nor had much rest, since leaving the farmhouse yesterday evening after the *Radio Londres* transmission, but they had achieved exactly what they had set out to do, disrupting an important section of the main railway track, preventing Jerry from transporting troops to combat the invasion, and cutting through phone and power lines, thus stopping any communication between enemy ranks.

When they reached the house on Rue de Carentan, where they had agreed to rendezvous with the rest of their circuit, Jacques and Louis practically fell through the door, followed by Peter. Looking around the empty building that had once been a bakery, it was clear they were the first to arrive. Peter prayed that the rest of his men had made it through the past twenty hours in one piece and would indeed turn up.

Too tired even to speak, the men signalled that they would check the rooms on the ground floor while Peter headed upstairs to check the top floor. Stomping back down the creaking stairs, Peter gave the thumbs up and Jacques and Louis did likewise. At last they could rest. They each found a space clear of debris and sat down on the stone floor, leaning their backs against the wall, faces towards the front door. Peter let out a heavy sigh, which went along with a surge of pride in the part they had all played. They had done it. They had succeeded. And they had survived. They had done their bit to help open the long-awaited second front. This was their last operation together. Possibly the last of this war, God willing. Peter looked at the relief on the faces of Jacques and Louis and knew it reflected his own.

Closing his eyes for a moment, he allowed himself to think of Rosie. He knew she would be proud of him. Despite her initial anger about him leaving for the war, she'd understood. One day he'd like to tell her about his undercover work here in a country that had been infested by evil for the past four years. Thinking of those men – and women – with whom he had worked and who had sacrificed their lives in this war against the forces of darkness, he knew he was lucky to be here now. And luckier still that soon he would be back home – with the woman he loved. Just imagining Rosie's face – of once again being with her after all this time – brought him a feeling of light and love.

He tried to fight the pull of sleep, but this was a battle he couldn't win. In the end he gave in and was just on the verge of dropping into a deep slumber when his whole body jumped on hearing a noise. Eyes wide open, Peter put his finger to his lips and looked at Louis and Jacques, who were now also on high alert. Scanning the floor, Peter saw a trapdoor. *The house had a cellar.* They should have spotted it on arrival. Fatigue was to blame. He got up and raised one hand, showing his palm, telling his two men to stay put; his other hand went to his gun. Treading quietly over to the trapdoor, Peter slowly pulled it open. Taking his torch out of his top pocket, he shone it into the cellar as he carefully climbed down the steep wooden steps. Yellow light pooled over the small area, illuminating a wine rack and a barrel.

Peter jumped for a second time as a rat suddenly came into view and scuttled across the floor, disappearing back into the darkness as quickly as it had appeared. Peter let out a loud laugh.

'*Juste un rat!*' he shouted up the stairs.

Turning to climb back up the steps, he heard Jacques and Louis joking that the rat had nearly finished them off by giving them heart attacks. Peter smiled as he put his foot on the first step. It was good to hear laughter. When his foot hit the second step, he heard a familiar whistling sound.

No, no, no! a voice in his head screamed.

And then there was an almighty explosion.

Peter felt dirt hit his face, blinding him, followed by something heavy and wooden hitting him on the head.

And then his world went black.

Chapter Thirty-Three

Wednesday 7 June

'Hi, Mam,' Bobby said as he came striding over to where the women were having their lunch. 'I've just heard that the ship that went down *definitely* wasn't *Opportune*. It was a Royal Norwegian Navy destroyer called *Svenner*.'

Since hearing the news yesterday that a warship had been hit, Bobby had read every newspaper he could get his hands on, scanning all the articles for news of any naval battles or ships sunk.

'Oh, thank goodness for that.' Gloria put her hand on her heart. 'I've been worried sick.' She blew out air. 'How do you know?'

'Jimmy,' he explained. Jimmy had, of course, given him the full rundown on *Svenner* – that she'd been built by Scottish shipbuilders Scotts, and had started life as HMS *Shark*, but had been lent to the Norwegian Armed Forces in exile.

All the women looked up at Bobby and smiled – all apart from Dorothy, who was getting to her feet, brushing crumbs off her overalls.

'I'll tell you if I hear anything else, but don't worry, Gordon will be fine. And if *Opportune* does take a bashing, you can rest assured he'll survive.' Bobby smiled. 'Gordon can swim like a fish. He could swim the Channel if he had to.'

Gloria smiled too. Her relationship with Bobby might be strained, but at that moment she didn't care; she was just glad he was home, safe and sound. Now all she wanted was the same for her younger son.

As Bobby started to turn, he found himself face to face with Dorothy.

'Now might be a good time to give your mam a hug. She's been worried sick.' She spoke out of the corner of her mouth so no one else could hear.

Bobby looked down at Dorothy's earnest, dirty, oil-smeared face. *God, he wanted to kiss her.* He opened his mouth to speak, but nothing came out. He wanted to tell her that he wished he *could* put his arms around his mam and give her a hug – make everything all right – but he couldn't. He wanted to tell Dorothy that sometimes things don't work out how you expect – or how you want them to. That sometimes your mind tells you to be one way, but your heart won't comply. But he didn't.

'I best get back to my squad,' he said instead, a look of apology etched into his face.

As Dorothy sat back down with the women, she forced herself to smile.

'You two heard from Toby or Quentin?' Gloria asked.

Dorothy and Angie shook their heads in unison.

'They warned us they probably wouldn't get the chance to call when the invasion started, didn't they, Ange?'

Angie nodded.

Neither woman said anything, but a lack of communication from their beaux was far preferable to them being overseas. Like Gordon or Tommy – or worst of all, Peter.

Gloria looked at Rosie.

'How yer bearing up?'

It was a question they had all wanted to ask since they'd arrived at work this morning but hadn't known whether to or not. Rosie was not one for talking about her emotions.

'I'm fine,' she said, before letting out a gasp of laughter. 'I don't think I'll have any nerves left by the time we win this war.'

Everyone chuckled. It was good to hear Rosie still sounding so upbeat. Whenever she talked about the war it was always *when* and not *if* it would be won.

'Besides, I'm not the only worried wife on the planet, am I?' Rosie nodded down at the *Daily Mirror*. 'Come on, then. Tell us the latest.'

Hannah spread out the newspaper. They all knew their 'little bird' was praying for a swift victory. If Europe was liberated, her parents would be freed from Auschwitz; God willing, they were still alive.

'"Invaders THRUSTING inland!"' Dorothy read the headline over Hannah's shoulder. Angie pulled her back and gave her a glowering look.

'Go on, Hannah,' Martha said. 'Read what it says.'

Squinting down at the small print, Hannah started to read.

'"Reports of operations so far show that our forces succeeded in their initial landings. Fighting continues. Our aircraft met with little enemy fighter opposition or AA gunfire. Naval casualties are regarded as being very light – "' she looked up and smiled at Gloria '" – especially when the magnitude of the operation is taken into account. Allied airmen returning from attacks on north France last evening reported that our troops were moving inland. There was no longer any opposition on the beaches now guarded by balloons."'

'Hurrah!' Dorothy shouted out. Seeing Bobby looking over, her smile morphed into a scowl.

'Gan on, Hannah,' Angie said, rolling her eyes.

'"One pilot saw the Stars and Stripes flying over a French town."'

All the women automatically turned to Rosie. She felt her face flush with excitement and hope. *Perhaps Peter was in that town?*

As Hannah continued to read the article, which boasted of the British, Canadian and American troops gaining footholds along the Normandy coast as well as several miles inland, Rosie only caught the odd word or phrase – her mind was on the flag flying over a French town.

It's a sign, she couldn't help thinking. *We're winning. France is being liberated. Peter is coming home.*

Sergeant MacLeod knocked and walked into Toby's office.

'Update, sir,' he said simply. They were all exhausted, having had next to no sleep for the past forty-eight hours.

'We're getting news through that there've been nearly one thousand acts of sabotage carried out by our circuits and the Resistance over the past forty-eight hours. I'm getting reports of huge disruptions to the German forces.'

'Excellent!' Toby said, sitting down and motioning his sergeant to do the same.

'And I've just had a memo saying that Bayeux has been liberated. The SS scarpered as soon as the invasion started. British troops are there now. There's not even been any need to drop a single bomb on the place.'

'Brilliant news!'

Sergeant MacLeod leant forward. 'There is some bad news, I'm afraid.' He paused. 'Regarding circuit Tempest.'

Toby sat up. 'Yes?'

'All the other networks have messaged in, but nothing from Tempest.'

'They might have got held up somewhere?' Toby said.

'A report has just come in that Sainte-Mère-Église has just taken an unexpected battering from a German counter-attack.'

'What? I thought the Yanks had taken Sainte-Mère-Église? Communications came through that the town had been one of the first – if not *the* first – to be liberated!' Toby said incredulously.

'It was, but it seems there was a sting in the tail of the retreating German troops. The place was hit badly. Peter and two Resistance fighters were seen arriving in the town just before the first bomb landed. They were spotted going into a house on the Rue de Carentan, which is where I've just learnt they were due to meet up with the rest of the circuit.' Sergeant MacLeod paused. 'Seconds later, the first bomb dropped. The house they were in took a direct hit. There was no way anyone was walking out of it alive.'

Toby clenched his jaw in anger. 'Bloody hell! Unbelievable! Bloody, bloody unbelievable.' He shook his head. 'The town's secure now?'

Sergeant MacLeod nodded. 'It is, sir. Reinforcements arrived this afternoon. Tanks from nearby Utah Beach.'

'And they've checked for bodies?'

'As much as they've been able to. The town's got eighteen of their own to bury. Sounds like it'll be a while before they're able to clear the site.'

Toby fought back his anger at the loss of more men – worse still, men he knew. He thought of Rosie. Pictured her face when he'd seen her last, unashamedly desperate to hear news of her husband.

Toby pulled out his top drawer and retrieved his bottle of whisky, as well as the letter he had hoped he would never have to send.

'Dorothy,' Mrs Kwiatkowski shouted up the stairs. It had just gone six o'clock and she had heard Dorothy and Angie trudge up to their flat just a few minutes earlier.

She waited a moment before shouting again, this time louder.

'Dorothy!'

She heard their door open and Dorothy appeared, still in her overalls.

'Toby is on the phone,' she told her.

'Really? I'm not expecting a call from him,' Dorothy said, stepping out of the flat.

'Well, go and see what it's about,' Angie said, nudging her from behind.

Dorothy hurried down the stairs. Mrs Kwiatkowski was glad to see she had taken her work boots off and was just in her socks. She moved to the side to let Dorothy pass.

Dorothy heard Mrs Kwiatkowski ask Angie how her day at work had been and knew she would stand there chatting until her phone call with Toby was over. Walking over to the receiver, she picked it up. She was not one for premonitions, but she had an uneasy feeling that this was not going to be good news.

Ten minutes later, Dorothy walked to the door to see that Angie was sitting with Mrs Kwiatkowski on the bottom step of the stairs that led up to their flat.

Seeing Dorothy's serious face, which looked unusually white, they both knew instinctively that something was wrong.

'What is it?' Angie asked.

Mrs Kwiatkowski eased her arthritic body into a standing position.

'Come on, let's get a cup of tea,' she said, squeezing Dorothy's arm as they all walked back into her flat.

'What is it, Dor?' Angie asked again, although in truth she didn't really want to know. She'd never seen such a look on her best mate's face and knew this was serious. Really serious.

Dorothy slumped into the chair by the kitchen table. Her eyes were bloodshot, and Angie could see the beginning of tears. Dorothy very rarely cried. When she did, they were generally crocodile tears. The ones starting to trickle down her face now were most definitely real.

Angie sat down next to her.

'It's Peter,' Dorothy said.

Toby had told Dorothy that Peter had been officially declared 'missing presumed dead', which they all knew meant he was dead, only they didn't have a body to prove it. Dorothy had asked him for more details, but Toby had apologised and said at this point in time they could not give any more information, but they believed Peter had been killed on the day of the invasion. He had told Dorothy that she could tell Rosie the news herself – with the support of the women around her – or he could do it through more conventional channels and send a telegram to her home. If he did that, though, Peter's letter – his final letter to Rosie – would likely come later. Without hesitation, Dorothy said that the news should come from her squad – and that Peter's letter might offer a minuscule drop of comfort. She knew her workmates would agree that Rosie should not be alone when she got the news, nor, indeed, hear it at this late hour.

Just after ten o'clock, four hours after her phone call with Toby, there was a knock on the main front door to the flats. Dorothy and Angie hurried down the stairs to the hallway and opened the door to find a young uniformed soldier standing at the top of the stone steps. He saluted and handed over the two letters. They offered the soldier a cup of tea and a sandwich, which he politely refused.

Dorothy and Angie were relieved. Neither of them were in the mood to make small talk. Angie told him to wait and quickly went up to their flat to wrap up the sandwich they had made in case he took them up on their offer.

Going back up to their flat, Dorothy put the two letters on the tallboy. For once, Dorothy had not the slightest desire to sneak a peek – especially not at Peter's letter. She thought her heart might break if she did. Toby had told her that most soldiers going into dangerous situations were advised to write letters to their loved ones in the event of their death. Some chose to. Some didn't. Sadly, some didn't have loved ones to write letters to. Dorothy didn't know which was worse.

Dorothy and Angie talked well into the early morning, recalling what they had all been doing the day Peter had died – how happy they had all been at work, and afterwards in the Admiral. They had all been so relieved. The day they had all been working towards, the day when the vessels they'd built and the landing craft they had pieced together so speedily had gone into battle. There had been an unmistakable sense of hope that the end of the war was in sight.

Sitting at the kitchen table, drinking cups of tea, Dorothy and Angie talked and talked, as if talking about it might make it better, but it didn't. Angie had nearly started to cry when they recalled how positive Rosie had been. It had been infectious. She'd even convinced Gloria that Gordon would be fine – telling her that most of the attacks were on land and that it appeared as though there were plenty of smaller vessels in the Channel that could rescue those on *Opportune* should she take a blast and sink.

Rosie had been acting as though she was privy to some inside information that Peter would be all right. That he was coming home.

How wrong she had been.

Chapter Thirty-Four

Thursday 8 June

As soon as Bobby saw Dorothy and Angie, he knew something was wrong. He always waited on the corner of High Street East so that he could catch the ferry with them – or rather, so that he could be in close proximity to Dorothy.

He wondered if she was aware he purposely waited for her, or if she just presumed it was because they both left the house at the same time. Bobby knew his habit of waiting for them was a little pathetic, but he didn't care. It gave him a chance to walk with Dorothy and chat as they made their way to work. Of course, it was always Angie he ended up talking to, despite Dorothy throwing her friend scowls of disapproval. Sometimes, though, Dorothy forgot she was angry at him and would join in the conversation. Dorothy, he had learnt, found it nigh-on impossible to keep shtum, no matter how much she purported to loathe him.

Looking at Dorothy and Angie now, neither seemed to have had much sleep, both had dark bags under their eyes and their arms were linked firmly together, as though they needed each other's support. Normally, he would have ribbed them about having had a night out on the tiles, but they did not look like two people who had been out painting the town red. Observing their wan faces caused him immediate concern.

'Everything all right?' he asked as he joined them walking towards Low Street.

Dorothy threw him a hard stare. All her anger about Peter's death suddenly had a target.

Bobby looked at Angie.

She shook her head. 'Not really.'

'What's happened? Is there anything I can do to help?'

Again, Angie shook her head. 'Don't think there's anything anyone can do about this.'

They walked in silence for a while.

Bobby looked down and saw that Dorothy was gripping two letters: one looked official, the other personal.

'Who's died?' he asked as they reached the ferry. He paid their fares and ushered them on.

They walked to the front of the old paddle steamer.

'Peter,' Angie told him.

'Rosie's husband?' Bobby asked. He looked at Dorothy. She had been the one to tell him about Detective Sergeant Peter Miller – the man who had helped his mam and had got shot of his dad. Rosie's husband had seemed like one of the good guys. There was no justice in this life.

'That's right,' Angie said. She usually complained about having to answer for Dorothy, but not today.

The three of them looked out to the mouth of the River Wear, each lost in their own thoughts.

After the ferry arrived at the north side, they all got off and walked in silence up to the main gates.

When they collected their time boards off Davey and started towards their workstations, Bobby looked at Dorothy.

'Good luck,' he said, his voice low and sombre. 'And just say if I can help in any way,' he added, looking at Angie.

'Oh, God,' Dorothy said. 'This is going to be awful.'

Seeing that Gloria and Polly hadn't arrived and that it was just Rosie and Martha standing by the brazier, chatting,

Dorothy looked at Angie. 'You still agree – we need to tell her when everyone's here?'

Angie nodded. They slowed their pace. 'Let's do it at lunchtime.'

'Yes, at lunchtime,' Dorothy said, feeling a slight sense of relief that she didn't have to drop the guillotine onto her friend's neck just yet. It was a temporary stay of execution, though. Whether they told her now or in a few hours, it would not make the news any less devastating, but at least she'd have her workmates there to support her in whatever way they could.

'Just act normal,' Dorothy said.

'Easier said than done,' Angie said, plastering a smile on her face as she wished Rosie and Martha 'Good morning' before declaring that she needed the loo.

Rosie and Martha watched as the group's 'terrible two' sloped off to the outside toilets – something they usually avoided at all costs.

'Do they seem a bit out of sorts to you?' Rosie asked Martha, who laughed and said that they were probably just hung-over.

By the time the klaxon sounded out the lunch break, Dorothy felt as though she was going to be physically sick with nerves.

'Shall we all have our lunch out here?' Angie said, cocking her head over to the stack of pallets by the quayside.

'Sounds a good idea,' Rosie said. 'I've got a packed lunch.'

'I'll just nip to the canteen,' Gloria said. 'I didn't have time to make anything today.'

Dorothy and Angie looked at each.

'Well, dinnit take all day!' The words – and the harshness with which they had been spoken – were out before Angie could rein them back in.

Gloria gave Angie a questioning look. 'What's up?'

'Yeah, you two have been acting strange all morning,' Martha said.

'Quentin and Toby all right?' Rosie asked.

The last question pushed Dorothy over the edge. She felt the urge to burst out crying, but managed to hold back. She had to be strong. Out of the corner of her eye, she saw Bobby and the rest of his squad settling down nearby with their packed lunches. She caught his eye and looked away.

'Actually,' Dorothy said, looking nervously at Gloria and then focusing back on Rosie, 'it's Peter.'

Everyone stopped dead.

Everyone was staring at Dorothy, who had put her hand into the side pocket of her overalls and had taken out Peter's letter.

She put her other hand in her other pocket and pulled out the official notification of death.

Rosie's eyes dropped down to Dorothy's hand. Suddenly everything became slow motion. Was that Peter's handwriting she could see on the front of one of the envelopes? Her heart lifted. *Dorothy had brought news. She had brought a letter from Peter.* But why did she look so serious?

'Is that from Peter?' she asked.

She watched as Dorothy nodded, her face grim, as Gloria stepped forward and took the other letter – the official one with typing on the front.

She watched as Gloria slid her thumb under the seal and opened it, casting her eyes briefly down the page before offering it to her.

Rosie could feel her hands starting to shake as she took hold of the letter. Her eyes scanned the typed words:

It is with the deepest regret that I have learnt that your husband, Mr Peter Miller, a member of the Special Operations

*Executive, has been recorded as 'missing presumed dead'
following an operation on 6 June in France. I wish to
express my admiration for the services he rendered and to
convey my profound sympathy in your sad bereavement.*

She stood staring, unable to move.

She sensed Angie was handing her the other envelope.
The one with Peter's handwriting on it. She heard Dorothy
say something about Toby, and that he'd asked Dorothy to
give it to her along with the notification.

She felt her body starting to tremble along with her
hands as she took the envelope, ripped it open and began
to read.

Dear Rosie,
*I hope that you will never read this letter, for if you do it
means that my superiors have received news that I am
dead.*

*It pains me to write this, but I know it is going to cause
you much more pain to have to read it, so I want to say
sorry to you. Sorry I have put you through this heartache.*

*God only knows, you have been through enough in
your life. But you've survived it – all of it. You kept going
when others would have given up, you forced a smile when
others would have cried, you made untold sacrifices in
your life for the sake of love – the love you have for your
little sister.*

*I know you understand the nature of sacrifice. You gave
up so much to ensure that Charlotte was safe from harm
and to give her the chance of a good life. And you did so
without any hesitation. You knew without any kind of
doubt that what you were doing was right.*

*I too have felt the same about the work I have been
doing since I left you that day at the train station in*

Guildford. There has never been any doubt in my mind that what I decided to do after we said our goodbyes as man and wife was the right thing, and – I can't stress this enough – so very necessary. I hope as you are reading this that you understand. And that you know I have no regrets. My love for you knows no bounds, but it also has to be sacrificed for the Greater Good.

Now I am writing, I realise there is so much I want to say – and which I haven't been able to say. First of all, about Charlotte – I do hope she is well and not making your life too hard. It's funny, but I feel like I know her even though we have never met, so say hello to her from me – and a reluctant goodbye – and tell her she has to be strong and brave, just like her older sister, and that she must now be there for you.

It took me some time to know what to write. I have sat here for a good while at the wooden kitchen table in the house where I am presently staying. It is dark and quiet, and it strikes me, as I sit and contemplate, how strange it is to write such a letter, but also very necessary – for us both.

When I first tried to put pen to paper, I didn't know what to say. But in my mind's eye I pictured you and the times we shared, and as I did, it started to feel as if you were near to me. I remembered the last time we were together at home in our bed and I could almost smell you – feel the touch of your bare skin on mine.

Just writing the words makes me feel sad – not for the loss of my life, but because I will never get to lie with you again, kiss you, or make love to you. But I will take it all with me, wherever that may be.

I need you to know that I have no regrets and that you must not either – for anything – nor any guilt. I have been around too much death these past few years and I know *the residue that death can leave behind, how it can taint a life and darken a future and I need to know that this will not be the case for you.*

It is why so many men – and women – have given their lives to this war: to fight the terrible darkness that will engulf the whole of humanity if we don't beat this evil.

The life we had together was incredibly special and was all that I believe true love to be. Don't ever forget that. And don't ever let it stop you loving again. You are young and life is precious.

But I know you don't want to hear that now.

What I'm trying to say is that the sacrifice of my life and the lives of so many others has been made so that love – not hate – can flourish.

So that the world can be one of light and not darkness.

Please, please don't forsake that because I am not here to enjoy it with you. Whenever you feel lonely, just close your eyes and I'll be there right by your side. And know I will always be with you. And I will always love you.

Forever yours,

Peter x

Chapter Thirty-Five

After reading the final words of Peter's letter, Rosie felt the life leave her body. Every ounce of energy drained from every part of her physical being. It felt as though she had suddenly taken a step back and was looking at reality from a distance; as though a protective see-through curtain had dropped between herself and life, and she was viewing everything from afar.

As she felt her legs lose their strength, she sat down on something hard and wooden and then the tears came. Doubled up, she cried from her very core, great heaving sobs. Through a blur of tears, she looked up and saw the women's concerned faces around her. Hannah disappeared and returned moments later with a glass of water. She saw her hand reach out and felt the cool liquid run down her throat, but it did not seem to quench her thirst. She saw Gloria move and sit down next to her. She looked at her friend's grave face and realised that she was talking to her. Her mouth was moving and her face expressed such sadness and concern, but all Rosie could hear were muted, mumbled words.

She caught movement to her right and turned her head to see Martha lowering herself down so that she too was sitting next to her, dwarfing her. She felt Martha's arm go around her shoulders as she gave her a hug. She felt her head slump onto Martha's chest and then she felt her body shuddering. More tears ran down her face and left the taste of salt on her dry lips.

She saw Polly's face, which seemed to be a reflection of her own. Tears were running down her cheeks, making white streaks through the dirt on her skin. Dorothy and Angie turned and disappeared. Time seemed to have taken on a different dimension, because it seemed as though they were back in the blink of an eye, with Helen in tow.

Then Dorothy was by her side, helping her up from her seat, her arm hooked into Rosie's. She was like a rag doll, her body unable to hold itself straight. She had a flash of the night she had been attacked by her uncle Raymond. The women had hauled her to her feet. They had been there then, and they were here now. Back then she had felt the same sense of exhaustion, of being beaten.

Looking up, she noticed Bobby. Where had he come from? She saw him flash a look at Dorothy. Worry mixed with deep sorrow was etched on his face as he reached for her other arm and helped her to her feet. She was standing, although her legs still felt as though they had not the strength to support her weight. She felt herself move, a little lopsidedly, with most of her weight being taken by Bobby. She looked up and realised for the first time how tall he was. She smelled the dirt and sweat of the shipyard on him. Noticed his tattoo of a dagger going through a rose. The image hit her. She couldn't take her eyes off it. She felt more tears streaming down her face. More salt on her lips. A rose. A symbol of love being destroyed.

She felt her boots clomp on the concrete as Dorothy and Bobby supported her across the yard. She felt the eyes of the workers on her – a squad of platers and their apprentices, a squad of women red-leaders whose overalls were speckled red, making her think of spilt blood. Reaching the timekeeper's cabin, she looked up to see Davey, his big, innocent child's eyes staring down at her, full of confusion and fear. And then Helen seemed to appear out of nowhere, walking towards a green sports car. Her green sports car. She was opening the passenger door. Now there was just Bobby holding her up, helping her into the front passenger seat, then gently shutting the door.

She looked to her right and saw Helen putting the keys into the ignition. Helen was talking to her, but she couldn't understand what she was saying, her mind unable to process the words. The car pulled away and as she looked out of the passenger window, she saw Bobby and Dorothy standing together, wearing identical overalls, their arms almost touching, both watching forlornly as the car drove off.

When Rosie arrived back home, she was still crying – it was now coming in waves, first small, then tidal and uncontrollable. Helen helped her up the stairs and guided her to the bed, suggesting she should lie down for a little while and that she would go and make them both a cup of tea. Rosie nodded. If Helen had told her to walk out of the house and in front of a car, she would have done so.

She heard a knock on the front door and Helen talking to her neighbour, Mrs Jenkins, in hushed tones. Five minutes later, Mrs Jenkins came into the room with a cup of tea and told her to sit up and drink it. For once her neighbour didn't chat on incessantly, as she was wont to do, but simply sat on the chair by the bed quietly while Rosie cried and took sips of tea, doing what she was told without question. Mrs Jenkins only left the room when there was another knock on the door and she went to answer it. She heard voices – a man and a woman. It was Lily and George. She heard Lily's heavy footsteps coming up the stairs and a quick knock before she bustled in. She walked over, took the teacup and saucer off her and put them on the bedside table. She held Rosie's face in her heavily bejewelled hands and told her, 'You will survive this, Rosie.' Then she told her to get up as they were going to the bordello. George, she explained, was waiting downstairs and had brought the car. Once there, she said, Rosie could rest.

Rosie started to speak, to ask about Charlotte, but Lily beat her to it.

'I'll see to Charlotte,' she said.

When they arrived back at the bordello, Lily took Rosie up to the guest bedroom, got her out of her overalls and into a nightdress and told her to get into bed. During the whole process, Rosie did not once let go of Peter's letter. Lily asked her if she wanted a brandy, or a sleeping pill, but she shook her head before curling up in a ball, holding Peter's farewell letter close to her chest.

Going back downstairs, Lily closed up the bordello and drew all the curtains to show there had been a death in the family. Maisie and Vivian, who had heard the news when Helen had come knocking on the door a little earlier, said they would keep checking on Rosie every ten minutes. George and Lily left for the Maison Nouvelle to tell Kate what had happened, after which they went to get Charlotte.

Waiting at the school gates, Lily used the opportunity to tell the group of boys also waiting there that if they ever did anything to hurt or upset her charge they'd spend the rest of their lives regretting it. Running out of the main doors as soon as the bell went and seeing Lily's face, Charlotte knew something was terribly wrong.

Chapter Thirty-Six

Over the next few days, people came and went. Rosie continued to be hit by waves of grief so deep she thought they would consume her whole being. Part of her wanted them to. She cried and cried. Helen brought Dr Parker to check on her. He left a bottle of sleeping pills with Lily should she feel Rosie needed them. There was no need to explain why he had given the bottle to Lily rather than leave them with Rosie. It was hard to tell her mindset as all she kept saying was that she was fine and just wanted to be on her own.

While Rosie was on leave, Helen put Gloria in charge and the women on 'pickup' work, touching up spots that had been missed or weren't up to scratch; she'd done so knowing their minds would not be on the job and that a lack of concentration might well lead to accidents – none of them needed any more tragedies.

All Rosie's squad took it in turns to go and visit, as did Georgina, who wondered how so much heartache could befall one person. They didn't stay long, just enough time to give her a quick update on what was happening at the yard and to tell her what she already knew – that they were there, should she need or want them. The problem was that the only person Rosie needed and wanted was Peter.

Through it all, Rosie barely let go of Peter's letter. She held it when she fell asleep and cried over it as she read it over and over again in the morning.

The day after Rosie had been brought to the bordello, Charlotte came into her room to find the letter had fallen on the floor while Rosie was asleep. Picking it up, she caught a glimpse of her own name and couldn't stop herself reading it. She stood stock-still as she committed to memory every word Peter had written to her big sister – how Charlotte had to be strong and brave, just like Rosie had been. She reread the lines on how Rosie had sacrificed her life for her own, and with tears stinging her eyes she resolved to show her sister that her sacrifice had been worth it – just as Peter's had been too.

Thereafter, Charlotte would take Rosie a cup of tea and a sandwich after school and she would sit by her bed and tell her all about what she had learnt. She would stay there until Rosie had eaten her sandwich and drunk her tea. Only then would she leave her in peace.

The magnitude of the aftershock from Peter's death was far-reaching. Every one of Rosie's squad and those who knew her and loved her was deeply affected. And the ways they were affected were varied.

When Martha had told her mam and dad the news, they had hugged her tightly. Mrs Perkins had cried for a long while. It was only later that Martha understood for the first time both why they had been so set against her ARP work and their relief that it had more or less come to an end. Martha knew that if anything happened to their only daughter, her parents, like Rosie, would struggle with the effort of living.

Secretly, Polly felt guilty. She hadn't told the women she'd received a letter from Tommy on the morning they'd heard that Peter had been killed. Tommy had written full of good humour and hope that victory was within their grasp, reassuring her that it was highly improbable that his unit would be involved in any more dangerous operations. Polly had confided her guilt to Bel, who had told her that from her experience, thinking back to when she was told that Teddy had been killed, the grief she felt had gone hand in hand with guilt. Polly and her sister-in-law had both cried. Their tears as much for Teddy as they were for Peter.

Like all the women, Hannah had saved her tears for when she was at home on her own. Peter, in her eyes, was a true hero. He had sacrificed his life and his love to try to stop the spread of malevolence unleashed by Hitler – a small man with a mammoth capacity for hate. Every night she prayed – every prayer devoted to Peter – asking God for a miracle, arguing that they needed to see that good could triumph and that there was light in a world that had become cloaked in darkness.

It was Dorothy out of all the women, though, who seemed the most affected by Peter's death.

'She keeps saying she feels like she's "the angel of death",' Angie confided to her workmates. 'I've never seen her so down. She didn't even get excited when Toby called the other night.'

'Dorothy's life is about happy endings,' Gloria said. 'Look at all her favourite films 'n the books she reads – they all have a *happy ever after*.'

She paused.

'And Rosie is not going to get her happy ending, is she?'

Helen, meanwhile, kept thinking about John. They had gone for a cup of tea after he had checked Rosie over and she had told him, 'I can't imagine what it must be like to lose someone like that.' She had looked at John and caught a flash of how it might feel should he die. It was an insight that had stayed with her and played on her mind. She couldn't help thinking that if John was suddenly taken from her, she would be filled with huge regret. She thought about her own tragedies in life – the most dreadful one, of course, being the death of her unborn child. And the more she thought about it, the more she realised that she would

311

not like to add the burden of regret to her own losses and adversities. She was edging to a decision – heading towards a course of action she knew she had to take. It was just a matter of when.

John had been hit by an equally strong revelation after tending to Rosie. Seeing her lying on the bed at Lily's, he knew he was looking at a woman who had loved truly and deeply and with all of her heart. Some might argue that the effect on Rosie of losing Peter was an argument for a person not giving their whole heart to another. The repercussions should that love be taken away – ripped from you unexpectedly or unjustly or by sheer misfortune – were too great. He wondered if Rosie would ever be able to recover. It was almost too unbearable to witness. And during the days that followed, he thought about the love that Rosie felt for Peter and which he was sure Peter had felt for Rosie too, and it made him wonder about his love for Claire – and the love he'd felt for Helen. *Still felt for Helen.*

Dr Eris had wanted to scream in frustration when John told her that Helen, a damsel in distress, had gone to him following Peter's death, asking him to check that Rosie was all right. The woman had only to snap her fingers and he'd come running. If anything, Helen should have been asking for *her* help. She was the psychologist, after all. Mental well-being was her domain. What did John know? He was a bloody surgeon. Besides which, there were plenty of other women the length and breadth of the country who were having to deal with similar news. And Rosie doubted very much there were many – if any – of those newly-made widows who were being checked over by a doctor. They simply had to get over it and get on with life. She would bet her bottom dollar that Helen had used Rosie's bad news as an excuse to see even more of John than she was already.

Walking towards the reception area, Dr Eris saw that Genevieve was waiting by the front door. Her young stand-in was sitting behind the reception desk, looking bright-eyed and bushy-tailed.

'Ah, Genevieve,' Dr Eris called out. 'You look lovely.'

Genevieve smiled. She had put on her best dress. It wasn't often she went out of an evening. Not at her age – and on her wage. She wasn't stupid, though, and knew there would be a reason Dr Eris had suggested they go out for a drink and something to eat. It wasn't the first time she'd been wined and dined in exchange for information. She was intrigued, though, to know what Dr Eris wanted to find out. Whatever it was, she was sure she'd have the answers. She'd been at the asylum for a long, long time. Decades. And she had been blessed with a memory like an elephant.

Chapter Thirty-Seven

Monday 12 June

On the fourth day after Rosie learnt of Peter's death, she got out of bed and went downstairs to have a cup of tea in the kitchen with Lily and Charlotte. Her little sister had the morning paper spread out on the kitchen table and she was giving Lily a resumé of the news in between mouthfuls of Marmite on toast. Neither of them made a fuss when they saw her, but simply poured her a cup of tea.

Rosie listened as her little sister read out the morning paper's headlines. Charlotte quickly skimmed through the main stories, which were all about France and the ongoing battles, now mainly happening inland, before finding an article that was not connected in any way to Peter.

'It says here,' she said, taking a slurp of tea, 'that German *women* prisoners are expected to land at a "British invasion port" today.' She read on. 'It doesn't say which port.' She looked up, her eyes going from Lily to Rosie. 'It's strange, but you don't expect women to be prisoners, do you?' She knew, of course, there were plenty in Nazi camps abroad. 'Not over here, anyway.'

Lily murmured her agreement and Rosie looked at her sister with glazed eyes that had a faraway look. She didn't appear to have heard what Charlotte had said.

'And we're being told to keep taking our gas masks everywhere we go,' Charlotte groaned. 'And we're not to let the children play football with them,' she paraphrased the story. 'The Germans, it says, have promised not to use gas, but they might go "Mad dog with defeat and resort to gas warfare".'

Lily tutted. '*Might* go mad dog – they've been going mad dog since the war began.'

'I'm going back to work today,' Rosie told them both when Charlotte started packing her satchel ready for school.

'You sure you'll be all right, *ma chère*?' Lily asked.

'Yes. It's time,' she said, simply. She looked at Charlotte. 'I'll see you back home this evening. Lily needs to open up shop. We all need to get back to normal.' Even as she said the words, inside her head she laughed bitterly. As if life would ever be normal again.

'All right,' Charlotte said, getting up and giving her sister a hug. 'I'll do the tea.'

Rosie gave a smile that was heartbreakingly sad. 'No, you won't. How about we get some fish and chips tonight?'

Charlotte wanted to cry because her sister was trying to be happy for her sake. Again, she thought of Peter's letter.

'Yeah,' she faked enthusiastically, 'I'd love that.'

And so Rosie returned to the world – even though inside she felt as though all life had been sucked out of her being. These past few days, she had cried more than she had ever cried before. She had read and reread Peter's letter and tried her hardest to take strength from his words. But she was beaten. Her heart felt numb. She had no more tears.

During the past four nights, when she had fallen into a fitful sleep she had not dreamed about Peter – instead she had dreamed of the day her life had changed when she was fifteen and her uncle had raped her after her parents' funeral. Her body had been violated that night, and she had known instinctively then that nothing would ever be the same.

Thinking back to the time following the rape, she recalled how she had learnt the skill of shutting off the horror, keeping it boxed up, only allowing it space every now and again, which had helped her to survive.

Now it was time to put the boxes in her head back in their place. It was the only way she could carry on and live this wretched, godforsaken life inflicted upon her. If not for herself, then she would do it for Charlotte. She could not abandon her sister.

Seeing Rosie back at work, no one would have guessed at the grief that lay just under the surface, as heavy as the metal sheets she and her squad were welding. The women knew, of course – just as they knew it was important that they play along and create a semblance of normality. And so they toiled as they always did with speed and determination. During break times, Dorothy and Angie worked hard at being the squad's 'terrible two' with their litany of jokes and jibes, pushes and shoves. As soon as they were home, though, they dropped their façades and with heavy hearts went to see Mrs Kwiatkowski, who always seemed to say the right thing – even if that was nothing.

Like Polly, Gloria suffered from feelings of guilt, even though she knew she had nothing to be guilty about. Her guilt, she realised, came from the fact that her sons had been spared – and hopefully would continue to be spared – while Rosie's husband had not. Sitting with a cup of tea in her hand and watching Hope play in the Anderson shelter, which had become redundant this past year, turning instead into a poor person's Wendy house, she resolved to tell Hope about Peter when she was older – and about all the other Peters who had given their lives so that her generation could grow up in a free world devoid of tyrannical masters and the terrors they brought with them. She thanked whatever God there might be that she had Bobby home – safe and sound. Deafness in one ear was an easy trade to make for his life. And as she thought of Bobby, she knew it was time to talk to him. To face up to what she had been running away from.

Similar thoughts were also going through Bobby's head. He might not have known Peter, but he'd seen the anguish his death had brought to all the women – and especially to Dorothy and his mam. They were putting on a good show, but at work he could feel their sadness. There was nothing like death to put life into perspective, and he had to admit to himself that his mam's new fella was a good man. There was obviously, judging by what Dorothy had intimated, a good reason why Jack had not been able to get a divorce – and it was clear there was no need to worry about Hope. She had a happy home. His worries had been unnecessary.

Lily and George's worries, however, were far from needless. They knew Rosie was only functioning because of her younger sister. And that Charlotte still needed watching over. Her clinginess might have abated somewhat of late, but she was still fragile and now it was more important than ever that she feel secure. They resolved to push on with their efforts to make the business legitimate – to turn their beautiful bordello into what it purported to be on the outside: a magnificent family home. Lily expressed the hope that if this happened, she might even persuade Rosie and Charlotte to move in with them and rent out Peter's home. George agreed. Neither thought it would be good to live in the shadow of the past.

Meanwhile, Kate was busy making Rosie a dress that was as beautiful as it was black. She knew that outside of work, her lifelong friend would not want to be clothed in colour. Not for a good while. Rosie was not one to wear her heart on her sleeve, but her clothes could go some way towards expressing the grief that Kate knew would cling to her for a long while yet.

Chapter Thirty-Eight

Dr Eris sneezed, then cursed. She was down in the bowels of the asylum. It was dusty, dirty and dark. All her increasingly foul mood needed now was the bulb to blow.

But still, needs must. Besides, she had come prepared with a torch. She was determined this would be her only trip down to the basement.

She hoped Genevieve was right. For a petite older woman, she couldn't half knock back the booze and she'd had no trouble demolishing three courses. Claire hoped the long and expensive evening she'd suffered would pay dividends.

She let out a long sigh and pulled out another deep drawer rammed full of bulging files stuffed with yellowing paper. Starting to root through them, she brushed off thick, sticky cobwebs.

She sneezed again.

This better be worth it.

Chapter Thirty-Nine

Lying in bed, Rosie held Peter's letter to her heart. He might be gone, but she needed to keep him close – at least his words and his memory. Tonight, as she did every night, she replayed in her head the film of their love affair, starting with how she had met Peter when he came to inform her that her uncle Raymond's body had been pulled from the Wear. The image of Peter standing in her bedsit was as clear as day. He had been wearing a smart but well-worn black woollen three-piece suit, with a narrow, perfectly knotted dark blue tie; his manner, like his attire, had been the epitome of professionalism.

Was that really just over three and a half years ago? Somehow it seemed longer.

Suddenly, Rosie's eyes flashed open as a thought occurred to her.

Had that been a sign?

A death had brought them together, therefore was it not inevitable that their relationship would end with a death?

Rosie sighed in the darkness.

Well, if it was a sign of things to come, she hadn't read it, and even if she had done, she wondered whether she would have paid it any heed, for after that first meeting they'd been drawn to each other – by chance and by an undeniable magnetism.

Rosie looked up at the ceiling, knowing that sleep was still a long way off. Forcing her eyes closed again, she brought to the forefront of her mind the image of Peter a few months later when she had bumped into him by the docks. Much as she had tried to fight it, she'd been attracted to this older man with his thick, grey-flecked dark hair and intelligent blue eyes. Then – on Valentine's Day of all days – they'd bumped into each other again and Rosie had agreed to go for a cup of tea with him at Vera's café. Peter had later admitted that he'd been smitten since first setting eyes on her.

Rosie smiled to herself in the darkness of her bedroom as she remembered his confession. She too had felt the same way. The chemistry between them had been obvious from the start.

Their courtship had never been a traditional one – or smooth-running. Rosie had known from the off that she was playing with fire as there was no way that Peter, a detective sergeant, could find out about her 'other job'. Still, she hadn't been able to stop herself.

Rosie opened her eyes and stared at the blackout curtains. She imagined she saw Peter in the shadows. The outline of his trilby hat, clutched in his hand, his coat loose and flapping open as he strode towards her; he always seemed so desperate to reach her. He had admitted later that his attraction towards her was unlike anything he had ever felt before – even with his first wife, whom he had loved dearly. 'You fascinated and intrigued me,' he'd told her, 'and you still do.'

Rosie folded Peter's letter.

They had been together until the day Peter had told her that he had joined the Special Operations Executive. Rosie had been so angry. Every time she remembered that awful night on New Year's Eve, she cringed, recalling how she had shouted, 'Damn you, Peter!' and stomped off. She wished more than anything that she could take those words back. *Had those words in fact damned him for real?*

Peter had left town without being able to say goodbye to her. He had written her a letter, but she had received it too late. She had run like the clappers in her hobnailed boots after she'd belatedly read his words – sprinted to the station to catch him, but had missed him by minutes.

Rosie sat up in her bed and wiped away her tears. Even now she still felt exasperated with herself for being so stubborn and so selfish. She should have been proud of Peter, not furious with him. He was prepared to sacrifice his life for his country and all she could think about were her own feelings. Their time together had been too short and made shorter still by her obstinacy.

Rosie leant over and switched on her bedside light. It was no use. Tonight, she was not going to sleep. Her body might be tired, but her mind felt on high alert.

Putting Peter's letter on the bedside cabinet, Rosie mused that the day she'd missed him at the station, fate had lent a hand. Peter had caught a glimpse of her as his train had left and on arrival in Guildford he had sent a telegram and a travel warrant for her to come and join him, which she had done – and they had married and barely left the hotel suite near the registry office where they had tied the knot. They had called it *their* hotel. Rosie tried to convince herself that she had been lucky they'd had that wonderful weekend together.

Getting out of her bed, Rosie retrieved the special box she kept in her wardrobe. It contained the few reminders of her husband she had been left with. Climbing back under the covers, she opened the box and took out the letter she had kept pristine these past two and a half years since she had picked it up from the doormat when she had moved into Brookside Gardens. Peter had sent it before leaving on his first assignment. She smiled as she reread his words of love – how wonderful it was being able to call her his 'wife', and how happy he was that she had made him her husband – his only regret that he wasn't there to pick her up and carry her across the threshold.

Another tear escaped as she read his words of encouragement, telling her how strong and resilient she was.

How she wished she still was.

He'd told her that if he didn't make it back, she had to live 'this wonderful life we have been given'.

But it doesn't feel wonderful, she thought, forcing back more tears.

She touched a fragile dried petal in the bottom of the box. Peter had sent her an envelope of petals a few months after he had left for France. They were the same as her wedding bouquet. Pansies. They had discussed their meaning – *thinking of you*. She remembered telling him on their honeymoon, 'I want you to know I'll always be thinking of you. When I'm working. When I'm not working. Even when I'm sleeping, I'll always be thinking of you.'

How true those words still were.

Her instincts had told her that Peter *would* return. That they would have a future together.

How wrong she'd been.

And with that thought, more tears came. It was always the same when her mind slipped to the future – a future without Peter in it. The thought of never seeing him again unleashed all the unrelenting, tireless demons of grief. She muffled her cries so that Charlotte would not hear her.

Eventually they abated. Perhaps now she might be able to sleep.

She switched off the side light.

As she started to drift off, she felt Peter's presence close by. *Why did she feel he was still here with her?*

She was keeping him here, in her thoughts – feeling the weight of her love for him. A love that was as strong now as it had ever been, and which she knew would never die. Not for as long as she lived.

Chapter Forty

Sainte-Mère-Église

Wednesday 14 June

It had been just over a week since the little town six miles inland from Utah Beach in Normandy had been liberated from the Germans; just over a week since the long-awaited and meticulously planned *Jour J* had finally happened. An old woman, her black shawl pulled tightly around her shoulders even though the weather was mild, walked past a huge mound of bricks and broken glass that had once been a *patisserie*. It had been derelict for a few years, Leon the baker having disappeared shortly after the Germans had goose-stepped their way into the town. Another *boulangerie* had opened up nearer to the market square, and so Leon's old shop had slowly gone to rack and ruin. Now the two-storey building was totally demolished, razed to the ground by Jerry's last-ditch attempt to reclaim a town that had never been theirs. The old woman covered her mouth with her shawl; the smell of burnt wood, soot and foul, stagnant water still lingered in the air. And there was another smell. One they had all become familiar with – death.

She stood for a moment and said a prayer for those who had been killed, and a prayer of thanks that their lives had not been sacrificed in vain. After four years of occupation – of living in fear and hearing the tongue of the Hun – they were once again free to come and go as they pleased, without the fear of saying or doing something that would bring them to the attention of their captors.

Now they heard American voices, but they did not mind – not one bit – for the brave paratroopers had come and saved them all. Her grandson and granddaughter, whom she was going to see now, would be able to grow up speaking the language of their forefathers and carrying on their Gallic traditions, not those of the Fatherland. She muttered another prayer of thanks and touched the rosary beads in her pocket as her mind wandered to what their futures might have been.

'Merci Dieu,' she muttered, crossing herself.

Looking across the azure skyline, her attention settled on the steeple of their ancient church. A parachute was still flapping in the breeze. The story going round the village was that the paratrooper had hung there for several hours while the battle raged around him and the church bells rang non-stop in his ears. She heard he had been cut down and captured by the Nazis but had later escaped.

She walked on, thinking of what she would cook her grandchildren for their evening meal. As she shuffled her way around the demolished building, her eye caught a movement. It was a big rat scurrying over the ruins. There'd been an increase of them since the fighting and the bombings. 'Charognards!' Scavengers! As she shouted, she grabbed a rock by the side of the pathway and chucked it with considerable force for a woman so old and arthritic.

'Va au diable!' The rock missed the rat but hit some soot-encrusted debris at the top of bomb site, causing it to tumble down the side like a miniature avalanche, taking other bricks and remnants with it. She was just about to carry on walking when she stopped and squinted hard, silently cursing her failing eyesight. What was that in the rubble? She made to go, but still something stopped her continuing on her way. She took a step forward. Squinted again. *Mon Dieu!* Was that a hand she could see? Or were her eyes playing tricks on her? No, she was sure it was a hand, the skin blackened with dirt.

A young boy ran past her, catching her long skirt as she did so.

'Garçon!' she shouted out.

The boy stopped and looked apologetically at the old woman.

'Pardonnez-moi,' he said, thinking the old witch was annoyed with him.

The old woman shook her head, showing she was not angry, but puzzled. She pointed to the mound of bricks – to what she was certain was a man's hand.

'Gee whiz!' the young French boy exclaimed. He had been learning a few American expressions. His mouth remained open, revealing a wad of chewing gum.

'Regardez! Regardez!' She flapped her free hand towards the ruins.

The boy didn't need any encouragement. He ran over, scrabbling across bricks and debris to the spot where he had seen the hand.

The old woman watched as the boy started flinging bricks to the side. Suddenly, he stopped. He swivelled around to face the old woman.

'C'est un homme!' he cried out. *It's a man!*

The boy started frantically throwing stones and bricks to the side. After a few moments, he stopped and stood up straight. Turning to the old woman, his expression was crestfallen.

'Il est mort,' he said. Looking down at the mop of blond hair, he thought the figure would have looked German were it not for his French clothes.

326

'*Venez!*' the old woman shouted.

The boy was about to do as he was told when he heard something.

A muffled banging sound, which seemed to be coming from deep within the ruins.

Chapter Forty-One

Thursday 15 June

Toby and Sergeant MacLeod were sitting in the smaller of the two conference rooms at RAF Harrington. The place was empty apart from Miss Sterling, the secretary, who sat at her desk at the far end of the room. The two men had been chatting about the recent air raids on London by what Germany was calling its 'secret weapon' – the V-1 flying bomb.

'At least only four out of eleven of the damn things hit their targets,' Toby said, pushing a clean ashtray across the desk.

'Six dead, though,' Sergeant MacLeod said gravely, casting a quick look over at Miss Sterling. They had been discussing the 'doodlebugs' over drinks last night. They had only just started to court and so were trying to keep their burgeoning romance under wraps for the time being.

'Revenge for France,' he added as he lit a cigarette and inhaled deeply.

They were quiet for a moment.

'What's the total of SOE casualties so far?' Toby asked.

'There's been at least a hundred and twenty-four either killed, wounded, missing or taken prisoner. At this stage, we're not sure how many are actually dead and how many have been captured,' Sergeant MacLeod informed him. He didn't need to look up the figures; the growing number of those reported or presumed dead was imprinted on his mind.

'I hope one day the sacrifices these men have made are honoured. They really are our unsung heroes,' said Toby.

'I cannae agree more, sir,' Sergeant MacLeod said, again shooting Miss Sterling a quick look and giving her a sad smile. 'Let's hope when all this is over, people realise that sabotage *can* cripple an army.'

Toby nodded. 'Albeit at a cost.'

The two men were again quiet for a moment. The stillness was broken only by Miss Sterling gently tapping on her typewriter.

'Right, back to the job in hand,' Toby said, getting up and walking over to the large map pasted on the back wall. He tapped his swagger stick on a place near to the French capital. 'About these drops ...' He rubbed his jaw as he inspected the terrain around the city. The second front was pushing inland. More soldiers and supplies were needed.

Suddenly, the phone rang. It sounded loud due to the acoustics in the near-empty conference room.

'It's for you, sir!' Miss Sterling called out across the half a dozen desks that separated her from the two men.

Toby walked back over to his desk and picked up the receiver. There was a click and the caller was connected.

'Hello, Lieutenant Mitchell speaking.' Toby tried to add a modicum of warmth to his tone, but failed. He was weary. This past week the deaths of his men had been weighing heavily on him.

He listened for a moment, stooped over the phone, his hand splayed out on the wooden desk, before suddenly standing up straight.

'Sorry, old chap, say that again,' he demanded, pressing the receiver to his ear, as though to make sure he was hearing correctly.

'Are you sure? Absolutely sure?' he asked, clenching his free hand. He wanted to punch the air but held back.

'Well I never,' he said, a wide smile spreading across his face. 'Perhaps there is a God after all.'

Sergeant MacLeod and Miss Sterling were watching Toby intently.

'What's that?' Toby asked the voice at the other end of the phone.

'Yes, of course. His wife will be informed. Immediately.'

Toby listened.

'King's Cross Station?'

He grabbed a pen and a piece of paper.

'When?'

Silence.

'Tomorrow?' He scribbled down the information, not that he needed to – every word of this phone call would be imprinted on his mind.

'Time?'

More scribbling.

'Yes, I will convey the message personally … Bloody brilliant news!'

Toby didn't think he had felt this shocked or happy for a long time.

'Tell him …' He paused. 'Tell him he's a bloody lucky bastard!'

Toby banged the phone down and looked at Sergeant MacLeod, shaking his head in disbelief, an elated look on his face.

'Well I never!' he declared. 'Agent Peter Miller of the Tempest circuit appears to have come back from the dead!'

Sergeant MacLeod looked over to Miss Sterling and cocked his head for her to join them.

'How's the lucky bugger managed that?' Sergeant MacLeod's smile now matched that of his Lieutenant, as Miss Sterling sat down on the chair next to him.

Toby pulled out the top drawer of his desk and retrieved the half-bottle of Scotch he kept there.

'God only knows,' he said, grabbing three mugs from the untouched tea tray perched at the end of his desk. 'Sounds like he was buried alive. Some young French lad found him – or rather heard him.' He sloshed a good measure of Scotch into each cup. 'Stuck in the cellar under a load of rubble.'

'And he's all right?' Miss Sterling asked, incredulously. They had all heard about Peter and the two Resistance fighters. Sergeant MacLeod had told her that it had hit Toby particularly hard.

'Hardly a scratch on him,' Toby said, again shaking his head in disbelief

He handed them each a mug and they clinked porcelain.

'We're going to win this bloody war, we are!'

'I'll drink to that,' Sergeant MacLeod said.

'We bleedin' well are, 'n all!' Miss Sterling said, her cockney roots revealing themselves in her excitement. Toby's mood was contagious.

They downed their drinks in one.

Toby looked at his watch and then back to Miss Sterling.

'I'll need a travel warrant drafted for Mrs Rosie Miller, whom I am going to take great pleasure telling is no longer a widow.' He looked again at his watch. 'And I need it as soon as possible, please, Miss Sterling.'

It took Toby an hour to pack an overnight bag and make sure that Sergeant MacLeod was briefed to cover for him for the next twenty-four hours. After picking up the travel warrant from his sergeant's sweetheart, he ran round to the car park, jumped into his Austin 8 and started his journey up north.

Chapter Forty-Two

Everyone looked as Toby came striding across the yard. It wasn't often you saw an army uniform – and a high-ranking officer at that – in the shipyard. The khaki uniform and peaked cap stood out against the oil-stained grey of overalls and tweed flat caps. In fact, the last time had probably been on Valentine's Day, when Toby had last been at the yard.

Other than surprise, Rosie felt nothing, unlike the past two years, when every time she'd seen Toby, or even heard his name mentioned, she'd been hit by a terrible fear and dread of the news he might bring with him. What she would give now to have that feeling again, for it would mean there was still hope that Peter was alive.

Rosie put her hand to shield her eyes from the sun and saw in her peripheral vision that her squad were all doing the same. It was a glorious day. The weather had been bright and sunny every day since she had been told that Peter was dead. When she had been at Lily's she'd managed to block out the sun by keeping the blackout blinds down all day, but when she had surfaced and forced herself to return to the outside world, it was unavoidable and she had found the radiance and the bright, cheerful faces that the summery weather brought with it so incredibly painful. It was as though the sun's rays were highlighting the doom and darkness that enveloped her and which she felt would be with her for the rest of her days.

She watched as Toby waved over at them all. Seeing the smile on his face, Rosie wondered if he was going to drop down on one knee and propose to Dorothy. There was no doubting that she would say yes.

Knowing that there was little chance of much more work being done, Rosie went round and switched off all their machines. When she stood back up, she saw Toby had got stuck behind a crane. He waited impatiently, shuffling about on the spot before he could jog past it. She saw him looking in Dorothy's direction and giving her a hundred-watt smile, but he didn't go to her as expected.

'Rosie!' Toby shouted out, marching towards her. He said something else, but his words were lost as one of the drillers started up a few yards away. By the time he reached her, Toby was still smiling. He leant into her ear and again tried to speak, but all Rosie caught was 'Peter'. The driller had been joined by another and now all Rosie could hear was thudding machinery. Toby stepped back and was still trying to tell her something, but it was no good, Rosie couldn't hear a word.

Turning to the women, she made the T sign and was met by a show of thumbs pointing up. Toby looked at Rosie and nodded. Checking that there were no spare rods lying around, ready to cause an accident, Rosie led the way across the yard, Toby by her side and Dorothy, Angie, Polly, Gloria and Martha all following – all with furrowed brows and quizzical faces. The rest of the workers in their vicinity were watching with interest. Dorothy caught Bobby's eye. He, Jimmy and the rest of their squad had stopped work and were watching the afternoon theatre with interest.

As soon as they were in the canteen and had shut the door firmly behind themselves, obliterating the din and chatter of the yard, Rosie looked towards the counter and, seeing Muriel appear from the kitchen, mouthed across 'Tea, please,' and made a circle with her hand in everyone's direction to show that it was for them all.

Muriel nodded, her eyes still betraying the sorrow she felt for Rosie.

Toby kept standing as the women pulled out chairs and plonked themselves down, their eyes darting from Toby to Rosie and then to each other.

Taking off his cap, Toby kept his eyes glued to Rosie.

'I've got some incredible news,' he said, feeling a sudden well of emotion. He kept himself in check and took a deep breath.

'I had a call this morning informing me that Peter is in fact still alive.'

There were quiet gasps from the women, their attention ping-ponging between Toby and Rosie.

Rosie stared at Toby, her face impassive. Uncomprehending.

'It's quite the miracle,' he said. 'From the reports we're getting in, Peter was trapped under a bombed building. He was literally buried alive.' He looked at Rosie and smiled. 'But he survived.'

There was a whispered 'Oh my God!' from a mesmerised Dorothy.

Rosie was still looking blankly at Toby.

'He's alive, Rosie,' he reassured. 'He really is alive.'

Rosie looked to her side, grabbed a seat and sat down. Just as when she had been told that Peter was dead her legs seemed to have lost the ability to keep her upright.

Gloria reached out and squeezed her arm but didn't say anything. She felt speechless herself.

'He's alive?' Rosie's question sounded more like a plea, her voice disbelieving. *'Really? He's really alive?'* She looked at Toby's face, needing to see the veracity of what he was saying as well as hear it.

334

'He is,' Toby said with complete certainty. 'One of my unit who knows Peter spoke to him personally. There is no doubt.'

'I can't believe it,' Rosie gasped, a tentative smile beginning to spread across her face. 'There's no doubt, no doubt at all?' She needed to be reassured. Needed to hear the words again and again. 'Someone who knows Peter spoke with him?'

'They did,' Toby said. 'Peter told him that he had been trapped for a week before anyone realised that he was there.' Toby purposely did not mention the other two men who had not been so lucky. He pulled out a chair, sat down, took Rosie's hand and squeezed it.

'I'm so sorry you were told Peter was dead. But we honestly did not think there was any chance he could still be alive.'

Rosie looked around at her squad – their faces showing their sheer amazement – and then back at Toby.

'Oh Toby, don't be sorry.' She took a deep breath. 'I want to be happy … I *am* happy.' She paused, bit down on her lip. 'But I don't think I will allow myself to believe it until I see him.'

Just then Muriel appeared carrying a tray with a large pot of piping-hot tea, a jug of milk and a small bowl of sugar. She was followed by one of her young charges, who set down a tray of cups and saucers.

'Everything all right?' Muriel asked as she started to unload her tray onto the table.

'Yes.' Rosie looked up at the woman who might be the town's biggest gossipmonger but whose heart was in the right place. 'They're saying Peter's alive.'

Toby looked at Rosie with intensity. 'He *is* alive. Really he is.'

'Oh, pet, that's wonderful,' Muriel said, wrapping her arms around Rosie, squashing her in a motherly embrace. 'I'm so pleased for yer, so pleased!'

She stood back up and wiped away a tear with the corner of her pinny, looking around at all the women welders.

They, too, had tears in their eyes.

'Eee, well I never.' She threw Toby a look of teary-eyed wonder as she left, shooing the young girl who'd been standing with her tray under her arm, staring at them all.

Just then the canteen door slammed shut and they all looked up to see Hannah hurrying across the empty cafeteria.

'What's happened?' Hannah asked, worried.

'Peter's alive!' Martha said, her eyes wide with incredulity.

Hannah looked at Rosie, who nodded, but still seemed in shock.

'They say he's alive,' she said to Hannah, although her tone still lacked conviction.

Hannah looked at Toby for confirmation; his face was testament that the news was bona fide. She hurried towards Rosie and flung her skinny arms around her.

Toby pulled out an envelope from his inside pocket.

'It really is true, Rosie. He's flying back as we speak. He's asked if you can meet him at King's Cross Station.'

'In London?' Angie blurted out. She and Dorothy were sitting with their arms linked, looking as though they were going to burst with pure rapture.

Toby looked at Angie and Dorothy, his gaze lingering on the woman he loved.

'Yes, King's Cross Station, London,' he said, looking back at Rosie. 'Is that all right?'

Rosie was half laughing, half crying. 'Oh, yes. That's all right. More than all right!'

She looked at the women and smiled for the first time.

They all beamed back at her.

She saw that Polly had tears rolling down her dirty, flushed cheeks, a hanky scrunched up in her hand.

'I think Peter wanted to see you as soon as possible,' Toby said, allowing himself a little chuckle. 'So, we've got you booked onto the five o'clock train. Peter will be waiting for you on the platform when you arrive.'

Everyone looked up at the canteen clock.

'It's three o'clock!' Gloria said. 'You better get going!'

All the women stood up, surrounding Rosie as they walked her to the canteen doors.

'Is there anything we can do?' Gloria asked, her mind whirring, thinking of anything practical Rosie might need.

'Ma can put you up some food for the journey and I can bring it to the station,' Polly said. She was still having to choke back the tears.

Rosie shook her head. 'No, honestly, I'll be fine. I just need to change,' she said, looking down at her scruffy overalls.

'Have you got something to wear?' Dorothy asked. 'We can run and get you an outfit from Kate, can't we, Ange?'

Angie nodded vigorously.

'Don't worry. I've got my red dress. The one I got married in. I've hardly worn it.' She stood and looked at her squad.

'I'll say goodbye to you all now,' Rosie said when they reached the door. She still felt dazed.

'I'll wait in the car,' said Toby. 'It's parked by the Admiral. I can take you straight home, or anywhere else you might need to go.'

'Thanks, Toby,' said Rosie. She turned to Martha, who gave her a hug, then Polly, Hannah, Dorothy, Angie and Gloria.

'Yer sure there's nothing we can do?' Gloria asked again.

'Sure,' Rosie said, wiping away tears that had started to trickle down her face.

337

'I love you all,' she said suddenly.

'We love you too,' the women chorused as Rosie, not trusting herself to refrain from bursting into tears, hurried out of the door.

Stepping out into the yard, Rosie hurried across to the admin building. Throwing open the door, she suddenly felt her energy return. She hurried up the stairs.

Peter will be waiting for you.

Toby's words kept looping around in her head.

Just like when he had met her off the train at Guildford.

She opened the door, looked across at Marie-Anne and pointed to Helen's office. Marie-Anne nodded.

'Helen,' said Rosie, knocking on the door to her office, even though it was open. She was hit by a smoky warmth.

'Come in,' Helen said, surprised, not just by Rosie's sudden appearance, but because she looked happy. 'Is everything all right?'

'Yes. Oh, yes,' Rosie said, swallowing back tears. 'I've just been told Peter's not dead.'

She paused, not wanting to jinx the words.

'He's alive.'

'He's alive!' Helen was gobsmacked. 'Oh my goodness, that's amazing. What happened?'

'I still can't quite believe it myself,' Rosie said. 'Sounds like he's been trapped – buried alive – and they've only just found him.'

'Oh, Rosie.' Helen got up and hurried around the desk to give her a hug. 'I'm so happy for you.' She stood, blinking back tears.

'Don't start!' Rosie said, her words choked. 'Otherwise I'll start and won't be able to stop.' She wiped away a stray tear. 'And I've got a train to catch!'

'What? Peter's back here? He's back in the country?'

'He will be in a few hours,' Rosie said. 'I'm meeting him at King's Cross Station.'

'What time?'

'I'm catching the five o'clock train.'

Helen looked at her watch. 'Well, you better get a move on!'

'Thanks, Helen. I wanted to check it was all right. Didn't want to just run off.'

'I would have understood if you had,' Helen said. 'Now go!'

Rosie turned to leave, but stopped and looked back at Helen.

'I also wanted to tell you the good news personally,' she said, tears making her eyes shine. 'You're a good friend. I didn't want you to hear it second-hand.'

Tears were now glistening in Helen's eyes.

'That's a lovely thing to be told,' she said. *'Now go! You can't miss that train!'*

Helen must have stood in the middle of her office for a good few minutes after Rosie left. Her mind felt as though it was fizzing. *Peter was alive!* It was nothing short of a miracle. Helen had looked at Rosie and had seen the full extent of what love could do. It had brought her friend back to life.

It was true, Helen thought, the most important thing in life was love. It was a discussion she'd had with Henrietta during her last visit to the hospital, when she had told her about Peter's death. Her grandmother had urged her to make the most of 'every day' and of 'every love'. Since then, Helen had been thinking a lot about those words. After the hurt and deception she'd endured during her relationship with Theodore, and the numbness that had followed her miscarriage, she had relegated love to a lowly position on her list of what was important in life. There was a war to be won, after all – and work, of course. But she'd been kidding herself. Love would always take the number-one spot, regardless of world affairs and no matter how important her work might be. Love infused everything else in life.

And that was when it came to her, like a flash of lightning, illuminating and energising. She walked over to her desk, picked up the phone and dialled a number she knew by heart.

'Hello, Denise, it's Miss Crawford. Can you pass on a message, please?'

She waited a beat.

'Can you tell Dr Parker I'm coming over and it's an emergency and can he meet me in our usual place, please?'

Helen listened as Denise asked if everything was all right and was there anything she could do to help?

'No, but thank you anyway, Denise, that's really kind of you to ask,' she said, smiling. She hung up. Reaching down into her handbag, she got out her lipstick and compact. Quickly adding a fresh layer of Victory Red and checking herself in the small mirror, she stood up, brushed down her olive-green dress, picked up her handbag and walked out of her office.

'Marie-Anne!' she called over.

Marie-Anne was chatting away to the women sitting around the sorting desk. Her face was animated. She had obviously heard about Peter and was spreading the good news. She swung round, her face showing her mortification that she had been caught gossiping when she should be working. She hurried over to her boss.

'Sorry, Miss Crawford, I was just—'

Helen waved away her apology. 'Don't worry, Marie-Anne. Can you take charge while I go out for a while? It will probably be for the rest of the afternoon. Something very important has just come up and I've got to go out.'

'Of course,' Marie-Anne said, a wide smile stretching across her freckled face, amazed she hadn't been reprimanded.

Helen turned and hurried out of the main office and down the stairs.

Her mission – to pursue her own happy ending and resurrect a love that she had tried to entomb for too long.

As soon as Denise hung up, she dialled the number for Dr Parker's consultation room and was surprised to find him there. She passed on the message as she had said she would and hung up.

Taking a deep breath, she then rang the number for the asylum.

'Ah, Genevieve, how are you today?'

The two receptionists exchanged pleasantries.

'Would you mind putting me through to Dr Eris, please? I've got an important and rather urgent message for her.'

She listened as Genevieve told her she would ring her office.

The line went silent. Denise wasn't sure whether she wanted Dr Eris to be there or not – whether she really wanted to tell her about Miss Crawford's 'emergency' meeting with Dr Parker. If she was honest, Denise had been relieved when Dr Parker had pulled her up about 'forgetting' to pass on a message from Helen. She liked Dr Parker and felt bad about deceiving him. And although she had never been a huge fan of Miss Crawford, she had started to warm to her of late.

'Denise ...' it was Genevieve back on the line '... I'm just putting you through now.'

'Thank you. Much appreciated.' Denise's heart sank. She knew what she was doing was wrong, that it would have repercussions and that the consequences of her meddling would not be good – not for Dr Parker or Miss Crawford, anyway. Still, it would put her in Dr Eris's debt – she would owe Denise a favour. Another introduction to an eligible bachelor from the Ryhope. An introduction that she was determined would lead to a ring on her finger, a walk down the aisle and a bun in the oven. She didn't particularly care if it was in that order. But it had to happen soon, before she was well and truly stuck on the shelf, dried up and destined to a lonely life of spinsterhood.

Chapter Forty-Three

Bobby had seen Toby turn up and had watched as he and the rest of the women welders had trooped off to the canteen. Toby's arrival in his officer's uniform had caught everyone's eye and when Bobby had seen him, he'd felt his heart lurch. *Had he come to propose to Dorothy?* The relief he'd felt when he saw Toby going straight over to Rosie had made him feel like sitting down, his energy suddenly drained. He really did have it bad.

He'd watched Dorothy and Toby exchange looks, but it was clear that Toby's visit to the yard was to see Rosie. Instinct told him it wasn't bad news. Toby had looked too chirpy. Besides, it wasn't as though Peter could die twice. Rosie had received the worst news imaginable – anything that Toby had come to tell her would pale into insignificance.

Bobby had worked on, keeping half an eye on the canteen. When he saw Rosie emerge and head over to the admin buildings, she'd looked in a daze, albeit a happy one. He hadn't seen her smile once since she'd been made a widow. *Had the War Office got it wrong and was Peter alive?* It wouldn't be the first time a woman had thought her husband was dead only for him to turn up on her doorstep.

Bobby continued to watch the canteen and had seen Toby leave on his own, which had raised his spirits. *He hadn't left with Dorothy.* Rosie had reappeared from admin and hurried out of the main gates. He'd then seen a snatch of Toby's black Austin 8 drive up the embankment.

A few minutes later he'd seen Polly, Hannah and Martha leave, followed by Dorothy and Angie. His mam must have stayed behind. He'd wanted to go after Dorothy but stopped himself. There was something he had to do first.

Tapping Jimmy on the shoulder, he shouted in his ear, asking permission to take a break. Jimmy nodded. Bobby had more than earned it. On top of which, the success of D-Day was making even the hardest of taskmasters soften. Jimmy grabbed Bobby by the arm and shouted into his good ear that he could take the rest of the afternoon off if he wanted to. Bobby mouthed, 'Thanks.'

Hurrying over to the canteen, he suddenly realised he couldn't get there quickly enough. He'd been a fool to leave it this long. Peter's death had been playing heavily on his mind, not because it was Peter who had been killed, but because it was a harsh reminder that life really was short. It was too precious to waste on resentments.

Opening the door, he looked around. There was just a smattering of workers dotted about. He could hear the clatter of dishes coming from the kitchen and was glad there was no one at the counter. He didn't want to have to deal with any small talk or quizzing from Muriel. Striding over to Gloria, who was sitting at the table on her own, sipping a cup of tea, he couldn't help noticing that she seemed lost in her own world. As boys, he and Gordon used to come back home and find their mam looking just as she did now – drinking tea, oblivious to everything around her, immersed in her own thoughts.

Gloria didn't realise Bobby was there until he pulled out the chair next to her and sat down.

'Bobby!' she said, surprised, snapping herself back into the present. 'Is everything all right?' She suddenly felt panicked. Bobby never came to see her at work. Never came to see her at all unless it was on a Friday evening, and that was only to see Hope – and Dorothy.

'Is Gordon all right?' Suddenly, Gloria felt terrified that something had happened to her other son. Peter's coming back from the dead might somehow be at the expense of someone else's happiness. She knew it was insane to think that, but still she couldn't help it.

'No, Gordon's fine,' Bobby said.

'Thank God.' Gloria breathed a sigh of relief.

'You never have to worry about Gordon, Mam,' he reassured. 'He's a born survivor.'

'Do yer want a cuppa?' Gloria asked.

Bobby shook his head. 'No, Mam, I just want to talk to you.'

Gloria caught Muriel's eye. She shook her head to show that they didn't want anything.

Bobby leant forward with his hands clasped on the table.

'I'm sorry I've been this way, Mam. You know – distant …' His voice trailed off.

Gloria nodded but didn't say anything. She knew words didn't come easily to Bobby.

'I couldn't help it. I tried to talk myself round … tried to force myself to be nice to you, to be loving and kind and all the things Dorothy has repeatedly told me I need to be.' He laughed. 'I have even tried just to please her.' Dorothy's serious face sprang to mind. 'But I just wasn't able to. I'm sorry, Mam.'

Gloria shook her head and put her hand on his arm to show he didn't have to be sorry, but she remained quiet.

'I was shocked when I came back and found out that you'd not only left Dad but you'd divorced him too – never mind set up home with some other bloke and had a

345

daughter together who you hadn't bothered to tell me and Gordon about.'

Gloria opened her mouth to defend herself but stopped. She needed to let her son speak.

'I wasn't angry, like Dorothy thinks I was, because you were a divorcee, living in sin and with a baby out of wedlock.' Bobby looked into his mother's sad brown eyes. 'But I think you've known that deep down. I don't care about things like that.'

Gloria nodded. Both her boys had never judged others, or been prejudiced in any way. It was something she'd always been so proud of.

'But when I saw you with Jack and Hope, I felt angry towards you,' Bobby said. 'And I feel a bit ashamed to admit why it was I was so angry ...'

'You felt resentment,' Gloria said finally. She had known it all along, but there was nothing she could do. She couldn't change the past, no matter how much she wanted to.

'Yes.' Bobby was surprised at her insight. 'I feel embarrassed saying this as a grown man, but I was angry with you because Gordon and I begged you to leave Dad so many times, and you promised so many times that you would leave him and you never did.'

Bobby rubbed his hand across the top of his head. 'He used you as his punchbag, Mam – verbally and physically.' He was going to add *and sexually as well*, but he didn't. It would not be proper, although he was under no illusion that his father had used his mother for his own gratification whenever the mood had taken him.

'And then we go off to sea and you meet someone else and not only leave Dad, but you divorce him to boot. Why couldn't you have done that when Gordon and I were at home – when we were young?' Bobby took a deep breath. 'I can still see it all now, as clear as day – still feel the

346

tension in that house. The fear, the nights me and Gordon lay awake, dreading him coming back from the pub, dreading him kicking off because his supper hadn't been kept hot, or it had dried out, or, God forbid, hadn't been made.' Bobby shook his head as the memories flooded back.

Gloria leant forward, wanting to take her son's clenched hand, but held back.

'I stayed because he promised he would change.' Gloria's voice was a monotone; her words were not a defence, merely a statement of facts.

'But he never did,' Bobby said.

'I just kept hoping – pathetic, I know,' Gloria said. 'He kept *saying* he wanted to change, but I know now that he didn't – not really.'

'He only said it so that you wouldn't leave,' Bobby said. *He had understood that as a child, so why hadn't his mother?*

'It's only now,' she said, her voice more animated, 'it's taken me this long to realise how stupid I was back then.' She sighed, again wishing she could change the past. Not for her own sake, but for the sake of her boys. 'How stupid was I to keep believing him.' She exhaled. 'I'm so sorry I put you and Gordon through all of that.' Gloria looked at her son and felt the most terrible guilt. Guilt she had kept buried deep inside herself for years. But her son's words had cut deep. Tears started to fill her eyes. Her whole life had been blighted by her one decision to marry Vinnie. She hated him, but she hated herself more because she had stayed with him.

Bobby looked at his mam and saw how the light in her being was dimming at the remembrance of that time.

'Bobby, I am so sorry. I could sit here and tell yer that I had no idea yer felt like that, but that would be a lie, because deep down I've always known. I should have simply packed our bags 'n left, but I didn't. When yer both joined the navy,

347

I felt such relief that yer had both done what I couldn't do. Yer'd left 'n I admired yer both for it – and I still do.'

Bobby gave Gloria a sad smile. 'It was the broken china that made my mind up.'

Gloria had to stop herself from bursting out crying. She'd never forget that day. Vinnie had come back home in a foul mood. He wasn't even drunk, but he'd let rip and smashed up all the crockery.

'The funny thing is,' Bobby said, 'I don't think he actually hit you that time, but for some reason all this terrible anger just rose up in me. It scared me because I didn't feel in control of it – all I could think of was going downstairs, opening the kitchen drawer, getting out the sharpest knife I could find and stabbing him to death.' Darkness clouded Bobby's expression. 'And that's when I knew I had to go – and if I was going, Gordon was coming with me.'

A lone tear had escaped and was trickling down Gloria's cheek. 'If I'm honest, I was scared,' she said. 'Scared of him. Scared of what would happen if I did leave. Ashamed because I didn't have the strength to say no and leave him. I just went round and round in circles. For fifteen years. And believe me – ' she looked at her son ' – there's not a day goes by that I don't regret that.'

Bobby looked at his mam. If he had any residue of anger or resentment, his mother's words had dissolved it all. And for the first time in a long, long while he felt unburdened. Free of the hold of the past. Free of the anger and resentment that had always been there, but which had marched to the fore since his return and clung to him.

'But I want yer to know one thing,' Gloria said. 'I didn't leave Vinnie because of Jack.' She paused. 'I wanted to be with Jack, of course, but the actual moment I decided to finally get shot of Vinnie for good was when he punched me while I was pregnant with Hope.'

Gloria stopped for a moment and took a breath. It was a part of her history it pained her to recall.

'Vinnie had no idea I was pregnant; it was just another punch to let off steam because he wasn't getting his own way.' She paused. 'But when I got him out of the house and bolted the door, I was filled with the most terrible dread that he had killed the life growing inside of me – my baby … I had not protected you and Gordon from that man who was your father – I was not going to fail again. That was when I went to the solicitors, took all the money I had saved' – Gloria had a flash of herself sitting in the musty-smelling office on John Street and opening up her bag in which she had stashed every penny she had – 'and told the solicitor that I wanted that man out of my life and I had the money to pay for it.'

Bobby sat up. He hadn't known anything about this. Dorothy's lectures had missed this part out.

'For a divorce?' Bobby asked.

Gloria shook her head. 'Not to start with. At first, the solicitor drafted out a letter that threatened Vinnie and said that if he laid another hand on me he would file charges against him on my behalf. And then he got started on the divorce.'

Bobby looked at his mam and understood. For whatever reason, Gloria hadn't been able to leave their dad when they were young, but she'd done it for Hope. And for the first time he felt proud of his mam. Proud of her true grit and her determination.

'Which is why you needn't have worried about Jack being another Vinnie,' Gloria said. It had broken her heart when she'd realised this was the reason Bobby was a regular visitor to the house, why he wanted to spend time with Hope – to make sure neither his mam nor his sister were being hurt in any way. She had wanted to tell him that there was no way she was going to make the same mistake twice.

'You knew that was why I was coming round?' Bobby asked.

Gloria nodded. '*And* why you got a job at Thompson's – rather than at Bartram's, where yer did your apprenticeship. Yer got to check on me here 'n on Jack working next door at Crown's.'

They were quiet for a moment.

'I don't think I've ever heard anyone say a bad word about Jack,' Bobby admitted. 'You look like you've got yourself a decent bloke there.'

'I have,' Gloria said.

Bobby half laughed. 'There might have been another reason I got a job at Thompson's.'

Gloria looked at Bobby and, seeing the look of love on his face, smiled.

'Dorothy,' she said simply.

Bobby nodded, a lopsided, almost sheepish expression on his face. He guessed she'd known how he felt from the off.

'Well, now we've put the world to rights,' Gloria said, 'will you please go and put that poor girl out of her misery and tell her yer've done as she's been mithering on at yer to do since yer first tipped up here, and have forgiven yer auld ma.'

Gloria could feel the tears starting and forced them back. She leant forward and put her arms around her son – her broad, handsome, stubborn, brave boy – and hugged him hard.

'Tell her we're gonna be happy families now, or as happy as real families in the real world get, outside of the ones they like to have acted out in all them films she's so keen on dragging us to see.'

Bobby bear-hugged his mam back.

'We just need to get our Gordon home now,' Gloria said, her voice muffled against her son's dirty overalls. 'Then we really will be a proper family.'

'We will, Mam,' Bobby said, letting go. 'We'll get him back.'

Gloria swallowed her tears. She could let them all out once he was gone.

'Go on, get yerself off.'

'I love you, Mam. And Gordon does too.'

'Oh, Bobby, I love you too. And Gordon and Hope. I love you all so, so very much.'

She watched as Bobby pushed his chair back, grabbed his haversack and strode out of the canteen. She had a feeling her son might well be telling Dorothy more than that he had done her bidding and made up with his mam.

Gloria smiled through her tears, which she could now let free.

God help the lad.

Chapter Forty-Four

As Toby pulled up at the end of Brookside Gardens, he jumped out to open the passenger door, but was beaten to it by Rosie, who was climbing out and grabbing her work haversack.

'I must apologise once again for initially giving you false information about Peter's demise,' Toby said, taking off his cap and putting it under his arm.

'Toby, I'm just so glad it was this way round and I didn't think Peter was alive only to be told a mistake had been made and he was dead.'

Toby smiled.

'So, you're all sorted,' he said. 'You've got your ticket?' They had stopped off at the train station to convert the travel warrant into an actual ticket. Toby didn't want any hiccups. He'd been able to check that the train to London was running on time and there weren't any delays. He had also upgraded Rosie's ticket to first class, which he had managed to do after telling the ticket inspector that Rosie was meeting a war hero, and slipping him a ten-bob note.

'Yes,' Rosie said, pulling out the ticket from her top pocket and waving it. Her face was flushed with excitement. 'I just need to spruce myself up a little ...' She laughed, looking down at her dirty overalls.

'I don't think Peter will mind what you wear,' Toby chuckled. He stepped forward and took Rosie's hands and squeezed them. 'I'm so happy for you – for you both.'

Rosie suddenly became sombre.

'I know it might sound like I'm being overanxious – neurotic even,' Rosie said, 'but Peter's safe now, isn't he? He's not in any danger?'

'None at all, my dear,' Toby said with confidence.

'I think … well … I was just thinking about his flight over – it'll be all right, won't it?'

'Don't worry. He'll be fine. The aircraft he's on has been across the Channel and back more times than I've had hot dinners – it's safe as houses.'

Rosie breathed a sigh of relief. She had been wanting to ask Toby this since they'd got her train ticket and he'd told her that Peter's plane would probably be landing at around the time her train reached York, giving him enough time to meet briefly with his superiors and get a lift to King's Cross.

'Are you off to see Dorothy now?' Rosie asked as Toby turned to get back in his car.

Her question was met by a wide smile.

'Most definitely, although I have a few errands to run first.'

Rosie narrowed her eyes. She wondered if Toby's 'errands' involved nipping to one of the jewellers in town. Toby had casually asked Rosie which shop she would patronise if she wanted to treat herself to 'a nice necklace, or the like'.

'Good luck!' she said, smiling.

Chapter Forty-Five

As Helen drove along the coastal road to Ryhope, she kept thinking of the many times she and John had spent together since they had become friends. She was now convinced that John *did* love her – *had always loved her*. That her feelings for him would have been reciprocated.

Why the change of perspective? She was unsure. Perhaps it was because previously she had been blinded by the traumas she had been going through, as well as by her mother's words, which had convinced her she was 'sullied'. Perhaps she now knew that John did not view her, or any woman who had been with another man outside of marriage, as second-hand goods. Perhaps she no longer saw herself as *less than*.

Or had her change in thinking come from the time she was spending with her grandmama? The books and poetry they read and discussed – and their many conversations about love.

As she glanced to her left, she caught sight of the long stretch of Hendon beach, with its dark wooden breakers, visible due to the low tide. She wished that Henrietta had been a part of her life when she was growing up. She would have loved to have been shown a different view of the world than the one her mother had instilled in her. For Miriam, looks, status, money and social standing came first, whereas her grandmother was the opposite. Henrietta's focus was on the mind – not just her own, but on the thoughts and opinions of others, those she came into contact with, and those she read about. Her looks were about expressing her individuality, and, unlike Miriam, she believed passionately that all men and women were equal.

As Helen turned right and drove past the village green and the old post office, she knew what her grandmother would say if she was chatting to her now. She would say that Helen should not look back in regret – nor wish that her life had been any different. Life, Henrietta would say, should be lived in the present – which was why she was about to do something she should have done a long time ago.

Dr Parker sat back in his chair. Helen's message had sounded very cryptic. An 'emergency', but not a bad one by the sounds of it, just news that needed to be imparted as a matter of urgency, although why the urgency, he was unsure. Dr Parker combed his mop of fair hair back with his fingers, then looked up at the clock above the door. He'd quickly check on his new recruits and then head over to the canteen. He could get a pot of tea ready for Helen's arrival. It would also give him time to think. Something he'd been doing a lot of lately.

When Helen pulled up outside the Ryhope Emergency Hospital, she quickly flicked the visor down and checked herself in the small mirror. She pushed it back up and took a deep breath. She was nervous but also incredibly excited. Telling John how she felt about him – how she had always felt about him – was daring and she risked being rejected, but that didn't matter any more. She just wanted to unburden herself to him. To open her heart and tell him of her love for him. If he didn't want her love, then that would be fine too. Of course, she'd be heartbroken, and probably more than a little embarrassed, but at least, finally, it would be out in the open.

Helen stepped out of the car and started walking towards the entrance. Hurrying up the stone steps, she suddenly felt impatient. She couldn't wait to see him. To tell him the truth.

She pulled open the main door – but came to an abrupt halt.

'I'm so sorry!'

She had come face to face with Dr Eris.

Damn! The last person she wanted to see.

'Dear me, Helen. You're charging in here like a steam train. Is everything all right? You look very flustered?'

'I'm fine, thank you,' said Helen. She stepped to the side so as to slip by, but found the way blocked as Claire niftily stepped to the side too, preventing her from entering the main foyer.

'I'm just meeting John in the canteen,' Helen said, making a point of looking at her watch as though she was running late.

'Well, then,' Dr Eris said, making no attempt to move, 'I've caught you at the right time.'

Helen looked at her nemesis, whose mouth was stretched into a taut smile. Her eyes were glistening with what looked like malice.

'I think we need to have a talk before you have your "emergency" chat with John in the canteen,' Dr Eris said, throwing her arm out towards the bench by the side of the entrance.

Helen glanced through the open door and saw Denise, who looked away as soon as she caught her eye. *Was that guilt she saw on her face?* Had Denise told Claire that Helen was meeting John?

Helen turned and walked back down the stone steps and over to the bench. The sun was shining. Squinting in the light, she watched as Dr Eris sat down next to her.

'Well, isn't this dandy,' she said, looking at Helen and smiling. 'I'm just so glad I caught you in time.'

Helen was feeling more uncomfortable by the second.

'Claire, if you've got something to say, can you make it quick, I really am in somewhat of a rush.'

'Clearly,' Dr Eris said. She smiled. 'As you wish. I'll get straight to the point.'

Helen thought Claire looked like the cat that had got the cream. Totally self-satisfied.

'I know who Miss Girling really is,' Dr Eris said simply.

Helen blinked. Her words felt like an affront. And they were totally unexpected. She had thought she was going to say something about keeping away from John; never in a month of Sundays had she expected this to be about her grandmother.

'What?' Helen asked, looking confused, playing for time.

'I think you know "what",' Dr Eris said. 'Miss Henrietta Girling is not just some "distant elderly relative", as you claim. Or a great-aunty as your mother claims. No. Miss Henrietta Girling is in fact Mrs Catherine Henrietta Havelock … Mr Charles Havelock's wife … Your mother Miriam's dear mama. *Your* grandmother.'

Helen felt a wave of panic hit her. She fought to keep her demeanour impassive.

Dr Eris sat back a little to observe Helen's reaction more closely. There was no denying she'd caught her off guard.

'What makes you think that?' Helen asked, furrowing her brow to give the appearance of confusion. She was hoping that Claire was hedging her bets and that she simply suspected this was the case – that she was guessing and trying to get it confirmed by catching Helen out.

'Helen, my dear, I would never dream of sitting here and saying this to you unless I had proof.' She dug in her pocket and pulled out a piece of creased yellow paper. Dr

Eris straightened it out. Helen could see the writing was old-fashioned, with elaborate swirls and loops.

'It took me a while to get this – many hours, many *boring* hours, of looking through a stack of dusty old files buried away in the dank basement of the asylum. But I got there in the end. It was worth all the hard work.'

She handed the document to Helen.

A quick glance showed it was an admissions report. The ornate handwriting made it hard to read, but she could clearly see her grandmother's name, along with the date of her admittance and *insanity and deliriums* clearly noted as the reasons for her confinement. As she scanned down the document, she saw her grandfather's signature.

'It wouldn't be the first time a wife was dumped in a sanatorium for the insane because her husband wanted shot of her,' Dr Eris said. She dug into her other pocket and pulled out another document. Helen saw that it was a replica of the first one, only with the name changed.

'The first should have been destroyed. If you're going to do a job, then do it properly, that's what I say.' She smiled. 'But lucky for me, they didn't.'

Helen looked at Dr Eris. She had felt a slight twinge of guilt beforehand about going to see John with the aim of taking him away from Claire. Of stealing him off her. Now she realised she would be doing him a favour. A huge favour.

'You're wondering what it was that piqued my interest, aren't you?' Dr Eris asked, not waiting for an answer. 'It took me a while to suspect foul play, but something just kept niggling me. Before you started to visit dear Henrietta, your mother had been quite vocal in her refusal to take her "great-aunty" out on day trips. That had always struck me as being odd. Most people would jump at the chance of getting their loved ones out – even if it was just for the day.

But of course, your mother wouldn't have risked someone recognising dear Henrietta, would she?' Dr Eris paused. 'Especially as I believe the story peddled out when your grandmother was incarcerated was that the poor woman had died of some tropical disease while out in India.'

Helen thought of her grandmother, locked up because she was going to hang her husband out to dry, having found out the man she had married was a monster – a monster who raped young girls. Young girls like Pearl and poor Grace, who had been found hanging from the bannisters. Helen could feel her heart thumping in her chest. Part fear. Part anger. She looked at Claire – *she was enjoying this*.

'And then I thought about your grandfather. How can anyone forget the money he has ploughed into the asylum – there's a plaque out front to remind everyone, should they forget. And that's when I put two and two together. His purported philanthropy was in reality him buying the silence of the powers that be.

'But to be honest, none of this really bothers me at all. What matters to me is it has given me something over you.'

Helen looked at Claire, and it was then that the penny dropped, hard and resoundingly.

'Let me guess,' Helen said. 'This is really all about John?'

'You *are* clever, my dear.' Dr Eris's tone was truly patronising. 'What is it people say – *brains as well as beauty*?'

Dr Eris shuffled in her seat so that she was staring at Helen. 'Which brings me to the crux of the matter.' She narrowed her eyes. 'If you *really do* have brains, then you will back off and leave John well alone. And if he should ever express any kind of interest towards you, other than that of a brother or a platonic friend, then you are to knock him back and make a convincing show that your feelings for him are purely chaste – those of a good friend, a sister, and nothing more.'

359

She smiled at Helen.

'And if you don't, I will spill the beans. I will tell the authorities that we have a woman under our care who is not who she says she is. A woman who might well have been restrained under duress. But most of all, as I'm sure you are aware, Helen, your grandfather and the Havelock name will be destroyed. And as Mr Havelock's granddaughter, your reputation will also be ruined. You'll be tarnished with the same brush. You're the same blood, after all. You'll be stigmatised the rest of your life.' Dr Eris paused. 'I'll have nothing to lose, so don't doubt I won't do it.'

Helen stared at Dr Eris. She really had no idea Helen didn't give a fig about the Havelock name being dragged through the mud; wouldn't care if she was also tarnished with the same brush – would, in fact, revel in seeing her grandfather get the comeuppance he deserved. He'd got away scot-free for too long. It had always irked her that her grandfather seemed to have an incredible capacity to glide through life without having to suffer any kind of punishment for what he'd done. For ruining the lives of those who had fallen prey to his perversions.

How Helen wished she could tell Claire to go ahead, *do it*.

Helen would love to shout the truth out from the treetops. But, of course, she couldn't. Nobody could. Her grandfather had made it more than clear that if the truth about Henrietta were ever exposed, he would wreak his revenge. He would ruin Pearl and everyone connected to her, for she had been the one who had threatened to tell the world about Henrietta's incarceration if Jack were not allowed back.

And he would almost certainly go to the Borough Police and inform them that Maisie was a call girl and the house in West Lawn was a bordello, no doubt greasing as many palms as necessary to ensure Pearl's daughter and all those she worked with had the book thrown at them. Bill would lose his licence, as the Havelock family had links with the town's breweries, and Pearl and her new husband would be chucked out of their home. And God only knew what her grandfather would have in mind for Gloria, Jack and Hope – and the dire consequences for Dorothy, Angie and Martha. Helen dreaded to think what would happen if their secrets were revealed.

It was endless.

Helen looked at Dr Eris. She would have to do as she wished.

Dr Eris looked at her watch. 'You'd better go and meet John at the canteen. He'll be wondering where you are.'

'You won't win,' Helen hissed, standing up. 'John'll see through you eventually.'

'I don't think he will,' Dr Eris said, standing. 'Not until he's walked me down the aisle anyway and then, let's face it, it'll be too late.'

'That's if you get there. You might have fooled John so far, but he's not stupid.'

Dr Eris laughed. 'All men are stupid when it comes to women, Helen, surely even you must have realised that by now?' She looked out at the landscaped grounds. 'There's only one obstacle that's stopping John from dropping down on one knee at the moment, and that's you. Once you're out of the way, he'll be proposing, mark my words.'

Helen shook her head.

'My dear, I'm a psychologist, don't forget. I can read people and John is pretty transparent. He loves me, but lately I can see that he's been wondering if perhaps your feelings for him are more than those of a friend. I saw the change after that wretched wedding reception in the east end.' Dr Eris pulled a face, showing her distaste at Pearl's working-class wedding celebration.

Helen stared at the woman she had never liked, though she'd never really had a reason to dislike, other than an instinct that she was not all she seemed – and, of course, because she was dating John. Seeing her now – hearing the words coming out of her mouth, betraying the person she really was – she realised Claire was much worse than she'd imagined.

'I think it might have been when he realised that you weren't dating that shipyard manager. I think you might have said something to encourage him,' she continued, her voice tempered with steel, 'but whatever it might have been, that was the start of the change. It was then I knew I had to put a stop to it.' She paused. 'Especially, as I'm sure you're well aware, as John's been holding a candle for you for quite a while.'

Helen looked at Dr Eris, trying not to show that her words had shocked her. Claire clearly believed it was obvious that John was in love with her. Helen could have slapped herself. *How had she not realised it herself?*

A smile spread across Dr Eris's face on seeing Helen's look.

'Oh dear, you didn't know, did you?' Dr Eris laughed cruelly. 'I had wondered.' Another sharp laugh. 'A case of confident on the outside, but crippling insecurity on the inside. A woman who has everything but self-esteem. How very interesting. And how very fortunate for me.'

Helen clenched her hands. How ironic that it had taken Claire to confirm her growing suspicion that John loved her. And how heartbreaking that she'd realised too late.

'And if I feel that Dr Parker is getting cold feet,' Dr Eris said, smoothing her hand over her flat stomach. 'There's always the oldest trick in the book. Like I said, men really are quite stupid.'

Helen looked at this vile woman in front of her. The thought of Claire getting pregnant with John's baby made her want to weep – just as much for John as for herself.

Dr Parker stirred the pot of tea and poured himself a cup. Helen was late, which he was glad of, as it had given him time to think. She clearly had something important to tell him, but he also had something important that he wanted to tell her – or rather to ask her. He had to know. Either way. And today was the perfect opportunity.

Looking up, he saw Helen walking through the entrance to the canteen, the door held open for her by one of the doctors. She smiled her thanks before scanning the room. As always, the sight of her took his breath away. She looked stunning in an olive dress that he had seen her in a number of times before and which never failed to raise his temperature.

Dr Parker stood up and waved across to her. She waved back and made her way over to the table. The canteen was only half full, but those who were there looked as Helen manoeuvred her way around tables to get to him.

'Helen!' He stepped forward to give her a kiss on the cheek, but instead she put her arms around him and gave him a long, tight embrace. She held on to him longer than normal.

'Is everything all right?' he asked as Helen released herself and sat down at their table, reaching into her handbag for her packet of Pall Malls.

'Oh John, it is,' she lied. 'It really is.' Helen lit a cigarette and blew out smoke to the ceiling. She swallowed back angry tears and forced a smile on her face.

'So, tell me, I'm dying of curiosity – what is the "emergency"?' John asked.

'It's Peter. He's alive!' Helen declared. Tears stung her eyes, causing her vision to blur slightly. She didn't stop them – couldn't stop them – but knew at least they would be construed as tears of happiness.

'Good God!' Dr Parker said, automatically grabbing Helen's hand. 'This is incredible news!'

Helen stubbed out her barely smoked cigarette and put her hand on top of the hand of the man she loved. She held it firmly, enjoying his touch.

'He got trapped under a bombed building,' Helen said, knowing this would be John's next question.

'And he wasn't injured?'

Helen smiled.

'No, by all accounts he came out of it pretty much unscathed, although the details are sketchy.'

'This is brilliant news. I'll bet you Rosie doesn't know whether she's coming or going.' Dr Parker had known of a few cases of wives and girlfriends who had believed the men they loved had been killed in action, only to receive a second telegram telling them otherwise. It was not an uncommon phenomenon of war.

'Well,' Helen let out a slightly strangled laugh, 'she's definitely *going*.' She smiled, looking into Dr Parker's brown eyes. 'Going all the way to London to meet him today!'

'Well, that's a turn-up for the books,' Dr Parker said, holding Helen's gaze. *God, he could look into those emerald eyes until kingdom come.* 'I'll bet you she's walking on air.'

'She was definitely floating when she came to tell me,' Helen smiled. This time her happiness was genuine as she recalled Rosie's face. It had been such a mix of emotions – euphoria, disbelief, shock and sheer joy.

Dr Parker looked down at Helen's hand, which was still clamped over his own.

'And it's lovely that you came to tell me in person,' he said. 'It's wonderful to hear some good news for a change. Really bolsters one up.'

They were quiet for a moment.

'It must be a wonderful feeling,' Helen said, unusually wistful. 'Knowing he's alive and that she's now going to be spending the rest of her life with him.'

'Yes, yes, it must be,' John agreed, looking at Helen and thinking she seemed to be momentarily lost in another world. Was she thinking of her own life and how she too would love to spend the rest of it with someone she loved? Could that other person possibly be him?

Dr Parker looked at Helen, a furrow on his brow.

'Was there anything else you came to tell me?' he asked, shifting on his chair. 'Odd question, I know. I just feel as though there's something you're not saying?'

Oh John, if only you knew.

'You can read me like a book,' she said, still holding his hand. 'I did come here to tell you something else ...'

Dr Parker's heart lifted.

'When I heard about Peter, I kept thinking of you ... kept thinking how lucky I am to have you in my life,' Helen said, forcing a smile. 'So lucky to have you in my life that I just wanted to tell you.'

Dr Parker looked at Helen. He still sensed she wanted to say more but couldn't for some reason.

'Are you sure that was all?' Dr Parker queried.

Helen released his hand and sat back.

'Dear me, we've not had our tea. It'll be cold.' She put her hand round the brown ceramic teapot. 'Still warm.' She started to pour.

'Helen,' Dr Parker said, his face deadly serious, 'I'm going to go out on a limb here and say that I think there's something else you came here to tell me, but for some reason you have decided to hold back.'

Helen put the pot down on the table.

Dr Parker leant forward so that both his elbows were on the tabletop. 'So, I'm going to take the reins and ask you something that I've wanted to ask you for a while now.'

'Since Pearl's wedding day?' Helen asked.

Dr Parker nodded.

'Do you know what I'm going to ask?'

'I think so,' Helen said, 'but ask me anyway.' She needed to hear it from John's own mouth. *No matter that it was all too late.*

Dr Parker cleared his throat. 'I know how much you value me as a friend, but would you ever consider me as more than a friend?' He expelled air. *There, he had said it.*

Helen paused for a moment.

'Would *you* consider *me* as more than a friend?' She batted the question back. She needed to hear him say it.

'Yes,' Dr Parker said, without hesitation. 'Very much so.'

Helen yearned to lean across and kiss him, to touch his face, his skin, his body. To show him her answer. To make love to him. But, of course, she couldn't. Instead, she took a deep breath. This was the hardest thing she had ever had to say in her life.

'That is so lovely to hear, John. Really it is.' *You have no idea.* 'It is such a huge compliment.' She swallowed hard. 'But I'm afraid we can only be friends ... just friends ... and nothing more,' she said, sitting back.

Dr Parker looked into Helen's green eyes. *Could she see the devastation her words had wrought in him?* Well, if she could, he didn't care.

'I don't understand?' He had thought she was going to say yes – that his feelings for her were requited. 'Why? Why can't we be more than friends?'

'Don't ask me why – please,' Helen said, once again taking hold of his hands.

There was a moment's silence.

'I just don't understand,' Dr Parker murmured, genuinely perplexed. 'Why can't you tell me?'

'I'm sorry, John. So sorry.' Helen looked into his eyes, pleading with him not to push her any further. 'I can't say any more than I have already. You just have to trust me. And believe me. There can be no future for the two of us.'

Dr Parker shook his head to show his confusion. His disbelief.

'But …' she squeezed his hands, desperate for him to know the inner joy his words of love had brought her '… I want you to know that I love you. I really do love you.'

Dr Parker looked into Helen's eyes. They seemed so sad – or were they simply reflecting his own desolation? 'And I really do love you too, Helen.' He took a deep breath. 'But I have to ask you, otherwise it will always plague me – it's not because of your past, is it? Because you know I don't care about what anyone has done in their past, or what might have happened to someone, don't you?' He didn't need to talk specifics.

'Oh, John, I do. I really do. And knowing that makes me love you all the more.' Helen let out a sad, soft laugh. 'But I can't love you in the way you want. I just can't. I'm sorry. So sorry.'

Dr Parker took another deep breath, as though he were about to say something else – argue the case for their love. For the possibility that Helen could love him in the way he wanted. He was sure of it. But she had said the words. He had to accept what she'd told him. Didn't he? Even if he didn't believe she was being truly honest – either with him, or with herself.

'If you need time, I can wait,' Dr Parker said, trying his hardest to get to the truth; trying hard not to sound as desperate as he felt.

'No, don't wait, please,' Helen said, suddenly terrified that Claire might carry out her threat. John had to understand the situation was hopeless. Which, in truth, it was.

'I don't need time. I know,' she said.

Dr Parker felt his body wilt. He knew he couldn't push any more.

'I love you, Helen,' he said in place of an argument. 'I've always loved you and always will. Regardless.' He looked once more into those emerald eyes, glistening with the beginnings of tears. 'And I'll always be here for you.'

Helen smiled, desperately forcing back the surge of emotion that threatened to weaken her resolve. 'And the same goes for me, too. I'll always be here for you. And I will always love you …' she paused '… even if it might not look that way.'

When Helen walked out of the main entrance of the hospital and got back into her car, she put the key into the ignition but didn't turn it.

Dr Eris might well have her in her grip – one that she saw no way of freeing herself from – but John loved her.

He loved her.

She would revel in that thought – in that feeling – for today.

Tomorrow was another day.

Chapter Forty-Six

'Charlie! Charlie!' Rosie shouted as soon as she spotted her sister coming out of school.

Seeing Charlotte look around, she waved frantically.

'What's wrong?' Charlotte's face was serious.

'It's Peter,' Rosie said, grabbing her arm and pulling her gently away from the rest of the girls spilling out onto Mowbray Road.

'Peter?' Charlotte was confused.

Rosie stopped walking and took hold of her sister's arms and squeezed them. 'Oh, Charlie – he's alive! Peter's alive!'

For a moment it went through Charlotte's mind that her sister might have lost the plot and become delusional.

'Really?' she asked, unsure. 'He's not dead?'

'No! He's not dead,' Rosie said. 'I know, it's unbelievable,' she said, grabbing Charlotte's arm again and tugging her towards Ryhope Road. 'But he's alive. Toby's just been to see me. Said they'd just got news through that he's alive.'

As soon as Charlotte heard that Toby had brought the news, she knew this was for real.

'Oh my God!' she said, sounding like Dorothy. 'That's amazing!' She stopped and wrapped her arms around her big sister. She squeezed her with all her might.

'I'm so pleased for you,' she said, tears pricking her eyes. She looked at Rosie and saw that she was also overcome with emotion, and that judging by the smudges on her face and her bloodshot eyes, she had already shed a fair few tears.

'The thing is,' Rosie explained as they waited for a tram to pass before hurrying across the road, 'he's flying back now.'

'What? Now?'

Rosie laughed. 'Yes, now. As we speak.'

Passing Christ Church, they continued walking down Mowbray Road.

'So, you're going to meet him?' Charlotte asked.

'I am, but it means I'm going to be away for at least a night. I'm due to catch the train in an hour.' She looked at her watch. 'Which means leaving you on your own.'

'That's all right,' Charlotte said. 'I can go and stay with Lily and George.'

Rosie looked at her sister and laughed.

'Never one to miss an opportunity,' she said, shaking her head.

'Well, you can't leave me on my own at home, can you? You know how much I *detest* being alone,' Charlotte said, poker-faced.

'Which is exactly what I thought you'd say,' Rosie said as they turned left into West Lawn, 'so I popped in to see Lily before I came to get you. She says she'd love to have you for however long I'm away.'

'Yeah!' Charlotte jumped up and stuck her hands in the air. She grabbed hold of her sister and gave her another hug.

'Thanks, Rosie, you're the best!'

When they walked through the door at Lily's, everyone was there to greet them: Lily, George, Kate, Maisie, Vivian, all beaming from ear to ear.

Twenty minutes ago, when Rosie had come through the door, breathless and bursting with joy to tell them the good news, Lily had hugged her tightly. Never before had she felt so relieved and thankful, for she had worried that Peter's death would be one blow too many for Rosie to bear.

Lily had told Rosie she was shutting up shop, so there was no reason Charlotte could not stay while Rosie was off being reunited with her husband. The second Rosie had left, Lily had gone to tell George the news before sweeping round the bordello, banging on all the bedroom doors, telling everyone that there was an emergency and they all had to be up, dressed and out the back door within five minutes. The clients might have thought they were about to be raided, were it not for Lily's high spirits. The girls were happy to leave as Lily had promised to reimburse them the night's earnings, and she had also told them as they had scuttled out the back that they were to take at least two days' paid holiday.

During the time it took for Rosie to go and pick up Charlotte, Lily had transformed the house from a den of iniquity to a perfectly innocent family home, all the while having the almightiest of hot flushes.

'Ma chère!' Lily enveloped Rosie in her arms once again, winking at an ecstatic-looking Charlotte by her side.

As soon as Lily released Rosie from her grip, Kate stepped in and flung her arms around her beloved friend. 'Oh Rosie, we are so, so happy for you.' It felt only right, in Kate's eyes, that Rosie had been given back her lover.

'As are we,' Vivian said, her tone sincere. Rosie had taken Vivian under her wing when she had first arrived at the bordello as poor and as plain as a church mouse. She'd brought her out of her shell and looked out for her, something no one had ever done before. She took hold of Rosie's hand and squeezed it. 'And don't feel like you have to hurry back. Enjoy every minute with that man of yours.' She winked at Rosie, knowing not to say more in front of Charlotte.

'Don't worry about Charlie,' Maisie said, putting her arm out and pulling Rosie's little sister close. 'We'll make sure she behaves herself, won't we?' She looked at Charlotte, who was nodding and grinning.

'Righty-ho!' George said, putting on his trilby. 'We better get you to that station. Don't want you to miss your train, do we? Don't want to keep that husband of yours waiting, eh?'

Rosie smiled. Just talking about Peter in the present tense gave her a feeling of elation.

As she grabbed her overnight bag and gas mask, which she had left at the door before going to fetch Charlotte, she turned to leave.

'Thanks, everyone,' she said. She wanted to say more but didn't trust herself. 'Thanks – for everything.'

She hurried down the steps and towards George's red MG. He was waiting with the passenger door open.

'Your carriage awaits.'

Waving Rosie off in the car, Lily turned to Charlotte. She couldn't wait to spoil her rotten. 'Sod the waistline, we're going to have a feast of fish and chips, and, *ma chérie*,' she said, gently pinching Charlotte's cheek, 'you can have as many mugs of hot chocolate as you want.'

They all made their way into the kitchen.

'And we're going to spend the entire evening talking all things *français*,' she said. *'D'accord?'*

'Vraiment,' Charlotte answered.

'And when George returns,' Lily looked at Maisie and Vivian, 'I shall get him to raid the cellar and we shall toast Peter with a glass or two of our finest champagne.'

It would be a toast not only to Peter but also to Rosie, for it was not just Peter who had been given back his life.

*

372

'We'll see you when you both get home!' George shouted after Rosie as she hurried to the entrance to the railway station.

Turning round, Rosie beamed back a smile. She waved and was then swallowed up by the throng of fellow travellers. She caught a glimpse of a newspaper. The headline declared that de Gaulle had arrived in France. The French were getting back their leader and she was getting back her man. As she made her way down the wooden steps and onto the platform, Rosie forced herself to take deep breaths. She put her overnight bag down on the ground and saw that her hands were shaking. Since Toby had told her the news, it had felt as if her heart was going to explode with a cocktail of excitement, relief and pure joy.

Breathe, Rosie, breathe, she told herself.

Looking at the railway tracks, she saw a rat scurrying around, foraging for food.

Rats had never bothered her or scared her. She'd seen enough of them at work. They were just trying to survive like everyone else. She felt a gusty breeze and knew that meant the train was approaching. She looked again at the railway tracks. How life could change in the blink of an eye. Just three hours ago, if she had been standing here, she would have had to fight the urge to fling herself in front of the train that was about to come steaming into the station. Now she had never felt so happy in her life – and she would feel happier still when she saw Peter walking towards her.

She heard the train before it appeared through the darkness of the underground tunnel. The brakes squealed and she squinted as the dust and dirt that had been kicked up by its arrival swirled in the air. As the steam filled the platform, the doors to the carriages were thrown open and Rosie climbed aboard and found her seat.

Sitting down by the window in the first-class carriage, she realised that her dream had come true twice over. She was not only going to have the family she had always wanted, with herself, Peter and Charlotte living at Brookside Gardens, but she also had an extended family in the women at work and the people who had just waved her off at the bordello.

At that moment in time she felt like the luckiest woman alive.

Chapter Forty-Seven

Peter looked down at the English Channel from the small passenger window of the Airspeed AS.5 Courier in which he was flying. Although the single-engine light aircraft had room for six, today there was only himself and the two RAF pilots. As the plane pitched up slightly, his eyes were drawn to the skies above. He saw a flurry of perfect white clouds and thought back to how, as a child, he had firmly believed that heaven was on the other side of those clouds and that if he were able to fly high, he'd be able to snatch a sneak preview.

While he'd been trapped under the ruins of the building in Sainte-Mère-Église, he had wondered, as he drifted in and out of consciousness, if he had in fact died and was languishing in limbo while the powers that be judged if he was worthy enough to pass through St Peter's pearly gates. Acting as judge and jury on his own life, Peter had lain there, with barely enough space to move his arms and legs, and had thought about the life he had led. Sitting here, strapped into a plane on his way back home – alive – he surmised that the celestial jury must have ruled in his favour.

A burst water main had kept him from dehydrating while he had been trapped under a blanket of bricks and mortar. Peter's survival training at Wanborough Manor had taught him that he could last without food for weeks, but only days without liquids. The water from the ruptured pipes had been tainted with mud and dirt, but it had served its purpose. And, of course, he'd had oxygen. The air had been dusty and acrid, but he had been able to take short, shallow breaths.

During the time he'd been buried alive, he had hypnotised himself to stay calm and not think about his inability to free himself, forcing his mind to think of a life beyond his concrete coffin. When he had felt dust and debris on his face and sensed movement above him, heard the voice of a young boy, he'd started banging hard on the wooden boards of the caved-in trapdoor. On hearing his rescuers he had experienced a rising feeling of insanity that, thankfully, he had managed to keep at bay for the time it took a team of men to dismantle the bomb site and reach the basement. As he'd been freed from his prison, he'd heard a French voice, which he guessed belonged to a doctor, telling the medics to blindfold him and give him a water-soaked cloth to suck on. And so he was kept in darkness as his body was hauled onto a stretcher and into a truck. He had felt the jolts as the vehicle drove over potholes and after losing consciousness he had woken in a darkened room in a makeshift medical centre. Apart from being dehydrated and having some cuts and bruises, he was told he'd had a miraculous escape.

The nurse charged with his care had been a chatty young girl and she had told him the story that had now gone around the town several times: how Madame Toulouse had originally noticed there was life amongst the rubble, but it had initially seemed like a false alarm, that the rat had been very much alive, but the man whom the rodent had unwittingly unearthed hadn't been. Peter expressed sadness that a young boy had been forced to see death up close, but the nurse had waved her hand and said, 'Ce n'est rien,' it's nothing, he had not only seen dead bodies before, but had witnessed men die. Peter didn't think he had felt so sad in his entire life, hearing the nurse's words. *What had become of the world where a little boy had become accustomed not only to death – but to cold-blooded murder?*

Peter had vowed to himself there and then that one day he would like to go back to Sainte-Mère-Église and thank both the old woman and the young *garçon*. Perhaps Rosie and Charlotte would come too. He knew Rosie would also want to thank them. He thought about the letter he had written to her. His unit had all been in agreement that they wanted their loved ones to be given their letters as soon as reports of their demise came through. They had not wanted their wives and families to wait longer than necessary, especially as they knew there was a good chance that their bodies might never be found or identified. It hurt him to think that Rosie would have read her letter by now. He knew how devastated she would be. It was why, as soon as he was conscious, he had asked to be taken to the commander in charge, who had facilitated his communication with London.

Whilst there he had also been given an update on the events of the past few days and his spirits had risen on hearing of the success of the Battle of Normandy. It was clear that *Jour J* had more than lived up to the Allies' hopes and expectations. Battles were still being played out, but the second front had been established. There was no doubt that this marked a decisive turning point in the war. Victory was not far off.

As his thoughts again wandered to his wife, Peter's stomach was suddenly in his mouth. The plane must have hit a pocket of air and momentarily lost altitude. He looked out of the window and could just about make out the White Cliffs of Dover. His heart leapt with joy. Not long before he saw Rosie. Not long before he could wrap his arms around her and hold her tight. He didn't think he'd ever let her go.

As they flew over the clifftops, it felt as though the plane was again losing altitude.

They seemed to be flying very low.

So low he could almost see the houses beneath.

He looked out of the window and saw smoke coming from the engine; the view below was now obscured by thick, billowing grey smoke.

He looked towards the cockpit as one of the pilots turned and looked over his shoulder.

'Strap yourself in and assume the brace position!' the pilot shouted.

Peter stared ahead for a moment. Both pilots were pulling back on the yoke with all of their might. He looked beyond them and through the window of the cockpit. He could see a flash of houses, then a mass of treetops. A forest. In the distance he caught sight of fields of sun-kissed wheat.

He put his head down to his knees and covered it with his hands.

There was an eerie silence.

It took him a beat to realise the engine had died.

He knew it would just be seconds before he felt the impact as the plane crash-landed.

He'd got so near. So near to getting home. To being with the woman he loved.

He thought of Rosie. Imagined her smiling face, determined that if these were to be his last moments on this earth, then she would be the last image he saw.

Chapter Forty-Eight

Bobby had left the yard in such a hurry he'd forgotten to hand in his clocking-off board. Davey hung out of the window, shouting to catch his attention, but it was no good. Bobby couldn't hear, and even if he had heard, he wouldn't have gone back. There was no time to lose. *Why he hadn't done this before, he did not know.* It was like everything had come to him in one fell swoop. Seeing Toby had somehow pulled away the chocks and now he was off there was no stopping him.

Racing towards the ferry landing and seeing the boat pull away, he leapt on board, grabbed the railings and climbed over the entrance barrier. Stan, the ferry master, gave him a look like the summons as Bobby apologised, digging in his pocket and giving him his penny fare along with extra for a pint.

'Something important has just come up,' he said, sucking in air and trying to get his breath back.

'Let me guess,' Stan said, speaking into Bobby's good ear. 'It concerns a woman.'

Bobby let out a loud guffaw. 'How did you know!'

The old ferry master walked away, smiling to himself and shaking his head.

As Bobby looked out at the Wear, for the first time he really felt happy to be back home. Since hearing the reports that Peter was dead, he had thought a lot about life and love. He had come to realise that his father still had power over him – was still stopping him enjoying his life with his mam, her new fella, his little sister and all the people they had around them. It was up to him to let go of his anger and resentment and to finally allow himself to be happy.

When he had left his hometown all those years ago, he had succeeded geographically in leaving the past behind, but it had stayed within him – no matter where he went. How strange, he mused, that it had taken his return to the home he'd run away from all those years ago for him to be able to let go of the past and move on.

It took Bobby five minutes to run in his steel-toecapped boots along High Street East, onto High Street West, then left down West Sunniside, before slowing to a jog when he reached the top of Foyle Street. The sun was still beating down despite it being late afternoon. He was dirty and sweaty. Reaching the main front door of the flat, he knocked, wiping his brow with the sleeve of his overalls. He really should have gone back home, cleaned up and changed, but he couldn't wait. He felt as though he were in a race and every second counted.

'Ah, *Bobby*.' It was Mrs Kwiatkowski. She stepped back and opened the large oak door wide to let him in. 'I'm guessing you're after Dorothy?'

Bobby gave a short laugh. 'I am. For my sins.'

Walking over the threshold, he took a deep breath and clomped up the two flights of stairs to the woman who had taken his heart captive.

Seeing that the front door was open, Bobby knocked loudly.

'Hello, anyone home?' he shouted through.

Seconds later, Dorothy appeared from the kitchen. She was still in her work overalls, but was in the process of freeing her arms and tying the sleeves around her waist. She didn't hide her surprise at seeing who her caller was.

'What do you want?' she asked.

Bobby laughed loudly.

'Do you mind if I come in?' he asked, thinking how she reminded him of that day by the quayside. His ardour for her had not abated since then but grown.

'If you must.' Dorothy turned and went back into the kitchen.

Bobby walked down the short hallway and into the small kitchen. Dorothy had her back to him and was making a pot of tea.

'So, to what do I owe this pleasure?' she asked, turning round and putting the pot onto the table, which already had two cups and saucers in place and a jug of milk.

Bobby looked around.

'No Angie?'

Dorothy made a show of looking under the table and around the room. 'It doesn't look like it.' She went over and opened the small kitchen window. She felt hot. A light breeze made its way into the room.

'She's at the shops,' she said eventually, 'or rather, standing in a queue waiting to get into a shop.'

Bobby smiled and opened his mouth to speak.

'And before you say it – I have not bullied her into doing the shopping. We take turns and today it's Angie's turn.'

Bobby chuckled. 'Actually, I wasn't going to say that, but it's good to know.'

Dorothy glowered at him.

'So, what *were* you going to say?' Suddenly, she felt a little self-conscious. This was the first time they had been in a room together, just the two of them.

Bobby stepped forward and put his hands on the back of one of the chairs.

'I was going to say what brilliant news it is about Peter.'

381

Dorothy's face immediately lit up. All awkwardness gone. 'Isn't it just! No one can quite believe it.' In the blink of an eye Dorothy's demeanour had changed from surly to sunny.

'See,' she said, 'you *can* have a happy ending in real life.'

Bobby laughed. 'You certainly can.'

He stood for a moment, taking in the vision of this woman whom he found irresistible. He had to stop himself going over, taking her in his arms and kissing her from here to eternity. He forced himself to push all amorous thoughts from his mind.

'And I think you might have another happy ending ...' Bobby let his voice trail off.

'Really?' Dorothy said. 'Two in one day?'

Again, Bobby smiled. 'Yes, two in one day.'

'So, what's the second one?' Dorothy was now genuinely curious.

Bobby inhaled.

'I've just had a chat with Mam – and we've managed to sort out our differences,' he said simply.

Dorothy's face lit up. 'That's brilliant news!' She looked at Bobby and for the first time saw that there was something different about him. He seemed happier. More at peace.

'Tell me more,' she demanded.

'Well, there's nothing much to tell,' Bobby said, suddenly feeling slightly ill at ease.

'*Of course* there's plenty to tell,' she said, putting out two cups. 'Sit down and drink some tea – I want every detail.'

Bobby smiled and sat down, watching as Dorothy sloshed tea and milk into the cups. How lovely, he thought, that she was so happy for both Rosie and Gloria.

'Come on, I want to hear all about it,' she said impatiently.

Bobby smiled. His heart lifted to see that the only barrier between them had been the problem he'd had with his mam. Now that had gone, so had Dorothy's animosity towards him. He took a sip of his tea, stalling a little. Talking about his personal feelings and his past was not his forte. It was something he rarely did – especially not with women, never mind with a woman he was mad about. Bobby knew, though, that he had to be open and honest if he was to win Dorothy over. And so he started to tell her the real reason why he had found it so hard to be a loving son to his mam. It was not as Dorothy had thought – he was not against divorce, far from it, and he didn't judge those who chose to live in sin. It was, he explained, because of his own feelings of resentment, the origins of which stemmed from way back when he was just a boy.

The more he talked, the more easily the words came and, after listening intently, Dorothy confided in Bobby about her own childhood, which, she said, had been in no way as bad as the one Bobby and Gordon had suffered living under the same roof as Vinnie, but it was, however, still something that had affected her. She knew how it felt to be young and innocent and to be an unwilling witness to the violence of a father – a man whose role it was to love, care for and protect his children.

They had been talking for quite some time when Dorothy glanced at the clock and jumped up.

'Oh my goodness, look at the time. I've got to get ready.'

Bobby knew why Dorothy had to get ready. Toby was in town. He felt a rush of jealousy. And also panic. He had been sidetracked into talking about his mam and his dad and now it looked like he was running out of time to tell Dorothy what he had really come here to say.

'I better let you get on,' he said, standing up.

'I'll see you out.' Dorothy stepped forward, but Bobby didn't move out of the way.

She looked at him and knew what he wanted. *Knew what she also wanted.* Now that her anger towards Bobby had dissolved, the feelings she had tried to deny were laid bare.

Bobby saw the look in Dorothy's eyes. He leant forward and kissed her. Softly. Gently. The feel of her full, soft lips on his own was the most sensuous feeling he'd ever experienced.

Suddenly, he felt Dorothy pull away. His heart was pumping at full force. He opened his eyes just as Dorothy raised her hand and slapped him around the face. His skin stung momentarily.

He looked at Dorothy, into those blue eyes, and saw not anger that he had overstepped the mark, but confusion and, dare he even think it – love.

He watched as she leant back into him, her eyes dropping to his mouth before she kissed him. He closed his eyes and was again lost in the sensuous feel of her lips. He pulled her close, feeling her body respond and pressing against his own. All he wanted to do in that moment was touch every part of her body, explore every wonderful curve and make love to her. He sensed she felt the same about him.

They stood, their bodies so close they could feel each other's chests lifting as their breathing became heavier by the second. He felt Dorothy kiss his neck and then whisper something in his deaf ear. He responded by kissing her neck, breathing in her scent, desperate to ask her what she had just told him, but not wanting to break free.

And then, all of a sudden, they heard Mrs Kwiatkowski's voice shouting up the stairs.

'You've got another visitor, Dorothy!' Her words were followed by the sound of footsteps taking the steps two at a time.

Bobby and Dorothy froze. They seemed unable to part.

'Oh my God!' Dorothy said, finally forcing herself to move away from Bobby.

She managed to put a little distance between them just in time.

'Where's that jolly gorgeous girl of mine?' Toby's voice could be heard before he appeared in the kitchen doorway. His face dropped as soon as he saw Bobby.

'Ah, hello there, old chap.' His voice was flat, he was clearly disappointed to see Dorothy had company and that company was Bobby. 'Didn't expect to find you here.'

Bobby simply stood there. He wanted to explain that this *jolly gorgeous girl* was no longer Toby's – that Dorothy was now *his* girl. They were meant for each other. It was as clear as day. Especially now they had kissed – her kisses spoke a thousand words.

'Bobby just popped round to chat about his mam,' Dorothy explained.

'Ah, is that so?' Toby asked. 'Everything all right, I hope?'

'All good,' Dorothy answered. 'Bobby was just leaving, weren't you?'

Bobby gave a tight smile, ran a hand over his jaw and nodded. His eyes lingered on Dorothy as he started to leave.

'I didn't catch what you said just then,' he said, touching his left ear.

Dorothy looked him in the eye. 'It wasn't important.'

Bobby turned, giving Toby a sharp nod farewell and throwing Dorothy one last look.

Chapter Forty-Nine

When the train pulled in, Rosie was already at the door and had the sash window down. She looked out, her eyes searching for Peter. The platform was partially obscured by steam and she felt a sudden pang of concern that he'd not been able to make it. The train slowly screeched to a halt. Above the noise she heard the conductor telling travellers that they had arrived in King's Cross Station and this was the train's final destination.

It was the end of the line.

But the start of a new life, Rosie thought.

One she would never have dreamt a week ago could possibly happen.

Stepping down onto the platform, Rosie hauled her bag off and stood, adjusting to the noise, smells and chaos of one of the capital's busiest railway stations.

She looked for Peter.

When the steam had cleared and all the passengers had got off, she was still standing.

Still looking.

Perhaps he had been delayed?

Stuck in traffic? Had a puncture?

Or perhaps his plane hadn't made it over the Channel?

Stop it! Rosie told herself.

Toby had said his journey back was not in any way dangerous. *As safe as houses.*

Peter is alive.

Nothing had happened to him.

Had it?

Chapter Fifty

Following Bobby's departure, Dorothy told Toby to wait downstairs in Mrs Kwiatkowski's flat while she got ready. She was sure their elderly neighbour wouldn't mind Toby's company for a little while. As soon as she was on her own, Dorothy sat and stared at the kitchen wall for a full five minutes, her head spinning. Seeing that time was ticking on, she realised she had to get a move on. She had to forget what had just happened with Bobby, push it to the back of her mind until she was on her own again.

Twenty minutes later, Dorothy looked at herself in the mirror. She had managed to plaster on the make-up as well as what she hoped was a convincing look of excitement and anticipation at her unexpected date with Toby. Before he'd left the yard, Toby had told her they were going somewhere special and to put her glad rags on. Walking down the stairs to Mrs Kwiatkowski's flat, Dorothy could hear Angie's voice. She'd obviously got back from the shops and was chatting away to Toby and their neighbour. As she reached the doorway of the flat, Dorothy took a deep breath, once again trying to obliterate any thoughts of Bobby.

Appearing at the doorway, Dorothy struck a pose, as she usually did for her audience of three, congratulating herself on being able to act so well and disguise the turmoil inside.

Toby whistled. 'Well worth the wait,' he declared, jumping up and putting out his arm.

'Have fun!' Mrs Kwiatkowski said, smiling at the young couple.

'Yeah, and dinnit forget to bring us back a doggy bag.' Angie forced herself to sound jovial, although she felt anything but. She had walked in on Dorothy and Bobby and walked straight back out again. Neither had noticed.

Toby smiled, saluted and bade them farewell, then guided Dorothy out of the flat, through the main front door and down the stone steps.

'So, what's all this about Bobby and his mam?' he asked as he took hold of Dorothy's hand and they walked down Foyle Street.

'Oh, huge drama,' Dorothy said, wondering how quickly she could steer the conversation away from him. She was still unsure if Toby had picked up that something had been going on between them as he'd arrived at the flat.

They walked on.

Toby laughed. 'Yes? And the *huge drama* being?' he asked. It was unlike Dorothy to need any encouragement to talk.

'Oh, he's finally sorted everything out with Gloria,' Dorothy said, trying to act as though she was not the least bit interested.

They turned right into Borough Road.

'Well, that's great news,' Toby said, eyeing Dorothy and wondering why she wasn't regaling him with every detail. She had spent the past three months giving him earache about bloody Bobby not doing what she wanted him to do, and now she barely had two words to say about the matter.

'So, he's forgiven her for divorcing his father?' Toby continued to probe as they crossed the road.

'Sort of,' Dorothy said, wishing now she hadn't gone on so much about the Bobby and Gloria situation to Toby. 'Although I don't think he was so much against the divorce.'

Toby stopped at the stone-pillared entrance to the Palatine, the town's most exclusive restaurant. Dorothy's eyes widened. Her mind had been so preoccupied with what had just happened with Bobby that she hadn't even thought about asking Toby where they were going.

'Oh my God!' she said. 'What are we celebrating?'

Toby opened the heavy swing door and Dorothy walked through.

'Peter being alive?' Dorothy made a guess. 'Us conquering Normandy?'

Toby smiled but didn't say anything.

The maître d' appeared and showed them to their seats. Dorothy guessed that Toby must have been in earlier to pick out a table for two set back from the main dining area.

'Oh, Toby, I feel thoroughly spoilt,' Dorothy said as the waiter pulled out her chair and she sat down. She smiled, desperately hoping the guilt that she was presently drowning in was not apparent.

'You deserve it,' Toby said as he too sat down.

Dorothy pushed back yet more waves of guilt.

Seconds later, the sommelier arrived with the champagne. Normally, Dorothy would have been desperately holding back a shriek of excitement. As it was, she felt terrible. Disloyal. *If only she hadn't kissed Bobby. What had she been thinking of when she already had Toby? Lovely, kind, handsome Toby.*

'A toast,' Toby said.

'A toast.' Dorothy pasted what she hoped looked like an ecstatically happy look on her face as they raised their glasses.

'To Peter and Rosie,' Dorothy said.

Toby smiled. 'Yes, to Peter and Rosie. And also, to us.'

'Of course, to us!' she said, clinking glasses a tad too robustly and causing a little champagne to spill.

As they took their first sips, the starters arrived. French pâté on toast. Dorothy thanked the waiter and widened her eyes at Toby.

'My favourite!'

Dorothy forced the first course down, making a show of enjoying every mouthful, clapping her hands in glee when the lobster thermidor arrived, all the while doing her best to banish images of Bobby and the kisses and caresses they had shared. If only she had stopped it and sent him packing. But she hadn't. When she had slapped him, it was as though she were slapping herself for not having realised that she had let herself fall in love with him. She felt herself blush as she recalled telling him so in his deaf ear.

Why did she have to fall in love with Bobby when she had Toby?

She loved Toby, didn't she? But the way she felt about Bobby was different and a little scary. He made her feel alive, and more than a little reckless. If Toby had not arrived when he had, she wondered if she would have been able to stop herself from going further with Bobby. She had held off sleeping with Toby – was determined to wait until she was married – but a few moments with Bobby and all those resolutions seemed to have vanished into thin air.

'So, tell me more about Peter and how you found out he was still alive,' Dorothy said. She needed Toby to talk while she dealt with the tsunami of thoughts crashing in her head.

Toby chatted on, telling Dorothy what he could. His own head, though, was full to bursting with other thoughts, and as they finished their chocolate mousse dessert – another favourite of Dorothy's – he started to feel the full throttle of nerves as they approached the reason they were there.

'So,' Dorothy said, playfully, 'you got me and Ange to deliver the bad news to Rosie, but the good news you drive all the way up here to divulge yourself!'

Toby laughed.

'Actually, there was another reason I put the old gal through her paces to get here in record time.' His face looked serious.

'And what would that be?' she asked.

Please, no, please don't. Not today. Not now.

She could feel the colour drain from her cheeks as she watched Toby dig his hand into his trouser pocket and pull out a small leather box.

Watched as he dropped to one knee.

This was all she had wanted for so long. But now it was really happening it was the last thing she wanted.

Damn Bobby!

'Dorothy Mary Williams …' Toby opened the petite red box to reveal a beautiful, sparkling diamond ring.

'Oh, my goodness,' Dorothy said, her hand going to her chest. 'It's beautiful.'

Toby looked at the woman he loved; her eyes were sparkling as brightly as the diamond he was offering her.

'Dorothy, I want you to be my wife more than anything else in the world. Will you marry me?' He looked up at the woman with whom he'd been madly in love since first setting eyes on her at Lily's.

Dorothy opened her mouth, but nothing came out. It was as though she had been struck dumb. For once in her life she had no idea what to say. She was aware of the other diners looking at her and Toby. She knew what she was supposed to say and do, but she couldn't. It was as if she had become temporarily paralysed.

Toby stayed a few more moments on bended knee, but, seeing the look of confusion on Dorothy's face and taking it to mean she was feeling overwhelmed, he pushed himself up and sat back down on his seat. He took her hand, squeezed it and smiled.

The curious diners, sensing that this scene was not about to be played out as planned, turned their attention back to their own partners and meals.

Toby scrutinised Dorothy. She looked as though she were about to burst into tears. He had never guessed she would react this way. *Had something changed? Had her feelings changed since he had seen her last?* Surely she was just overwrought. The news about Peter had affected them all.

'Are you all right?' he asked gently.

Dorothy nodded vigorously, but still didn't speak.

'I'm guessing this has been all a bit too much. What with the news about Peter and now me springing this on you?'

Again, Dorothy nodded; tears had started to well in her eyes. Tears of guilt.

She looked at Toby and all she could see was Bobby.

'I'm so sorry,' Dorothy said, choking back the tears.

She gave him an apologetic smile.

'I just don't know what I want.'

Or rather, who *I want.*

Chapter Fifty-One

Peter hurried as fast as his exhausted body would allow through the main entrance to King's Cross Station.

He was late, but at least he had made it.

He hated to think what it might have done to Rosie, having been told he was alive, for her to have arrived in London expecting to meet him, only to be told once again that he was dead – and that this time it really was true.

And he would have been dead had it not been for the skill of the pilots. The plane had lost all power, yet they had somehow managed to glide the aircraft down to the ground, avoiding a village and a forest, before crash-landing in a field. Peter could only surmise that the long stems of wheat had acted as a cushion of sorts and had helped to break the speed of the plane as it skidded to a halt. Clambering out of the little hatch door on the side of the aircraft and looking around, he'd shaken his head in disbelief that the nose of the plane was just inches from touching the fence bordering the field. The two pilots were unbuckling their belts and hauling themselves out of the shattered windows of their cockpit. After they'd jumped down, they had both looked at Peter and smiled.

'Sorry about the rough landing, old chap,' one of the pilots said, deadpan.

'We managed to radio in our position, so you should still be able to get to your *very important meeting*,' the other said with a smile. They knew the reason for Peter's trip back to Blighty.

Laughing, Peter had walked over and slapped them both on the back.

It took him a little while before he'd realised he was thanking them in French.

'Long time overseas,' the pilot said. His understanding of French was basic, but he had caught the gist of Peter's gratitude.

'Too long,' Peter said.

They had landed in a field in Kent, luckily near an RAF base that had immediately dispatched an army ambulance and truck. After being checked over and given a clean bill of health, Peter had managed to persuade the truck driver to transport him, at speed, to King's Cross Station, where he was now hurrying towards platform number five.

When Rosie saw Peter, she almost didn't recognise him. He looked as thin as a rake, and his once salt-and-pepper hair was now completely grey. As he hurried towards her, she saw the life in his eyes and the smile on his face and knew he was all right.

She didn't run towards him, instead she simply stood there and devoured every second of seeing that he was really alive. The man she had grieved for and had believed was dead was here in the flesh. It was only now, watching him striding towards her, his eyes sparkling with love, that she was sure it was true.

Peter was alive.

When he reached her, neither spoke. No words were needed. Instead, Peter took Rosie in his arms and kissed her. And kissed her again. And Rosie kissed him back with the same fervour, enjoying the feel of his lips on hers as her lover, her husband, her friend, her soulmate kissed her over and over again.

Wrapping his arms around her, he nuzzled her neck and breathed in her scent.

'Rosie ... Rosie ... Rosie,' he mumbled, kissing her neck before once again finding her lips.

He broke off and looked at her, put his hand on her face, touched her cheeks, her blonde hair, her gorgeous face – a face he would never tire of looking at and which he hoped now to be seeing for the rest of his life. He gazed into her blue eyes – eyes he had pictured while he had been buried alive and that he had seen again when the plane had gone into a nosedive and he had thought the gods had reversed their decision and decided to lay claim to his soul. He had clearly been given a last-minute reprieve. And by God was he going to make the most of every moment he had left on this earth. Starting with this one.

He looked down at Rosie and kissed her once more before forcing himself to pull away.

'We're not staying in London,' he said. He didn't say that he felt it wasn't safe. The pilotless bombs that Hitler was dropping on the capital made it too dangerous. He took her hand, grabbed her overnight bag and started walking.

'Where are we going?' Rosie asked, not that she cared. Not one jot. As long as she was with Peter.

Peter didn't answer.

'Is Charlie all right?' he asked as they walked down the platform. 'You're OK leaving her for a little while?'

Rosie laughed. 'Oh yes, she's more than OK. Overjoyed that you're alive, and happy as Larry about where she will be staying while I'm away.'

Peter gave her a quizzical look as they reached the end of the platform and turned left.

'I'll tell you all about it later,' she said. 'It's a long story. Very long.'

'But with a happy ending by the sounds of it?' Peter asked as they reached the adjourning platform. There was a train waiting.

'A happy and rather unconventional ending,' Rosie said, looking at the train, steam streaming out of the engine. Passengers had started to board.

Peter walked towards the top of the train, to the first-class carriages, and pulled open the door.

'All aboard, Mrs Miller,' he smiled.

She stepped from the platform into the carriage.

'So, where are you taking me?' Rosie asked.

'Guildford,' said Peter, hauling their baggage in and stepping on board himself.

Rosie's face lit up.

'Guildford!'

Peter took Rosie into his arms and kissed her.

'I've booked us into a lovely little hotel just a short walk from the registry office.'

Rosie's eyes were glistening. *Their hotel*. She had never felt so happy in her whole life.

They heard the stationmaster's whistle screech and the door to the carriage slam shut.

'We're going to have a second honeymoon,' Peter said. 'Only this time, I'll be coming home with you.'

Welcome to

Penny Street

where your favourite authors and stories live.

Meet casts of characters you'll never forget,
create memories you'll treasure forever,
and discover places that will stay with
you long after the last page.

Turn the page to step into the home of

Nancy Revell

and discover more about

The Shipyard Girls...

Dear Reader,

It was only when I had finished writing *The Shipyard Girls on the Home Front* that I realised the theme of this book is actually sacrifice. Peter is prepared to give up his life for the sake of humanity, as is Bobby. Bel gives up her need for retribution so that Hope can have a father. Helen sacrifices romantic love for the well-being of her friends and their families. And Lily is prepared to change her life and her livelihood to give Charlotte the security she craves.

This got me thinking about the act of making sacrifices – of giving up something valued for the sake of something else deemed more important or worthy.

I wondered if perhaps by making sacrifices a person can sometimes find themselves gifted with something else – and perhaps even end up with more than they relinquished. Bel certainly does! The idealist in me would hope so.

Until next time, Dear Reader. I wish you all love and light – and lots of it – in your lives and in the lives of those you hold dear.

Love

Nancy
x

HISTORICAL NOTES

I just had to share with you this image of women shipyard
workers taken during the First World War at a shipyard in
Wallsend, Tyne and Wear. Little is known about the women
shipyard workers during the Second World War and even
less is known about those building ships during the first.
Amazing and inspirational women. Let's not forget them!

© Tyne & Wear Archives & Museums

Chapter One

June 1944

Mr Havelock was sitting alone in the large dining room in his very grandiose home in Glen Path, one of the richest areas of the town known as Ashbrooke. His mood had plummeted after he'd perused the headlines over breakfast. There was no denying the success of the Normandy landings and the opening up of the Second Front. You didn't need to have a crystal ball to see that an Allied victory was on the horizon; it was just a matter of when. The photographs and illustrations of *The Sunday Pictorial* said it all. 'WE'RE SQUEEZING IN – NOTHING CAN SAVE HITLER NOW!' screamed the banner at the bottom of the page in bold, black ink.

Reading the piece, Mr Havelock's appetite left him and he pushed his plate of bacon and egg away. Lighting up a Winston, he smoked and drank his tea, flicking ash onto his untouched food before stubbing the half-smoked cigarette out in the middle of the perfectly fried egg. He knew it would hurt his housekeeper, Agatha, to see food soiled and wasted during these times of rationing. It gave him a smidgeon of sadistic joy.

Scraping his chair back, he made his way across the large oak-panelled dining room, banging his walking stick on the polished parquet flooring as he headed out of the door and made a beeline for his office. Stepping into the room, its size condensed by the walls lined with shelves stacked with books, Mr Havelock slammed the door shut and went straight to the safe situated behind his mahogany desk. Unlocking it and letting the small, heavy door swing back, he started foraging around. Finally, under the thick parchment of his 'Last Will and Testament' and other important waxed sealed documents, he found what he was looking for – his membership of Oswald Mosley's now defunct political party, the British Union of Fascists. He had kept it in the hope that Hitler would win the war. It would have been proof of his political leanings and alliances. Had the Nazis successfully invaded the British Isles, Mosley would have been installed as a head, albeit a puppet head, of a pro-German government.

Mr Havelock muttered blasphemies under his breath as he took the souvenir of a future that would never be over to the fireplace. Pulling out his silver lighter from his trouser pocket, he clicked it open and held the flame under the thick card, on which the letters B.U.F. had been heavily embossed in black. It slowly caught alight. Leaning one hand on the mantelpiece he watched it burn, letting it go at the last minute.

He had to accept that there really was no chance of Hitler making any kind of a comeback. Why the British were so against him he did not know. His policies made good sense. His own people certainly thought so, otherwise why would they have voted him in?

Mr Havelock turned and sat down at his desk. His mind wandered, as it often did of late, to his wife, Henrietta. A wife who, on paper, had died of a terrible tropical disease in India but who, in reality, was very much alive and well. If only she really had died, he would not be in his current predicament.

He was being controlled.

No one had ever controlled him in his entire life.

And it was all because of Henrietta.

Mr Havelock sat forward, his elbows leaning on the leather-embossed top of his desk, his hands clasped as though in prayer. He thought again about Mosley. And Hitler. And the hoped-for future that now had no chance of becoming a reality.

He thought of Hitler's policies. He thought about Henrietta. Insane. Or at least she was deemed to be on paper. He thought of the controversial T4 Euthanasia Program adopted by the Führer at the start of the war, which sanctioned the killing of the incurably ill, the elderly, the physically disabled – and the mentally ill.

The mentally ill.

Those housed in lunatic asylums.

Like the one in Ryhope.

Mr Havelock turned and looked out the lead-paned window of the office, still covered in anti-blast tape even though there hadn't been a single air raid in well over a year. He sat quite still and thought. And slowly an idea started to take shape in his head, and as it did so, it grew at a rapid rate of knots.

He knew what he had to do. It was as clear as the day outside. And with that knowledge came a sudden wave of impatience. He sat up in his chair and picked up the receiver of his gloss black Bakelite phone. He dialled a familiar number.

'Good morning, Inverness 4356.' His eldest daughter's soft voice sounded down the line.

'Margaret!' Mr Havelock shouted down the phone.

'Well, hello there, Father.' The tone no longer soft. 'You do realise that most people start their telephone conversations with, "Hello, how are you?" rather than simply bawling their name down the line.'

Mr Havelock ignored the reprimand. 'When's Miriam coming back?'

'She's not,' Margaret said simply.

There was silence down the phone.

'Again, I have to inform you, Father, that it is customary in civilised society to ask how someone is if they have been unwell. Especially if that person is your daughter.'

'For God's sake, Margaret—' Mr Havelock forced the words out. 'How's she doing?'

'*She's* doing just fine, Father,' Margaret tried hard to remain civil.

'Well, if she's doing *just fine*, then why is she not back home where she belongs … She's got a divorce to sort out if nothing else!'

He heard Margaret take a deep breath.

'Miriam's on the mend, but she's not well enough to return home just yet.'

Margaret would have liked to ask why it was her father wanted his daughter home, but knew it was unlikely she'd get either a straight or an honest answer. Her father, she had learnt over the years, was a pathological liar.

'Bloody hell, how long does it take to squeeze someone dry?' Mr Havelock yelled down the phone in exasperation.

For God's sake, he needed her home. And sooner rather than later. He waited. Silence. A click as his daughter hung up. Then dead air. He banged the receiver down, fighting the urge to pick it up again and smash it down on the cradle. Repeatedly.

Even as a child Margaret had always defied him. Always answering back. Never doing what he wanted. It had been a relief when he'd got shot of her and she'd buggered off over the border to marry that husband of hers. He wished Angus had answered the phone. He'd have got more joy, and certainly more information, from his son-in-law.

'Eddy!' Mr Havelock bellowed. It felt good to shout. Flicking open his box of cigars, he took one out, clipped the end, and lit it impatiently, puffing on it so hard he was soon surrounded by a fog of smoke.

'Yes, Mr Havelock?' Eddy's voice could be heard before he appeared through the half-opened doorway.

'I need a drink – and quick!'

Eddy gave a curt nod, disappearing as quickly as he had arrived, and returning a few minutes later with a silver tray on which there was a bottle of his master's favourite brandy and a large brandy glass.

Seeing the bottle, Mr Havelock started to calm down. Shooing Eddy away, he took the Remy and poured himself a good measure. He'd just have to be patient, remind himself of one of his long-held beliefs.

Slowly, slowly catch the monkey.

He'd have to hold his horses until Miriam got back.

Then he could put into play his plan of action.